Praise for *Prospero's Daughter*

"[Nunez] critiques colonialist assumptions about race and class in this ambitious reworking of *The Tempest*, set in her native Trinidad in the early 1960s. . . . With its strong themes and dramatic ironies . . . readers will find her love story—which has a refreshingly happy ending—very sensitively told."
—*Publishers Weekly*

"Nunez is a gifted writer, and her story not only recalls the despoiling of the Caribbean by Europeans, but brings hope for reconciliation and healing."
—*Bookpage*

"[*Prospero's Daughter* is an] exquisite retelling of *The Tempest*."
—*Kirkus Reviews* (starred review)

"*Prospero's Daughter* is a rich story that moves back and forth easily between the past and the present, between reality and fantasy, and between falsely perceived truth and the truth that ultimately sets the characters free."
—*Black Issues Book Review*

"[*Prospero's Daughter* is a] page-turning delight."
—*Entertainment Weekly*

"American Book Award winner Nunez . . . is in top form with this ambitious interpretation of Shakespeare's *The Tempest*. . . . Along with characters who virtually demand attention, the novel's intense imagery, powerful themes of race and class, and keen evocations of Caribbean land- and seascapes create a complex and emotional narrative with broad reader appeal."
—*Library Journal*

Praise for *Grace*

"Extremely deserving of its title, this gorgeous, meditative book is a graceful rendering of one couple's journeys and explorations toward and away from each other. A moving love story, it shows us how a deferred dream can erode a marriage and how grace can sometimes put us to the test, even as it redeems."
—EDWIDGE DANTICAT, author of *Breath, Eyes, Memory*

"An exquisite love story . . . Once again, accomplished author Elizabeth Nunez lends readers her remarkable voice in this masterfully crafted story."
—*New American*

"Highly recommended . . . a deeply felt and compassionate novel. Wise and resonant, it will strike a chord with readers."
—*Library Journal*

"Nunez is able to write the interior monologue of a changing mind, to show grace at work in the human heart."
—*Book Street USA*

"Nunez's skill as a writer and storyteller is . . . evident. *Grace* speaks to our propensity for self-delusion that cripples our relationship with ourselves and with those we care deeply about."
—*Black Issues Book Review*

Praise for *Beyond the Limbo Silence*

"This fine coming-of-age novel possesses the clarity—and courage—of an intensely personal narrative of the sixties." —PAUL GIDDINGS

"[A] haunting story . . . [that] bears witness to the struggles of an African Caribbean woman as she seeks to find her place in America without selling her soul." —BEBE MOORE CAMPBELL, author of *Your Blues Ain't Like Mine*

"This powerful illumination of race and culture by the light of dreams, ritual, and Vodoun will remind many of Toni Morrison or Alice Walker." —*Booklist* (starred review)

"The reader has the pleasure of experiencing Sara's discovery of American life through Nunez's wonderful, descriptive voice." —*The Bloomsbury Review*

Praise for *Bruised Hibiscus*
Winner of the American Book Award

"An American masterpiece . . . Elizabeth Nunez, a superbly gifted writer, has delivered a powerful and unsettling novel for all time and all people." —SAPPHIRE, author of *Push*

"Hypnotic, searing . . . a story so explosive and disturbing, so brilliantly wrought, its images will haunt us in our dreams." —KIANA DAVENPORT, author of *Song of the Exile*

"Nunez weaves a complex story of race, class, culture, and gender in a polyglot society rife with rumors and memories, superstitions, old grudges, and simmering tensions. This multilayered, beautifully textured novel pulls you in and holds you from beginning to end." —*Ms. Magazine*

"Moving, powerful, and haunting." —*Black Issues Book Review*

Praise for *Discretion*

"A complicated story to be relished and enjoyed by complicated people. *Discretion* is a journey, no, a pilgrimage to the gulf between love and honor." —COLIN CHANNER, author of *Waiting in Vain, Satisfy My Soul,* and *Passing Through*

"Elizabeth Nunez's writing is lush and dense, like a rain forest letting in light. Her imagery is so rich, and mastery of storytelling so compelling and fluid, it's hard to believe a woman is actually telling this story from a man's point of view. Ms. Nunez has managed to capture the complexities of political responsibility and the burdens that come with it which interfere with passion and unfiltered love. I applaud her for helping me appreciate the dichotomy between pride and social obligation. A tough one. But she's pulled it off. I recommend this novel ten times over. I was due for a smart, well-written novel with depth of breadth and scope, and I got it in *Discretion*. —TERRY MCMILLAN, author of *Waiting to Exhale*

ALSO BY ELIZABETH NUNEZ

Grace

Beyond the Limbo Silence

Bruised Hibiscus

Discretion

When Rocks Dance

Prospero's Daughter

BALLANTINE BOOKS

NEW YORK

Prospero's Daughter

A NOVEL

ELIZABETH
NUNEZ

2006 Ballantine Books Trade Paperback Edition

Copyright © 2006 by Elizabeth Nunez

Published in the United States by Ballantine Books, an imprint of The Random House Publishing Group, a division of Random House, Inc., New York.

BALLANTINE and colophon are registered trademarks of Random House, Inc.

Originally published in hardcover in the United States by Ballantine Books, an imprint of The Random House Publishing Group, a division of Random House, Inc., in 2006.

Library of Congress Cataloging-in-Publication Data
Nunez, Elizabeth.
Prospero's daughter : a novel / by Elizabeth Nunez.
p. cm.
ISBN 0-345-45536-3
1. Human experimentation in medicine—Fiction.   2. Conflict of generations—Fiction.   3. Fathers and daughters—Fiction.   4. Caribbean Area—Fiction.   5. Scientists—Fiction.   6. Islands—Fiction.   7. Exiles—Fiction   I. Title.
PS3564.U48P76 2006
813'.54—dc22   2005051260

Printed in the United States of America

www.ballantinebooks.com

2 4 6 8 9 7 5 3 1

Book designed by Caroline Cunningham

For my parents,

Waldo and Una Nunez

All men are created equal—all men, that is to say,

who possess umbrellas.

—E. M. FORSTER, *HOWARDS END*

ACKNOWLEDGMENT

My gratitude to Shakespeare for attributing some of
his most lyrical lines to Caliban.

The
Englishmen

ONE

He tell a lie if he say those two don't love one another. I know
them from when they was children. They do anything for one
another. I know. I see them. I watch them. I tell you he love she
and she love him back. They love one another. Bad. He never
rape she. Mr. Prospero lie.

> *Signed*
> *Ariana, cook for Mr. Prospero, doctor*

*J*OHN MUMSFORD put down the paper he had been reading and
sighed. He did not want the case, but the commissioner had assigned it to him. Murder and robbery were the kinds of crimes he preferred to investigate. Hard crimes, not soft crimes where the evidence
of criminality is circumstantial. He preferred a dead body, a ransacked
house, a vault blown open, jewels and money missing, tangible evidence of wrongdoing, not cases that depended on *her* word against *his*
word.

In 1961 no one had figured out that dried sperm on a woman's dress
could be traced irrefutably to its source, at least no one in the police department in Trinidad. So as far as Mumsford was concerned, notwith-
standing the fact that there could be some damage to the woman—torn
clothing, scratches on the body, sometimes blood—these matters of

rape were better handled as domestic quarrels, some of which could certainly end in murder, but in the absence of murder, not worth pursuing. In the end, there was always a persuasive argument to be made about a woman dressed provocatively, a woman alone, in the wrong place, in the dead of night. A woman flirting. A woman asking for it.

There was the case the week before, buried in *The Guardian* on the fifth page. A black woman from Laventille had filed a complaint with the police claiming that her fifteen-year-old daughter had been gang-raped in a nightclub in Port of Spain by three American sailors who had locked her in the restroom and stuffed her mouth with toilet paper. The reporter presented the facts as they were apparently given to him by the mother of the fifteen-year-old, but he went on to comment on the sad conditions of life for the residents of Laventille: "Houses, no hovels," he wrote, "packed one on top of the other, garbage everywhere, children in rags, young people without hope, dependent on charity. It's no wonder."

That "no wonder" set off a deluge of letters to the newspaper. Four days later, on its second page, *The Guardian* printed three. "A wonder, what?" one person wrote. "A wonder that her mother wasn't in the nightclub also selling her body? What do those women expect when they dress up in tight clothes and go to those clubs? Everybody knows the American sailors go there for cheap girls. She had it coming. How could her mother in good conscience call what happened to her daughter rape?"

That seemed to be the consensus of God-fearing people on the island. Soon witnesses surfaced who swore they had seen the girl the night before with the same three sailors.

Mumsford agreed with the consensus: The girl had asked for it. Yet for no other reason than that the hairs on the back of his neck stood up at the mere mention of Americans, he also believed that the sailors had taken advantage of her.

It was a matter of schadenfreude, of course. Mumsford was English, and though he readily admitted his country had needed the Americans during the war, they irritated him. They were too boisterous, too happy-go-lucky, he thought. They waved dollar bills around as if they were useless pieces of paper; they laughed too loudly, got too friendly with the natives.

Trinidad's black bourgeoisie didn't approve of the Americans either, but they knew it was the English colonists who had given them this leave to swagger into town as if they owned the island. Which, indeed, they did, partially, that is, when the British gave them Chaguaramas, on the northwest coast of the island, not far from the capital, Port of Spain, to set down a naval base, and then Waller Field in central Trinidad, for the air force. It helped that the British explained that they needed the twenty battleships the Americans offered in exchange, but not enough to quell rancor in some who were making the American military bases a cause célèbre in their demands for independence.

Still, the simmering resentment of the American presence, shared by both the colonizers and the colonized, though for different reasons, was not enough to gain sympathy for the girl. How could it be rape when she was dressed like that, a fifteen-year-old girl with her bosom popping out of a tight red jersey top, and a skirt so short that, according to the nightclub owner, you could see her panties?

But, of course, the case the commissioner had assigned him was different. The woman in question, the victim, was English; the accused, the perpetrator, the brute, was a colored man.

The commissioner himself had come down to the station where Mumsford was posted and had spoken to him in private. "Mumsford," he said, "you are the only one I can trust with this job."

The job involved going to the scene of the crime, Chacachacare, a tiny, desolate island off the northwest coast of Trinidad, where the reputed rape had occurred, and taking the deposition of Dr. Peter Gardner, an Englishman, who had lodged the complaint on behalf of his fifteen-year-old daughter, Virginia.

"It is a delicate matter, you understand," the commissioner said. "Not for a colored man's ears or eyes."

The commissioner was himself Trinidadian. He was born in Trinidad, as were his parents and grandparents and great-great-grandparents. He was what the people in Trinidad called a French Creole. He was white. That is, his skin was the color of what white people called white, though it was tanned a golden brown from generations in the sun. Local gossip had it, though, that none of the white people in Trinidad whose families went back so many generations had escaped the tar brush, and indeed the telltale signs of the tar brush were evident in the commissioner's high cheekbones, his wide mouth and full lips, and in the curl that persisted in his thick brown hair. These features made him handsome, but skittish, too, for he had a deep-seated fear of being exposed, of finding himself in good company confronted by a man whose resemblance left no doubt that he was a relative with ancestors who had come from Africa.

The French had come in 1777 at the invitation of the king of Spain, who had neither the time nor the inclination to develop the island, one of the smallest of his "discoveries" in the New World. Preoccupied with the more alluring possibilities of gold in El Dorado on the South American continent, the king opened Trinidad to the French, who already had thriving plantations on the more northerly West Indian islands, thanks to slave labor from Africans they had captured on the west coast of Africa. The Spanish king thought he had struck a clever bargain, a cheap way to clear the bush in Trinidad while he was busy with weightier matters. The French brought thousands of African slaves to Trinidad from Martinique and Guadeloupe. Twenty years later, in 1797, the British seized Trinidad from the Spanish, but the French stayed on, claiming ownership of large plots of land, even after Emancipation in 1834.

Mumsford knew something of this history. He knew, too, that though the French Creoles on the island were linked to the English by the color of their skin, they were, nevertheless, culturally bonded to the Africans in Trinidad who had raised their children. More than once this knowledge had caused him to wonder whether, in a time of crisis, he could count on the commissioner's loyalty. Would he side with the English, or would he suddenly be gripped by misguided patriotism and join forces with the black people on the island? He was always a little put off by the commissioner's singsong Trinidadian English, though he had no quarrel with his grammar. On the question, however, of how to respond to Dr. Gardner's allegation, the commissioner put him completely at ease.

"Only *we*," the commissioner said, stressing the *we* and sending Mumsford a knowing look that sealed his trust, "can be depended upon with a matter of this delicacy. Don't forget, Mumsford, that girl, Ariana, has already come up with her own lies and can make a mess of this for all of us."

Us. The commissioner had a French-sounding last name, but Mumsford was satisfied that he was on his side.

Mumsford picked up the paper he had shoved aside and read Ariana's statement again. *He never rape her.* She had written *she*, not *her*, but he could not get his tongue to say it. Dropping the *d* from the verb was bad enough.

"Attempted rape, not rape," the commissioner had cautioned him. "In fact, Mumsford," he said, "if you can avoid using that word at all, so much the better. We can't have that stain on a white woman's honor."

And so it would have been—the nightmare of any red-blooded Englishman who had brought wife, daughters, sisters to these dark colonies—had that man, that savage, managed to do what no doubt had been his intention.

He had to remember to be careful then. It was not a rape, not even an attempted rape. There was no consummation. He must not give even the slightest suggestion that consummation could have been possible, that the purity of an English woman, that her unblemished flower, had been desecrated by a black man.

The woman, Ariana, had not put her letter in an envelope. She had glued together the ends of the paper with a paste she had made with flour and water. Mumsford was sure it was flour and water she had used, not store-bought glue. He was there when the commissioner slit open the letter. The dried dough, already cracked, crumbled in pieces, white dust scattering everywhere. He had leaned forward to clear the specks off the commissioner's desk and was in mid-sentence, rebuking Ariana for her lack of consideration for others—"What with the desk now covered in her mess"—when the commissioner interrupted him. It was good she had sealed it, whatever she had used, the commissioner said. They needed to be discreet. Then he paused, scratched his head, and added, "Though there is no guarantee she has not told the boatman. People here talk." He wagged his finger at Mumsford. No, they had to nip this in the bud. If they were not careful, the whole island would soon be repeating her version of what had happened on that godforsaken island. Soon they would be whispering that a white woman had fallen in love with a colored boy.

" 'I tell you he love she and she love him back.' " The commissioner read Ariana's words aloud. He threw back his head and laughed bitterly. "A total fabrication," he said. "How could it be otherwise?"

Mumsford did not need convincing. *They love one another. Bad.* That had to be a lie.

But it was not only Ariana's reference to rape and the pack of lies she wrote in defense of the colored boy that irritated Mumsford this morning. It was also her presumption—what he called the carnival mentality of the islanders, their tendency to trivialize everything, to make a joke of the most serious of matters, turning them into calypsos and then playing out their stories in the streets, in broad daylight, on their two-day Carnival, dressed in their ragtag costumes. Yes, an English doctor of high repute would be addressed as Mister, but he was sure Ariana did not know that, and certain that she knew that the doctor's name was not Prospero, but Gardner. He was Dr. Peter Gardner—Gardner, a proper English name—not Mr. Prospero, doctor, as she had scrawled next to her name.

Ordinarily Mumsford would have left it at that, dismissed the name Ariana had given to Dr. Peter Gardner as some unkind sobriquet, loaded with innuendo, taken from one of those long-winded tales the calypso-rhyming, carnival-dancing, rum-drinking natives told endlessly. For Prospero had no particular significance to Mumsford, though he had guessed correctly that it was the name of a character in a story. What story (it was a play by Shakespeare, his last) he did not know. Mumsford was a civil servant who had worked his way through the ranks of Her Majesty's police force. Like all English schoolboys he had read Charles Lamb, not the plays, and then not the story about Prospero. Nevertheless, he was on a special assignment and could leave nothing to chance. He had the honor of an Englishwoman to protect. So he made a note to himself to question Ariana. *Question for Ariana,* he wrote in his notebook. *Why do you call Dr. Gardner Prospero?*

He would have to speak to her separately, not in the presence of Dr. Gardner. That was the directive from the commissioner. Mumsford would have preferred otherwise. He wanted to expose her in front of Dr. Gardner for the liar she was, but when he argued his point, the commissioner stopped him. "I don't think that would be wise," he said.

For a brief moment, the tiniest sliver of a gap opened up between the Englishman and the French Creole. Would he, in the end, choose *them* over *us?* the Englishman wondered. For they could not always be depended upon to be grateful, even the white ones born here. The man stirring up trouble in the streets of Port of Spain with his call for independence was not grateful. And yet there were few on the island that England had done more for. England had educated him, England had paid his way to Oxford, but when he returned to Trinidad, the ungrateful wretch bit the hand that fed him: *Independence now!* Thousands were gathering behind him.

"You mean Eric Williams?" he asked the commissioner.

The commissioner ignored the question but he winked at him when he said, "We'll have time sufficient to deal with the girl."

Was the wink conspiratorial? Did he mean that England still had time in spite of the ravings of this troublemaking politician? Mumsford tried again. "This is still a Crown Colony," he said.

The commissioner slapped him on the back. "Let's not cause the good doctor more grief, okay, Inspector?"

Mumsford had to be satisfied with his response, for the commissioner kept his hand firmly on the small of Mumsford's back and didn't remove it until he had walked the inspector out of his office.

But though Mumsford could not say with certainty whether or not the commissioner sided with the Crown or with the burgeoning movement for independence, on the matter of race the commissioner had made himself clear. He would protect a white woman from malicious insinuations. Mumsford was to go alone to Chacachacare without his usual police partner, who was a colored Trinidadian, and, therefore, as the commissioner pointed out, could not be trusted to be objective.

"He will take the side of the colored man against the English girl," he said to Mumsford without the slightest trace of irony. "You'll have to do this alone."

Mumsford shut his notebook and reached for the official statement the commissioner had prepared for the press just in case Ariana had been indiscreet. He had placed the statement next to his brass desk lamp with the bottle-green glass shade, along with two sharpened pencils and his navy blue Parker fountain pen, which he had filled earlier that morning with black ink in preparation for the notes he would take later when he arrived in Chacachacare. Carefully, and reverentially, he unfolded the paper. It was the original copy. It bore Her Majesty's seal and was typed in blue ink on expensive ivory linen stationery. In the official statement, the commissioner had avoided the word *rape* altogether. Instead, he had written *attempted assault*. He had not named the victim, referring to her only as "a young, innocent girl, a fresh flower, an English rose," but he had identified the assailant: "Carlos Codrington, a colored man on the island of Chacachacare."

Mumsford's pencil-thin lips curled downward, an inverted *U* on a face on a cartoon, and he shook his head in disgust. *Carlos Codrington.* They were two names, he was sure, which would never be found together in his beloved England. But, as he had resigned himself to accepting, he was not in his beloved England. He was here, on this mixed-up, smothering, suffocating, sultry island, on this stifling, godforsaken, mosquito-ridden, insect-infested, sweat-drenched outpost, with its too, too bright colors, its too, too much everything: too much rain in the rainy season, too much sun in the dry season, too much blue in the sky, too much green in the grass, too much red in the creeping flowering plants, too much turquoise in the sea, too much white on the sand. Too, too many black people. And here there would be a Codrington who was a Carlos.

Mumsford had not come to Trinidad for the black people, of course. He came for the sun, the warmth, when the thought of another winter, another month of gray skies, of the perpetual drip, drip of rain and the smothering fog in England, threatened to drive him insane. These days it often crossed his mind that he had indeed gone crazy, mad, to think this would have been better. This would have been what he needed to end the ceaseless colds that pursued him season after season in Birmingham, and the damnable pollen in the spring that found its way always to his sinuses, leaving his eyes bleary and itchy, his nose red and runny.

The muscles at the base of his head formed a knot, and he reached for the pair of silver tongs his housekeeper had placed on a silver tray on his desk, as she did each morning before he left for work, along with a crystal bowl filled with ice cubes, an empty glass, and a pitcher of water. He was a fairly young man, not much over thirty, slender, but already with a middle-aged paunch from too many beers in the pub after work. He had thick, light brown hair, a neatly trimmed mustache, hazel eyes, and a complexion that was naturally ruddy, his cheeks rosy as apples in England, though here, under the constant sun, sweat dampening his face no matter how often he mopped it with his handkerchief, he looked baked, or, rather, boiled, his skin a startling pink as if it would erupt.

And it was startling pink now as he thought of the brochures that had lured him here, pictures of happy English families frolicking on the beach, their blond hair swept by tropical breezes, which he knew now to be either blisteringly hot or so thick with moisture they would hardly have been able to breathe.

Wielding the tongs between his fingers, he lifted two ice cubes out of the bowl, dropped them in the glass, and filled it with water. His head was throbbing. Behind God's back, that's where he was. They should be shot, lined up one next to the other in front of a firing squad, those liars who wrote those ads, who ensnared innocents like him to this outpost.

He had jumped at the chance to escape England's soggy weather when he was offered the post of assistant to the commissioner of police in Trinidad, and since he was an only child and his father was dead, he had brought his mother with him.

"The sun is not the only advantage," the recruiting officer had pointed out to him. When he looked puzzled, the officer clarified. "You can improve your class, your station in life. In the colonies, young man, every Englishman is a lord."

Yes, Mumsford thought, remembering, the Empire was still standing, crumbling, weakened at the knees—they had lost India, most of

China, Africa was slipping from their hands, and there were rumblings in the West Indies and the East Indies—but there were still years left for an Englishman in the colonies.

He brought the glass to his lips and drained it. The cold water coursing through the heat in his chest felt good. The knot in the back of his head loosened. He had to admit it: Aside from the sun and the crawly things, he lived like a lord—housekeeper, cook, chauffeur, gardener, a house with three bedrooms, an English car with leather seats, tennis and ballroom dancing at the Country Club, tea at four at Queen's Park Hotel, golf at St. Andrew's, yachting down the Grenadines. He began to feel better, his nerves soothed, as they had been soothed in the past, by the realization that it was not all a loss. There was much to gain. Why, last month, for example, there was an invitation to cocktails at the Governor's House when a relative of royalty was visiting. What stories he would have for the people back home in his English village! He, Mumsford, rubbing shoulders with royalty! The sickening humidity and the too, too bright colors were almost worth the sacrifice. He gathered the papers on his desk, his mood much improved. He had a job to do and he would do it well. The brute, after all, was Carlos, not Charles. A dead giveaway.

He was practically smiling when he bent down to put his papers in his briefcase, consoling himself with his conviction that even without meeting this Carlos, anyone who mattered would know "he was not one of *us.*" Charles Codrington would have made perfect English sense; Carlos Rodriguez would have been logical. But Carlos Codrington? He was still mumbling happily to himself, reassured by the false comfort he had given himself, when he saw the ants, tiny little russet ones, so small as to be almost invisible, crawling up the sides of his briefcase, from a brown trail that began at a quivering mound in a corner of the mahogany wood floor, and his mood swung back. He had done it again. Last night, tired, his head reeling from more alcohol than he should have had, he had left the briefcase on the floor—a habit he had not broken from his life in England.

It was probably no more than a crumb or a speck of jelly from a tart. In England it would lie there until someone had noticed it. Here, in an instant, an army of ants appeared out of nowhere. His mother no doubt had had her tea in here. He had warned her. Drop the tiniest spot of food and in seconds they would swarm over it. Peel an orange, put it down, turn away for just a few minutes, and they would materialize. In the wet season, they were bigger, fatter. After a rainstorm, some grew wings. At night, they flitted around his bedside lamp before landing on the walls, their flimsy new-made wings fluttering nervously. In the morning, the floor was covered with them, their wings discarded, their bodies like tiny cargo trains, carriages and all, heading toward the next pickup, the next port of food. He had made it a practice to check for them, especially for the tiny russet ones that were the most insidious. Often he would find them when it was too late, when he had already opened a book and they had crawled down its spine into the shafts of hair on his arms, when they were in the folds of the papers he had put into his briefcase. Or when, after he had put on his pajamas and was safely under his mosquito net, they would scoot up his back like thieves, their tiny legs tingling his skin.

This was not a place, Mumsford had discovered, where a man could go to the lavatory in the dark. In the daylight, spiders, lizards, centipedes, water bugs, cockroaches hid in the crevices near the pipes in the bathroom, but at night, they were everywhere: next to the sink, next to the lavatory where more than once a water bug had scuttled across his bare feet when he was sitting down, his pants at his knees, his bare bottom exposed, his legs tucked under unprepared for flight. He had learned, finally, from these unpleasant experiences not only to turn on the light but to wait behind the closed door, even if his bladder was bursting, giving them time to scatter back to their hiding place.

Last week, just as he was stepping into the shower, naked as he was born, he was attacked again. A thing had fallen, or jumped, from the ledge of the window near the shower, onto the shower floor. Splat! He heard the disgusting sound. It was not a water bug. It was larger and uglier than a water bug, six inches long, with a multitude of feet.

It was the two fangs—he was sure they were fangs—jutting out of its head that caused his heart to lurch and the veins in his neck to flood and bulge out thick. He flew out of the house, barely managing to wrap a towel around his waist, which nevertheless loosened when he clutched the gardener by his shoulders, exposing his soft penis nestled against a scraggly bush of long, thin red pubic hairs.

"Is just a millepatte, sir."

Terrified, but humiliated also by the gardener's casual response to the fear that gripped him (not to mention the exposure of his penis, which he was certain would become fodder for gossip), Mumsford could only stutter out a command: "Get it out of here!"

But the gardener's face broke into a wide grin. "Is your lucky day, sir. Kill it, sir. Is good luck, sir, when you see a millepatte yourself, sir. You get plenty money if you kill it yourself, sir."

It took all of Mumsford's English stiff upper lip to get the gardener to understand he wanted the thing removed from his bathroom. *Now!*

He would learn later that a millepatte, as his gardener called it, was a kind of scorpion. If it had stung him, he would have been in the hospital burning with fever. He could have died. But it was a millepatte to his gardener, a lucky charm, called simply millepatte because of its many feet. Mille, the word for a thousand in French.

How they remembered everything, these people, though they never got the history right! Their capital was Port of Spain, but England had won her wars with Spain more than three centuries ago. They had villages with names like Sans Souci, Blanchisseuse, and Pointe à Pierre and yet the French were never their colonizers. Their singsong sentences ended with *oui*, which, at first, though it made no sense to him, Mumsford understood as *we: I tired, we. I gone, we.* Then he found out that it was *oui. Oui,* as in the French, meaning *yes.*

In the country districts, they spoke a patois, French laced with some African words they remembered and the English imposed on them. They had Amerindian and African blood in them, and though Mumsford shivered to think of it (but he knew what had happened in those battles for conquest of these islands, and in the days of slavery), they had European blood in them, too—Spanish, French, Dutch, and, as he was forced to admit, English.

Now it was fashionable: the impurities. Now, the days long gone when his people could pick off the best of them, the prettiest, and she would lie down for the man who had ordered her to, who had demanded, because he was master, because she was his slave and had no choice, the tables were turning. They would choose. Carlos, the colored boy with the English last name, would choose, would think he could choose. The chief justice would choose, the chief medical officer would choose. They would think they could pick out the prettiest, the best. They could marry an English rose.

For that was what they had both done, the black chief justice and the black chief medical officer. His mother was with their wives that very morning, at the Country Club, playing croquet as if nothing had changed, as if it were natural, the normal evolution of things, that black men would marry white women now that England was about to relinquish yet another colony (indications were everywhere in Trinidad), now that her reign was about to end. But it would never be normal for him. Never for him.

I tell you he love she and she love him back. He would see about that. He would trap that lying Ariana.

Mumsford brushed the last of the ants off his briefcase. He was ready to go. He pulled up his khaki knit high socks over his pink calves, adjusted the wide brown leather belt on his khaki shorts, patted the gleaming buttons on his well-pressed khaki shirt, lifted his stiff khaki policeman's hat off the hat rack, checked it for ants before putting it on his head, picked up his polished dark brown policeman's baton, gave himself a last look over in the mirror, made a soldier's right turn for Good Old England, there, in his drawing room, to the surprise of no one, not to his housekeeper, and certainly not to the driver who had come to collect him, and marched down the steps.

Left, right. That was what he did to show his loyalty to England before this ungrateful lot, biding their time until he was gone, until all the English were gone. Well, let them have it. He, for one, would not be sad to see independence come. Let them have the whole damn place, damn insects and all, damn miserable, stifling weather, damn mixing of bloods. Bloody impurities.

March. He would march down the steps. He was wearing Her Majesty's uniform.

"Mr. Inspector, sir. Your briefcase, sir."

He turned to see his housekeeper, one hand over her mouth, choking back her laughter, the other extended with his briefcase. He snatched it out of her hand. Let them snicker. He was an Englishman.

Once inside the car, he breathed in deeply, closed his eyes, and leaned back against the plush, dark brown leather seat. He would set things right. He would see about the choosing Carlos Codrington had done. It would be his word against the word of an Englishman. In Chacachacare he would settle the score for every Englishman whose daughter and sister had become prey these days of the colored man.

TWO

CHACACHACARE, where Mumsford was heading that morning, was a leper colony. It was not always so. In the eighteenth century Spanish and French settlers brought their African slaves to the island. Within a year, working the Africans mercilessly, they turned Chacachacare into a thriving cotton plantation, one so successful that the Amerindians, who were summarily chased off the island but continued to fish close by, named the island Chacacha, the Amerindian word for cotton. By the mid-nineteenth century, though, cotton plantations in North America made growing cotton on Chacachacare no longer lucrative and the island became a seaside resort for the sons and daughters of former slave owners.

Whalers had also made a fortune in the waters around Chacachacare. Gulfo de Ballena, Gulf of the Whales, the Spanish settlers called the Gulf of Paria, the body of water cupped in the embrace of the two strips of land that extended off the western coast of Trinidad, the northern entrance guarded by the Dragon—the Dragon's Mouth—the southern by the Serpent—the Serpent's Mouth. Like cotton, however, whaling had come to an end long before the century closed.

Chacachacare was not a seaside resort when Dr. Peter Gardner arrived on the island with his daughter, Virginia, who had recently turned three. And strictly speaking it was not a leper colony either. Though the leprosarium continued to operate on a small scale, it was officially closed in 1950 when the Dominican Sisters of St. Catherine of Siena, who had ministered to the sick there, left the island enfeebled by age and the relentless sun, and unable to replenish their ranks because of a world war that had halted recruits. The Dominicans were replaced by the Sisters of Mercy from America, but life on the island among the lepers proved more than the American nuns were willing to endure. Count Finbar Ryan, archbishop of Port of Spain, had left them no room for compromise. "Sign a blank check," he counseled those who answered his call, "and honor whatever the Lord may write on it."

The Lord wrote more than the new nuns could bear. They lasted barely five years, until 1955, not long after a fisherman found a nun's white habit floating on the sea off Chacachacare, a suicide attributed to depression.

In fairness to the Dominicans, they had not abandoned their patients. By the time they left, new sulphonic drugs were halting the progress of the bacteria that caused nerve ends on the afflicted to wither and die, the skin to rot, and fingers and toes to fall off. Nevertheless, the lepers begged them to stay. "The doctors seem to give us up [to] death," one of the patients wrote, expressing the sentiments of the others in a petition sent to the governor. "The Sisters on the contrary care for us. The more miserable, pitiful, sinful we are, the more they show us love. They care for us until they have closed our eyes."

The Dominicans had come to Trinidad from France in 1868 at the request of the British government. The leprosarium that the British had established in Cocorite, on the outskirts of Port of Spain, the capital of Trinidad, had failed to contain the disease. It was spreading like wildfire to the city and beyond, and the British colonizers were terrified.

They were responsible, of course. It was they who had caused this disease to run amuck on the quiet, idyllic island of Trinidad, where hibiscus and bougainvillea bloomed in the sun, anthuriums in the shade, and where, in the dry season, the hills were aflame with gold and crimson blossoms from the branches of the flamboyant and dotted with the brilliant reds, yellows, pinks, and whites of the poui rising beneath a sky dazzling blue, clouds white and fluffy as new cotton.

A man could feed his family with what he hunted and fished in those days. For if you saw Trinidad from the height of an airplane, what you saw was an island floating in the delta of the Orinoco, a sliver cut off from the rain forests of the Amazon, its flora and fauna stranded with the divide. There, unlike any other island in the Caribbean chain, agouti, deer, tattou, lapp, manicou, and cats ferocious as tigers ran wild; fish and crustaceans—shrimp, lobster, crab, oyster—everyday table food. *National Geographic* sent in scouts. Everything they could find in the Amazon, they could find here, and there were swampy mangroves, too, and sea the color of turquoise, beaches ringed with coconut fronds and the leaves of wide sea-almond trees.

It was greed that caused the epidemic. Slavery had been abolished and the Africans, scarred by nightmares of the horrors of the plantation, had fled to the cities. Left with no workers to cut the sugarcane, process it into sugar, and ferment the juices into alcohol, for which they had developed an addiction, the British raked the slums of their continental colonies in the east. Five acres of land after five years, they promised, if the workers wanted to stay, or passage back home. Thousands came from India. They came with the disease.

At first the nuns treated the patients topically with chaulmoogra oil from the seeds of tropical trees in Asia belonging to the genus Hydnocarpus, and with cod liver oil from codfish, but the oils did not work. The disease still gutted faces, lopped off limbs. So they injected the oils, once a day, in the afternoons, and startled birds from their evening roosts when bloodcurdling screams from children, full-grown women and men, too, rent the air. Then, from late afternoon until well after the sun had set below the horizon, the sky was filled with the frantic flapping of wings, and as far away as Cocorite across the sea, street dogs howled and tears sprang from the eyes of villagers.

They ran away. They would not stay, the ones subjected to these treatments. The cure to them, the searing pain of those injections, was

a million times worse than the disease. So the epidemic spread. The
nuns gave the colonial government a choice: a colony in Chacachacare
or the end of Trinidad. The British sent in troops. One of the nuns'
diary dated May 10, 1922, records the day:

> At 6 a.m., the patients were seized with horror when the news spread
> throughout the wards that the whole place was surrounded and cor-
> doned off by policemen on foot and on horseback. A dead silence set
> in . . . since it was impossible to escape, all had to be resigned to their
> fate. Some were sobbing, others fainted, and others again were seized
> with fits. The sisters could hardly bear the sight of the distress. Even
> the policemen were moved with compassion. A crowd of onlookers
> gathered outside to see the patients being escorted by policemen to
> the Cocorite pier, where a steamer was waiting to take them to Cha-
> cachacare.

The sons and daughters of slave owners who had got rich on the cotton plantations on Chacachacare did not sob and faint, but it was no
less difficult to pry them away from their vacation homes. Chacachacare was Crown land; it belonged to the British royal family.
When the governor issued the order, the vacationers were obliged to
leave. They were compensated, of course. Even today, the descendants
of some of these slave-owning families hold rights to large plots of
seafront land on the offshore islands. Ninety years they were given in
exchange for a meager fee, and for at least one of them, a lease that
would not expire until the year 2051.

In its own way, the clergy smoothed the way for the colonial government by fanning the flames of superstition already raging in the
Caribbean. To most people in this part of the world, leprosy was a
curse from God, a disease of the poor and the slovenly. Even after it
was renamed Hansen's disease, after the Norwegian Armauer Hansen,
who had identified it in 1874, it still bore this stigma that had its roots
in the Old Testament.

But leprosy was caused by bacteria, not God's curse, and it was not
absolutely clear that it was sufficiently contagious to warrant the isola-
tion of those infected from the rest of the population. In eighty-two

years, only two of the nuns succumbed to the disease. To the religious, of course, this was not proof that the disease was not contagious, but, rather, evidence of Divine intervention, God protecting those who had given themselves willingly to Him in His service. In the case of Sister Rose de Sainte Marie Vébert, who, in the opinion of many, deserved to be canonized, there seemed to be merit in this faith they had in God's mercy. It was said that the disease had so ravaged her that it took both her tongue and her sight, though for eighteen years she continued to nurse the sick.

When she died, the hand of God was evident. Another entry in a nun's diary dated June 17, 1937, tells the story:

> The sisters kept singing hymns and canticles by her bedside to help her regain her calm when the terrible fits shook her poor body. Finally she breathed her last, gently. The sisters transported her body to the chapel. While she lay there exposed, something extraordinary happened: all traces of the awful disease disappeared from her face; and it was looking most beautiful . . .

The sisters remained in Chacachacare for twenty-eight years. Few spoke English when they first arrived and they had to rely on hand gestures and drawings before they managed to pick up the rudiments of the language from the patients. But this was not their only challenge. There was no electricity or running water in Chacachacare, and during the war years, from 1939 to 1945, when there were constant fears of German U-boats patrolling the waters, which, after all, were British waters since Trinidad belonged to England, service between the leprosarium in Chacachacare and the mainland was often curtailed, and food was scarce. Patients, who in the past were not allowed to fish or cultivate the land, now fished and grew vegetables, and, troubling for the nuns, were also permitted to work side by side with members of the opposite sex. This liberal attitude of the colonial government posed a moral problem for the nuns. They would not be the conduit for sin, for base carnality. They had taken pains to prevent this occurrence and in this holy endeavor, the island had been their natural ally.

Chacachacare was shaped like a horseshoe. It was fairly flat in the middle with two fingers of hilly land that curved out to the sea on either side. The nuns arranged for the doctors to be on one end of this horseshoe and for them to be on the other (the doctors being male and they female). In the middle, they put the hospital and living quarters for the patients, which were strictly segregated by gender. Men and women came into contact with each other only under the supervision of the nuns or medical personnel. But all that changed with the war. The colonial government was struggling to keep its empire intact and there was no time for Chacachacare, for enforcing laws to appease the consciences of nuns.

But there were other considerations. There was the matter of babies born of the couplings of men and women riddled with the disease.

Years later, the sisters would say that the most painful task they were ever called upon to do was to take these babies away from their parents and place them in the orphanage in Trinidad. The mothers were inconsolable. They cried for weeks on end. Some, refusing to eat, died within months. Those who lived to be cured often faced rejection from their children when they went to the orphanage to collect them. *No, no, you are too ugly to be my mother.*

But the Chacachacare Mumsford was on his way to was a different place. There were better drugs, better treatments, and patients stayed on the colony because they chose to, because the disease had so deformed them they feared ridicule on the mainland, because they preferred to be treated at the leprosarium in Chacachacare than at the outpatient clinics in Trinidad, where they were seen as pariahs. In fact, for a brief time, between 1950 and 1952, visiting doctors performed surgeries in Chacachacare to excise and graft sagging lips, build bone nose bridges where the tissue had been eaten away, correct "claw hands," and open eyes closed by the disease.

There was one doctor left on the island now, the commissioner had informed Mumsford. Most of the doctors had been Europeans who had come to the colony primarily to conduct research. Once that research had produced a cure, he said (Mumsford thought with some bitterness), they left for new adventures.

Was the remaining doctor Dr. Peter Gardner? Mumsford asked reasonably.

Oh no, not Dr. Peter Gardner. Yes, Gardner was a medical doctor, but he was referring to the other doctor, a local man who sometimes stayed on the island and took care of the remaining patients.

"Then what is Dr. Gardner doing there?" Mumsford asked.

The commissioner had no answer, but to Mumsford's second question as to the character of Dr. Gardner ("What sort of man is he?" Mumsford had asked), he was quick to respond. "A gentleman. A rare breed. A white man who is not intimidated by the goings-on on the island these days."

The harshness of his tone puzzled Mumsford. There it was, without the least prompting from him, the commissioner had spoken disparagingly about "goings-on," and yet it had been impossible to draw him out to say unequivocally that he supported the Crown against the movement for independence.

"What goings-on?" Mumsford took the chance to ask.

"Colored people getting too big for their shoes," the commissioner said.

And because on that point Mumsford could agree, he didn't press him for more, he didn't ask, as he wanted to, if he didn't think the people in Trinidad owed a debt to England for the progress they had made, and, if owing England, they shouldn't be willing to remain, as the French colonies of Martinique and Guadeloupe were willing to remain, a loyal Crown colony.

The commissioner's orders to Mumsford were to get Dr. Gardner's deposition and to bring the alleged assailant (he could not bring himself to say rapist) back with him to Trinidad. Mumsford was not to question the English girl. In his letter, Dr. Gardner had specifically requested that no one interrogate his daughter. She was only fifteen. He did not want her involved in a scandal. He had done his part: filed the complaint and locked the savage in a pen in the back of his house. All that was left for the commissioner to do was to arrange to have the brute taken to prison.

"Of course we cannot do that," the commissioner said to Mumsford.

"Cannot?" Again, a shadow of a doubt darkened Mumsford's brow.

"Everything will be on the QT, of course," the commissioner said.

"Nothing in the newspapers, or anything like that. Still, there is the matter of the law, due process. You can't put someone in jail without some inquiry, at least the semblance of one. The monks at St. Benedict's owe me a favor. They will keep the boy until we can lock him up."

How long? Mumsford wanted to know.

"All the facts have to be gathered and corroborated."

"Corroborated?"

"There has to be evidence to support the allegations. That's your job, Mumsford. That girl Ariana has made things a little messy for us. She is a bloody liar, of course, but we need to get the evidence from Dr. Gardner. In the meanwhile, we will remove the boy. Dr. Gardner has him secured, but he can't remain on the island with the girl, in the same house. It's not decent."

It was this point of decency, or rather indecency, that Mumsford was mulling over in his head as he sat back in the car that was taking him to the dock not far from Cocorite, where he would get the boat to Chacachacare. It was not only indecent for the boy to remain on the island and in the same house, it was indecent, he believed, for him to have ever been there at all.

"He was not alone," the commissioner had explained when Mumsford raised his eyebrows. "There was also Ariana. They were both Dr. Gardner's servants. Anyhow, there was nowhere else for them to stay."

The explanation was not satisfactory to Mumsford. Servant or not, it was imprudent, reckless, for an English father to permit a black boy to live in the same house as his young white daughter.

Who was this man? Who was this Peter Gardner who had been so careless as to have risked the virtue of his daughter, as to have endangered her life and limb on this Land of the Dead?

He did not want to go. If the commissioner had not insisted, if Ariana had not sent a letter by the boatman full of her malicious lies, if (and this was the most compelling of all the reasons) Trinidad was not all riled up with talk about independence and colored people were not looking for any excuse to blame their failures on England, there would have been no need for him to go. The message Dr. Gardner had sent, written by his own hand and on his stationery, would have sufficed in spite of the commissioner's admonition about the law and due process. Now he had to face the half-hour sea crossing.

He leaned forward on his seat and tapped his driver on the shoulder. "I say, what's the sea like at this hour?" he asked.

The chauffeur looked at him through the rearview mirror. "Good, sir. Calm seas, sir," he said.

And the sea was calm, but the chauffeur had not warned him about the jellyfish. There were hundreds of them, transparent little blue buoys, their tentacles splayed out behind them like carnival streamers, bobbing in the water around the sides of the boat. He wanted to be brave (he had felt the quivering in his neck from the moment he spotted the jellyfish), but when he raised his leg to step into the boat, his English reserve abandoned him and he found himself waving frantically to his chauffeur, who was leaning casually against the parked car, chewing a toothpick that dangled from his bottom lip.

"Driver!" he shouted. "I say, driver!"

"Sir?" The chauffeur raised his head and turned in his direction, but he remained where he was and Mumsford was forced to be explicit.

"Help me!"

In the end, though Mumsford could not avoid noticing the group of dark-skinned young men snickering in the background, he clutched the chauffeur's arm, digging his fingers into the chauffeur's hard flesh with such desperation that the blood drained from his hand, turning his knuckles white as chalk.

And the chauffeur had not mentioned that within minutes of leaving the calm waters of Trinidad, the boat would skirt the edges of the Dragon's Mouth. When the boat began to rock, Mumsford found himself again at the mercy of a dark-skinned man. For the commissioner, insisting on secrecy to protect the good name of Dr. Gardner's daughter, had not sent the government's launch, manned by a uniformed navigational officer; he had rented a pirogue, and the man at the tiller was a fisherman, a local boatman.

"Nothing to worry about." The boatman grinned when Mumsford turned anxiously toward him. He was sitting sideways with the insouciance of a man on his way to a picnic, one hand steering the engine and the other waving in the air as he spoke.

A fancy man, Mumsford thought. His life was in the hands of a fancy man. *A saga boy.* It was a term he had learned from the officers at the station.

"Just the wash from the first boca, sir. We go pass far from it and I go take the boat easy, easy, past the second and the third one."

Mumsford clamped his hands down hard on the sides of his seat and braced himself.

The Dragon's Mouth. It was the channel that connected the Atlantic Ocean to the Gulf of Paria. Across it were underwater rocks, some visible above the surface of the sea, three large enough for the rich to build vacation homes on them.

"The Dragon teeth," the boatman shouted from the back of the boat. "The first two big teeth call Monos and Huevos. The last one I taking you to is Chacachacare. Is a boca in the space between each big teeth. The water bad there. It rough. He have four mouth, the Dragon."

Mumsford pressed down harder on his seat. Cerberus, lips drawn back in a grin of fangs, one more head to strike terror in the heart of the condemned.

"You have nothing to worry about, sir." The boatman's voice rose above the drone of the boat engine. "You in good hands with me, sir."

In good hands? He was barefooted, dressed scantily in a loose navy T-shirt and red shorts. How could he be in good hands with this man who could not even speak proper English? He should have put more pressure on the commissioner to give him the launch, Mumsford thought, demanded he send him a man in a uniform.

"We just pass one of the Dragon small tooth," the boatman called out merrily. "We does call it Scorpion Island. Well, we don't call it Scorpion no more. We call it Centipede Island now. They have more centipede there than scorpion. Centipede long, long. 'Bout twelve, fourteen, inches."

Mumsford looked back and saw the tiny island topped with green vegetation.

"Don't know if centipede long like that eat the scorpion or the centipede more frisky than scorpion. Know what I mean?" The boatman

winked at him, but Mumsford was in no mood for winks. He was terrified.

"And on Chacachacare?" he asked nervously. "Are there scorpions . . .
centipedes, there?"

"Maybe one or two scorpion, I think. Telling you the truth, sir . . ."
The boatman scratched his head and wrinkled his nose. "I never hear
'bout leper dying from scorpion bite." The idea seemed to strike him
as funny. He laughed out loud. "Scorpion catch leprosy before leper
die from scorpion bite. You know what I mean, sir?"

Mumsford's face remained resolutely serious. "So are there scorpions on Chacachacare?" he asked.

The boatman wiped his mouth with the back of his hand. "I never
hear about that, sir. It only have centipede, and if centipede bite you on
your leg, you don't have to bother. Just have to mash the centipede in
rum and pour the rum over where they bite you. You be surprise how
your leg heal up fast, fast."

Mumsford gritted his teeth and faced forward in his seat. He had
only to step on the poisonous millepatte, the gardener had said to him,
and he would get rich. Now the boatman was recommending an anti-
dote to a centipede bite. Crush the centipede in rum, he said. Thank
God he was born in England, where medicine was based on science
and not in this godforsaken part of the world, where he would have
been at the mercy of the superstitions of ignorant people!

The boat rocked, but slightly, as they neared the second boca between the islands of Monos and Huevos. True to the boatman's word,
they passed its outskirts without much difficulty.

"Dey name is Spanish. You know, from the time when Columbus
and the other Spanish people came down here. Monos is monkey in
Spanish," the boatman said proudly, "and Huevos mean egg."

Mumsford already knew the literal translation from his Spanish
classes in grammar school and he conveyed his disinterest to the boatman.

"You don't want to know why? The tourists and them always asking
why. Why this, why that. Sometimes just to satisfy them, I does make
up things I don't know nothing about, but I know about Monos and
Huevos."

Mumsford was not impressed. He was more concerned about what he needed to look out for when he got to Chacachacare. "Are there monkeys on Chacachacare?" he asked.

"It don't have no monkey on Chacachacare," the boatman said, and undeterred, though Mumsford had positioned his back firmly against him, he informed him that the Spanish people killed all the monkeys on Monos. "They name it Monos and then they kill the Red Howlers. You think they would've change the name after that, right? But you wrong."

Mumsford looked steadily in front of him.

"Is turtle egg they have on Huevos," the boatman went on. "The turtle swim out in the sea after they lay they egg on the beach. That is how the Spanish people make it in the early days. They eat turtle egg and turtle meat. When they leave here and gone on their way discovering, they used to turn the turtle upside down on the ship so the turtle stay alive. I just can't believe they was so bad that every day they cut off a piece of the turtle and leave them bleeding till they finish them off. But you know," his voice became grave, "those Spanish people did some bad, bad things to the Africans they made slaves."

Mumsford wanted him to shut up. "If there are turtle eggs on the island, the Spaniards must not have killed all the turtles," he said mockingly. He was tired of these stories about what white men had done to Africans. The past was the past. The slaves were free now. The present was what concerned him, and in the present, his body was on fire. If the trip lasted much longer he would burn, and then in a matter of days he would start shedding like a common reptile.

"You right, sir. So I suppose you could say in the case of Huevos, the name still fit. Correct, sir?"

"Correct," Mumsford said without enthusiasm.

The boatman said nothing more for a while. When he spoke again, his voice was so soft that Mumsford was not quite sure he had heard him correctly.

"I suppose you know the princess was there." That was what the boatman had said, and it was only his tone that made Mumsford ask him to repeat himself, for a sly intimacy had entered his voice and Mumsford wanted to be sure.

"Yes, Princess Margaret sheself," the boatman said.

Mumsford glared at him.

"She come with the governor-general, two, maybe three years now. She like the tortoiseshell she find there. Papers say she plan to make a comb and spectacles for sheself."

It was not tortoiseshell; it was the shell of the hawksbill turtle, unique for its translucent amber color, some of which was speckled with black, others with green, red, or white. A letter written by a self-styled naturalist was printed in the papers warning of the extinction of the turtles if "certain royalty" insisted on killing them for combs and spectacles.

"He doesn't dare mention the princess by name," Mumsford had said to his mother when he read the complaint. "The coward. These are Crown lands and Crown seas. The Crown can do whatever the Crown wants with Crown property."

"She say the water in the bay in Huevos so nice, she find it hard to leave. She bathe here all the time in she bathing suit. Between you and me," the boatman continued confidentially, "she could have bathed naked if she want. Hardly anybody here."

His mouth quivered slightly and Mumsford took notice when he passed his tongue across his bottom lip.

"I lucky. I get the chance to see her one day. She cheeks pink, pink, like a rose. But I never did see her in she bathing suit. If only . . ."

It was too much for him. The body of Her Royal Highness exposed to the lecherous fantasies of a common boatman! Mumsford cut him off. "How much farther?" he barked.

But if the boatman had been hurt by Mumsford's rebuff, he soon got his revenge. They were now entering the tail end of the third boca on the approach to Rust's Bay in Chacachacare. Waves swelled and fell in quick succession like the folds of a fan. Mumsford clutched his seat. "Hold on tight!" the boatman called out to him. The boat rose high in the air and then slapped down hard on the water. Mumsford lurched forward.

"Hold up your back!" the boatman shouted. Before Mumsford could respond, he was walking toward him. "Yes, just so," the boatman said, and passed him, making his way to the helm of the boat. "See, I can stand up because I accustom." He spread out his arms and legs, balancing himself perfectly though the boat pitched up and down, flinging long sprays of water at them, almost blinding Mumsford. "This is nothing. We do this all the time. I know how it bad for you people from the big countries," he yelled over the loud thudding sounds of the hull hitting the water. "Is just a little rough passage. We go pass it soon. Don't be frighten. Is a little thing."

The nerves at the ends of Mumsford's fingers were still tingling, his stomach still churning, when the boat reached calmer waters, close to the right prong of the horseshoe that was the island of Chacachacare. His face was scorched, and in spite of the seawater that had soaked his jacket, he was hot, sweaty. Only after the boat rounded the bend and a pleasant assortment of pink and ivory angles appeared at the edge of the sea, nestled in the forest of trees that fanned up an incline, did the tightness in his jaw begin to loosen.

It was the A-framed structure, with wings behind it, on top of another floor with a covered veranda, that calmed him. For suddenly in front of him were not the contours of a tropical house but of a Swiss chalet. Snow, an icy wind blowing through pine trees were what he was thinking of when he took out his handkerchief and dried the perspiration that had gathered on his brow.

"Dr. Gardner's house, one presumes," he said to the boatman, and allowed himself a faint smile. But the boatman said no, it was not Dr. Gardner's house. It was the real doctor's house.

"Real?"

"The doctor who see about the lepers."

Disappointment brought the stiffness back in Mumsford's jaw.

Misinterpreting the change in Mumsford's face, the boatman added quickly, "Maybe you see him another day. He don't always be here. He come to the island now and then to give the lepers they medicine. If you want to see him, maybe you come another time."

Mumsford bit his lip. The house was still as a grave. As they drew nearer, it seemed all but abandoned. The pretty pink that had caught his eyes was in fact rust. The entire galvanized roof, apparently neglected for years in the sun and rain, was stained with it. In parts the rust had turned bright orange, in some places a pale pink. Close up he saw that the ivory ripples below the roof were wood slats that were spotted and scraped, in need of fresh paint. The whitewash on the concrete walls on the bottom floor was recent but it barely camouflaged the places where the concrete had begun to crumble. The wooden shutters and doors were closed. Here and there Mumsford could make out where a shutter was broken, a slat dangled from a nail. Weeds and thin patches of high grass sprouted between the dirt and stones near the concrete pillars that held up the house. The only sign of life, if it could be called a sign of life, was a brown burlap hammock on the veranda swinging listlessly in the slight breeze. Someone had strung one end to a nail on the wall of the house and the other to one of the four unpainted wood poles that supported the rusty galvanized roof covering the veranda. But there was nothing, no other trace, not a piece of clothing, not a piece of paper, not a kitchen utensil, to indicate the existence of that someone.

He was in the Land of the Dead. There were no rivers, no ponds, no freshwater anywhere on the island, the commissioner had told him. No water except what one chanced to collect when it rained.

"And the lepers?" A chill ran up his spine.

"Not to worry. They never come here. They on the other side. 'Rond the bend. They can't see you from this side."

"And Dr. Gardner?" It was an effort to keep his fear from affecting his voice.

"Up yonder," the boatman said, pointing to the distance beyond the doctor's house. "Way behind there."

All Mumsford could see was a thick nest of trees and interlocking branches. His eyebrows converged.

"It have a road," the boatman said sympathetically. "You get there easy."

But no road was in sight when the boatman steered the boat to the low stone wall that separated the doctor's house from the sea, and once on land, on the pebbled dirt yard that bordered the doctor's house (for there was no beach), what the boatman led him to was not a road but a dirt track, bounded on either side by bushes thinned out by the sun and entwined with vines whose brown stems were as thick as rope. Stiff dried branches stuck out across the dirt track and poked his legs.

"You lucky is the dry season," the boatman said, "or you need cutlass to pass here. The bush thick when it rain."

Mumsford asked him about snakes. In the dry season they crawled close to houses looking for water.

"Only horsewhip," the boatman said.

"Horsewhip? Is it poisonous?"

"We does call it horsewhip because . . ."

Lines of sweat were trickling down Mumsford's forehead into his eyes. He lost his patience. "For God's sake, man." He swiped his hand across his eyes. "I don't want to know *why* you call it horsewhip. I want to know *if* it is poisonous. Can you answer that simple question?"

"Everybody from England does want to know," the boatman said defensively.

"*I* want to know if it is poisonous. Can you tell me that? " Mumsford had moved to the middle of the dirt track, far from the edge of the bushes, and was examining the area around him.

"Is a thin, thin, green snake. Like a whip. Just sting you when it whip you. It don't kill."

Not poisonous. But Mumsford had no chance to savor his relief. Just when he felt the tension ease from his shoulders, the boatman reached between his belt and the waistband of his shorts and pulled out his machete.

"What?" Mumsford drew in his breath.

"Iguana," he said, peering into the bushes. "They big like little dragon here."

For Mumsford the trip on foot to Dr. Gardner's house was a nightmare. His heart raced, beads of sweat collected dust on his top lip and down the sides of his bright red cheeks. He clutched his briefcase close to his chest.

"Carry that for you?" the boatman offered.

But for Mumsford the briefcase was a lifeline. It was England in a world shot backward to the heart of darkness.

Then suddenly it all changed. Then suddenly, at the end of the path where the bushes had grown wild, though now, in the dry season, were almost leafless and brown, was a meadow, a field of green stretching before him. And at the end of the field of green was a blaze of color, and behind it a white house with eaves and alcoves and large baskets of luscious green ferns hanging from the ceiling to the railings on a glorious porch.

"Dr. Gardner." The boatman stopped. He waved his machete in the direction of the house. "Is here he live. I come back for you here. In an hour."

It was frightening, too, all that green. Never had he seen such green, never on any lawn he knew, never even in England. For it was not simply green, it was brilliantly green. Plastic, artificially, brilliantly green. As he walked along the paved path that led to the house, he saw that the flowers, too, were brilliantly colorful, artificially colorful. But what made him suck in his breath was not the brilliance, the artificiality of color, but the variety, not of plants, but of the colors on a single plant. There, along the front of the house, were rose plants, and on each plant were flowers of every hue, and bougainvillea (yes, he was sure; he leaned in close to be sure), their petals splashed with polka dots, blue upon pink, violet on orange, yellow on red, the petals on some opened out flat like lilies.

THREE

"THE MIRACLES of the latest research in botany," Dr. Gardner said and satisfied Mumsford with his logical explanation for the shapes and colors. "I've been experimenting." He had an answer, too, for the plastic-green lawn. "A special fertilizer, and I have a reservoir. I store water in the rainy season and pump it into my garden. I've built a generator in the back. We can take a look when we're done here."

They were already well inside the house when Mumsford asked his questions about the lawn and the flowers, and only because he was prompted, only because Dr. Gardner said to him, "What do you think about my lawn and my flowers?" Yet as he had walked toward the house no other questions had consumed him more, no other questions had been on the tip of his tongue causing him to lose memory temporarily of his only reason for coming. The green of the grass, the texture, the shapes and colors of the flowers, disturbed him but thrilled him, too. He wanted to know how the Englishman had done it. But when the Englishman appeared, the thrill he had felt subsided and his head spun with confusion and disappointment.

Dr. Gardner had met him on the porch. He had come through the front door tucking a white shirt down the back of his tan cotton pants. He was a tall, thin, wiry man with tiny nuggets of steel blue for eyes and skin tough like leather, burnt to a deep olive brown. His hair fell down in scraggly locks to his shoulders. It was a dark reddish color but the ends were light, bleached by the sun.

"It's Mumsford, isn't it?" he asked and he held out his hand. "I mean it's not Mumford, or Munford, is it?"

"Yes, yes, it is Mumsford."

He shoved the rest of his shirt down the front of his pants, pulled a blue elastic band off his wrist, and tied back his hair. "Servants," he said. "Ariana told me an Inspector Munford was here to see me, but I knew she had made a mistake."

Ariana.

Before Gardner appeared, Mumsford had knocked on the door, and when there was no answer he had peered through the window. He was certain he had seen a naked woman dashing across the drawing room. He had caught a glimpse of her back before she disappeared through another door. A tumble of wild black curls swished across her bare bottom, back and forth like the pendulum of a clock.

"Ariana," Dr. Gardner called out. "Ariana!"

Perhaps it was another woman.

"Come, come, Inspector," Dr. Gardner urged him. "Don't stand there in the sun. Come inside. It's nicer inside."

She reappeared hovering behind him. The same tumble of hair. Ariana.

"Don't stand in the doorway." Dr. Gardner pushed her aside. "Make way, make way."

Ariana, Dr. Gardner's servant. Ariana, naked in Dr. Gardner's drawing room. Ariana who should not be questioned in the presence of Dr. Gardner. Images collided in Mumsford's head: the naked woman, the man tucking in his shirt. *Did he know she had written a letter to the commissioner?*

Dr. Gardner led him into the drawing room. "Drinks for the inspector," he said as he brushed past Ariana.

Mumsford kept his eyes focused on the room in front of him, too embarrassed to look back at her.

"Bit of a shock, isn't it, young man?" Gardner was speaking to him.
Yes, but more than a bit of a shock.

"One never gets quite used to it." Gardner chuckled. "I mean, after the blistering heat outside."

The muscles on Mumsford's face tightened.

"Relax, old man." Gardner gave him a friendly tap on his back. "It's only air-conditioning."

It wasn't that he had not felt the difference the instant he entered the room. Suddenly he could breathe, suddenly the pores on his neck and face contracted pleasantly, and his undershirt, seconds ago damp, sticking uncomfortably to his back, was a cool compress soothing his blistering skin. But it was a sensation he experienced almost unconsciously. His conscious self was preoccupied with sorting out the shock: the certainty that it was Ariana he had seen. He was not wrong about the hair, the lithe body, the liquid flow of brown skin. He was not wrong about the loose shirttails hanging out of Dr. Gardner's pants, which were unbelted and, he could swear, unbuttoned at the waist.

"So what do you think?" Dr. Gardner's voice penetrated his brain and Mumsford pulled himself together.

"I didn't think the technology had been advanced for domestic use," he said.

Gardner grinned. "Not for everybody, my man."

She was still standing there, waiting, he supposed, for Dr. Gardner's order. Dr. Gardner had not said what kind of drinks. Perhaps she was waiting to know exactly what he wanted her to bring.

"But it has advanced, it has advanced," Dr. Gardner was saying, taking no notice of Ariana.

This was not his business, Mumsford reminded himself. He was not here to discuss her or her dealings with Gardner.

"And my lawn? What do you think about my lawn and my flowers?" Dr. Gardner came closer to him. So Mumsford asked and Gardner replied, "The miracles of the latest research in botany. I'm a scientist, Inspector."

How logical was his answer, how simple. He was a scientist; he was experimenting with shapes and colors. Mumsford managed a smile. "And all this?" He cast his eyes around the room.

"For my Virginia," Dr. Gardner said. "A little of England for her."

Yes, that was what his subconscious mind had registered: *England*. He fixed his back resolutely toward her so he could not see her. *England*. There were no wicker and bamboo here, no couches covered in fabric with overlaying patterns of coconut fronds and bright red hibiscus. His eyes took in more: proper English armchairs, proper English love seats. Dr. Gardner had not been snared, as some of his compatriots on the island had, into succumbing to the foolish romantic notion of local color. In the drawing room where he stood, the chairs were upholstered in English fabrics, refined damasks in English floral patterns: sprays of pink, white, and red roses extending off long, leafy green stems against a pale yellow background. The drapes on the windows matched the yellow of the damask. On the mahogany cocktail table that separated the love seats were picture books of English gardens and a bronze sculpture of Don Quixote on his horse. He looked down to the rug on the floor.

"Persian," Dr. Gardner said before he could inquire. "An original. Handwoven, not one of those modern machine-made imitations."

No straw mats, either, on the wood floors.

One wall was completely lined with books. Mumsford could not read all the titles, but he was sure they were by English writers. Shakespeare—the name stood out—and then there were others: Milton, Byron, Shelley, Wordsworth, names he had learned in grammar school. England's heroes, her geniuses. Racial pride flared through him like a brush fire. Whatever distaste he felt for Gardner when the image of his unbuttoned pants flashed across his brain was replaced now with genuine admiration. Here was an Englishman indeed.

"Sit. Sit." Dr. Gardner pointed to an armchair. "Give me your hat and baton."

Mumsford relinquished them with a slight bow, clicking his heels in military fashion. Gardner laughed and laid his hand lightly on his shoulder. "For heaven's sake, at ease, young man. Don't be so stuffy. Make yourself comfortable."

Mumsford blushed. He had not intended the bow and the click, but he was overtaken by an enormous sense of relief. After the bugs, the scorching sun, the stifling scent of sweaty bodies, vegetation that was too green in the wet season, too brown in the dry, but always haphazard, always out of control, he was overjoyed to be in a room that reaffirmed a world he had been taught was his, a world of order and civility, though he did not know it personally, except from pictures his teachers had shown him and in the books he had read in school that reassured him of his heritage.

"I haven't seen anything like this, sir," he said. "Not in Trinidad."

Dr. Gardner was pleased. "It's all for my daughter," he said. "So she'll know. She was three, you understand, when we left."

Mumsford put his briefcase on the floor next to the armchair, drew his fingers down the front seams of his pants, and sat down. "It must have been difficult for you, sir," he said.

"Difficult?" Gardner fastened his eyes on Mumsford.

"What with a three-year-old, sir."

"My daughter, Inspector, is that for which I live."

His words sounded strange to Mumsford's ears, melodramatic, theatrical, but he nodded his head sympathetically. After twelve years in the Land of the Dead, it was to be expected. A man could be excused under those conditions for being melodramatic.

"Quite. Quite," he said. "And that is understandable, sir."

But Gardner was not finished. "I have done nothing," he said, continuing to keep his eyes on Mumsford, "but in care of her."

Strange words again, but it was clear that Gardner meant exactly what he said. The intensity of emotion in his eyes made Mumsford uncomfortable and he looked away. *He did nothing except for her? In care of her?* Still, Mumsford managed to say, "You must love your daughter, sir."

"Immeasurably."

When Mumsford looked up, he saw that Gardner's eyes were misty. "I mean it is admirable, sir," he said, feeling obliged to say something more. "All you have done here." He extended his arm in a sweeping gesture across the room. "This room, this house. The furniture."

The praise seemed to snap Gardner out of the sudden morose

mood that had come over him. He turned his head, following the arc of Mumsford's arm, and his lips curved upward in a self-satisfied smile. "I did my best," he said.

"You should be congratulated, sir."

"Music?"

Mumsford's face flushed with pleasure and then he remembered he was on assignment for the commissioner. "If you please, sir, when we are done, sir."

"Oh, I don't mean calypso," Gardner said, assuming there could be no other explanation for Mumsford's discomfort. "Our music. Mozart's concerto for oboe and strings. Do you know it? The concerto for oboe and strings?"

Mumsford did not know it. It was not his music; his music was not classical music. His music was popular music. He listened to Tommy Steele, Billy Fury, Cliff Richard. He liked Kenny Weathers and the Emotions, but he lied. It felt good to be in the company of a cultured Englishman, to be considered cultured himself. He was not in a hurry. He had time to ask his questions. "Haven't heard it in a long time, sir," he said.

"Then I will play it for you." Gardner walked toward the console on the other side of the room.

"I'd like that, sir."

"We have our own world here, you know, Mumsford." Gardner picked up the record and balanced it between his open palms.

"In spite of the lepers, sir?" Mumsford asked, for it seemed miraculous to him that Gardner should have made a paradise here, in the Land of the Dead.

"The lepers take care of themselves." Gardner put the record in the record player, raised the arm, and placed the needle carefully in the first groove. "Close your eyes, Mumsford. Listen. Be transported. England."

He had dismissed his question about the lepers, but Mumsford did not mind. When the music poured out, encasing him in a warm cocoon, he, too, did not want to talk about lepers, he, too, did not want to spoil the moment by raising the specter of deformed flesh. He closed his eyes, as Gardner urged him to do, and let the music take him back across the Atlantic.

But Gardner allowed him only minutes before he pulled him back. "Now you will understand my distress better, Inspector," he said.

Mumsford opened his eyes to see Gardner conducting, his arm rising and falling rhythmically through the air. "Now that you are here," he said, still conducting the concerto with an imaginary baton, "you will know why I insisted that the commissioner send an Englishman, not a native."

"I do, sir," Mumsford said.

Gardner dropped his arm. "I wanted you to see for yourself. To understand the circumstances. My outrage. The depth of this insult to my person," he said. He lowered the volume on the record player.

Mumsford sat up. "To your person, sir?" he asked. The music was barely audible now and he was no longer in a cocoon.

"To the person of all honorable Englishmen, Inspector. To the person of my daughter." He closed the console and recrossed the room. "When you meet her, Inspector, you will find she will outstrip all praise and make it halt behind her." He hummed a few bars of the concerto and sat down on the armchair next to Mumsford's. "A piece of England for my daughter," he said.

He meant Mozart, and at the very least Mumsford knew that Mozart was not English, but it did not matter. He understood.

"Before you get the boy, I will show you my orchids and the rest of my garden."

Yes, Mumsford thought, he could get the boy when he was done, after he had taken Gardner's deposition. But Gardner did not wait for his response. "Ariana!" he shouted.

She was still there. She had not left the room. Gardner need not have raised his voice. She stood near the back door, twirling a strand of her long hair between her fingers.

"Ariana, the drinks!" She dropped her hand and swung it behind her back. It was the only acknowledgment she gave that she had heard him.

Mumsford had not been unaware of her presence. From time to time, in spite of his pleasure over the furniture, the crispness in the air, the reassuring music, his eyes had strayed in her direction. A will-o'-the-wisp, he had thought. They flitted over the marshes on hot summer nights. A speck of light too fleeting to be brilliant.

Ethereal. That was the word he had been searching for, yet it was a word that was inconsonant with her deep brown skin, her black wavy hair. Consonant, though, with her slight frame, her small bones, her long arms that dangled from their sockets, her long legs, her bare feet, her long, long hair, her huge eyes, which one noticed next, or first, if one saw her from the front and not from the back. They were round and bright, and made the rest of her face—her satiny smooth cheeks, her flat nose, her tiny mouth—seem inconsequential. She was probably Indian, though something about the curls in her hair and the flattish nose bridge told him that perhaps there was an African parent or grandparent. Doogla. That was what she was. It was the name the native people gave to such mixtures. Yes, she was a doogla.

But a will-o'-the-wisp, too. She could be blown away with a puff of breath. The fabric of her yellow dress, which was tied to the back in a girlish bow, was thin, almost transparent. He glanced at her again. He could make out shadows behind the thin fabric. It struck him that there was no inconsonance between the word that had occurred to him and the person he was seeing, the brilliance of her yellow dress flashing now against her dark skin not unlike the ethereal light flitting across the dark night in the marshes in England.

"Gin and tonic for you, Inspector?"

Mumsford was so deep in his ruminations, unsettled somewhat by the likeness he had made between the slight woman before him and England (though the comparison he had made was not with her and England but with her and a fairy, not a person in England) that he literally jumped when Gardner's voice cut across his thoughts.

"Something the matter, Inspector?" Gardner asked.

Mumsford patted his hands down his jacket and folded them over his belt buckle. "I was dreaming," he said hastily. "Of England. All this reminded me."

Gardner smiled. "It happens to me sometimes. So will it be gin and tonic, or rum punch?"

"Neither, sir. I can't have alcohol, sir. Not on the job, sir," Mumsford said.

"Neither?"

"No, sir."

Gardner considered his answer for a moment and then threw up his hands. "Then so it will be. But none of the formalities, John, okay? Call me Peter."

"If you don't mind, sir," Mumsford said, "I'd prefer to call you by your surname, sir."

Gardner frowned and crossed his legs. "If that is what you want."

"And me, sir. I'd prefer if you'd call me Inspector Mumsford, sir."

"By God, John, we're in my house."

"I'm here on an investigation, sir. If you don't mind, it should be Inspector Mumsford, sir."

"Then it shall." Gardner slapped his knees. "Ariana, ask Inspector Mumsford what he'd like to drink."

Ariana stepped toward them.

"Orange juice will be fine," Mumsford said.

"Orange juice and my drink," Dr. Gardner said to Ariana. She lifted her eyes to his and then quickly lowered them. "So go now," Gardner said and fluttered his fingers in an exaggerated gesture of irritation. She hesitated. "Go," Gardner said softly. Her lips parted in a brief smile, and then she turned and walked to the door, her hair swinging behind her, thick and dark, the two tiny globes of her backside clearly outlined under her thin dress.

"And pin up your hair, for God's sake."

Yes, Mumsford had no doubt; it was she he had seen dashing across the room without a stitch of clothing on her body. There was no mistaking that, nor the desire palpable in Gardner's voice.

"They are all the same," Gardner said and tugged his lower lip. "She, a little better than the others, but for the most part, they have such natures that nurture can never stick."

"Nurture, sir?"

"Upbringing, Inspector." His head was still turned in the direction of the door that had closed behind Ariana. "They have no upbringing. And it is a waste of time to educate them." He dropped his hand and settled back in his chair.

Mumsford reached for his briefcase on the floor. "Well, to the matter in question, sir."

"The matter in question?" Gardner looked at him, the furrows tightening on his brow as if he didn't understand.

"The reason I am here, sir," Mumsford said. "The boy."

"Ah, the boy." The furrows smoothened, then tightened again.

"Carlos Codrington, sir." Mumsford brought the briefcase to his lap and opened it.

"He is the one on whom nurture can least stick," Gardner said. He sat up and flicked off a piece of lint from the leg of his trousers. "You can have no idea of the pains I took to help him. Did you know I taught him to read?"

"You taught him?"

But Gardner was not listening to him. "Ariana!" he shouted, and when she did not answer him, he called her again. "Ariana, the inspector didn't ask you to pick the oranges. How long does it take to pour orange juice in a glass?"

The sound of glass clinking against glass filtered into the drawing room.

"Ariana!" Gardner raised his voice for the third time. This time there was silence behind the door, a quiet so complete that though Gardner had set the record player to its lowest volume, the music seemed suddenly loud, the mournful sighs of violin and piano as the needle moved to another track on the record framing the tension in the room.

"I'm not very thirsty," Mumsford said.

Gardner looked from him to the door and back again at him.

"You were telling me you taught the boy." Mumsford tried again, hoping to refocus him.

"I taught him to speak properly," Gardner said.

Mumsford took his notebook and pen from his briefcase. From the corner of his eye, he could see the door crack open, a slight sliver of a crack, a line, but enough to reveal yellow flickering in the narrow space between the door frame and the door.

"Now he speaks like an Englishman," Gardner was saying.

"He, sir?" It was Mumsford's turn to be distracted.

"Carlos. We are speaking about Carlos, Inspector."

"Yes, yes. Carlos." When he looked again, the yellow was gone.

"He was speaking like the rest of them when I came here," Gardner said. "Dat and dis and dey, as if there were no th's in the English language. He used to say, *I 'as* instead of *I do.* Now, you wouldn't believe it. Like a proper Englishman."

Mumsford opened his notebook. *He must have made a mistake. There was no yellow near the door.* "So you would say, sir," he said, writing determinedly, "that in some instances nurture stuck."

"Stuck?"

"What you were saying, sir, about nature," Mumsford said.

"Yes, I know what I was saying, Mumsford."

"That will be Inspector Mumsford, sir. If you don't mind, sir."

"Yes, I know what I said, Inspector Mumsford, but if you had waited a while you would have heard the rest. Carlos speaks like an Englishman only when he is sober. The rest of the time, which is most of the time, he speaks like a common sailor."

"An English sailor, sir?" Mumsford scribbled more notes in his notebook.

"Yes, yes, by God, an English sailor, Inspector. And he curses as one, too."

"So you'd say on the night in question . . ."

"It wasn't night."

"Then day, sir?"

"Yes, day."

"Well, you'd say on the day in question he was drunk?"

Gardner became agitated. He bent his head and picked nervously at the loose threads on the pocket of his shirt. Mumsford could see the roots of his hair. Red, English red, he was certain that was the color of Gardner's hair before the sun had stripped it. *Dirty color rust,* he scribbled in his notebook.

"What are you writing now, Inspector?" Gardner snapped back his head and glared at him.

"The details of the case," Mumsford said. And at that moment he felt a surge of pity for him. He had been sun-dried, bleached like a piece of driftwood.

"I haven't given you the details of the case, Inspector," Gardner said gruffly.

"About the event happening in the day, not the night, sir."

Gardner sighed and sat back in his chair. "He was not drunk on the day in question," he said. He looked tired, a wrinkled old man, though he was not much past fifty.

Not for me, Mumsford thought. I will not turn into a leathery old man before my time. After this matter has ended, the perpetrator put in jail, I will submit my resignation, return to England, marry a young English girl, settle down in some quiet English countryside. Next year will not find me here.

"Yes. That would have been quite another matter, indeed," he said to Gardner, the picture he had formed in his head softening his tone.

"Another matter?" Gardner asked.

"One can never tell what a man is capable of doing when he is drunk," Mumsford said.

"Well, he wasn't." Gardner sat up. "Not that day."

"Other days then?" Mumsford asked. He did not want to agitate him again, but the deposition had to be precise.

Gardner smoothed back the wrinkles on his cheeks. "Other days," he said. "Other days." His voice trailed.

He must have been handsome once, Mumsford thought. In England his skin would not have turned to leather. In England his red hair would have been streaked with bronze, not rust, the detestable sun would not have hardened his eyes, and there would have been muscles, not wires in his arms.

"When?" he asked. "Which other days?"

But Gardner's mind was on Ariana again. He turned toward the door through which she had exited moments ago.

"Ariana!" He was calling her again. "Ariana!"

This time Mumsford was certain of the yellow. He saw it move. She had been standing there all along, behind the door, listening to them.

"Ariana!"

The sliver of yellow widened and she was in the room, smiling, balancing a tray with two glasses on it, one the color of orange juice, the other a disturbing blue.

"I come to answer your best pleasure, Dr. Gardner. Whether you want me to fly, to swim, to dive into the fire, to ride on the clouds. I come to do your bidding task." She batted her eyes and swung her hips.

Mumsford strangled a gasp. He could not believe the change in her. Minutes before she was surly, pouting, refusing to answer him.

"Moody today, aren't you, Ariana?" Gardner got up and took the glasses from the tray.

"Your thoughts are mine," she said.

"And so they should be, Ariana." Gardner stood close to her, so close that he would only have to lean forward slightly and their lips would meet.

"Tell me your pleasure, my commander. Is there more toil?"

Mumsford had to strain his ears to hear her.

"No," Gardner said softly, his voice a caress. "There is no more toil."

Their whispered intimacy embarrassed Mumsford. He flipped through the pages of his notebook, busying himself. The whispering continued, Ariana's voice gliding seductively across the room, Gardner's at once gruff and plaintive but so low Mumsford could not discern the words.

Mumsford coughed again and shifted his body nosily in his chair, but nothing worked. Then, when he least expected it, Gardner's voice changed from an anxious drone to a harsh whisper and then to a command. "Well, be off with you," Mumsford heard him say. He caught Ariana's eyes. There was something curiously submissive in her expression. He had seen that look before—many times it seemed lately—when he apprehended a native: a shading over the eyes that did little to mask fear, feelings of powerlessness, of defeat, and yet somehow beneath the fear, defiance.

Gardner raised his voice again and ordered Ariana to leave. She threw her head back and walked slowly and deliberately out of the room, tossing her hair over her shoulders and swaying her hips seductively from side to side as if she knew, as indeed it was true, that Gardner's eyes would be glued on her.

When the door clicked shut, Gardner explained: "She wants something. They are childish that way. They pout, and when that doesn't work, they turn on the charm. Soon she'll sulk."

What was it she wanted? The question formed in Mumsford's mind, but he knew better than to ask it. The commissioner's instructions were explicit. He was not to arouse suspicions in Dr. Gardner that Ariana had betrayed him, that the day before she had sent a letter by a boatman with an accusation of her own: *He tell a lie. Mr. Prospero lie.*

"I taught her those words." Gardner handed Mumsford the glass with the drink the color of orange juice. "Quite an actress, wouldn't you say?"

Mumsford brought his glass quickly to his lips to hide his consternation. A performance, perhaps, but more natural than artificial, Gardner's words about nature and nurture still lingering in his head.

"Mine is special," Gardner said, holding up the drink with the bluish hue and regarding it from the distance of his arm. "It's something I've concocted. It builds the mind." He pointed to his right temple.

It looked like poison, Mumsford thought, but that was none of his business. Nor was Gardner's relationship with Ariana. Whether Gardner was putting on his clothes when he came to the door, whether Ariana had been naked and had run to the back of the house to dress, whether she and Gardner had been fucking like pigs, none of that mattered. That was not why he was here. He took two more sips from his orange juice, put down the glass, reached into his pocket for his handkerchief, dabbed his lips dry, and began "So, sir, back to the business that brings me here." He sat forward on his chair, his pen poised over his notebook. "Can you tell me, sir, what happened exactly on that day? I am assuming, of course, we are speaking in privacy."

"Ariana is in the kitchen." Gardner continued to regard his drink.

"Can't she hear us, sir?"

Gardner swirled the blue liquid in his glass. "It's no matter," he said vacantly.

"And the young man . . ."

"As I wrote to the commissioner, the young man, as you call him, is safely locked up in the back of the house."

"Yes, yes. But your daughter, sir?"

"My daughter has gone to Trinidad for a few days."

The commissioner had not told him that, and Mumsford wondered whether he knew.

Gardner seemed to read the puzzlement on his face. "It so happens that her intended . . ."

"Her intended? Is she engaged, sir?"

"I didn't say so, Inspector. Her intended, the man who intends to marry her . . . It so happens he is here on holiday."

"She is fifteen, isn't she, sir?"

"She is fifteen, Inspector." Gardner stated the fact bluntly, his eyes challenging Mumsford to make more of his statement.

Mumsford looked away. "A bit young, don't you think, sir?" he asked. He softened the inflection at the end so his question would not sound as harsh as the thoughts that ran through his head: *Fifteen?*

"I am her father," Gardner said. "I will be the judge of that."

"I was just saying, sir . . ."

"You said it. You think she is too young, but let me tell you, Inspector." Gardner put his glass down on the table. His movements were measured, as were the next words that came out of his mouth. "If . . ." His hand was still on the glass and he twirled it between his thumb and middle finger. "If you don't direct the hormones when they start jumping . . ." He left the sentence hanging in the air, unfinished.

"Jumping, sir?" Mumsford pushed him to complete his thought.

"Have you forgotten when you were fifteen, Inspector?" He picked up the glass. "Yes, jumping. I can't have her hormones going in the wrong direction, toward the wrong person, can I, Inspector?"

Mumsford did not like the coarse reference to hormones, but he shrugged off his discomfort. "And I take it, Dr. Gardner, the young man here on a holiday is the right person?" There were no traces of sarcasm in his question. He was simply seeking clarification.

"A medical student," Gardner said.

"Studying to be a doctor, like you, sir?"

Gardner swallowed a mouthful of the blue liquid. "Yes. Like me, Inspector."

Mumsford came closer to the edge of his seat. "This may seem an impertinence, sir, but I assure you none is intended. Is she alone with him, sir?"

Gardner reddened. "It is an impertinence, Inspector Mumsford."

"He is in Trinidad, is he not, sir?"

"The young man comes from a good family, Inspector. From Boston. They have kept the old ways in Boston." Gardner spoke in clipped tones.

"American?"

"From New England. You've heard of New England, haven't you, Inspector? It is as it says. *New* England."

"And your daughter, sir, is with this American from New England?" Mumsford's pen moved rapidly across his notebook.

"Not by herself, as you seem to want to imply, Inspector. She's well chaperoned. By Mrs. Burton."

"Mrs. Burton?" Mumsford raised his head.

"An Englishwoman. And the young man is not here alone. He is with his father."

"With his mother, too, I take it, sir?"

"No. Not with his mother, Inspector. His mother is dead."

Mumsford pursed his lips.

"The young man is quite respectable," Gardner said.

Mumsford scratched the side of his head.

"Quite respectable. Father and son are staying in a hotel and my daughter is staying with Mrs. Burton."

"Indeed, sir."

"They would all be here if that devil had not attacked her." Gardner threw back his head and drained his glass.

Attacked was a specific word. Mumsford prided himself on being thorough. He had been properly trained. *Attacked* indicated action. Violence to a person.

"Attacked, sir?" he asked.

"*Attempted,* Inspector." Dr. Gardner corrected himself and put the empty glass on the table. "As I said to you before, that beast Carlos *attempted* to put a stain on my daughter's honor."

After *Daughter in hotel with boyfriend,* Mumsford wrote in his notebook *No violence with the colored boy.*

"Still writing, Inspector?" Gardner stretched his neck in Mumsford's direction.

"Just notes, sir."

"The inspector on duty," Gardner said drily. He glanced once more at Mumsford's notebook and then closed his eyes briefly. When he opened them again, he was still fixed on the point of establishing the propriety of his daughter's trip to Trinidad. "The young man would be here," he said, "if it had not been for the present situation. You understand? The attempt."

"Yes, sir."

"And he and my daughter will be here as soon as you remove that savage from my premises. Don't you think I know about fire i' th' blood?" His eyes bored into Mumsford's.

"Fire in the blood, sir?"

"Sexual passion. Carnal lust. You understand passion and lust, don't you, Inspector?"

And in truth Inspector Mumsford did not understand, not in the way he felt Dr. Gardner implied. He had read books about carnal lust, dirty books he still stuffed under his mattress, for he lived with his mother, though it was the other way around now that she had followed him to Trinidad. But he had no experience with carnal lust. He had never been to a brothel.

"I have given the young man strict instructions," Gardner said, when Mumsford did not answer him. "He is never to ask her to his room. They can go for walks, meet in the hotel lobby, that sort of thing. Public places only. Oh, he swore to me that he would respect her. That he would not touch her before they were married. But you know, Inspector," he lowered his voice, "the strongest oaths are straw to fire i' th' blood. I told him so." He examined his fingernails. "One must avoid all situations where the temptation may be too great or it is good night your vow," he said.

Did he imagine it, Mumsford wondered, or had he not detected a trace of sadness in Gardner's voice? "Yes," Mumsford said, "it is always best to avoid temptation."

"It's her greatest treasure, you know." Gardner raised his eyes to him again.

"Her treasure, sir?"

"I speak of her virginity, Inspector. It is the jewel in her dower."

Mumsford's neck felt hot. It throbbed with the rush of blood that rose from his chest.

"Yes, yes, no need for double-talk, Inspector. I will be plain. It is her jewel. I said so to Alfred. That is the young man who wants to marry her. Break her virgin knot, and it is all over. Nothing can follow but disdain after that. I told her that, too. A man may promise you the stars, but if you surrender to him, that which made you so special will be tarnished. Light winning makes the prize light. You understand? We are hunters, Inspector." He leaned forward conspiratorially, the nuggets he had for eyes hard and shining.

Every instinct in Mumsford urged him to recoil—the man was making him uneasy—but he held his ground. He was here on police business. He was a professional. He would remember that.

"I would agree with you," he said to Gardner. "Anthropologically speaking, sir."

Gardner slapped his thighs and let out a loud guffaw. " 'Anthropologically speaking, sir?' " he mimicked him. " 'Anthropologically speaking, sir?' "

How had he allowed himself to feel pity for this man? Why did he think he seemed sad minutes ago when he talked of oaths and temptation? "Are you making fun of me, sir?" Mumsford asked.

"Did they teach you to speak like that in police school?"

"Am I amusing you, sir?"

"No, no, Inspector. It was a good word. *Anthropologically speaking.* Those are good words. Precise." Gardner wiped his eyes on the shoulder of his shirt. "And anthropologically speaking, Mumsford, as you know as well as I do, there is no sport after the kill." Gardner was no longer smiling. The hardness had returned in his eyes. "Yes, it is her jewel. They will both hate each other if it loses its sheen. Discord will come between them when they marry. Barren hate. He would know it was spoilt meat he got when he married her, and she would hate him for spoiling her before she had taken her vows."

Mumsford felt he could not take much more of this talk of virgin knot, sexual passion, jumping hormones, carnal lust, spoilt meat. It was talk better for the pub among like-minded companions, or in a sleazy motel, perhaps with a prostitute. *He was her father, for God's sake.*

Dr. Gardner had called him stuffy, and perhaps he was. He was not a city man. He did not have city ways. He was raised in the country, in England, where it was improper for a father to speak this way about his daughter. His stomach felt queasy. They were inappropriate, Dr. Gardner's intimate references to his daughter's sexuality, not normal for a decent father.

"So you see, Inspector, that born devil would have destroyed all that if he had succeeded," Gardner was saying, and in a flash Mumsford saw his mistake. Good detective as he thought he was, he had missed the point of Gardner's tirade: first, to establish that there had been no assault, but, rather, an attempt to assault, thus leaving no doubt of his daughter's purity. Then (his real purpose) to lay the foundation that would seal his argument that that very attempt had threatened her future, the plans he had in place for her.

"A good boy from New England would not marry a slut," Gardner concluded.

Yes. Yes, it was clear now. He should have known.

"A woman who had been broken into. Used. You understand me, Mumsford?"

He understood him now. He turned to a clean page in his notebook. "I would need to know the beginning," he said.

"The beginning?" Gardner's eyes drifted across to the record player.

"Can we start from the beginning, sir?" Mumsford asked quietly.

"The adagio." Gardner was not listening to him. "Mozart's clarinet concerto in A." He was conducting again, lifting his hand when the music arced, lowering it when it descended.

"Sir?" Mumsford tried to rouse him. It was mournful, the music, though he could barely hear it.

"She was a piece of virtue," he said.

"She?"

"My wife." His hand fell to his side. "Faithful to me. Pure as driven snow. She died shortly after Virginia was born. Twelve years we are here."

"A long time," Mumsford said.

"There is no doubt Virginia . . ."

"Tell me about her, sir."

"No doubt my daughter. Her mother said she was my daughter." He glanced at Mumsford as if daring him to contradict him.

Not missing the challenge in the glance, Mumsford said quickly, "Indeed, sir. The commissioner said there is a great resemblance between you two, sir."

"A virgin when I married her, Inspector. Never been touched. A piece of virtue."

Afraid he was about to launch into another lecture about virginity, Mumsford interrupted him, but not unkindly. "If you don't mind, sir, could we start at the other beginning, the time immediately before the incident, sir?"

Gardner rubbed his eyes. The edges of his mouth had hardened, and nothing remained of the slackness that moments ago had caused the skin there to droop so that the lines along his chin had deepened. "They had a cure for the disease when we arrived," he said abruptly.

It was not the beginning Mumsford wanted, but it was a beginning closer to the present.

"The nuns had left," Gardner said, "but there were still a few patients. The doctor here was old and tired."

"Is that why you came, sir?" Mumsford encouraged him.

"What?" Gardner seemed momentarily perplexed

"Why you came, sir?"

"Yes. It was why I came."

"And why you stayed, sir?"

"Yes, yes. I came for the lepers and I stayed for the ones who were still here."

"But I understand, sir, you no longer take care of them."

"And your understanding is accurate, Inspector," he said angrily.

The glare from the cold light that shone from Gardner's eyes forced Mumsford to look down. His remark to Gardner had not been benign. He wanted to know why Gardner was still on the island; why, since he no longer took care of the lepers.

"When you came here," he began, trying another approach, "did you find Carlos here, sir?"

Gardner pushed back a thin lock of hair that had gotten loose from the elastic band on his ponytail. "He was six," he said without emotion. "His mother had just died."

"And his father?" Mumsford fumbled through his notes.

"She was a blue-eyed hag."

"Sir?"

"His mother. Sylvia. Carlos's mother. She was a blue-eyed hag," he repeated.

"Blue-eyed?"

"And that whelp she gave birth to was freckled."

"She was white, his mother?"

"I said blue-eyed, Inspector."

"So Carlos is white?"

"Freckled," Gardner said.

"Half white?" Mumsford asked, straining forward in his chair.

"She didn't know the father, that hag. But he was a black man."

"There was more than one?" Mumsford fought the anger rising in him. *Damn mixing of the bloods—the impurities.*

"She screwed them all on the island," Gardner said.

"The lepers?"

Gardner narrowed his eyes. "She birthed a misshapen bastard," he said.

"Because of the disease?"

"Because of his father's black blood," Gardner said.

"So he is deformed?"

"Freckled," Gardner said again.

Mumsford looked puzzled and then, as if finally making sense of what Gardner had said, he drew in his breath. "Ah," he said knowingly.

"Freckles all over his body," Gardner said.

"I've heard that happens," Mumsford said.

Gardner raised his eyebrows.

"When the two bloods meet."

Gardner's eyebrows arched higher.

"Sometimes it makes black and brown dots on the white," Mumsford said.

At first Gardner's jaw simply dropped and his mouth gaped open.

No sound came out of it, and then he was choking, laughing uproari-
ously, kicking up his feet and making scissorlike movements with his
legs in the air. "I say, I say . . ." The words came sputtering out of his
mouth. "Black and brown dots on the white." He was fighting for
breath. "When the two bloods meet." Tears streamed down his face.
"When the . . ."

Mumsford fiddled with his collar, adjusted the buckle on his belt,
and tried to look dignified.

"I mean . . ." Gardner swallowed the cough rising in his throat. "I
mean, didn't they teach you anything about biology in police school,
Inspector?" He dried his eyes with the back of his hand.

"We were not training to be doctors, sir," Mumsford said stiffly.

"The fundamentals. Just the fundamentals, Inspector."

"I didn't intend to entertain you, sir."

"I mean, colored people don't leave dots on white people. Or
stripes, for that matter. A black and a white horse don't make a zebra,
Mumsford."

"I'm sorry you should find me amusing, sir."

"No. I suppose it's not your fault. I suppose I shouldn't have
laughed." Gardner patted his cheeks dry. "I should beg your pardon. I
should apologize."

"No apology is needed, sir."

"I suppose you shouldn't be blamed."

"A misunderstanding, sir."

"But one would have thought the colonial office would have prepared you men better before they let you come out here."

"They prepared me, sir."

"But surely, you've seen a freckled white person?"

Mumsford's face hardened. "He lived here in the house with you?"
His voice was loaded with exaggerated formality.

"Carlos?" Gardner seemed surprised by the question.

"I am here to discuss Carlos, sir. Did he live here?" Mumsford
crossed off *misshapen* in his notes.

"Here?" Gardner looked around him.

"Yes. Did he live here?"

"From the first day," Gardner said.

"With you and your daughter? Twelve years?" Mumsford pressed his questions.

"I thought he would be someone to amuse her. I let them play together." Gardner stroked the legs of his pants.

"Them?"

"Carlos and my daughter. Then, when I started teaching her to read—she was four, he was six at the time—he stood nearby listening. He picked up what I was saying to her. Later he would take her little books and try to read on his own. Sometimes I would see him reading to her. Many times I was busy in my garden." He paused, and checked the buttons on his shirt. The top one was undone. He buttoned it. "My orchids, you know, Mumsford. They are the rarest in the world. If we have time, before you leave . . ."

But Mumsford would not let him change the subject so easily. Biology might not be his expertise, he might know nothing about botany, he might not be able to grow grass that looked like plastic or make polka dots appear on the petals of bougainvillea, but he was an expert in detective work. He could keep his focus in a deposition. "So he read to her?" Mumsford cut him off in mid-sentence.

"I gave him my books. I taught my daughter and he listened," Gardner said.

"Your daughter did not go to school?"

"We don't have school here, Inspector. It's a leper colony. Or haven't you noticed?"

"Surely her education?"

"Fire i' th' blood, Inspector. These tropical climes arouse a man's sexual desires. We men are old goats. I could not put her at risk sending her to school in Trinidad."

"Surely in a boarding school?" Mumsford asked, malice curling around the edges of his question.

"There are never sufficient protections. Besides, Inspector, she could do no better than to have me as a schoolmaster. Others might not have been so careful."

"Careful?"

"To teach her what she needed to know."

Mumsford was struck by his emphasis on *needed* but he stuck to his objective, which now was not merely to gather information, but to make Gardner pay for humiliating him. "But Carlos?" he asked, taking no little satisfaction in noticing that his line of questioning was agitating Gardner.

"If she were a princess in a castle, she could not have had a better tutor," Gardner said.

Mumsford made himself clearer. "Was Carlos there all the time when you were teaching her?"

"I'm not sure what you are implying, Inspector, but yes, he was there sometimes. I took interest in him when I saw how quickly he learned. He had some aptitude for science. I gave him my books."

"Was he a help to you, sir?"

"A help?"

"When you were working with the lepers, sir."

"I was not needed to work with the lepers. I thought I made that clear, Inspector."

"Ah, yes. Then in the garden, sir?"

"The garden?"

"Did he help you in the garden? With your orchids, sir?"

"Ah, my orchids." A grim smile cut across Gardner's face. "He excelled there. He learned quickly about crossbreeding, cross-pollination. He was a bastard, you see. A crossbreed himself."

"And you think it was that he wanted to do?"

"*That?*"

"With your daughter, sir. Was it crossbreeding he was thinking of, sir?"

Gardner got up abruptly and paced the room. He ran his hand over the top of his head down to his neck. The elastic band that held his ponytail slid off and his hair hung in limp locks above his shoulders. "None of this. None of what I say to you must leave here." He came close to Mumsford. The muscles in his face were taut as wires.

"Only to the commissioner," Mumsford said. "Only between us."

"He came to me and said he wanted to have children with her." Gardner was breathing hard. A vein popped out along the length of his forehead, slight at first and then thick, blue, hard, ugly, pushing against his leathery skin.

"He said that? Those words exactly?" Mumsford was taking notes.

"No. He used an ancient language from one of my books."

"Which book?"

"Never mind." Gardner massaged the back of his neck. "He said he wanted to people the island with little Carloses."

"People?"

"Make babies."

"But his exact words, sir? Do you remember his exact words?"

"He said he wanted to people the island with Calibans."

"Calibans?"

"He meant himself."

"But he didn't give you any indication to suggest . . ."

Gardner did not let him finish. "Do you take me for an idiot, Inspector? I know how to guard my daughter's honor."

"But when you were in the garden, sir. Were there times they could have been alone?"

"I resent these insinuations, Inspector."

"I am sorry, sir. It's my job, sir. I must ask. The commissioner will expect me to ask."

Gardner's hand tightened around the back of his neck, and his head fell on his shoulders. With infinite patience, as if he were speaking to a child, he said, "When I was not with them, Inspector, Ariana was always there. She was my spy."

From the moment Gardner opened the back door in the kitchen, Mumsford was accosted by the stench. It came on the first wave of heat that, after the cool of the interior, felt like a blast from a blowtorch on his face. The combination of heat and foul odor almost knocked him off of his feet. His knees buckled and his head felt light. It was shit: cow shit, dog shit, pig shit. It stank as if the sun had vaporized all the shit in the world into the very particles of the air he breathed. He put his handkerchief to his nose, but even the cologne he had dampened it with that morning could not mask the stench. The hairs stood up on the back of his neck, and goose bumps ran down the length of his arms.

"Stink, isn't it?" Gardner said, smirking.

In front of them it was green, an immaculate plastic lawn that had recently been cut, or, as the discomforting thought snaked its way into Mumsford's consciousness, had never needed cutting, stretching out to a chain-link fence behind which the bush grew tall and wild. There was no animal in sight, no mound of shit anywhere.

"Where?" Mumsford looked over the handkerchief he held plastered to his nose and mouth.

Gardner grinned and motioned him to follow him.

What registered first in Mumsford's brain when they turned the corner was color, a mirage of color. He saw color first because the sun dazzled him, because here, on this side of the house, there was not a sliver of green, no grass, no trees, just dry, brown dirt and beds of gray pebbles; because when he squinted to protect his eyes from the glare, it was the macabre shimmering of color that arrested him; because though he could not have missed the chain-link fence enclosing a tiny area behind the color and the outlines of the man inside, it was easier, less painful, to focus on the color.

"My orchids," Gardner said.

Never in all his years of police work had Mumsford seen a sight more terrible. Never had he smelled a stench more foul.

"They are my pride and joy," Gardner said.

The mirage cleared and the outlines took shape. A young man— Mumsford guessed he was about seventeen; seventeen it would be exactly, for Carlos Codrington was two years older than the girl—was sitting on a rock in the scorching sun, penned in an area hardly more than six feet by six. In front of him were Gardner's orchids, a blaze of purple, pink, and white flowers springing out from a maze of brown roots clinging crablike to gray stumps of coconut tree trunks cut in half and sunk into beds of gravel.

"My prizewinners." Gardner was beaming.

Mumsford's throat burned, nausea mounted his upper chest. Except for black boxer shorts, the man was naked, his torso, his arms, thighs, and legs bare and blanketed with red bumps. Some of the bumps had turned into sores, and Mumsford could see blood seeping slowly out of them. Some were already pustulant. At his feet, on one side of the base of the rock, was a pool of putrid water, on the other mounds of foul-smelling brown dirt Mumsford was certain was excrement. Mosquitoes buzzed around the water, in and out of the excrement, and lit upon the young man in clusters on his face and over his body. The young man did not move. He did not swat them away. He sat still as a statue, his hands clutched to his knees, his head bent. Only when Gardner approached did he give any sign of life. He must have heard the gravel crunch and when the sounds stopped, he raised his head.

"I've brought the police," Gardner said.

The young man looked at him with hatred in his eyes purer than any Mumsford could ever have imagined.

"He is filth," Gardner said.

Mumsford turned away in horror. "Get him out of here! Now!" he shouted at Gardner.

Gardner smiled cruelly. "A lying slave whom stripes may move, not kindness."

"You have not beaten him?" Mumsford glanced quickly at the young man.

"The cat-o'-nine-tails for what he did to my daughter."

"You have not struck him?" Mumsford asked again.

"No, I have been kind to him, filth that he is."

"Clean him up," Mumsford said. Nausea clogged his throat.

"He deserves worse than a prison."

"Now, Dr. Gardner! I say now! Take him out of there!"

"I put him there on that rock for endangering the honor of my child." Gardner curled his lips.

"Clean him up, I say, Dr. Gardner!"

"People the island with Carloses, eh?" Gardner taunted Carlos. "Let's see you people now."

"Enough, Dr. Gardner. Get him ready. I will take him now."

Gardner came closer to the fence. "Filth," he shouted.

"For God's sake, Dr. Gardner, he is harmless now. Leave him be."

Gardner curled his fingers around the loops at the top of the fence. His chest was pumping up and down. "Worse than filth," he shouted.

"The commissioner will handle the situation," Mumsford said. "I will take him to Trinidad."

"To jail," Gardner said.

"The commissioner will know what to do." Mumsford tugged Gardner's arm.

"You're a lucky boy." Gardner shook his finger at Carlos. "If the inspector had not come . . ."

Mumsford pulled his arm harder and with a parting curse to Carlos, Gardner let go of the fence.

At least, Mumsford thought, Carlos had not been beaten. At least he had seen no evidence of stripes on his body, only sores.

Inside the house, Gardner shouted orders at Ariana. "Clean him up! See he takes his things with him. I want nothing of his left here."

He invited Mumsford to wait in the drawing room, but Mumsford declined. He was not prepared to call Gardner a torturer, but he could not bear to stay a minute more in his presence, tempting though it was to sit in the cool of the air-conditioned room. He mumbled something about needing to get on his way and said he would wait on the porch.

The boy had been tortured. When he replayed Gardner's words, he thought tortured for nothing. His better self, his English self, his more noble self, told him that. For nothing. For expressing a wish, a desire.

Did intent warrant such torture? Consummation—there was no question—consummation would have been repulsive to him, but Dr. Gardner had given him no proof of consummation. *Attempted* was the word he used, and the accusation was a garble of words about peopling the island.

Male concupiscence. Lust. Lascivious intent. Mumsford could find the young man guilty of no more than these. Contemptible, yes. The boy, like the rest of his kind, was prone to carnal lechery, but he had done nothing more than reveal his dirty longings to Gardner.

But why? Mumsford's detective mind churned. What was his motive for exposing filthy thoughts to Gardner? Only a fool would be so stupid as to make his intentions known to the very person he intended to hurt. Only a predator gone daft in the head would warn his prey, and yet the boy did not look like a fool. No one capable of sustaining such control over his expression while he was being taunted was a fool.

Surely the boy knew that Gardner would not have welcomed his crude overtures toward his daughter. But were his overtures crude?

People, Gardner said Carlos wanted to do. *People* as in make babies with his daughter.

Crude overtures, yes, because she was an English girl; crude because he was a colored man. But Mumsford had seen the chief medical officer get away with this sort of crudeness. He and the chief justice had married Englishwomen and had brown babies with them. These were indecencies to him, and he presumed to all red-blooded Englishmen—to Gardner—but one did not imprison a man for these indecencies.

Was there more? Was Gardner hiding more? Was it possible that his daughter's jewel, her virgin knot as he called it, had been broken? Had the boy done more than reveal his dark desires, his criminal intent?

Was it shame, embarrassment, that caused Gardner to hide the crime? He said, he intimated, that his daughter's chances for marriage with the American from Boston had been in jeopardy. The man from New England would not marry a slut, he said. Yet Mumsford was certain that Gardner would not have let Carlos off so lightly had he done this, had he raped his daughter. He would have told the commissioner, he would have secured Carlos's punishment—his death possibly—discreetly, in secret. No, it was not likely that Carlos had raped Dr. Gardner's daughter.

Mumsford had already arrived at this conclusion when Carlos appeared from the back of the house, alone. There were no restraints whatsoever on his body. There would have been restraints if he were wrong, Mumsford thought. If the boy had committed such a crime, Gardner would not have let him leave without at least manacling his wrists. He wanted him off the island, that was all, Mumsford decided. He wanted him out of the way when his daughter returned, out of the way in case desire turned into actuality, in case the next time the boy would not declare, but would do what he so foolhardily confessed to be his intention.

Now cleaned up, dressed in beige pants and a pink long-sleeved cotton shirt, the boy seemed harmless to Mumsford, incapable of that kind of barbarity.

Misshapen? He had seen him bare-chested. His shoulders were broad, his torso muscular, his hips slim. Was it the shape of his backside that had caused Gardner to tell that lie? Mumsford had heard the snickering in the Country Club. *Tails.* No one believed it, but it made for raucous laughter when the blacks left and they had the billiard room to themselves.

Mumsford blushed remembering how his eyes had strayed there, but he had felt compelled to examine the boy as he walked toward the house in front of him. His torso was shorter, his buttocks more pronounced than the average Englishman's. High, but not misshapen.

He was facing him now and the blood and pus had been washed off. He had to admit he was handsome; even the freckles were not unattractive. There were pink blotches on his face for sure, and around his ears and neck where the skin was broken, but the freckles spread across his cheekbones seemed to him like chocolate dust sprinkled over a butterscotch brown cake.

It bothered Mumsford that this pleasant image should come to him at this moment, dredged from a happy time in his childhood. Yet something about Carlos's face, his skin—butterscotch brown was indeed how he would describe his color—reminded him of toffee and chocolate, and the brown cake he loved as a child.

And perhaps his gaffe with Gardner had its source from these times, too, when he was a boy, in the early years after the war. He had known better, of course. He had seen freckles on many an Englishman's face. But the talk in those years in the streets where he lived in England was about the coloreds, the flood of immigrants from the colonies, coming to England now that the country had been battered. "Reverse colonization," his father called it. "They come to take what we have worked for."

Signs warned dark-skinned immigrants that they were not welcome. *No dogs. No coloreds.* Some were more humiliating: *Pets. No coloreds.* But nothing stopped these sons and daughters of the Commonwealth. They came in droves from India, Pakistan, China, Africa, the West Indies, from every corner of the world where the sun set on lands the British had colonized, trusting in the propaganda of the Mother Country, believing in her gospel of fair play and justice. When asked, their response was naïve. Their oil, tobacco, cotton, sugar, bananas had made the Mother Country rich. Surely it was their turn.

The fear among the men was, naturally, the vulnerability of the women. What would happen if a colored man fucked a white woman? Mumsford and his school chums spent many an amusing hour making up answers—*Stripes like a zebra, spots like a leopard. Freckles*—all the time trying to smother hysteria.

Say something enough times and myth becomes fact, lies truth, Mumsford now admitted to himself. Carlos had freckles and the skin color of a colored man, but, as he grudgingly had to accede, the facial features of many an Englishman he knew: broad brow; thin lips; a wide, substantial chin; blue eyes undoubtedly inherited from his mother.

The blue eyes made Mumsford uneasy. They were disconcerting, strange to him on a brown face.

"Have you taken all you'll need?" Carlos was standing in front of him, obviously ready to leave, but he had not uttered a single word. "Ready?" Mumsford jerked his head toward the black duffel bag he was holding.

The young man nodded, but his lips remained sealed.

He could not figure him out. He could not tell if he was afraid or relieved to be going with him. His eyes told him nothing. They were blank, empty of any expression Mumsford could discern. "Well then," Mumsford said, when it was clear that Carlos would not answer him, "I'll let Dr. Gardner know we are leaving."

But before he could step forward, the front door opened and Gardner came running out, his shirttails flapping behind him. "See that he rots in jail," he shouted to Mumsford.

Carlos made a gurgling sound and puckered his lips.

"Until his flesh rots." Gardner had reached where they were standing.

What happened next so paralyzed both Mumsford and Gardner that neither man moved, stunned by the audacity of it, shocked by the intensity of the rage that had produced it. Had Mumsford been looking at Carlos at the time and seen his eyes narrow to slits and the venom pooled there, he might have anticipated it when he heard the gurgling coming from Carlos's direction. But he was facing Gardner, and he saw what happened after it happened, after Carlos had done it.

He saw the stream of spit jetting forward, he saw it land with absolute accuracy on the tip of Gardner's nose; he saw it slide and drain onto his top lip, and his feet, like Gardner's, froze to the ground.

Carlos came close to Gardner. He was breathing hard; his nostrils flared. "You taught me your language well and I use it now to curse you. May you burn in hell, motherfucker!"

Gardner's face lost color, and then his body thawed, and like a dog tucking its tail between its legs, he turned and walked away.

Mumsford had brought handcuffs, but he did not use them. After Carlos spat on Gardner's face and cursed him, he seemed ready to leave, anxious even. "Can we go now?" he asked Mumsford. His voice was as cool as ice.

Why had Gardner not retaliated? Why hadn't he struck him or insisted that Mumsford beat him with his baton? Why, when they faced each other, was Gardner the first to turn away? The conclusion Mumsford came to was the same one he had arrived at minutes before: Carlos had committed no real crime. The expression of his desire to have babies with Virginia was an insult to Gardner, no more. Still, to spit in the face of an Englishman!

"That was disrespectful." He said so to Carlos.

"He deserved it." Carlos's breathing had slowed. He spoke without emotion, as if merely stating an obvious fact.

And perhaps it was an obvious fact. The boy had been tortured. It had irked Mumsford when the commissioner had told him to take Carlos to the monks. Jail, he thought, would have been more appropriate for the perpetrator of a crime against an English girl. But he was grateful now for the commissioner's insistence, now after he had witnessed Gardner's cruelty.

"I'm not taking you to jail," he said, wanting to put the boy at ease. "The commissioner has asked me to bring you to the monks at St. Benedict's."

The young man remained stubbornly silent, but Mumsford saw the muscles on the side of his face loosen and his jaw relax.

"There will be no more punishment, Codrington."

He wanted to say more to him, but decided it would be imprudent. The fact remained that the investigation was not yet over. He had yet to speak to Virginia, to get her side of the story.

The boatman was waiting at the spot where he said he would be. The moment he saw Carlos, he came quickly toward him. "Is good you leaving, Mister Carlos," he said. He grabbed his hand and shook it vigorously.

Mumsford frowned at him, unsettled by the honorific. *Mister?*

The boatman paid no attention to his frown. "You lead the way, Mister Carlos," he said.

Carlos smiled and walked in front of him. Mumsford had no choice but to follow, and the boatman picked up the rear.

No one spoke on the brief walk to the water, the silence broken only by the swish of branches, the call of birds, the occasional pebble rolling downhill. Once a twig snapped and then another, rapidly, behind it. Mumsford turned around sharply. "Iguana," the boatman said. "Plenty in the bush." But when they neared the clearing, Mumsford saw the unmistakable flicker of yellow between the greens and browns in the bushes.

Ariana!

He told the boatman to wait in the boat with Carlos and he went to the place where he had seen the yellow. Ariana parted the branches and appeared before him.

"I tell you a lot about Carlos and Miss Virginia but not now. I can't stay." She held up her hand.

Mumsford brushed aside the flicker of irritation that flashed through him and concentrated. "Can you come to the station?" he asked.

"I come tomorrow. Tomorrow is Friday. He study on Friday; read he books all day. I come ten o'clock."

"Ten o'clock is fine. But won't he miss you?"

"Prospero miss nobody when he read his books."

It was not the time to ask the question, but Mumsford could not help himself. "Why do you call him Prospero?" he asked.

She shrugged. "He prosperous. He rich."

"So that is it?"

"Ask Carlos. If it have another reason, Carlos know. Is he who give him the name."

But it made no sense to ask Carlos then or during the sea crossing to Trinidad. It was clear he was determined not to speak, to remain in stony silence no matter what was said to him. When he did speak, as he was getting off the boat in Trinidad, it was to utter only four short sentences. He said them not to Mumsford and not to the boatman, either. It was as if he were speaking to himself, having felt a need to hear his own voice.

"My mother," he said, "was blue-eyed, but she was not a hag. She was beautiful. The house was hers. He stole it from me."

FOUR

*P*ETER GARDNER, as Mumsford could have surmised from his cagey answers, had not come for the lepers. He did not stay because of them. He would never have chosen this hellhole to raise his daughter. If he were forced to tell the truth, he would have said it was his innocence that had brought him here. His naïveté. His trust sans bounds and confidence in a brother who, next to his daughter, of all the world he loved. A brother who had clung to him like ivy but only to suck him dry. Only to hide his talent from others.

They were doctors, he and Paul, when he used to live in London. Peter and Paul Bidwedder, before he changed his surname to Gardner. His parents, ardent Christians when their sons were born, named them for the loyal disciples of Christ, but regretted their decision later, with the war, after the deaths of so many of England's most promising. After an explosion in a field in France brought their father back home a quadriplegic. By the time he and Paul left for medical school, their parents were proselytizing atheists.

It was because of their father that he and Paul decided to become doctors. He chose research, for unlike Paul, he was happiest when he was in the library, his head buried in a pile of dusty books. He told his father that he believed it was possible to grow new arms and legs for him in the laboratory. He was sure it was only a matter of figuring out the right cells and stimulating them. Then, when they multiplied into arms and legs, he would attach them where the old limbs had been amputated.

Voodoo medicine, Paul called it, but their father grabbed on to the hope Peter offered. "Maybe not as perfect as the ones you had before, Father, but they could grow back almost as strong."

Paul scoffed at him. He was the realist, the practical man. He spoke of a future of mechanical artificial limbs. Better still, robots that could respond to human command.

"You wouldn't have to do a thing," Paul said to his father. "It would be like having a personal servant."

His father preferred the fantasies Peter spun for him.

"All it would take is figuring out the human genome," Peter said. "Then we would have the secret to life. We could even make a clone of you, Father."

Their mother, who loved Paul best anyhow, was horrified. "Dr. Frankenstein was a monster," she said.

Peter waved her away. "Oh, those ideas are passé," he said, "No one is planning to use the dead."

"Playing God," she said.

"Yes, playing God," Paul repeated after her, but even when he was ridiculing Peter envy was eating him up.

In medical school, it was obvious that the professors admired Peter. He was the brain, the smarter of the Bidwedder men. But the students loved Paul. He was the popular one. They consulted Peter when they were faced with a difficult problem. At examination time, they stuck to him like flies to honey, but it was with Paul they went to the pub. Peter's ardor, his focus, his single-mindedness on curing every illness he came upon, made them uneasy. His patients were not human to him. To him, they were a mass of cells, tissue, blood and bones, not people, not living, breathing men and women with feelings and desires.

Peter became more human to them when he married. He still worked hard, but he no longer slept in the lab, as he often did when nothing mattered except the project that engaged him. His wife was beautiful: blond hair, blue eyes, a perfectly shaped oval face, and the pale alabaster skin that so many Englishmen loved. But what Peter Gardner boasted about was her virtue. He had married a virgin. So certain he was that no one could seduce her that he offered to put his head on a block to be chopped off if anyone proved him wrong. "Her virtue is nonpareil," he said. Paul's friends called Peter "Nonpareil" behind his back, but not only because of what he claimed for his wife, but because of what he claimed for himself. No one was smarter than he, he seemed to imply by his serious demeanor. And, indeed, all that he touched turned to gold.

Then his wife died, three years after giving birth to a daughter, and he was his old self again.

Except for his little girl, Virginia, Peter became, in all his human interactions, cold and distant. Inhuman, Paul accused him of being when Peter refused to lend him money after he lost his savings and three months' salary at a gambling table. "Keep it up and you will kill someone one day." It was a matter of time before Paul's words proved prophetic.

Peter had not intended to kill the woman. He had intended to cure her. He had given her one of his concoctions. Put it in her IV drip.

It was not the first time he had given one of his patients the experimental medicine he had mixed himself. Some improved. A few died, but, as he always reasoned, most were already terminal, and nothing, except this chance he was prepared to take, would have saved them.

This patient, however, was not fatally ill. She was the patient of another doctor. Peter Bidwedder just happened to be in the ward when she was admitted. He wanted to test a medicine that had worked on his rats. He gave it to her. She died within hours. She was rich, important. The wife of a government minister. There would be an inquest.

He was terrified. He went to his brother. His brother said that an inquest would lead to others. The hospital authorities would find out about the patients who had not been cured by the medicines he had given them. The ones who had died. When Peter said to Paul that they were dying anyway, Paul reminded him that he had enemies, colleagues who hated him.

Paul recommended Trinidad. He told Peter he would hide him at a friend's flat in London and the next day his friend would drive him to Liverpool. From there he could take a ship to Trinidad. It would cost money, lots of money. He would have to sign over his bank account to him. His house and his inheritance from their parents, too.

When Peter bit his lips and cast his eyes from side to side nervously, Paul was quick to reassure him. "I won't need *all* the money," he said. "But if that woman tries to sue, I want to be sure there is nothing left in your estate for her to take. Then, when things clear up, I'll send you what's left."

"When things clear up?"

"Surely there have been no cures without fatalities. One day people will understand that and acknowledge your genius."

Peter was in a bind. He had to trust his brother.

Paul said he knew someone with connections who could arrange for him to go to Chacachacare, a little island off the northwest coast of Trinidad. It was a leper colony, he said, but it was virtually abandoned. Most of the lepers were cured and had returned to Trinidad. There was a doctor there, taking care of the few patients who still remained, but he was old, hardly likely to ask disturbing questions. It would be a perfect hideout, he said to Peter.

Peter Bidwedder knew about the cure for Hansen's disease. Contrary to popular belief, the disease was not easily contracted. That it was not easily contracted, however, was not the same as saying it *could not* be contracted by contact with infected persons. Still, the chances were so slim that a reasonable man could conclude that even on a leper colony, if he kept some distance away from the lepers, he would be safe. In any case, Peter Bidwedder had no intentions of practicing medicine with lepers. His brother was right. A leper colony was the perfect hideout. No one would think of looking for him there. All that remained was to change his last name.

It was more than two hours now since Carlos had left. Peter Gardner sat on the porch in his rocking chair, staring at the sky and brooding, his head flopped backward on his neck.

Twilight. The time in the evening he loved best. Night hovered as in the wings of a stage, waiting its turn, while the sun glittered above the darkening clouds. But this evening the sun had cast an eerie white light on the sky—electric—that had made the darkening clouds darker.

The gods frowning. The words flitted, light as gossamer, through his head and he shut his eyes, willing his brain to mount a defense.

It is he who had wronged me. He who would misuse my daughter. He who would screw her.

When he opened his eyes, he was rewarded. Forgiven, he chose to believe. For below the clouds, the sun splashed her magnificent colors: red that bled to purple, yellow that burned to orange—the exquisiteness of a sunset found only here, on these Caribbean islands.

It was art: a great painting in the sky. Dark clouds but a fire below them. In the foreground, statuary—the tall bushes at the end of the lawn outlined in the silvery light. For after science, it was art Peter Gardner worshipped: music, painting, sculpture, literature. Poetry, best of all.

He groaned and clasped his fingers across his forehead. He had no talent for poetry. In England he had tried some verses and failed. It was the boy who was the poet.

> *To walk silently*
> *   in the forest,*
> *and not shake a leaf, to move*
> *and not disturb a branch.*
>
> *At twilight*
> *let me walk—*
> *   to the drum of impending*
> *   rest, caught between sleeping and waking—*

when rocks turn
malleable in the growing night, softening
to the touch of deepening
   shade.

He did not want to think of him, to remember the boy's poem he had memorized in two readings, patched together from scraps he had retrieved from the garbage after a fit of envy had caused him to tear it to pieces.

"Soft." He waved his hand across the still air. "Soft," he murmured again, looking around him, listening. But there was no sound, soft or loud, in his backyard, only the birds, their calls fading with the dying light. No mumblings between Ariana and the boy, no hushed whispers. He was gone. Left with the inspector. To jail. Yes, that was where he belonged.

He patted the pocket of his shirt as if to reassure himself that the packet of smoking papers was there where he had put it. He took it out now and picked up the flat thin box at the foot of the rocking chair. A bundle of letters bound in red ribbon lay close to the box. He would read them next. Carefully, laying out one sheet of the paper on his lap, he shook out the contents of the tin box until he made a thin line along the middle of the paper.

Tobacco and marijuana. He did not smoke one without the other. He was suspicious of things unaltered. Nature to him was a traitor, bringing disease to roses in bloom, blight to crops before harvest. Cancer to humans.

Rain made floods. Drought dried grass and sucked moisture from fruit. But on his land the grass was green; flowers blossomed in the dry season.

If Mumsford had not run off with the boy, he would have shown him what he had done with orchids. He would have taken him to his nursery to see the anthuriums he had grafted to calla lilies.

He rolled the paper into a cigarette, put it between his lips, lit it, and sucked the smoke deep into his lungs. The tobacco was for the taste, the marijuana to increase its potency, to calm his nerves. And this

evening he needed to calm his nerves: the boy had spat in his face. This
evening he needed to remind himself why he was here, why he could
not return to England.

He reached for the letters. Some were in envelopes, some simply
folded. He was a scientist. A meticulous man. The folded letters were
his, copies of the ones he had written to his brother. Of the ones in envelopes, only two were from Paul, the others his, returned unopened
to the sender. Slowly, gingerly, he unfolded the first one he had written
to his brother.

July 15, 1950
Cocorite, Trinidad

Dear Paul,

How long must I wait for the boat to Chacachacare? Virginia and
I have been here three weeks now, living in a shack in Cocorite. This
can't go on much longer. When will that man come to take us there?

Don't think I don't appreciate all you are doing for us. I shall
repay you well, I promise.

Your brother,
Peter

He refolded the letter and opened one still in its envelope, the first Paul
had sent.

July 31, 1950
Lancashire, England

Dear Peter,

By the time you receive this letter you would already have had
the answers to your questions. The bearer is a friend of a friend. He
will take you and Virginia to Chacachacare.

All is well here. There was an inquest, and, as you anticipated,
blame was placed squarely on your shoulders. Everything is out
in the open. Her husband wants blood. Your blood absolutely, and
so do the others. Even the ones you cured have become afraid.

They have made you into a monster. They say your medicines were
meant for animals. A woman claims that she has grown hair on her
arms and chest, a man that he laughs like a hyena. Lies, of course.
All lies.

Not to worry. I won't tell where you are hiding. Place your trust
in me.

Your brother,

Paul

Place your trust in me. Peter Gardner had laughed scornfully when he
first read those words. Trust him? *As a serpent's egg.* He needed him but
he did not trust him. He had turned their mother against him. He had
put her up to comparing him with Frankenstein. He was sure of that.

Playing God? That's what she had accused him of, and yet she had
claimed she did not believe in Him. They were hypocrites all. But he
had to be careful. He was in his brother's power. In his next letter he
was obsequious.

November 12, 1950

Chacachacare

Dear Paul,

We have arrived safely. The friend of your friend must have told
you so. I apologize for having taken this long to write, but I was not
sure it would be prudent. I wanted to wait a while. There may have
been spies checking your post box. Four months, I think, is long
enough. They would have given up by now, certain you have no
knowledge of my whereabouts. In any case, they love you and would
not want to harm you. You have been a kind and generous brother
to me. You cannot know how much I am grateful to you.

The weather here is rotten, unbelievably hot, but at least now it
is dry. The incessant rains have come to an end, though, alas, not the
mosquitoes. My poor Virginia suffers, but I have managed to make a
salve for her and to procure some netting.

We stayed for a while at the doctor's house. As you said, he asked
no questions, but he does not need me. The patients here can take

care of themselves, and the doctor, though quite old, is more than enough for the few who may need his help.

I have now found a better house for Virginia and me. It is not England, but it is not uncomfortable. I am, as it were, lord again of my own manor. I have a housekeeper, who does my cooking and cleaning. I don't think she is long for this world, but she has a daughter who helps.

Yes, and there is a boy, Carlos. He gabbles like a thing most brutish. Hardly language, as you and I would call it. A sort of English, I think he means it to be, with dats and dises and deres. No ths whatsoever, and not a verb to match its subject.

Maybe I'm not altogether out of the business of improving the lot of humans, though at this moment I would hardly call the little savage human. Maybe I shall teach him to speak so at least he'll know his own meaning. We shall see. But he makes an amusing playmate for Virginia. She is quite taken with him.

Give me news about the situation at the hospital. Do you think the matter will blow away soon?

Yours always in trust and gratitude,

Your brother,

Peter

For eight months he did not hear from Paul. He wrote to him again and the letter came back, unopened, the envelope stamped with the words *Return to Sender. Addressee Unknown.* He wrote again, four more letters. All returned. Addressee unknown. Then this one, the last. When he saw the date, he knew he had been betrayed. March 15. The Ides of March. *Et tu Brute?*

March 15, 1951
Lancashire

Dear Peter,

This is the last letter I will write to you, and I suggest you cease writing to me. Though I know you have been careful to mail my letters to people who could post them to me from other countries, it is still dangerous to send them. Your letters may be traced. I do not like being questioned, either. The postman mentioned to me the other day that he has noticed I get foreign letters without a return address. It will only be a matter of time before he tells that to the authorities.

Yes, I have many friends. People like me, the postman likes me, but loyalty and friendship cost money. I can bribe the postman. I have bribed your colleagues already. They take the money as a cat laps milk and have sworn to secrecy about your experiments.

Did you really think, Peter, you could grow limbs in a test tube? My God, what you did to those animals! One of your colleagues showed me a rat with six legs. Were you mad?

But now they have the money, your colleagues will keep your secrets, though I may need to pay off those who may still want more. Promise a man enough money and he'll tell the clock the time. He will swear eight o'clock if you tell him that that was the time when you were in such and such a place. Those grand doctors who used to drink with me and think me foolish and you the genius now do my bidding. Money, my dear Peter, talks and walks. You would not think how much they praise me now. There is no better doctor in London, they say. Fools!

Here it is, Peter: I have taken the house in Lancashire, the money the parents left you, and your bank account, what was left of your bank account after I paid out the bribes. Remember, you transferred everything to me. Of course, I am aware of our agreement. But, my dear brother, I have no intentions of returning your money to you, or giving you back your house.

You asked if I thought "the matter" would blow away soon. It will never blow away, dear brother. That woman's husband and her family will hunt you down forever. So it is no use thinking you can come back. There is no coming back for you.

But, perhaps, you think I should send you some money. Let me tell you this, brother. You have no estate. Your estate is mine. I feel sorry for your daughter. I feel sorry that because of you she is stuck in that savage place. But she will be able to leave one day, when she is old enough. A bit of advice, brother. Marry her to an Englishman. He will bring her back and restore to her what you have deprived her of. But you can never leave. Not ever. Don't trouble your mind with that thought. I will be the first to turn you in.

I do not feel sorry for you, Peter. I never liked you. You always thought you were better than me and so did Father. Now see who has the last laugh.

Conscience? Surely a man who has no conscience cannot ask me such a question. But if you were to ask, Peter, here is my answer. If my conscience were a corn on my big toe, I would wear special shoes. But the truth is, I do not feel that deity that so many claim troubles their souls. I feel no guilt. Indeed, I think I deserve what I now possess, as you deserve your exile.

Take heart, dear brother. What's past is prologue. The future is yours to discharge, as it is mine. Now that I have the means, I will make the best of mine. Make the best of yours. You have your books.

Paul.

He could recite the letter by heart. He had read it at least a hundred times. *You have your books.* All he had were two volumes of *The Complete Works of Shakespeare*, a couple of science texts, and some novels. He wanted to take more but Paul said no. "Too much baggage. You're a man on the run."

The ribbon lay on his lap. He picked it up and retied the letters. His head ached, his eyes stung. The sun had all but descended. There were embers still, but the day was over. Done.

What's past is prologue. He had his red leather-bound book; he had his notes; he had the formulas for his inventions.

"Ariana!" He called for her. "Ariana! Don't you hear me call?"

She came softly, a leaf floating on a breeze.

He was sleepy, so sleepy. The marijuana. His brother.

She touched his arm to stir him.

"Patricia?" He was thinking of his wife. "Patricia?" He reached up and stroked her cheek.

"You love me, Master? No?" she asked.

Not alabaster skin. Not Patricia. Brown. Too brown to be alabaster skin tanned brown.

"Ariana?"

"You love me, no, Master?"

He sighed. "Dearly. Dearly, my delicate Ariana."

FIVE

HEY HAD ALSO seen the sunset. At first Mumsford thought Carlos had not noticed it. He had not moved nor uttered a single word since they had entered the car that was waiting for them at the dock in Trinidad. He sat with his back erect, his arms folded stiffly across his duffel bag and looked straight ahead of him, no expression on his face except a dour rigidity.

Mumsford was certain it was all a pretense; he was convinced the boy was afraid. He had to be. He was in the custody of a police inspector—an Englishman—accused by another Englishman of improper advances to his daughter. The politics were changing in Trinidad, but the island was still a colony of England in spite of the saber rattling. *Machete rattling.* Mumsford grinned, for that was what he thought of the protest gatherings in the town square, mere machete rattling that England could suppress whenever she wanted to.

It bothered him that England did not seem to want to, that she seemed ready to cave in, that she had lost her will to fight back. But he was not blind to the cost of the war with Germany. Resources, what remained of resources, had to be conserved, used for reconstruction.

Still, there were colored people in Trinidad who would fight for England, who would give more credence to what an Englishman said than to anything one of their own would counter. That much Mumsford understood about the workings of colonialism, how a tiny island like his had managed to rule the world.

It was simple actually: a matter of changing the native's sense of the beautiful, a matter of controlling the mind. Even now the films the people rushed to see in the cinemas popping up all over the island reinforced the message: white skin was beautiful; blue, green, gray eyes were beautiful; blond hair was beautiful; straight black or brown hair was beautiful; curly hair without kinks was beautiful. Even now in the schools it was English history the teachers taught, the English way. Always the heroes were English, always the achievements and accomplishments were theirs.

Give the native something to strive for: your beauty, your accomplishments. An impossible goal for him to achieve, but his yearnings will keep him loyal.

What was Carlos thinking? Did he think the monks would save him? Did he think they would believe his word over the word of an Englishman?

Yet Mumsford was wary. The monks were known to be do-gooders. The poor flocked to them by the hundreds. The rich came, too, frightened by a world tumbling backward since the end of the war: traditions, the social order of respect for elders, respect for those in charge—the English who had helped them secure their fortunes—unraveling, falling apart.

The monks had opened a boarding school for boys in the early fifties. By the time the new decade began, it was overcrowded. A new music and a new movement, hippies, were pulling children away from their parents. Now not only Indian farmers smoked ganja rolled into fat cigars, the sons of the rich did, too.

Perhaps, Mumsford thought, the commissioner had sent his recalcitrant son to the monks. But what if the monks had taken his son's side over his side? Mumsford glanced again at Carlos. His face was a mask, immobile.

He would not be intimidated; he would not allow the boy with his

implacable exterior to throw his imagination into a tailspin. The commissioner's decision made sense. He understood his purpose. Accusing
a black boy of assaulting an English girl would be suicide given the politics in Trinidad. Better to hide behind the monks' skirts, better to have
them do the accusing.

The monks belonged to the order of the Benedictines who were
fleeing from religious persecution in Brazil. They had come to the island in 1912. When they arrived, like other orders of monks, they
searched for a hill. They found it above the village of Tunapuna.
Mount Tabor. Halfway through the century, few people remembered
its name. Mount St. Benedict, the little mountain came to be known.

It was up this mountain that the car bearing Mumsford and Carlos
was winding its way, curling around the tight bends of the narrow road
that in parts dropped suddenly to precipices so steep Mumsford held
his breath, resisting the urge to ask the driver to slow down for fear he
would think him a coward. He had seen him look into the rearview
mirror, exchanging glances with Carlos, and though Carlos's face remained unchanged and the driver had said not a single word, Mumsford was certain that a current of empathy had passed between them.

Well, let them feel sorry for each other. Mumsford gritted his teeth
and looked resolutely in front of him. The sun was descending, and its
last rays glittered over the tall palm trees that lined the road, casting a
fretwork of light and dark patches on the ground beneath them. When
the car rounded a bend that faced westward, Mumsford caught a
glimpse of the descending sun. It was only a glimpse, but a glimpse so
arresting that in spite of his resolution, he was pulled to it, and for the
remainder of the trip, it was not forward he looked, but backward.

He had seen nothing like it before, the flaming colors, yes, but not
the white light, electric under charcoal-gray clouds: a halo. It had so
frightened Gardner he shut his eyes and pleaded for vindication.

Only in paintings had Mumsford seen such radiance, such lumines-
cence, which would have blinded him were it not trapped in oils, were
it not confined over renderings of saints, over pictures of the Virgin
Mary and of the risen Christ. The radiance almost blinded him now. It
pierced his soul and set him off thinking of the power of God, of the
reward He rendered to the good and the innocent, and the punishment

He doled out to the bad and the guilty. Like Gardner, at that very moment, he thought of Carlos, and glancing over to him saw that he, too, was looking back, transfixed as he had been by the sunset. Mumsford breathed in deeply and slowly let out his breath, glad he was on his way to take the boy to a monastery and not to jail, as Gardner had wished.

Brother St. Clair was waiting for them outside the front door of the rectory. When the car pulled to a stop, he came running toward them, his face shining with excitement, his arms extended, the wide sleeves of his bright white cassock spread out like wings. He was a short, plump man, a caricature of a monk, a Friar Tuck with a monk's tonsure encircling his balding head and a belly that rolled over a brown rope tied below his waist and jiggled as he rushed out to meet them. "Did you see it? Did you see it?"

Mumsford was already out of the car. He held out his hand and the monk wrapped his fingers tightly around it. "God's sign," the monk said and cast his eyes upward.

And if the sunset was God's sign, Mumsford thought, looking around him, then this place, this particular spot, was His paradise. Not for the first time since he had come to live in Trinidad was he forced to admit that there were some compensations, that besides the social advantages, sometimes the landscape pleasantly surprised, sometimes it was reward enough. In front of him was a breathtaking panorama of shapes and colors tumbling down the hillside and spreading wide across green plains to the sea. A cluster of tiny houses, broken here and there by larger residences, clung to the hillsides, and beyond, a dizzying array of villages. To the west, the city of Port of Spain, its highest building— the skyscraper it was called, though less than twenty stories high— loomed above an entanglement of pretty-colored buildings and narrow streets. At its border the blue sea glistened, bloodied by the sunset.

Mumsford pointed to the railing at the edge of the sheer drop. "May I?" he asked the monk.

"Of course, of course."

And for more than a few minutes, standing behind the railing, both men seemed to forget Carlos.

"The Gulf of Paria," the monk said, indicating the sea. "Not so long ago, Gulfo de Ballena, Gulf of the Whales. Then the Japanese came with their trawlers looking for lobster and shrimp. They dredged the seabed and the whales swam northward."

It sounded like a made-up story. Mumsford pressed his lips together and turned to the east, to the grasslands.

"The Aripo Savannah," the monk said, following the line of Mumsford's head. "It's dry now because of *la sécheresse,* this terrible drought, but green most of the year. If you look farther you will see the Caroni Swamp. Now all manner of fowl nest there in the mangrove, crustaceans, too, but not for long." He sighed and his chin sank into his collarbone. "If they don't control the hunters and those people who come here from overseas to gawk, the birds will disappear. Just like the *ballena.*"

The monk did not accuse him, of course. He did not say he was one of the hunters, or one of those people from overseas, not even the "they" who should be protecting the fowl and the crustaceans, but his pious tone grated against Mumsford's nerves. The goodwill that had overtaken him began to slip away.

"It's sad to see . . ." the monk began again.

"The boy," Mumsford stopped him before he could finish. "I've brought Carlos Codrington."

"Yes, yes." The monk wiped his hands nervously down the sides of his cassock, and the rope from his belt swung back and forth against his thick thigh.

"The commissioner said you would be expecting him."

"Yes, the boy." The monk looked embarrassed, ashamed of his outburst.

"I'll get him now," Mumsford said. But before he could take a step forward, the monk touched his arm.

"He's doing the right thing," the monk said.

"He?"

"The commissioner."

Mumsford felt cross again. He had not come there for the monk's approval. Not with the best motives he said, as he walked with the monk toward the car, "You have a castle here."

It wasn't a castle. It was a chapel, a tall rectangular tower that rose high above a sprawling collection of two- and three-storied cream-colored buildings topped with red roofs. Behind the buildings, the jungle climbed farther up the mountain, thick, dense, and lush, even now in the dry season.

"We began with a tapia hut," the monk said, almost apologetically. And Mumsford regretted his malice, for it was an incredible feat of imagination and determination to have constructed such a grand building, no small thing to have put the monastery there, to have cut through the mountain, hacked down the jungle, and kept the constantly encroaching vegetation at bay. It wasn't a castle, but it looked as magnificent as a castle.

"The commissioner has always admired what the monks have done," he said, ashamed of his insolence. "He appreciates your help with the boy."

The monk was pleased. "Where is he? Let's have a look at him." The car door was open, but Carlos had not come out.

Mumsford tilted his head to one side and jerked it forward toward the car. The monk understood and peered into the car's interior. "Come." He waved his hand, urging Carlos to join them. "Come. We won't hurt you."

But he was not prepared for what he saw when Carlos emerged. He flinched. His cheeks lost color. "What? What?" he stammered. He spun around to Mumsford. "His face. My God! The sores! What on God's earth?" The words came out of his mouth in a jumble.

Inside the monastery Mumsford did his best to explain.

"Has he no heart?" the monk asked.

"He was afraid for his daughter," Mumsford said.

They were standing close to each other in the sparsely furnished reception room. Four wood-framed Morris chairs fitted with stiff burgundy cushions were arranged around a plain wood cocktail table on which were a Bible and a collection of religious magazines. Except for an enormous crucifix facing the door, the white walls were bare.

Carlos was sitting on one of the Morris chairs. The monk had invited Mumsford to sit, too, but he had declined. He didn't want to sit; he didn't want to stay with the boy longer than was necessary. He felt drained. Having to recount to the monk what he had witnessed in Gardner's backyard had drained him. He was anxious to go, to leave the boy in the monk's hands and return to the normalcy of his house. His mother would have been back; she would have given the cook instructions on what to make for his supper. Perhaps they would have roast lamb with mint tonight, and baked potatoes. He had left her a note, put it in her room before he went to Chacachacare. He had not requested roast lamb and baked potatoes, but he had told her about the ants, that someone had left crumbs on the polished floor of his study. He was a respectful son; he didn't say that someone was she, but he knew she would get his meaning. Lamb for supper would be her way of making amends. Buoyed by these pleasant thoughts of what awaited him, he chose to disregard the grimace that intensified on Carlos's face the more he struggled to find the right words to explain to the monk that Dr. Gardner had wanted only to protect his daughter, that she was all he had in the world.

"But I was led to understand that nothing happened to the girl," the monk said.

"If Dr. Gardner had not prevented him, who knows what could have happened."

Carlos made a fist with one hand and pushed it into the open palm of his other hand, grinding it around slowly. This time it was not as easy for Mumsford to ignore him.

"And this is what he did?" The monk, too, was looking at Carlos. "Shame, shame on him."

Mumsford twirled his pith helmet between his hands. He wanted to say that Carlos had given Dr. Gardner some cause, that he had taunted him, but he could not say so in good faith. His conscience would not let him. "The commissioner is indebted to you," he said to the monk.

The monk had not taken his eyes off Carlos. "How old are you?" he asked him.

Carlos did not answer.

"Seventeen," Mumsford said.

"Just a boy," the monk murmured.

"We are grateful," Mumsford said. "The commissioner did not want to put him in jail with the older men."

"But you don't have proof . . ."

"Maybe I'll get a chance to speak to Dr. Gardner's daughter tomorrow," Mumsford said. "She is here. In Trinidad."

Carlos's leg slid forward and the sole of his shoe squeaked against the polished wood floor. Both men heard it; both men were fully aware that Carlos was paying careful attention to what they were saying, but for Mumsford there was special meaning in Carlos's sudden, agitated movement. For it was when he mentioned that Dr. Gardner's daughter was in Trinidad that the boy sat up and his leg jerked forward.

Ariana's lies. It disturbed Mumsford that he would think now of her lies.

"Carlos," the monk began and then hesitated. "Is that how you want to be called, my son?"

Carlos pulled in his leg, but did not speak.

Perhaps it was mere coincidence, Mumsford thought. And because he preferred to think that way, because he could not bear to entertain for a second that there might be some truth in what Ariana had written, he suppressed the temptation to doubt himself. Carlos's face registered nothing, no emotion, no concern, no anxiety.

"He does not speak much," he said to the monk.

"And it's clear why not." The monk walked over to Carlos and stood in front of him. "I'll take you to our clinic, son. Brother Henry will give you something for those sores. Then you can have something to eat. After that, I'll show you to your bedroom." His eyes lingered on the dried blisters that were clustered on Carlos's face. "Are they everywhere?"

The question was for Carlos, but Mumsford answered. "All over his body. I saw them."

"What kind of beast . . . ?" The monk shook his head and the loose flesh on his cheeks wiggled back and forth. "I thought he was a doctor," he said to Mumsford.

"His interest seems to be botany," Mumsford said.

"Botany?"

"He is a gardener." Both men's heads swung back to Carlos. They were the first words he had uttered since his arrival. Others followed. "He specializes in grafting. He likes splitting the seeds of plants and implanting the seeds of other plants inside them. He likes binding cuttings of live plants from different genera. His interest is cross-pollination. His grass does not need watering."

Mumsford did not like Dr. Gardner. He had insulted him more than once that morning. But they were countrymen, Englishmen together in an English colony. He glared at Carlos. "He keeps a reservoir," he said, and paused as if waiting for Carlos to contradict him. When he didn't, he repeated for the monk what Gardner had told him. "It's the miracles of modern science, Brother St. Clair. Dr. Gardner is also a scientist."

"That was why I left the garden." Carlos spoke again.

"*The* garden?" The indefinite article arrested the monk.

"*The* garden," Carlos repeated.

"Are you speaking of Eden, my son? We all left the garden."

"He means Dr. Gardner's garden," Mumsford said. "You should see it. Orchids . . ."

"Adam is my hero," Carlos said.

The monk blushed. "He was a sinner, my son."

"Eden is a European myth meant to keep servants and slaves in their place," Carlos said.

Mumsford cleared his throat.

"Had Adam remained in the garden, he would not have been his own man," Carlos said.

"That is heresy, my son."

Mumsford came between them. "You are here on the kindness of the monks," he said to Carlos. "Remember that."

"That is not the point of the story," the monk was insisting.

"Really, Brother St. Clair," Mumsford interrupted him. "The boy doesn't know what he is saying."

"You are wrong about Adam," the monk said.

Carlos pressed his lips together.

"Wrong," the monk repeated.

Carlos looked down at his feet and did not respond. Mumsford was relieved. He did not want trouble. He had delivered the boy and now he wished to go home. In the morning he would call the commissioner. In the morning he would give him the details in an official report.

"I'm afraid I must be on my way, Brother St. Clair," he said. The monk mumbled something that he did not hear, but he didn't mind. He didn't want to be drawn into a foolish argument with the boy. "Call me if you have any problems." Mumsford was already walking toward the front door. "But I don't expect you will have any trouble from him." He paused. "Right, young man?" His hand was on the doorknob.

Carlos continued to look down at his feet.

"Right?" Mumsford asked again.

The monk shook out his skirt. It billowed out and fell in folds around his bare ankles. "He'll be okay," he said. "I will take care of him."

Mumsford was not satisfied. He expected some gesture of gratitude from the boy, some appreciation for having spared him the horrors of Her Majesty's Royal Jail. "You should thank Brother St. Clair," he said to him.

But Carlos remained still with his lips firmly closed.

As soon as he arrived home, Mumsford called the commissioner. He told him he had given the boy to Brother St. Clair. He said Dr. Gardner had him locked up in some kind of pen in his backyard; he said the boy went quietly with him; he had given him no trouble.

"He's an odd one," the commissioner said.

And from his tone Mumsford was puzzled, unsure of which one he meant: the boy or Dr. Gardner, so he asked.

"Dr. Gardner, of course," the commissioner said. "Keeps to himself. I've invited him here once or twice but he never shows up."

An odd one, indeed. Mumsford decided that tomorrow would be soon enough for the commissioner to know exactly how odd, to tell him about the odd flowers and the odd green lawn. Tomorrow he would tell him, too, exactly what Dr. Gardner had done to the boy in his backyard. He wanted to be able to see the expression on the commissioner's face when he told him. Would he, as Brother St. Clair had done, feel sorry for the boy, say that Dr. Gardner was heartless? He, too, had thought Dr. Gardner had not had justification enough. But he had been loyal, he had kept his thoughts to himself. Would the French

Creole be as discreet, be as loyal? Tomorrow he would record the details in the report; tomorrow he would submit it and see. For now he wanted his supper, a glass of red wine, light banter with his mother about her day at the Country Club, nothing to remind him of the boy.

Yet that evening as his mother blithely carried on, buttering her baked potato and cutting into the slices of roast lamb on her plate (he was right; she was to blame for the crumbs near his desk, and lamb and baked potatoes were her peace offering), he could not put Carlos's words out of his mind. *Eden, a European myth meant to keep servants and slaves in their place.*

In England, *he* had been kept in his place. He had come here to escape that place. The recruiting officer had dangled that promise like a gilded carrot and he had grabbed on to it. Here, he had servants. There, he was a bobby on foot patrol. And after he saw those glossy ads—smiling faces, windblown hair, children frolicking in a sea bluer than the sky—he asked no questions.

"Went to Cambridge."

Mumsford jerked his head upward, startled. An echo from his mind. He had not been paying attention to the monotonous drivel coming from his mother's direction, but when he looked up, he saw that her lips were moving. *Went to Cambridge.* The words had blasted out at him just as he was thinking of those lucky rich blokes who didn't have to be bobbies, who went to the right schools—Cambridge.

"Imagine, a colored man!"

Mumsford slumped down in his chair. She was at it again, her favorite subject these days.

"But I suppose Mary Hinsdale made a good bargain. After all, he's the chief medical officer. Do you know anybody who went to Cambridge, John?" She arched her eyebrows as if her question were genuine. And yet she knew better. And yet she knew no one in his social class had managed to rise so far.

"The world is changing, John." She sighed. "It's the colored man's turn."

The colored man's turn. Yes, the boy got a chance. Dr. Gardner had taught him, been kind to him. Wasn't that what he said? Still, Mumsford could not get his brain to obey him, to blanket the memory of the boy's eyes, the intensity of the hatred naked there, the glitter that bounced off his eyelids when he spat on Dr. Gardner's face.

A spasm of pain rippled through his stomach and he pushed his plate away, his appetite, so huge moments ago, suddenly vanished. He had been whipped by his schoolmasters in England. All the boys in his grammar school had been. "Lucky for you the stocks are outlawed," one particularly brutal beater had said to him.

Later that night as he settled in bed, the two memories conflated: the whippings he had suffered at the hands of his schoolmasters; Dr. Gardner jeering. He had insulted him, laughed at him when he used the word *anthropologically.* But it was a new word for him and it had taken him no little courage to speak it.

Little by little, sinking into the mattress that was too soft for his aching back stiff with tension, Mumsford found himself moving dangerously close to empathizing with Carlos. And then, just as he was on the verge of capitulating, a mosquito saved him.

He had hung the netting from the hook on the ceiling and had tucked the ends tightly under the mattress. Still a mosquito had managed to sneak its way inside. It buzzed past his right ear and he flapped his hand forward to strike it down, but it rose, circled his head, and returned, this time to his left ear. He swiped his hand across his face, punching the pillow on either side. The mosquito buzzed past his head again and lit on his neck, sinking its probes deep into his flesh. He bounded up on both feet on his bed, flailing his hands in the air. His fingers got caught on the holes of the netting above him and the netting collapsed and fell over him, trapping him like an animal in the wild.

When he disentangled himself, he felt the sting of the mosquito bite and he was bitter again, cursing the bad luck that had brought him here, to the tropics; pitying Dr. Gardner for his leathered skin, his rusty, dull hair; swearing to himself, as he had sworn in Dr. Gardner's drawing room, that not many more months would find him still here. He had improved his status, but he would take his chances in England. Whatever the cause, Dr. Gardner must have had good reason for imprisoning the boy.

Ariana was late, but as far as Mumsford was concerned that was to be expected. The natives, Mumsford believed, lacked the English understanding of the importance of punctuality, the English sense of order. They arrived when it suited them, always unapologetic, never concerned with any inconvenience they could have caused. Everything for them was a joke. "You too uptight," they were likely to say if you were foolish enough to complain, or if you had not lived long enough in the tropics to know that whatever time you had set, you had in fact made a tacit agreement to add an hour or two to it. *Relax, man. Don't give yourself a heart attack. The world not going nowhere.*

Their carefree attitude irritated Mumsford, mostly because it had the effect of turning the tables on the one who complained. Suddenly, you were the stupid one; you were the one willing to risk a heart attack for the sake of mere minutes. If you made the case that they were not mere minutes but an entire hour, if not more, you would be accused of not being manly, of suffering from nerves like a woman, of being neurotic. *Take it easy, man. Is only sixty minutes.*

He had learned. He came to his office prepared, anticipating that Ariana would be late, as they all were late. He brought the notes he had taken in Chacachacare and the ones he had jotted down on his way home from the monastery. Now he read them over carefully, for he wanted to be accurate, he wanted to be able to substantiate all he was going to write. He stuck paper in the typewriter and began. First, he recorded his notes on what Gardner had said about Carlos and his mother. He left out the part where Gardner had called Carlos freckled. He did not want to take the chance that in recalling what Gardner had said, he would suggest what he, Mumsford, had intimated. But in his bones he felt sure Gardner had meant something more, something accusatory when he spat out *Freckled.* Mumsford decided instead to type what Gardner had asserted: Carlos's mother was a white woman, perhaps English. His father was colored, a black man.

Let the commissioner make of it what he would, Mumsford thought. He was not going to insinuate his opinions on interbreeding in his report. Yet as he described the flowers and the grass Gardner had grown, as he typed the word *cross-pollination* and then the word *cross-breeding,* he couldn't help wondering if he weren't right when he sug-

gested to Dr. Gardner that perhaps he had encouraged Carlos in thinking of the possibility, in planting in his head the idea that interbreeding
of the races was acceptable, preferable even.

Peopling. It was the word Dr. Gardner said Carlos had used. Mumsford had not heard it before. A strange word, but, he reasoned, Carlos
would not have dared to say it outright. He would not have dared to
say to Dr. Gardner's face, "I want to fuck your daughter." He would
not have been so reckless, for that would have been justification
enough to jail him, for Gardner to do his worst, to lock him up, as he
had done, in that stinking pen in his backyard.

All the while Mumsford was finishing the report, typing what he
had seen of the condition of Carlos's skin, the stink that had assaulted
his nostrils as he approached the fenced-off area, he couldn't let go of
the interpretation he had given to peopling. *I want to fuck your daughter.*
Like the canopy of vines that blanketed the tops of trees in the rainy
season, shutting out light, siphoning off oxygen, the words weighed
down on him, clouding his brain, choking off other possibilities.

For a brief moment at supper with his mother, when his mind had
drifted, he had understood. For a second he had sympathized. He, too,
like the boy, had been expected to stay in his place. But now *I want to
fuck your daughter* left no space for alternatives, and he did something
that he prided himself in avoiding during an investigation. He inserted
his opinion in the report. When he typed the conversation at the
monastery, what Carlos had said to the monk, he wrote: "The boy is
obviously misguided. He seems intelligent, but not educated enough
to understand that Adam had disobeyed God and deserved his punishment."

Ariana arrived at noon, two hours after she had said she would. She
came toward him mumbling a convolution of half sentences strung together in no order that Mumsford could make sense of, except that she
seemed to blame Dr. Gardner. It was he who had made her late. "He
need me," she said.

Mumsford stopped her. There were probably dishes she had not
washed or floors she had not swept. He had the same problem with
servants in his house. Always finding ways to avoid work. He did not
need to hear her excuse. He had already filed his report. As far as he

was concerned there was nothing she had to say that would convince him that the English girl was in love with a colored boy. He had more or less come to the conclusion that the boy had not raped her, but that did not mean he was prepared to accept that he was in love with her or she with him. Yet there was the question of intent. If Carlos had attempted to assault Virginia, it was a crime, and it would be his duty to investigate. Ariana, he thought, could be useful. She could shed some light on why, if Carlos had not raped his daughter, Gardner had been so cruel.

Ariana, however, did not come to talk to him about Carlos and Virginia, as she had said she would. It was *her* story she wanted him to know.

"I hate him." That was the first of many things she said that shocked Mumsford that morning. Had he not seen her bat her eyes coyly at Gardner? Had he not heard them whispering like lovers? An act, Gardner claimed it was, but if it were, it seemed to Mumsford it had been rehearsed so often that it had become real for them now.

"He take advantage of me."

She was an adult, almost twenty years old. Her relationship with Gardner was her own private affair. Mumsford told her so.

"I was nine. Is okay if I was nine years old?"

She wore white this time, the cotton fabric as thin as the yellow dress she was wearing when he met her at Gardner's house. *Was she naked under it?* Shame forced him to look away when that thought reached his conscious mind, and when he turned back again he saw it was an illusion. There were no traces of nipples puncturing her bodice, no curves outlining her backside, only dark shadows shifting beneath the folds of her dress.

The men in the station must have made his same mistake. They pivoted on their chairs and stared when she passed, and, like him, in seconds they lowered their heads, ashamed. She seemed a child, a wisp of a thing, a virgin in that white, her hair tumbling freely down her back, her eyes stretched wide and round in girlish trepidation. The place had to be frightening to her with its rank odor of sweat, men in khaki police uniforms, their wood batons propped against their desks, metallic ceiling fans beating the heavy air.

Mumsford had asked the matron to be present when he questioned her. He ushered them into his office and closed the door. Immediately, the matron pounced on her. "Did you forget your slip, miss?" She was a stocky woman. She wore her hair pulled tightly in a bun at the back of her head, and it gave her an aspect of severity that belied her title. Like the other officers, she was in uniform, though unlike them her baton—her beating stick, Mumsford had heard a prisoner call it—was attached to her belt. "Did you?" she asked Ariana.

Ariana touched the hem of her dress. Fearing that she was about to lift it, Mumsford said quickly, "No. That won't be necessary."

She let go of the hem. "I don't have on a slip," she said, "but I wearing bra and panties. They black."

The matron glared at her, her lips tight with disapproval. "Didn't your mother teach you to wear a slip when you go out?"

Mumsford did not wait for Ariana's answer. He pointed to an armless cane-backed chair and told her to sit. "What's this you have to tell me?" He decided to get straight to the point, to her reason for coming to see him. He was ready for the lies he knew she would tell him, but that was when Ariana said, beginning at a place he could not have imagined: "I hate him."

"No," he said now, feeling a weariness that dragged his body even farther down on the leather chair he had pulled out from behind his desk. "It's not okay if you were nine years old."

"I 'fraid to tell my mother when he start touching me," she said.

From the corner of his eye Mumsford could see the matron chewing her bottom lip. How her expression had changed! Moments before she was glaring angrily at Ariana. Now concern was spread across her face. Not quite a French Creole, Mumsford had thought when he first met her. Her skin was too brown, her nose too flat, but her hair was straight, honey-colored with streaks of gold. French Creole, but with more than the usual helping of Creole.

"He touched you?" She came closer to Ariana. Mumsford put his finger to his lips and with a nod of his head, he warned her to be silent. *When trouble comes, they close ranks. But it was his job, not hers, to question Ariana.* "What do you mean he touched you?" he asked Ariana, not giving her a chance to respond to the matron.

"I was only nine when Prospero start to interfere with me," she said.

"Dr. Peter Gardner," Mumsford explained to the matron when her eyebrows shot up.

"Carlos tell me to call him Prospero," Ariana said.

"Dr. Gardner," Mumsford tried to correct her.

"Prospero," Ariana said as if he had not spoken. "He do a little bit at first. He don't do everything. But he start for real when Miss Virginia turn woman."

"Turn woman?"

"When she have her period."

Mumsford brought his chair closer to his desk. He shuffled the papers in front of him. He could feel sweat oozing from his pores. *What if she were telling the truth?* "Why were you afraid to tell your mother?" He kept his tone light, but he dared not look at her.

"She used to work for Miss Sylvia."

"Miss Sylvia?"

"Carlos mother."

The hag? The blue-eyed hag? The blue-eyed hag was dead. "I believe she was long gone and buried when Dr. Gardner came to the island. Or did Dr. Gardner begin doing whatever it is you claim he was doing even before he came to the island?" Mumsford asked sarcastically. He picked up a sheet of paper and fluttered it noisily in her direction.

"Before he came?" Ariana wrinkled her forehead, confused.

"What," he asked, his voice straining with exaggerated patience, "does Sylvia Codrington have to do with what you are telling us now about Dr. Gardner?"

"She hated me," Ariana said.

"And why was that, Ariana?" He was not interested in her answer. He did not care whether Sylvia Codrington had liked or disliked Ariana or what reasons she could have had for feeling one way or the other, but he preferred this turn in the alarming tale she was telling. Better to question her about Sylvia Codrington than to let her go on with her devastating accusations against Gardner.

"Why were you afraid to tell your mother if Miss Sylvia was dead?"

he asked, balancing his pen between his fingers. His notebook lay open on the desk, but he had not written anything on it.

"When I was a child," she said, "she catch me wearing her clothes. She say she tell my mother."

"Her clothes?" the matron scoffed. "That is nothing, girl."

Mumsford saw a red flag immediately. He had warned the matron, but she was ignoring him. He had to be careful even if she had sworn to uphold the law.

"All little children like to dress up in grown-up people's clothes. Isn't that so, Inspector?" The matron looked expectantly at him.

Mumsford held his tongue though he was tempted to point out the difference: It was not simply a matter of a little girl in grown-ups' clothes. It was a little colored girl in a white woman's clothes, a woman who was her mother's employer.

"She put it down in a letter," Ariana said.

"You must tell us who," Mumsford said. He tried to catch the matron's eye, but she had turned her head away from him. "You must be clear when you speak, Ariana, or we won't understand you. Who put what down in a letter?"

"Miss Sylvia put it down in a letter," she said.

"That you wore her clothes?" the matron asked.

Mumsford glared at her, but it was clear to him that she was not about to let him silence her.

"Is not only the clothes," Ariana said. "She find out."

"She found out what?" the matron asked.

"I take her diamond earrings."

"You took her earrings?"

"They was shining. She show me one day. She put it under the light and I saw the colors. Like the rainbow. Then she wear them for me in the night. She turn this way and that. The moon was shining, but I think nothing shine brighter than the diamonds on her ears. No matter how she turn, they bright. I only want to try them," Ariana said. She looked up at the matron.

"And did you put them on?"

"That's all I want to do at first when I went in her bureau and took them out. But I like them. I like the way they shine on my ears, too, and I wanted to keep them for myself. I was small, you see, not big like I am now. I didn't think about what she do to me if I keep them, so I keep them."

"You stole Miss Sylvia's diamond earrings?" Accusation only, not a shred of sympathy, was in Mumsford's voice.

"She was a child," the matron said to him. He frowned, disapproving.

"I didn't plan to steal it," Ariana said.

"But that is what you did," Mumsford barked.

"Did Miss Sylvia know you took her earrings?" the matron asked.

"She find out. She say she tell my mother and then she tell the police. They lock me up, she say."

"You can't lock up a child," the matron said.

"She say they lock up me and my mother."

"Nonsense," the matron said. "She only wanted to frighten you so you wouldn't touch her things again."

"She write it down in a letter and she hide the letter. She say if she catch me touching her earrings again, she give the letter to the police. When my mother die, Prospero find Miss Sylvia letter."

"And what did he do?" Mumsford asked this question, though he didn't want to, though ice was collecting in the pit of his stomach.

"In the night when everybody sleeping, he come on top of me with his thing. He say if I tell anybody he touch me, he show the police the letter. Even lunchtime he make me come in his room and Miss Virginia and Carlos think is message he giving me. And when my mother still living is true is message he giving me. He telling me what to cook and how he like me to cook it. He treat me nice, nice, nice. He pretend he watching out for me and he like me. I believe him. Then my mother die. He bring me in his bed after that."

"Why didn't you leave?" Mumsford's voice was hoarse. "Dr. Gardner has been in Chacachacare for twelve years. You must have had chances to leave."

"And is twelve years he use me."

"Why didn't you go to the police?"

"They lock me up, Prospero say. For stealing Miss Sylvia diamonds.

Every day he promise he tear up Miss Sylvia letter if I do what he say. He not only mean sleep with him. He want me to spy on Carlos when he go in his garden and Carlos alone with his daughter. He tell me if I tell him everything, he free me. I do all he ask. I don't grumble. I don't make mistakes. I don't lie. I tell him everything I see. And I ask him when, when will he tear up the letter. He get angry. He say, 'Every month I have to remind you how I save you from what Miss Sylvia was going to do to you. You always forgetting.' But he didn't save me. He do worse than what Miss Sylvia do. I can't leave. I must cook his food, I must serve him, I must do his bidding. I must spy on Carlos and Miss Virginia. I must open my legs for him even if I hate him. I must fuck him."

Ordinarily Mumsford would have ordered her out of his office. Ordinarily he would have demanded that she apologize. There was a certain decorum he required, and she had transgressed it. No subordinate of his dared use such language in his presence. But his world had begun a tumble downward and he needed to restore it.

"I heard you, Ariana. In Dr. Gardner's house. You asked him if he loved you."

"I think if he love me, then he free me. He tear up the letter." She wiped her mouth with the back of her hand. "That's why I treat him good. Why you think I come late? He want me again and I let him have me."

Two hours. She was two hours late.

"I know you blame me, but is not my fault I late."

What could he have done to her in two hours? When the picture formed in his head, Mumsford had to avert his eyes from hers.

"Is only because he tired, he let me go."

He had to find a way to defend the Englishman. "It seemed to me you wanted his affection," he began.

"I pretend," she said.

An act, a performance, Gardner had said so himself. "That is not what I saw," Mumsford said.

"I don't mean it when I ask him if he love me. I don't care, but he always answer, 'Yes. Dearly,' as if he love me. Still he don't free me. When I beg, he say in a year. If I good to him, in a year he free me. But a year pass and still he keep me in his bed. He still hold the letter. So I tell on him. When he lock up Carlos, I write the police. I say he lie. Carlos never do nothing to Miss Virginia. I see them kissing."

Mumsford pressed his body over his desk. "But that was a lie, wasn't it, Ariana?"

"No. I don't lie."

"Just the way you don't lie when you tell Dr. Gardner you love him, right?"

"No. I lie when I tell Prospero I love him, but I tell the truth about Carlos and Miss Virginia. He kiss her, but she kiss him back. Is the truth. I don't tell him and I don't tell nobody before I write the letter. I know what he do if I tell him or tell anybody."

"Do?"

"To Carlos, if he find out. He tell me he want to marry off his daughter to a rich American man. The American man come. I see him. Carlos see him, too. That's why Carlos propose."

"Propose?"

"That's why Carlos tell him he want to have children with Miss Virginia. But Prospero lie. Carlos never do nothing to Miss Virginia. He love her. He never hurt her."

Mumsford had to stop her. The matron had heard too much. He could not trust her. "That's enough, Ariana," he said. "No more lies."

"I not lying."

"Why now?" The matron had been so quiet that Mumsford was startled when she spoke. "Why are you telling this story now?"

"Carlos," Ariana said. "He make me brave. He say, 'I must eat my dinner.' "

"Dinner?"

"He don't mean dinner. He tell me he mean he will take what Prospero do to him. He won't say he sorry, like Prospero want him to. He say if you want to be free, you disobey him. I disobey him now, because I want to be free. I tell on him and take my punishment for the earrings."

"Nobody will do anything to you for that, Ariana," the matron said gently.

When he told her, as he had had to do before Ariana arrived, what

Gardner had alleged, the matron was suspicious. Have you questioned the boy? she had asked him. Did you find out what he has to say for himself? Was it because Carlos was colored that she had been so ready to doubt Dr. Gardner? Was it because Ariana was black she was ready to take her word as the gospel truth?

"That was in the past," the matron was saying. "A long time ago. You were a child, Ariana."

"But I don't want him to do me like he do Carlos."

Mumsford got up. He had to put an end to this now. He didn't want Ariana telling the matron about the prison behind Dr. Gardner's house. If she had been suspicious when he told her of Gardner's allegations, what would she think now if she knew about the mosquitoes, the stink, the blazing sun, the sores all over Carlos's body? He couldn't take the chance that what Gardner had done would be so repulsive to her, so inhumane, that her loyalties to the department would evaporate. What if she told the other police officers? What if the newspapers found out?

"The situation is under investigation." He spoke directly to the matron. "The commissioner has assigned the case to me. I've been to Chacachacare. Until the matter about Carlos is settled, I don't want any more discussion about him. Understand?"

But the matron was not interested in Carlos. It was to Ariana that her heart went out. "And the girl?" she asked him. "She can't go back there."

Mumsford allowed her the girl. He would put Ariana in her custody, he said, but there was to be no more talk about Carlos until the commissioner had given permission. All that was said in his office was confidential. She could be brought up on charges if she divulged any part of it. Then he told Ariana in his sternest voice that she was to say nothing more about Carlos, not even to the matron. He would help her. He would ask the commissioner to find her a place to stay, but only if she promised.

"But it have more for me to tell," Ariana protested. "About Miss Virginia and Prospero."

Mumsford held up his hand. "You've told enough for today," he said.

It did not occur to him that she could have anything significant to tell him about Dr. Gardner and his daughter, and he was in no mood to listen to her complaints about some domestic dispute, about something he was sure either Dr. Gardner or his daughter had asked her to do, something like scrubbing the floor on her hands and knees, or re-doing the washing when the clothes she claimed to have cleaned were still spotted with stains. What she had alleged was so despicable, so perverse, he could think of nothing else. He had before him a clear case of sexual abuse. *Child abuse.* He had to do something about it.

Mumsford was not a complicated man. His sense of morality left him no room for shades of good and evil. One was either good or one was evil. A good man did not commit evil acts; a bad man was never good. If Dr. Gardner had committed the sin Ariana had accused him of, then Dr. Gardner was a bad man, and he would have to conclude that the charges he had made against Carlos Codrington were untrue, that they were lies.

Yet he must have more proof, more assurances. He did not like Dr. Gardner—his air of superiority, his patronizing attitude toward the men on the force—but he balked at the idea of involving an English-man in a scandal on the island. He would not be party to such a scandal. And yet what to do?

When the door closed behind Ariana and the matron, and he was alone, finally able to think calmly, he decided he would speak to Virginia. He would go to see her at Mrs. Burton's. It was Dr. Gardner who had placed the injunction against questioning his daughter. He would tell the commissioner what Ariana had said. He would ask his permission to get Virginia's side of the story. If Ariana was right, if Virginia and Carlos Codrington were friends (he could not bring himself to consider a relationship between them deeper than friendship), then he would make an offer to Dr. Gardner: Withdraw his charge against Carlos Codrington and he would see to it that Ariana kept her silence, that her story go no further than where it had reached—the matron's ears and the ears of two white police officials who could be trusted. He closed his notebook, reached for his baton, and put on his policeman's hat. Yes, he said to himself. That was what he would do.

Carlos

SIX

I CALL IT the Miranda test. Pass it and I believe you. Fail it and all you say about the races being equal, that character, not color, is what matters, becomes theoretical.

It had never occurred to Dr. Gardner, of course, to conceive of me as an equal, but he taught me as if I were an equal, as if he believed I could learn as well as any Englishman. But I was an experiment to him, and when, in my own way (which I am prepared to say was not the best way), I declared my love for his daughter, my intention to marry her (for I had not conceived of having children with her without marriage), he hollered rape and threw me in the prison in his backyard.

I will begin at the beginning.

The house we lived in was my mother's house. She left it to me when she died, but Gardner used his cunning to cheat me out of it. He appeared one morning, after a terrible rainstorm, with his daughter, Virginia. I was six then. I lived with Lucinda, my mother's housekeeper, and her daughter, Ariana, who was nine at the time. Though we were shadowed always by the dark cloud of my parents' deaths (both had died within a year of each other), we were reasonably happy and wanted for nothing. My mother had many very expensive jewels. After she died, Lucinda needed only to sell a few of them to buy us food and things for the house.

It was a big house. It had many rooms: a drawing room, a dining room, a large kitchen, and four bedrooms. I had my own room, Ariana and her mother slept in another, and we used the other two bedrooms to store things or to play games when the sun was too hot to go outside, or when it rained. If we needed anything, the lepers helped us. They lived on the other side of the bay, far away from us, and though there was a narrow dirt path behind our house that led to their colony, we rarely used it, Lucinda preferring to send messages to them by the boatman, who did errands for us on the mainland. They always came. They never refused us. They would row over in their pirogues, whenever Lucinda asked, to fix our roof when it leaked, to repair the toilet when it got clogged, to sweep the yard when it was covered with leaves, or to cut back the bushes when they grew thick in the rainy season.

I was not afraid of them. I did not find them repulsive. I was accustomed to their deformities. I had known them from birth. To me they were simply different, their limbs shaped in another way from mine, but just as human, in every other way just as normal.

If I ever felt any unhappiness in those days it was because of my memories of my mother and my father, and because sometimes, when Lucinda thought I was not looking, I would see her crouched on the floor clutching her stomach. Whenever I asked her what was the matter, she would brush me away. Ariana told me her mother was dying. Cancer, she said it was.

So when Dr. Gardner came that morning, Lucinda had more than one reason to believe he was sent to her by God. I thought he looked like the devil, with his long red hair draped down to his shoulders and a branch in his hand that was forked at the top. Only the sight of his daughter, whose eyes reminded me of my mother's, made me not insist that he leave our yard, as I could have done. For the house was my mother's and so mine, and Lucinda would have followed my wishes.

We had had a terrible storm the night before and in the morning the sky had turned white with salt that powerful winds had blown from the sea and dropped on the clouds. But behind the whiteness was a glorious light. It gilded the horizon and sent rays of gold streaking up the white sky. God's miracle, Lucinda said it was. Which was why, even before she knew what Gardner had to offer, Lucinda was certain he had been sent by God. And why, that evening, when I sat in Inspector Mumsford's car, looking straight in front of me, determined not to move my head nor speak a word to him, knowing that no matter what I said he would not believe me, I weakened. For the light that lined the black clouds above the sunset that day on Mount St. Benedict reminded me of the shimmering gold that edged that salt-filled sky the morning after the storm, and I pressed my face against the car window as much in awe of it as in fear of what it could portend.

It is impossible for me to forget the night that brought us that strange sky the next morning. Rain had slashed down from the sky in torrents, whipping through our yard with a force as sharp and lethal as the blade of a machete. At any time, it seemed, it would slice through the roof. When the thunder came roaring in rapid succession, Ariana and I scrambled under the bed for cover. The house shook and shuddered with each blast, and we feared that at any moment it would collapse and fall on us. Then the lightning left the ocean. It was pitch-black outside but when lightning struck inland, each bolt brighter and eerier than the last, it set the house ablaze, making it seem like daylight, as if the sun were high and bright in the sky. Then came the big one. It split the sky in two and pitched a fiery fork of light into the chennette tree near my window. One half of the tree fell against the side of the house and broke into my bedroom wall, close to the spot where Ariana and I were huddled together, trembling.

"It is the devil himself working his evil tonight," Lucinda said.

I thought he came the next morning.

Water gushed through the hole where the tree had fallen and Lucinda pulled Ariana and me into the drawing room and shut the door behind us. But the water kept seeping under the door, rolling toward where we were standing. We watched, terrified, as it gathered and swelled. Soon it was no longer rolling, but climbing inch by inch, higher and higher, to my waist and then higher and higher to my chest. I thought I would drown, and I wrapped my legs around Lucinda's waist and clutched her neck. She was praying and I began praying, too. *Our father, who art in heaven* . . .

I have heard dogs howl at the moon many times since, but their cries were pitiful baying compared to the wailing of the wind that night. It was as though the gates of hell had opened and Cerberus himself, that three-headed monster, along with his minions, had been sent to devour us. Nothing was more terrible and frightening than that infernal howling. When it met with resistance, it growled like a thing alive, blowing out the Demerara shutters on one side of the house and butting its head against walls and the closed doors. Outside it had stripped the trees bare, and once inside, it hurled leaves and twigs on top of us, flinging its body here and there in every corner of the house, frantic for escape. When it abated, retreated, the rain, thunder, and lightning with it, Lucinda put me down. We were soaked to the bone, our clothes plastered to our bodies with mud and leaves, but alive, convinced that only by a miracle had we been saved.

Gardner came in the morning offering to help us. We had heard that a doctor from England and his young daughter had recently moved in with the old doctor who lived in the big house at the edge of the bay, but we had never seen them. It had seemed odd to us, with the leprosarium closing, that the old doctor would need additional help, and we were curious.

He could fix the house for us, Gardner said when Lucinda came out to greet him.

"How much?" she asked.

"Just room and board," he said.

We should have been suspicious of him then. Indeed, Lucinda asked the question that was on all our minds: "Don't you get room and board in the doctor's house?"

"The doctor does not need me," he replied.

There was nothing on our island except the leprosarium. Why would he want to stay if the doctor did not need him? But Lucinda was too polite to say the obvious: If the doctor did not need him, he should go back to Trinidad, and if not Trinidad, to England, where he came from.

He could see us hesitating. "Look at the damage," he said, and pointed to my bedroom wall. "That hole cannot stay that way. And your roof needs fixing. I can repair them both."

"The lepers can help us," Lucinda said.

"But are they strong enough to lift that tree trunk out of your house?"

"They always help," Lucinda said, but there was uncertainty in her voice and she had glanced down when she answered him. Gardner, his ears pricked up like a hunting dog, heard the slight inflection at the end of *help* and smelled her vulnerability.

"I would make the house like new. I would clean up the mud, sweep up the leaves, clean the yard." His words flowed smoothly off his tongue, but I was not fooled. I did not trust his red hair, his forked stick. I tugged Lucinda's skirts. "We don't need his help," I said to her.

"Better than new," he said, his eyes on me.

"We like it the way it is," I said, already brazen for my age.

"I can build you a porch," he said to Lucinda.

I tugged harder at Lucinda's skirt.

"Wouldn't that be nice?" His syrupy voice repulsed me.

Lucinda patted my head. "It would be nice to have a porch. Not so, Carlos?"

"We don't need a porch," I whined.

"You can sit on your rocking chair, Miss Lucinda, and watch the moon climb the sky."

It was the last time he called her Miss Lucinda and she never saw the moon from her rocking chair on the porch he eventually built.

Lucinda caved in. But first, out of respect for my mother, and so for me, she excused herself, and, leaving the strange white man in the yard with his daughter, I was already beginning to like, she took me into the house and gave me her reasons.

"We need the protection," she said.

"Why?" I asked her.

"There are people who don't like us. We don't know if the men who killed your father would come for you next," she said.

I remembered my father, his bloodied body on the dining room table. But Lucinda had sat many nights by my bed convincing me that we had nothing to fear. If my father had not gone fishing so far out in the sea, they never would have caught him, she said. "They too 'fraid they catch leprosy." Now she was trying to persuade me otherwise.

"They could come and the lepers can't do nothing to protect us. They can't protect themselves," she said.

"I don't want him here." I stamped my foot hard on the ground.

She grabbed my arms. Lucinda was a broad-shouldered, high-waisted woman with big breasts. Whenever she pulled me to her, I always felt shadowed by all that generous flesh. But this time was different. She had never held me so tightly before. "Stop it, Carlos!" She shook me so hard, my cheeks flapped and jiggled above my jaw. When I finally quieted down, the creases on her brown face, tanned beyond its natural biscuit brown by the sun she loved, softened, and she loosened her hold on me. "I am sick, Carlos," she said. Lucinda was a kind woman, with the gentlest eyes, but now they drilled into mine. "We'll need his help. He's a doctor."

Dr. Gardner moved into my house the very next day.

The first thing he did was to cut down the chennette tree. He went into the shed in the backyard where my father stored the tools he used when he was building our house and took out the saw and the wheel of rope hanging on the wall. Then he climbed up the tree and began sawing off the branches. Chennettes rained on the ground and scattered everywhere. I screamed. Lucinda put her arms around my shoulders and drew me to her. I yelled at Gardner to stop. He sawed another branch. More chennettes rained on the ground. "Stop! Stop!" I was inconsolable.

Lucinda called out to him for my sake. "They his favorite fruit. Don't cut it down, Doctor."

Gardner was patient in the beginning, almost kind. He climbed down the tree, and stooping next to me, he took my hand and explained. "If I don't cut it down, Carlos," he said gently, "the other half will fall with the next big wind."

But he did not stop with the branches. The next morning he hollered out to a fisherman who was passing in his boat across the bay, close to our shore, and offered him money to help him saw off the trunk. The next day, again engaging the fisherman's help, he attacked the chataigne tree. Every day, for one week, the fisherman came, and from sunrise to sunset, he and Gardner sawed and roped down branches and tree trunks. When they were done, not a single one of the trees my father had planted was left standing: not the coconut tree, the breadfruit tree, the chataigne tree, or the avocado tree, and not one of the fruit trees, neither the plum, orange, grapefruit, sapodilla, soursop nor the two mango trees that were in our yard.

As each tree went down, the fruits I loved tumbling to the ground when the branches were lopped off, I bawled as if my life itself were threatened.

"Disease," Gardner hollered. "Fruits attract flies and bats. Flies and bats carry disease. Disease will kill us."

Lucinda tried to fight back for me. "But Carlos likes fruits," she pleaded with Gardner. "Leave him one tree, for God's sake."

"They have worms," he declared and, dismissing her, signaled the fisherman to keep on sawing.

We could not make out what he said after that. His face was a mass of frowns and grimaces. Once in a while he would shout out something. *Disease* was the only word we heard clearly.

During that week, he confined Virginia to his bedroom and asked Ariana to keep her company, though it seemed to me, and it turned out that Ariana thought so also, he ordered, rather than asked, her to do it. I saw him frequently, but I rarely saw his daughter. Lucinda made meals for all of us, but we did not eat them together. Virginia and Gardner ate apart from us, in their bedroom. And, in truth, I did not mind, for I felt ashamed of my babyish behavior. I had made up my mind to be a man when my mother died, and I had failed. I did not want Virginia to know that I had blubbered like a weakling.

When all the trees were down and the yard was a mess of chopped tree trunks, branches, and leaves, Gardner told us that he was ready to build his garden.

Lucinda was as shocked as I. "Garden?" He had destroyed all the fruit trees and with them the flowering shrubs that grew in patches around them. He had trampled on them or cut them down. "I thought you didn't want garden," Lucinda said.

"Ah, but the flowers I am going to grow won't get diseased," he said. "Not like your flowers."

He meant the ixora plant I loved, with its bouquets of tiny red flowers clustered at the tips of stems crowded with dark green leaves; he meant the flaming wild poinsettia bush we called chaconia; he meant the chain of love, a vine with heart-shaped bright pink buds that looped over my father's shed in the backyard. He meant the bright yellow buttercup flowers that Ariana threaded into garlands, passing her needle down the tube of each trumpet-shaped flower.

I supposed it was thinking to soothe us, having the unmitigated gall to believe we could be compensated for the destruction he had wrought, that Gardner added, "I'll clean up the lawn in front of the house, too. I'll make it green."

We had not thought of the front yard as a lawn, but that was what he called it before he made it a reality.

"And when will you do the repairs on the house?" Lucinda asked. He had put up a makeshift board against the hole in my bedroom wall where the chennette tree had fallen, but he had done nothing else.

"Soon," he said. "Soon."

Soon never seemed to come. When we were not standing in the yard, me crying, Lucinda wringing her hands, we were busy cleaning the house. It was my father with his fanciful ideas about house construction that was to blame for all the work we had to do. None of the rooms followed any sort of logic that would be recognizable in an ordinary home. (This, too, Gardner would rectify.) The drawing room faced the back of the house and my parents' bedroom, the front. My mother said it made no sense to her that the most important room in the house, the place where she and my father spent most of their time together, where I was conceived and born (and where in the end she died), should be in the back where the bushes were. She wanted to see the sun in the morning, so her room faced the east and all the other rooms followed, zigzagging haphazardly, one to the side of the other, separated by a long corridor. My room came first, since I was their son, then Lucinda and Ariana's room a little to the right of it, but not directly, and to the left, the room we used as a playroom, and finally the kitchen, which had its own door to the outside and partially shared a wall and beams with the drawing room.

Air flowed equally through all the rooms, for my father had a carpenter cut into the top two feet of the wood panels separating each room and carve out flat sculptures of birds and flowers. My father wanted to remind us that the island where we lived belonged first to the flora and fauna we found here. It was this effort he made to teach me to love and respect nature that was the cause of most of our problems after the storm. The wind had been able to sweep unhampered through room after room, tunneling through the spaces in the carvings, dumping debris everywhere.

While Gardner chopped down trees, Lucinda and I packed garbage bags with water-soaked leaves and twigs, scraped mud off the floors, swept and mopped. On the third day, exhausted and irritable from all the cleaning and scrubbing, Lucinda dragged Ariana out of the room where she was sitting on the bed with Virginia. Ariana whined and cried and tried to pull away, insisting that Dr. Gardner had told her to stay with Virginia. She was afraid of disobeying Gardner, but Lucinda lost her patience. "Dr. Gardner be damned!" she said.

Though the three of us cleaned and scrubbed, the house remained a mess. Finally, frustrated, Lucinda reminded Gardner again of his promise. "Carlos can't continue to sleep in his room the way it is," she said. "Your *soon* will be too long for him."

It had rained twice that week, and in spite of the planks of wood Dr. Gardner had leaned against the hole in my wall, water leaked through the spaces at the sides and soaked my floorboards.

"In time, in time," Gardner said. "There's no hurry for the house. I'll get to it when I'm finished with the trees."

Having not the faintest suspicions of the intensity of Dr. Gardner's revulsion of leprosy, though his hatred for disease should have prepared her, Lucinda said defiantly, "Then I'll ask the lepers to help us."

A deep, guttural, animal roar rose up Gardner's throat. A tiger about to pounce on its prey. "No-o-o-o!" he shouted.

Startled, Lucinda stumbled backward and grabbed onto a chair nearby. I remained transfixed to the ground. But, then, suddenly, before my eyes, like the chameleon, Gardner's skin changed. The red stain that had rushed up his neck and spread over his face subsided.

The fire went out in his eyes. He stretched out his hand and helped Lucinda steady herself on her feet. "My daughter," he said softly. "For my daughter's sake, we cannot have the lepers."

Whether he was truly sorry for frightening us or whether he had been kind because he knew Lucinda was dying and it would not be long before he would not have to contend with her, I could not tell. What was certain was that the lepers would no longer be permitted to come to our house. What was clear to me was that the carrot and stick he had used with Lucinda was beginning to work, for never again did she oppose him.

Yet Gardner did in fact stop what he was doing that day and began to build a proper wall for my room. When he was finished with the wall, he went back to his garden, and when he had finished digging the rows and rows of beds in which he would plant his flowers—it took two months—Lucinda was dead.

I cannot say he killed her. She was in agony. She would stuff the sheets into her mouth and bite down hard when pain cut through her body. When I saw her like that, her teeth sunk into the sheets, her eyes popping out of their sockets, I pleaded with him to help her. "Anything. Do anything," I begged him, tears rolling down my cheeks. "Make it stop."

He would go to his room and return with a syringe filled with morphine, and he would inject it deep in her arm. She would grow quiet then, and the light in her eyes would dim.

It was hard for me to look at her after Gardner gave her morphine. I hated to see her lifeless eyes, glazed like the eyes of dead fish. But I preferred her so to writhing and thrashing on the bed, her fingers digging frantically into the edge of the mattress, her knuckles straining against the thin skin on her hands that, like the rest of her body, had turned a sickly yellow.

Sometimes, in the haze of the morphine, she forgot my name and she would call me by my mother's name or by my father's name. She would plead with me to forgive her. She had done her best, she would say. "He promised. He will help him. He will be good to him." I knew she was speaking of Gardner, and though I did not believe what I said,

I placed my hand over hers and tried to comfort her. "Don't cry, Lucinda. He will keep his promise. He will help me."

So I cannot say Gardner killed her. Morphine probably caused her death. She suffered unbearably. When the morphine wore off, terrible tremors erupted through her body and she called out to God, her dead mother and father, anyone, to help her, to put an end to her torture.

After she died, Gardner made changes inside the house. When he was done, the house was no longer mine.

SEVEN

IRST, HE BURNED my mother's bed. Only a week had
passed since we buried Lucinda. He must have figured out—
it wouldn't have been difficult for him to do, what with my blue eyes
and freckles and my brown skin so much lighter than Lucinda's or
Ariana's—that some blood other than African ran in my veins. He may
have asked Lucinda before she died and she may have said to him that
it was from my mother I got my eyes. So he burned her bed. A slut, he
called her, for lying down with a black man.

I will never forget that fire nor what he did that day. From the moment he picked up the ax, an aura of evil shadowed the house. He
struck the headboard first and I grabbed his shirt, pulling and tugging
at it to drag him away. He turned and slapped me.

I did not think he intended to slap me in front of Virginia. She was
standing near the doorway and when I cried out in pain, she screamed.
He left me at once and ran to her. On his knees, speaking in the gen-
tlest of tones, he said to her that there was something bad in the bed.
He had to destroy it. For her sake, he said. For *our* sake: his, mine, and
Ariana's. For our safety's sake. He had not meant to hit me. He merely

wanted to get me out of the way. Then he told Ariana to take Virginia to his room. When I turned to go also, he said, in a voice that made my heart flutter, "Not you. You stay."

He wanted me to witness the end of my mother. That was what he said, his eyes shooting darts at me, evil and menacing. "She's finished. Nothing in here belongs to her now. All is mine. I am lord of it all."

He dragged the mattress off the bed frame. Over and over his ax went down on the headboard and on the board at the foot of the bed. I had quieted down—I did not want to be struck again—but every time his ax cut into the bed frame, breaking apart the place where my mother had slept, where, before she became catatonic with grief over the death of my father, I had spent my happiest hours curled into her arms, my heart broke into pieces, too, and tears poured heavily down my cheeks and into my mouth. My mother's bed had become my bed since her death, her room my room. He was demolishing her bed, but he was also demolishing mine.

When Gardner was finally done chopping up the bed frame, he picked up the pieces and carried them, armfuls at a time, to the backyard. At one point, returning to the bedroom for the larger pieces, he looked over to me. I was standing in the spot where my mother's bed used to be, still whimpering. He ordered me to help him. "Stop crying like a little girl. Be a man. Hold that end." He pointed to a large plank of wood. I had no other choice but to help him.

After the pieces of my mother's bed were stacked in the backyard, he went to the shed for the can of kerosene we kept there for those nights when our oil supply was low and we needed it to fuel the wicks in the lamps. He put the kerosene next to me and warned me not to move. Then he returned to the house. When he came out again, he had changed his clothes. He was wearing black pants and a black T-shirt, and over them, a cloak draped across his shoulders and his arms, falling down to his ankles. It was not an ordinary cloak. I had seen nothing like it before. It was red, made of a thick velvet material that deepened and lightened in color when he moved. Gold stars were scattered over it, and at the collar was a gold string, which he had tied in a bow at his neck.

In one hand he carried a book bound in red leather and embossed with gold letters, and in the other a cane. I would see him with this cane and book many, many times afterward, when he worked in his garden. It was gnarled, coarse knots protruding on the polished dark brown wood, ending just below the top, which was covered with a silver cap. Later, when I had the chance to look at it closely, I saw that there were tiny figures engraved on the cap, centaurs, four of them in a ring, holding hands, dancing. I shuddered when I saw those smiling bare-chested men, their horses' legs raised in the air.

Gardner made a pyre of the pieces of my mother's bed, doused it with the kerosene, and lit it. Immediately, my mother's bed burst into a roaring fire. He opened his book, shook his cane over the fire, and began to chant words I did not understand. The higher the fire grew, the more violently he shook his cane and the louder he chanted. His face turned to a red the color of dried blood. The wood snapped and crackled, embers shot into the air and fell in a shower of sparks. He began to prance now, like a horse, round and round the flames, his cloak flying behind him, his red hair, like the fire itself, rising and falling as he galloped around the pyre.

From time to time he paused to douse more kerosene on the fire. Each time the flames roared higher, he cursed my mother. A witch, he called her. He would exorcise the evil spirits she had allowed in the house. "Whore! Slut! Witch! Blue-eyed hag!" He shouted out these curses as orange flames licked the night sky. He put his cane into the flames. It did not catch fire.

Ariana must have heard him when he began to pray. For at night she used to frighten me with his words. "Elves with printless feet will chase you if you do not keep quiet," she used to whisper to me. "Midnight mushrooms will smother you." But the threat I feared the most was the one I partially remembered: "I command the graves to open and wake their sleepers. Let them come forth!" Gardner had said.

I have been told that only black people in the Caribbean do obeah. That night I saw a white man call on the spirits, and he had learned his art not here, not in the Caribbean, but there, in England.

After the fire died down, Gardner sent me to bed in Lucinda's room. My mother's room was now his room, he said, my room Virginia's room. Ariana would sleep in the playroom.

I fell asleep with Gardner's chants ringing in my ears, his curses against my mother bombarding my dreams. Several times I woke up in fright, remembering it all again: *Whore! Slut! Witch! Blue-eyed hag!*

For weeks afterward, Gardner continued to curse my mother. He called me a bastard. My mother did not know who had fathered her child, he said, giving me the full force of his embittered eyes. But he was wrong. My mother knew my father. She loved my father. They did not marry, but my father had given me his name: Carlos.

My mother told me (Lucinda reinforced the bits I remembered) that my father was a fisherman. He saved her from drowning when, on a dare, as the cruise ship she had boarded in Algiers approached Trinidad, she dove into the swollen waters.

When Gardner was told the same story, he called my mother a party girl. He said she was hired by the ship to amuse the sailors and when they were done with her, they dropped her here. But my mother did not need to amuse the ship's crew for money. My mother was rich. She had her own money.

My mother said she hit the water with such force, she broke a rib. When she surfaced, she could barely breathe. The crewmen laughed at her. She was pretending, they said, yelling out for show. She had boasted that she was a champion swimmer (which she was), but the waves were mountainous and the undertow insistent. When she went under for the third time, believing it was for the last time, two arms scooped her to the surface. They were my father's arms. He had been fishing that day and saw the whole thing: the dive from so high up he thought she would die. He pulled the string on the rusty motor of his pirogue and sped to her.

My mother never forgave the crew. She returned to the ship, took her things—her money and her jewels—and left that day with my father, who had no home to take her to, for he was already in hiding from the men who ultimately killed him, and was living on the beach, off the coast of Manzanilla, in a shed he had made out of dried coconut fronds and branches from sea-almond trees.

My father was a poet and a dreamer in a country where people thought that what he did, writing poems endlessly on bits of paper, was an excuse for indolence. He had finished secondary school and passed exams for an entry-level position in the post office, but he could not get the sorting and filing right. Not that he lacked the skill to do this fairly simple job, but his mind often drifted, and he inevitably did things like filing surface mail in the airmail box or sending mail to Europe in the bag for China. But each time he did such things, a poem emerged from his head, whole, intact, beautifully formed. His bosses, however, were not impressed.

When one day he was offered the chance to bring flour and rice from Venezuela on his pirogue to the market in Trinidad, he thought he had found an end to his troubles. He did not know then that the men who offered him this job were part of a drug ring that trafficked in heroin in Venezuela. He thought he was lucky.

My father was a lover of nature. More than anything, he loved the sea. What he loved best was its vast openness, the seemingly infinite stretch of water, canopied by an equally endless sky. It was there, on the sea that he wrote his best poetry. He used to go alone in his pirogue, but after he found my mother (she was like a mermaid descending into the deep, he said), he took her with him whenever he went. She came to him as a gift, a present from the gods, he believed. That she was a champion swimmer and loved the sea was all he needed to know to have no doubt she would be his life companion.

On his way back from Venezuela, with his very first load to deliver in Trinidad, something white spilled out from one of the burlap bags. Supposing it was flour, he bent down to put it back and was struck by its texture. He slit another bag. It was rice this time, but something among the rice grains caught his eye. Then another bag, a smaller one. He opened it and white powder spilled from its insides.

He should have known better, of course. Any other person but a dreamer would have been suspicious from the start. Why would two well-dressed Venezuelans approach a lone fisherman with an offer of a month's wages at the post office for four runs a month to Venezuela? But to my father their offer was a chance in a lifetime.

It was my mother's idea that they go to Chacachacare. My father had told her about the leper colony. She persuaded him that no one

would look for him there. One year later, they began building their
house behind the doctor's quarters. Every day my mother would take
the ferry to the mainland to shop for building materials—wood, cement, galvanized nails, hammers, screwdrivers—things like that, and,
as the house began to take shape, she added tiles, pipes, sinks, shower-
heads, furniture for the interior.

Our house, before Gardner came and claimed he was going to save
us and bring us out of the dark ages, was not without modern facilities.
We had a small generator, a Delco, which powered a pump that
brought water into the house from two huge water tanks in the backyard where my father collected rainwater. Even today, all it would take
would be the rhythmic drumming of rain on the rooftop to remind me
of those days, of the tick, ticking of the Delco that used to lull me to
sleep.

We did not have electric lights. Gardner rightly could take credit for
that. At night oil lamps lit our house, but I preferred the soft light from
the oil lamps we had to the harshness of the light from the electric
bulbs when Gardner installed a more powerful generator and wired
the house. Gardner thought I should have been pleased, but it was hard
for me to show my gratitude. I had not forgotten the games I played
with my father at night when he folded his hands into shapes that
seemed unremarkable until struck by the lamplight. Then all sorts of
creatures—dogs, cats, agouti, manicou, iguana—leapt across the walls,
the shadows of my father's fingers and palms moving in a multitude of
directions to please me.

It was the construction of our house that probably helped my father's killers track him down. Every delivery of the goods my mother
had ordered must have been an occasion for much excitement on our
little island, and not just for the small band of inhabitants who lived
around the bay opposite to ours. My mother was pregnant with me
when they were building the house, and I imagine it had to have been
a strange sight for the men from Trinidad who unloaded our cargo to
see a blue-eyed blond woman, her belly swollen with child, locked arm
in arm with a black man who gave them orders.

Lucinda said that what she most admired about my mother was her
thoughtfulness, her consideration for my father's pride. His manhood,

she said emphatically. She explained that my mother never gave the slightest hint to anyone that the money was hers and my father was financially dependent on her. Which was why, when the news went back to Trinidad that my father was building a big, big house for a white, blue-eyed woman, it made sense that the drug lords would conclude that there could only be one way that my father could have got the money: He had siphoned off the white powder, sold it for a fortune.

There is not much I remember about my father. I remember that he had bushy eyebrows and a thin mustache that he cut every day. I remember that his nappy hair was so thick I could lose my fingers in it. I remember that he used to let me stand on his shoulders to reach the ripe mangoes on the mango tree. I remember that he taught me not to fear the iguana or the horsewhip green snake, or the white-tailed nightjar that made hooting sounds in the night and used to frighten me. I remember his joy, how it filled his eyes and, it seemed to me, every part of his body. I have this memory of him hopping from one spot to the other, his hand extended, his finger pointing to something he wanted me to see—a butterfly, flowers clustered on the branches of a tall tree—or, suddenly, in the midst of saying something to me, lowering his voice to a whisper: "Listen. Listen." Then puckering his lips, he would whistle, each time a trill so distinct that the bird he imitated would respond, and no other: a yellow keskidee, a gray long-tailed mockingbird, a yellow-headed green parrot. I would twist my head from right to left, like a weather vane, from him to the trees and back again, not knowing from where the sweet sounds came, so perfect was his imitation.

I remember, too, how happy he was when he had the carpenter carve birds, flowers, and animals into the wood panels above our walls. But those are the good memories. For I also remember his lifeless body stretched across the dining room table, blood congealed around the gashes the drug lords had cut across his chest and on his head.

How does a child, even if only five, blot out that memory? How does he forget the rain of tears that fell down his mother's face, or her deadening silence afterward, when she did not eat, did not bathe? When he hated the stench of her body and ran from her in disgust, even when she begged for his embrace? When, in less than a month, able. The thousand twangling instruments he heard in the whisper of a breeze, in the rustle of leaves in the bushes.

I was too young, of course, when Ariana made me ashamed of my freckles to have arrived at the conclusion that shocked that monk at Mount St. Benedict, but it was likely that the seeds of the war I would wage with the story in Genesis were planted then. I date the awakening of my conscious self to that singular event at the standpipe. There were penalties: the loss of innocence, the loss of bliss—the same penalties doled out to Adam when he was expelled from the garden and felt ashamed of his nakedness. But by the time I was seventeen, the age I was when Gardner imprisoned me, I had come to believe that the advantages far outweighed the penalties, and Adam became my hero. The exchange he made for Eden seemed to me better than the alternative: happiness with no cognizance of bad and ugly, and therefore no consciousness of good and beauty. For how to know good except by knowledge of what is bad, of what it is not? How to know beauty except by knowledge of what is ugly, of what it is not?

Sometimes, baffled by Gardner's outrageous arrogance, his cool assumption of superiority over me, I would try to make sense of his behavior in the light of this logic. Perhaps Gardner thought this way, too. Perhaps he said to himself: *I am unfreckled and pale, and Carlos is what I am not, and therefore he is ugly. I am good, and Carlos is not what I am, and therefore he is bad. I speak with an English accent, and Carlos does not, and therefore he gabbles like a thing most brutish; therefore he does not know his own meaning.*

But shame was all I felt that day at the standpipe, and I began to see my freckles as a sort of disfigurement (Ariana, when her mother could not hear her, would keep reminding me that they were). The next time I bathed at the standpipe, I put on my underpants.

Virginia's smile and touch restored in me the possibility of ease with my body, for when her hand caressed my face, brushing it with her sunshine, I was no longer that ugly boy Ariana said I was. "Freckles," Virginia said, and smiled at me. Gardner countered, *Freckled,* but he was already too late.

I was not the only one, however, who profited from Virginia's generous smile. The boatman who brought Virginia and her father to our

whispering his name, the name of his father also, she breathed her last breath?

I believe that Gardner spoke of my mother in this disparaging way to ease whatever shred of conscience he had left that pricked his soul in the night. Perhaps I give him more credit than is warranted. Perhaps he had no soul, or if he had, it was so tattered and torn with sin as to have barely existed at all. But it is also possible that in his diseased mind he had convinced himself that my mother had polluted the house and, therefore, had not deserved it.

My father thought my mother bewitching; Gardner called her a witch.

I grasp at straws no doubt, but there are days I seem to need to find some logic, *something,* that would help me make sense of Gardner's unrelenting arrogance, his overweening hubris. He had come to us homeless, an unwanted lodger in the old doctor's home, and yet he believed that we should be indebted to him and not the other way around. His bold-faced presumptions still astound me to silence, that he should act as if he thought he had discovered us, as if before his arrival we had not existed at all!

EIGHT

$\mathcal{B}$UT I LIKED his daughter right from the start, and not only because her eyes were the color of mine and re-minded me of my mother's. That first day, while Dr. Gardner was trying to persuade Lucinda that we needed his help, I caught her look-ing at me. When my eyes met hers, she ducked behind her father's back, but later that day, when Gardner returned with all his belong-ings, which were few—two duffel bags and a satchel strapped to his back, which led me foolishly to hope that his stay with us would not be long—she looked up at me again and this time she smiled. Her two front teeth were missing, and the pink gap on her gums was wide. I would have kept my lips closed if my front teeth were missing, but she spread hers apart and waved at me. At the top of the front steps, she stretched her hand toward me. I bent down and she touched my face.

"Freckles," she said.

She was walking behind her father. He spun around and pulled her hand away. "Freckled," he murmured gruffly. His eyes were stern, threatening.

That was how Virginia and I began—with a bond struck instantly

between us by the similarity of the color of our eyes, and a kindness she extended to me that I greedily accepted.

For I *was* self-conscious of the tiny brown dots that covered most of my body, though less so on my face. Only a few months earlier Ariana had convinced me that they were hideous. I had been accustomed at the time to bathing outdoors, from the standpipe at the back of the house. I would strip off my clothes regardless of who was there to see me: Ariana or Lucinda or anyone else. I thought no more of the ap-pendage hanging between my legs than of a convenience necessary when my bladder needed emptying, and my freckles, no different from my blue eyes, odd, because I had seen them on no one else, but famil-iar because they were mine. One day, probably because she was tired of the attention Lucinda was paying to me (my father had just been killed and my mother had died soon after), Ariana pointed to my sex and jeered: "Look at that teeny, weeny little thing you have."

"So what?" I said. My penis had shriveled under the cold water and was a knob lying limp next to my scrotum.

"So what, you stupid boy? Girls not going to like you, that's what."

"I don't care if girls don't like me," I struck back.

"You wait and see. When you get big, you going to want them to like you, and they not going to like you because your thing too small."

Instinctively, I cupped my hand over my penis.

"And, mostly," she added, taking pleasure in my discomfort, "girls not going to like you because you polka dot."

I looked down at my body, my thin arms and legs, the stump be-tween my upper thighs, the brown spots that marred my skin, and for the first time I felt ugly, for the first time I knew shame. I became con-scious of a self apart from the self of the carefree boy I was, a boy wh spent his days and nights with no awareness of his physical self exce when the need required it, except when the urges of his bodily fu tions demanded it, a boy who reveled in the delights of the w around him: white clouds drifting with the wind across a sun blue sky; the bay still, silent, and glittering before the coming of storm; birds whose whistles he was learning to imitate by hea he climbed without fear; cicadas whose crying in the night him comfort when grief over the death of his parents seeme island said that when the villagers at Cocorite, in Trinidad, first saw Gardner on the beach raking the sand for scraps of fish the fishermen had left behind, his flaming red hair draped down to his shoulders and the forked branch in his hand put them in mind of the devil, just as they had done me. They would have stayed far away from him and burned candles to ward off his evil spirit if it weren't for his daughter, they said, for she smiled and won their hearts.

In those days, while Gardner waited for the contact his brother had made to materialize and squirrel him away to Chacachacare, Virginia's hair was wild and unruly. I still find it hard to envision her hair this way, because when Gardner moved in with the doctor and got his hands on scissors, he did what he always did when confronted with disorder in nature: he trimmed, he slashed, he pushed back. So Virginia's hair was short and cut close to her head when I met her. But then, on the beach at Cocorite, masses of blond curls encircled her tiny face. When the sun struck the light wisps of hair, fraying at the ends, she glowed. Like an angel, the boatman said. The villagers wanted to protect her. They fed her, and because he was her father, they fed him, too.

It astonishes me still that he was not grateful. They had saved his life and had never asked for a penny.

Maybe it was the fuss they made over his daughter that gave Gardner this sense of privilege. Maybe something more malign. Though I know now he was an escapee from the law, a man for whom knowledge was its own reward, to be acquired without regard for his fellow men, perhaps in his mind he thought he was better than us, that what the villagers had done for him was no more than he was due. He was, after all, on an island that was part of his country's empire. He was an Englishman.

Even before he burned my mother's bed, Dr. Gardner had begun making changes in my house to erase my memory. Our food was to be cooked differently, not the way my mother used to cook it. My mother used pepper in her food, and seasoned the meat with vinegar or limes and with lots of garlic, onion, chives, and herbs, just as other women did in the Caribbean.

My mother had learned to cook this way in Africa. She was born in Algiers to English parents, in a country colonized by the French and native to Arabs and Africans. Her English parents must have felt alienated twice over in that place, strangers in a strange land where even the Europeans were foreign to them. And their daughter, too, must have seemed alien to them, swaddled in cloths they could not have recognized and snuggled in the arms of the black-skinned midwife who brought her to them in that hot, sticky room where she was born, in a hospital in Algiers. The pungent smells, the vibrating whir of an overhead fan whose purpose was not so much to ease the oppressive heat as to chase away the flies that were forever buzzing around the breasts of nursing mothers, must have repelled my grandparents.

My mother told me many stories about her life in Africa. As I grew older, I began to make sense of all she had told me. I understood that her parents hated Africa. They tolerated Africa only for the money they could make. They were in the import-export business, importing exquisitely handwoven rugs they bought for a song from Arab traders, and exporting them to rich buyers in the West. The business kept them busy, so busy they had little time left over for a daughter. They put her in the care of a nanny who was an Algerian. Black, not Arab. The black, not Arab, Algerian taught my mother everything: about her gods, about her history, about the days when the white man came with sweet words about his god of love, his god of brotherhood, his god who declared all men equal, who loved them all the same. She told my mother about the resistance of her people and the white man's impatience: The Bible took too long; the gun was more persuasive.

My mother's parents knew nothing of what the African nanny was teaching their daughter, except that she had taught my mother her language. For this they were grateful. At ten years old, my mother was already their interpreter, translating for them from Arabic to French, from French to English. But they had not counted on my mother loving Africa. When they left her upbringing to an African, they did not think she would fall in love with an African. They were aware, when she was in primary school, that her playmates were African, but in the colonies, African children were allowed to play with European children, to amuse them, to entertain them. That all came to an end, of course, when the European children crossed the threshold into adolescence. Then, the European children were in training to don the mantle of their parents; then, it was time for them to learn about their awesome heritage, their terrible burden. Then, there could be no commingling with the inferior, no fraternizing with the native. My mother never learned these lessons. Left in the hands of an African nanny, she learned what the African taught her, she loved what and whom the African loved.

Ultimately my mother became an embarrassment for her parents when her friendships with Africans persisted into secondary school. Nothing, however, was more embarrassing, more shameful, for them than my mother's announcement, on her twenty-first birthday, that she was in love with an African. My father, it seemed, was not the first black man my mother loved.

Soon after that birthday, the African disappeared. My mother blamed her parents. She cut off her relationships with the few European friends she had, believing that they, too, had a part in her lover's disappearance. Day and night she searched for him in the African quarters. Humiliated by my mother's persistence, her unbridled passion for a black African, my mother's parents tried to bribe her with clothes, jewels, money. My mother took them all, and, convinced that she would never see her lover again, left for a cruise around the world.

On the cruise ship the word got out. Gossip spread. *Nigger lover.* That's what the sailors called my mother behind her back. *A partying nigger lover.*

In Gardner's version of the story, the sailors threw my mother overboard when the ship reached the Caribbean. It was the version he chose to believe and thought justified, but my mother told me a different story: After my father rescued her, she walked off the ship on her own.

Sometimes I think the truth is somewhere in between. Perhaps when my mother returned to the cruise ship, after my father rescued her, it had not been her intention to leave. Perhaps the sailors had laughed at her when she came onboard, leaning on the arm of a black man. *Nigger lover.* It is likely that was what they called her.

The way to a man's heart. Lucinda would laugh and wink at me when she said it was my mother's cooking, what my mother had learned from her African nanny, that bound my father to her. For my father would eat food cooked by no one else, not even by Lucinda. Every morning my father took my mother with him on his pirogue and they would drift far out into the bay, though not too far (for the threat of the drug lords was always present), and my mother would lay her head on his lap and he would compose poem after poem that poured from his heart like music.

"It's all that good food your mother cooking for him," Lucinda said.

Ariana took her words literally. When Lucinda could not stand longer than ten minutes without clutching her knees as pain knifed through her from the cancer that was eating her insides, Ariana became our cook. Lucinda called out instructions from her bed and Ariana did as she was told.

In the beginning Gardner seemed pleased. He praised Ariana lavishly. The chicken was tender, the fish was fresh, the vegetables crisp, just as he liked them, he said. Magnificent. He would smile his false smiles and pat his lips with his napkin, a formality he insisted on (he had cut some fabric in squares and given each of us one), and Ariana would wilt before him, her eyes sweeping the floor, her lips twitching in an effort to suppress her delight. So greedy did she seem for his attention that I believed she heard nothing more. But I was not fooled. I heard the *buts* as Gardner pushed his chair away from the table: "But less pepper next time." "But less salt next time." "But not red pepper. Pepper, but black pepper."

Soon Ariana was strutting around the house with an air of self-importance, ordering me around. "Cut it this way, Carlos," she would say in an officious tone when I helped her in the kitchen. "*He* likes it this way." She acted as if Gardner had promoted her to chief of staff in his household, which I suppose she was, chief of a staff of one, namely of me. She had to speak to Gardner about this or that, she would say, never naming what this or that was. I always thought it was about cooking, never guessing that, after Lucinda died, her many visits to Gardner's room had nothing at all to do with cooking.

Lucinda was still alive but weak and in pain when Gardner announced that he was going to take Ariana under his wing, show her how to cook the English way. We were no longer to eat dasheen, yams, edoes, cassava, or any of the other tubers we called ground provisions. They were filthy, Gardner said. They grew in dirt. No garlic, either. No chives, no thyme, or any other green stuff, as he called it. He did not like fish. Rather, he liked fish, but not the way I used to like it. He wanted Ariana to stuff the fish with cubes of stale bread, or if she wanted to fry it, he wanted her to fillet it.

Poor Ariana had no idea what Gardner meant by fillet. He spent a morning showing her how, and when he was finished, there were bright red slits on each of her ten fingers.

Still, she wanted to please him. Lucinda had taught her to squeeze lime juice over the fish ("To cut the fresh, fishy taste"), but her fingers were so raw that she could not touch the rind of the lime without wincing.

"I sorry," she apologized to Gardner, sucking her fingers in an attempt to dilute the sting of the lime. "I sorry I can't lime it."

"Lime it?" he hollered.

It was the last time we used lime to season our fish or our meats.

Little by little our food changed. Our only seasonings were salt and black pepper. We no longer ate rice. Too much starch, Gardner said. It would put weight on his daughter. Chicken, but not stewed, only baked. In fact, anything baked: potatoes, which he allowed—"They come from Europe, where people practice hygiene"—macaroni baked with cheese, and vegetables I had never yet eaten, which had to be done, he explained to Ariana, "au gratin."

No tropical fruits were allowed in the house, and the fruits we were permitted to have could not be eaten raw. They had to be boiled, stewed, or baked. Apples were put in the oven, pears and peaches had to be simmered on the stove in water and sugar or taken from cans. Acknowledging that his daughter needed vitamin C, he let us have orange juice, but it came pasteurized and in bottles. "Disease!" he would shout. Nature was the enemy, and here in the tropics nature threatened to destroy us. At times I felt we were at war: nature on one side and art on the other, the interventions Gardner used to suppress what he called "nature's insidious power."

I had complained to Lucinda, when she was on her deathbed, about the changes Gardner was making to our food.

"You'll get accustomed," she said.

I tried to warn her that there was more. I had seen him with a measuring tape, measuring the drawing room walls.

"He thinks the house is his," I said.

"Maybe it's best," she said. "You will need a man in the house."

She never lived, thank God, to know what Gardner meant by needing a man in the house, what that would mean for her daughter, what that would mean for me.

In her final days, Lucinda handed over my mother's money and her jewel box to Gardner.

"It belongs to Carlos," she told him. "Use what you need for the house, but keep the rest for him when he becomes a man."

I never became a man in Gardner's eyes. I never again saw my mother's jewels, except for her diamond earrings. Ariana wore them, and I took it for granted that my mother had given them to her. I knew she loved shiny things: an ordinary stone if it glittered in the sunlight, asphalt that shone after the rain.

Ariana was a strange girl. She had a dreamy quality about her that made her seem almost incorporeal. She was very thin; the only parts of her body that seemed to grow were her arms and legs. Her hair was long, thick, and wavy. Lucinda would plait it, but minutes later Ariana would loosen it and it would flow around her shoulders like a cape. When the wind blew, her hair fanned out and seemed to pull her upward as if she were a puppet and the strands of her hair the strings of a puppeteer. A stronger wind and she would fly away.

Yellow was her favorite color. When I was a little boy I used to stretch out next to her on the floor watching her color a drawing with a yellow crayon. It was from her I first learned about the possibilities of nuance and subtlety, the variations of meaning and feeling evoked in shadings, for with that single color she would make me see a multitude of colors, a multitude of images. My father was the poet, but he did not live to teach me about the subtleties in poetry. Certainly not Gardner. Ariana taught me with her love of yellow. In return, I trapped fireflies in a bottle for her. After dinner, before Gardner came and changed our lives, she used to sit alone under the sapodilla tree with the bottle in her hand, mesmerized by their flickering lights. Sometimes we would find her in the morning, under the tree, the bottle clutched between her fingers.

When Dr. Gardner began to grow yellow flowers in yellows that ranged from those so delicate they were almost white to others that outshone the sun, Ariana became his servant, a willing lackey to a god who could make such magic. So it seemed to me. I would remind her of the necklaces she once made with the yellow trumpet-shaped flowers from the buttercup flower tree and she would stare at me wide-eyed as if I told a lie. I never suspected there was more to her seeming affection of Gardner. I did not know about the letter my mother had written. I did not know this letter was the reason for her sycophantic behavior.

My mother was not the most attentive parent—she loved my father more than she loved me—but she was not a blackmailer. She was a storyteller. I am convinced that all she meant to do was scare Ariana. More than likely it was nonsense she had scribbled on a piece of paper. When Ariana saw the letter in Gardner's hand, she must have been terrified. It would not have taken much for Gardner to trick her into confessing. Then it was easy for him to convince her that her life was in his hands.

NINE

$\mathcal{U}$NDER DR. GARDNER'S RULE, our days and nights were rigidly structured. We woke up at five, had breakfast at six, Virginia and Dr. Gardner in the dining room, Ariana and I in the kitchen after we served them. At seven, while Ariana and I washed the dishes and cleaned the house, Gardner tutored Virginia in his room. At nine, Gardner went to work on his garden, and I was at the beck and call of Ariana, helping her with whatever she wanted done. At noon, when the sun's rays were blinding and the heat so intense that perspiration rolled down our backs like rainwater, Gardner returned to the house for lunch. After lunch he called Ariana to his room, ostensibly to discuss household matters with her. Ariana reappeared an hour or so later, and Gardner remained in his room until four. For that hour or so when Gardner was with Ariana, I was alone with Virginia, though not alone in the strict sense of the word, for she was instructed to stay in her room and I in mine. From four until six, Gardner went back to work in his garden. At six-thirty, we had dinner. After dinner, until seven-thirty, he tutored Virginia, again in his room. At eight o'clock he turned off the lights.

In the beginning Dr. Gardner did not permit the slightest deviation from this strict schedule. If breakfast was served five minutes after six, Ariana and I were given five demerits, one for each minute we were tardy. We got demerits for waking up late, demerits for serving lunch or dinner late, demerits for going to bed late.

Punctuality, Gardner said to us, was the mark of a civilized man. I was late because I was lazy, because I had given in to my animal desire for sensual gratification: one more minute in bed, one more minute daydreaming or lollygagging instead of focusing on the task he had assigned to me. He did not call me a savage directly (soon enough he would make it plain to me that that was what he thought of me), but he let me know that a civilized man is one who allowed reason, not the flesh, to guide his actions.

It was his burden to civilize Ariana and me, he said. He despaired that such a goal could prove impossible, but he was determined to do his bloody best, his bloody, bloody English best.

When I was a child it puzzled me that he would be willing to spill his blood for something we did not want. Soon I understood that it was I who had to do his bloody best, that if blood were to be spilled it would be my blood, not his.

He kept his watch in his pocket. If we were late, he pulled it out, recorded the time in his notebook, and calculated our demerits. At the end of the week he doled out his punishment, but not without a lecture.

We had to sit around the kitchen table, Virginia, too, when he lectured us. He might not have been certain he could civilize us, but he had no doubt that she would understand the lesson he hoped to teach us. He seemed to imply that her genetic inheritance, the pure English blood that ran in her veins that had given her white skin, blue eyes, blond hair, had also given her English intelligence and so the capacity for acquiring English civility.

The first time we were subjected to his lectures, he stacked a bundle of sticks in the shape of a pyramid on the table. "Pick one," he said to me, pointing to the bundle. I picked up the stick at the top of the pyramid. He got flustered and gave me a dirty look.

"I said, 'Pick one.' "

"But I picked one," I insisted.

"Not the top one."

It was obvious to me that if I took any other stick, the others would fall down, but that, of course, was Gardner's point. When I hesitated, he warned me again. "Not the top one."

Ariana, afraid (I would like to believe) of what he would do if I disobeyed him, stretched out her hand. "I do it," she said, and pulled out a stick from the middle tier. The top stick fell down and struck the sticks below it, and they in turn struck the other sticks, scattering them across the table. I remember clearly that Gardner smiled. I remember he patted Ariana's hand and praised her. I remember this because I expected him to chastise her. *Speak only when you are spoken to.* It was another Gardner rule warranting demerits. He had addressed me, not her. But little by little, I was beginning to realize that rules that applied to me did not necessarily apply to Ariana.

The lesson was about law and order, who was to lead and who was to follow, who was in authority. The lesson was about the consequences of challenging authority.

He swiped his arm across the table, sending the sticks in all directions. One or two tottered at the edge but he grabbed them in time and prevented them from falling.

"God is a good God," he said, and his lips spread into a brief, cold smile. "He loves us. He wants the best for us. But God is in charge."

I was never certain of Gardner's religious convictions, whether or not he was a true believer. He was familiar with the Bible, but his interpretation of biblical stories always led to the same conclusion: They justified his right to be my master, and so he used them this time. He collected the sticks and while he formed the pyramid Ariana had dismantled, he told us the story about Lucifer, how he lost his place in heaven, how God had given him everything, how He had made him the most handsome of the angels. "Yet Lucifer was ungrateful," he said.

He looked directly at me when he said that, and a trembling began growing under my skin, for I knew what he was thinking. When Lucinda was still alive and I was foolish enough to feel protected, I had refused to eat the food Ariana had prepared for us. She had already started cooking in the way he demanded and had baked the chicken, not stewed it. Worse still, she had not seasoned it with garlic, thyme, chives, onion, and pepper, as Lucinda used to. Without seasonings, the meat was tasteless. One particular meal was so bland that I threw it away in the garbage. Gardner saw me, and he made me take it out. I was an ungrateful child, he hollered, shoving the chicken down my throat. I gagged and vomited but he kept putting more and more chicken into my mouth, all the time chastising me for my ingratitude. If it were not for him, I would starve, he said.

I wriggled away from him and ran to Lucinda. I fell on my knees by her bedside and begged her to help me. She was moaning in pain. Couldn't I see she was dying? "Try, Carlos," she implored me. "Listen to what he says. Who take care of you when I die?"

Gardner was standing at the doorway. "He's a spoiled brat," he said. "He needs to learn discipline."

Lucinda tried to defend me. She said I was a good boy, a kind and loving boy. Gardner shook his head and walked away.

When she was sure he could not hear her, Lucinda clawed at my shirt with her emaciated fingers. "Don't fight him." Her voice was hoarse, urgent. "He bigger than you."

I said it was not fair. The house was mine. I was the boss.

"You need him now."

"And if he never leaves?" I asked her, tears streaming down my cheeks. She let go of my shirt. "In time," she said and closed her eyes.

At first I did not understand her. I begged her again to do something. To speak to Gardner. To force him to leave the house.

She opened her eyes. "If not now, then in time," she said.

"Make him go away," I said.

"Come." She drew me closer to her. "Boys grow up to be men," she whispered in my ear.

Now Gardner was reminding Ariana and me that ingratitude was Lucifer's sin, that God had been good to Lucifer but Lucifer disobeyed Him.

He gives the orders in the house, Gardner said. We must do as he says.

He asked me to take a stick out from the bottom tier of the pyramid he had rebuilt. I braced myself for what I knew would happen.

When the sticks scattered across the table, Gardner pushed them farther away, this time letting several of them tumble over the edge.

He called Virginia to him and put her to sit on his lap. We were all assigned places, duties, tasks, he said, speaking pointedly now to Ariana and me. If we stayed in our place and did our jobs well, we would be rewarded. We would get food to eat, water to drink, a roof over our heads. If we did not stay in our place, if we challenged his authority, if we questioned his right to rule us, we would fall as the sticks had fallen. He picked up the sticks and broke them into little pieces. Without him to help us, he said, we would end up broken into pieces like these sticks. "God sent Lucifer to hell for challenging His authority," he said to us.

He had equated himself with God and made us Lucifer: Ariana and me. I say Ariana and me because at that moment he was holding Virginia close to his chest. Because, as he told us about the greater and lesser angels, the ones closer to God when Lucifer had fallen, he made it clear that though Virginia, like us, must obey him, she was better than us. Her place, he said, was on the second tier of the pyramid, ours on the last, firmly on the bottom, my place slightly above Ariana's.

He permitted me to call Virginia by her first name, but instructed Ariana to address her as Miss Virginia. I found no fault with this distinction he made between Ariana and me, and neither did Ariana. She was Lucinda's daughter and Lucinda was my mother's cook. Lucinda, of course, had a surname, Bates, but I never addressed her as Mrs. Bates. My mother had met her on one of her shopping trips to Trinidad. Lucinda's husband had abandoned her and she had nowhere to go. My mother offered her a job and a place to stay. She was an adult, with a child older than I, but even as a toddler, I was permitted to call her Lucinda. Before long, though, had she lived, she, too, as the boatman now did, would have had to address me as Mr. Carlos.

I did not like it when Gardner made me eat in the kitchen with Ariana, but I fooled myself into coming to terms with his arrangement, convincing myself that it made sense for him to prefer to eat alone with his daughter rather than with people he hardly knew. Now Gardner made it plain to me: Familiarity had nothing to do with his preference. I was his daughter's social inferior.

The system Gardner devised for correlating demerits with punish-

ment was consistent with his conviction of a God-ordained social hier-
archy. For one demerit for being one minute late, Ariana and I had to
wake up ten minutes early. The punishment for Virginia was more
equitable: one minute for one demerit. Being tardy a mere six minutes
meant that Ariana and I had to be up at four in the morning, but often
Gardner pardoned Ariana. Me, never once.

Gardner's rule about punctuality was not confined to tardiness,
however. One particularly sun-filled morning I had woken up at dawn.
I was sitting in the kitchen having my breakfast when Gardner walked
in. As soon as he saw me, he glanced down at his watch. "Five demerits," he said. It was five minutes to six. He had stipulated that breakfast
would be at six. His lesson this time was about good manners, good
breeding. A civilized man, he said, does not arrive at the home of his
host before he is invited. He knows that it is as inconsiderate for a guest
to arrive early as it is for him to be late.

I knew it was Dr. Gardner and his daughter who were the guests,
not Ariana and I. But in those early days, just the memory of Gardner's
face, red, distorted with his fury and hatred for my mother, rippling
with the reflection of the flames that burst out of the fire he had ig-
nited on her bed, was sufficient to keep me in line. And when I was not
quick enough for Ariana, or failed to help her as she thought I should,
she reminded me of the curses he hurled on my mother and the power
he had to open graves, wake the dead, and to command elves with
printless feet to attack me. "He could poison you with midnight mushrooms," she said. So I let Gardner be the king of my castle. For that
was how my childish mind conceived of his relationship to me. He was
king, but the castle was mine. When I was old enough, when I had
learned enough from him, I would assert my right to rule it.

Yet it was not as difficult as it might seem for me to sustain this fantasy. Gardner was not always cruel to me. Indeed, it was not long before
he began to pay attention to me and I became a source of pride to him,
his first successful experiment with humans, after his failures in England.

Virginia had just turned four when Gardner decided it was time to
teach her to read. He began with the alphabet. I heard him one morn-

ing shouting out the letters at her. It was the second or third day since he had begun to teach her. "How many more times do I have to say it?" His voice rose angrily as he listed all the letters. "A, B, C, D . . . Say them now!"

I was in the kitchen. Ariana was washing the dishes and she had just passed a plate to me to dry. I was so frightened I almost dropped it.

"L, M, N, O, P," Gardner yelled. "Not L, N, P, O!"

I could not hear what Virginia was saying, but when Gardner shouted L, M, N, O, P again, I knew she had said the letters in the wrong order. For some minutes afterward, though, there was silence, and in those minutes I felt such a rush of relief for Virginia, assuming she had finally got the letters right, that I turned to Ariana and said, "Good for her." Ariana gave me a withering glance that let me know without a word how foolish she thought I was to feel sorry for someone better off than I.

My assumption, however, was wrong, for soon Gardner was yelling at Virginia again. "For God's sake. O, P, O, P, not P, O." When the door finally opened, I held my breath, hoping his anger would not fall on me, too. But Gardner seemed unruffled. He was smiling when he came out of the room, his arm draped across Virginia's shoulder. Before he left for his garden, he kissed her and whispered something to her in tender tones. She bit her lip and looked across at me. The flesh around her eyes was swollen, and there were red streaks running down her cheeks. I could tell she had been crying, and yet had I not heard Gardner distinctly, I would never have guessed he had been the cause of her tears.

That night she must have taught herself the alphabet, for the next morning I heard Gardner say to her, "Good. Good." Then he began with the sounds of letters. "A: ahh. B: buh. C: cuh." Over and over, he repeated the sounds of the letters. On the third day, he moved to rhyming words. "Man, can, ran. Hit, sit, bit." He began slowly, patiently. He said the words loudly, but not roughly. "Man, can, ran. Hit, sit, bit." When I heard him repeat them the next day, fear gripped my heart. He was saying them now menacingly, threateningly. Morning after morning it was the same, sometimes new words, sometimes words he had shouted out to her the day before. Virginia was not a stupid girl. She was smart, intelligent. It would not have been difficult for her to memorize such phonetically similar simple words, but I was certain she was frozen with fear, as I was frozen with fear, her brain focused on one objective: to shield herself from her father's rage.

"Bat, cat, rat. Sam, Pam, jam!" Each time Gardner's voice rose with his growing impatience, a deafening silence followed. I worried more about the silence than about the shouting itself. I felt sorry for Virginia. I wanted to help her. I cringed when I saw her tear-stained face. Yet when Gardner reemerged from his room with her, always there was a smile on his face, always his arm caressed her shoulders, always he spoke to her in loving tones, but always, in spite of his embrace and kisses, her face was pale, her eyes strained with fear and anxiety.

If Gardner loved her, it was a strange kind of love, a love that had at its center not a warm, pulsating heart, but a stone, cold, hard, unmovable. Virginia had made him angry but she would not dissuade him. He would give her kisses and hugs at the end of each lesson, but only, I felt, to ease the way for his next onslaught. Whatever the plan he had for her, he would not let her deter him. I had the feeling then, even in those early days, that behind his efforts to teach her was an intention grander and far larger than any that seemed apparent.

At the end of the week, unable to bear the silence buffeting against the rising crescendo of Gardner's angry commands and the piercingly sorrowful glances Virginia sent my way, I decided to help her. She had been kind to me. She had loved the part of me Ariana and Gardner had tried to convince me was ugly. "Freckles," she had said, and touched me.

The problem was to find a time and a place to be alone with her. Gardner had put Ariana in charge of her, and Ariana never let me near her. I suppose I could have gone to Virginia's room when Ariana was with Gardner in his room, in the afternoon, but Ariana had frightened me with Gardner's curses. "Stay away from her," she had warned me.

One late afternoon, however, when Gardner was back in his garden after his midday nap, I got my chance. A little red bird had flown into the house. This was not an unusual occurrence. Birds often flew into the house through an open window, but they always flew out as quickly, sensing the difference in the air, the turgid stillness uninterrupted by even the merest ripple of a breeze, the domestic smells of cooked food, washed and unwashed clothing, the absence of greens and browns in trees and bushes. But this bird was different. Mistaking (I would like to believe) the flora and fauna my father had had a carpenter carve into the top panels of the interior walls of the house for real flora and fauna, it flew deeper into the house rather than out of it, passing through a wide space between the carvings of flowers into Virginia's room.

Virginia was beside herself with joy. "A bird! A bird!" she squealed. She frightened the bird, and it flew out of her room. "Ariana! Carlos!" she called out to us. "A bird! A bird! A pretty bird! Come see!" She bolted out of her room and down the corridor. Her slippers flip-flopped noisily against the wood floors and her pink cotton dress billowed out behind her.

Ariana tried to stop her. "Leave it alone. It will fly out on its own."

But there was no stopping Virginia. She clapped her hands and hopped excitedly from one foot to the other. "I want it. I want the bird. Catch it for me, Carlos!" she pleaded with me. "Please! Please, Carlos."

The bird, dazed and lost, flew from one partition along the corridor to the other, cawing in terror, its little wings beating rapidly against its body.

"Please, Carlos. I want to put it in my room." She tugged my shirt. Ariana pulled her away. "No, Miss Virginia. Let it alone."

My father would not have approved of what I did next. Many times I had begged him to trap a bird for me that had caught my fancy. I wanted to put it in a cage, to keep it in my room, to have it sing for me, but he never allowed it. "All living creatures desire freedom," he said. "The bird will die if it cannot be free." I fought with him. The lepers had birds that lived in cages, I told him, and he answered that he did not know one that sang as sweetly as the birds that lived free in the trees. Yet this was the first time since Virginia had come to my house that I had seen her so happy. I wanted to please her. I wanted to give her some joy after those tear-stained mornings.

"Please, Carlos," she begged me.

I told her not to make a sound. I would catch the bird for her, but she had to be still. She must not scare it. The bird had to settle down.

But when the bird settled down, it perched itself near the ceiling, on a branch carved out at the top of the wood partition, between two clutches of hibiscus flowers, far too high for me to reach it. Its little chest pumped in and out and it rolled its beady eyes at us. Then, from nervousness (or, perhaps, sheer revenge, gloating), it shat, not once, not twice, but a rain of shit that bounced off the wall, sprayed the side of my face, and fell with a splat on the floor.

Virginia was laughing hysterically and I was brushing off the excrement that had fallen on me, when, from the corner of my eye, I caught a glimpse of Ariana biting her fingernails, and a half a second later, Gardner standing behind her.

Had she gone for him? I had not noticed when she disappeared from the room, but with the knowledge I now have of the hold Gardner had on her, the terror she must have felt of imprisonment, she might have called him, she might have been, even then, already his spy.

He was holding a broom with long green bristles. Before I could warn Virginia, he was swinging it angrily at the bird. Pieces of the wood carvings broke off as the broom struck the delicate designs at the top of the wood panels. He cursed me; he cursed the bird. Virginia implored him to stop, but neither her tears nor her words had any effect on him. He swung the broom again and again, chasing the bird through the house, all the time hollering: "Filth, filth, you filthy bastard!" The bird flew frantically into the corridor. Gardner reached up on his toes and swatted at it again. This time the bristles of the broom grazed the bird's wing and the bird dipped downward. I rushed to catch it, but it was a strong little bird. It flapped its wings, and with heroic effort, it pulled itself upward. Before Gardner could hit it again, it found an open window.

It was gone, but Gardner was not done. "Filth, filth, you filthy bastard," he continued to shout, his words this time directed at me.

When he calmed down, he ordered me to clean up the bird droppings. "With your bare hands," he said, his lips curled in disgust. "Filth, like the filth you are."

After he left, taking Virginia with him, Ariana, pitying me, handed me a bucket and a rag.

The next morning Gardner woke me up before six and ordered me to bring him plywood from the back of the house. He wanted to board up all the open spaces between the carvings at the tops of the interior walls. "Fetch the wood, you lazy bastard. Do you think all I would have you do is housework?"

I should have guessed it would have only been a matter of time before he would make me work in the garden.

I fetched the wood, and when I was done, he made me stand on a chair beside him and hand him nails that he hammered into the plywood to cover the spaces in the carvings. Afterward, he had me sweep up the chips that had fallen on the floor.

"Next week you begin," he said. "No more lazing in the house."

After lunch, after Ariana had followed him to his room, Virginia came into mine. She could not forget the bird. I must find it for her, she said.

I was afraid and told her to leave. Her father would punish me if he found her in my room, I said.

"They stay in there a long time," she said.

I looked away from her, feeling strangely and unaccountably uncomfortable. "He will hear you," I said. But she knew that could not be true. Her room was too far from his room for him to hear our whispers. Her room—my mother's bedroom and my room after she died—was in the front of the house. Gardner had assigned me to a room in the back of the house.

"No," she said. She came closer to me.

"You must leave," I said.

"Ariana will be with Father a long, long time," she said. *Sometimes longer than an hour.*

"Find the bird for me," she pleaded.

The bird was hurt and I knew I could find it easily. It had to be somewhere nearby, cowering. I had seen when the bristles of the broom struck its wing. But I lied. "I don't think I can find it," I said.

"Please." She grasped my arm.

"I don't know," I said, trying hard to be firm, but it was not easy to resist her. A tear had pearled in the canals of her eyes, and a slight tremor had worked its way to the edges of her mouth. "I will love you forever," she breathed in my ear. "If you find the bird for me, I will love you always."

We were children. Neither of us had any notion then about romantic love. She was promising me friendship, loyalty, affection, and I was orphaned, no mother, no father, no one to love me afterward except Lucinda, and she was dead (I could not count on Ariana).

"Forever," she said. And I found myself latching on to her promise for every hope it offered.

"I will love you, too," I said. "Always."

The next day, by the purest of good luck, I found the bird. It was crouched down on a pile of dry leaves, in a corner of the front yard, shivering. One of its wings was spread out slightly, the tips drooping down limply. When I approached it, it opened its red-rimmed eyes, but, too weak to defend itself, it shut them down again and shuddered.

Virginia called me her prince when I told her I had found the bird, and for the rest of that week, while Ariana and Gardner were in Gardner's room, she and I nursed the bird together. I made a cast with matchsticks for its broken wing; she fed it with an eyedropper she had filled with milk and bread. We were careful. When either Ariana or Gardner was in our presence we avoided looking at each other; we did not speak to each other. We feared our excitement would brim over. We feared Ariana and Gardner would somehow sense the bond that was cementing between us, that Ariana would discover the affection we had for each other. We did not discuss these feelings; we did not plan how we should act. Instinctively, we each knew what we needed to do. So, stealing moments together to save the bird her father had almost killed, Virginia and I began our secret life together.

TEN

IRST WE FREED the bird. It didn't take much to convince her. She knew as well as I that her father would not let her keep it.

"It will fly away on its own when it's ready," I said. We were crouched over the bird. I had a razor in my hand and I was cutting the thread I had wrapped around the matchstick I had used to prop up the bird's broken wing.

She seemed not to be listening to me, or, rather, to be listening to words I had not spoken. "Father is a kind man," she said.

I was not surprised when she said that. I would have defended my father, but we both knew that we would not have had to tiptoe through the house, holding our breaths for fear he would hear us, had there been the slightest chance her father would have allowed us to care for the bird.

I said her father must have been a kind man when they were in England. She said she could not remember when they were in England, but she was sure he was a kind man in England. He was a kind man *now,* she said. He didn't have a wife to help him like other men. Her mother was dead. He had to take care of her. "All by himself." She opened her eyes wide in awe as if she thought that for him to do so required extraordinary, superhuman effort. He had told her not many fathers took care of their daughters all by themselves. She was special and she had a special father.

As she spoke, I kept my eyes focused on what I was doing. I cut the thread and stroked the bird's wing. The wing had not healed completely, but I was certain that in a few days the bird would be able to fly. "We'll have to bring it food," I said, "but you won't have to use the dropper."

Her mind was elsewhere. "He's teaching me to read," she said. There was a slight flutter in her voice. "Father is nice, but I am stupid. I give him trouble."

I did not know what she wanted from me. She could not doubt that I had heard her father shouting at her. Our eyes had met many times when she came out of his room. She could not doubt that I had seen the red streaks that marred her cheeks. Kind? Nice? He was not kind, he was not nice. Not the way my father had been kind and nice to me.

"He works hard. He tries his best. I am stupid," she said again.

I stopped stroking the bird. "I can teach you to read," I said.

Her eyes brightened. "You know how?"

"When I was little my mother used to read to me," I said.

They were adult books that my mother read to me, books far advanced for my age. I fell asleep to the sound of words at night, and in the daytime, after lunch, curled next to her in the drawing room in my father's armchair, the curtains drawn to shield us from the piercing noonday sunlight, I would nod off, rocked to sleep by vowels and consonants while my father snored in the bedroom, driven from his beloved sea by the scorching sun.

My mother would have preferred to have read children's books to me, but there weren't many children's books in the stores in Trinidad. In a colony where the only escape from poverty was through education, people had neither the time nor money to waste on reading 'nancy stories to children, which they had memorized anyhow and could recite by heart. Reading was for learning, for big books that held important words, told important stories, foreign stories about foreign things, foreign facts, information they would need in order to pass English exams set and marked in England. Exams that would lead to a placement in the right secondary school and to a passport to university in the Mother Country.

My mother was not thinking of these exams when she read to me from the books she bought for herself, but these were the only books she could find, and so she settled on making them interesting to me. She dramatized everything, turning fact into stories more exciting than fiction. Which was why it was easy for me to believe that her letter that Gardner had found was not intended to blackmail Ariana, but only to scare her.

"And Churchill ordered bombs to rain on Berlin," she would read aloud from her history books. Her hands would fly into the air; she would twist her body in horror. "Swoosh! Voom! Boom! Bang!" I saw exploding fires in the changing colors on her face, buildings blown apart, rubble tumbling into streets, people running, screaming.

It was the same when she read to me from her science books. "Homo sapiens is one little twig on the branch of life." She would spread out her fingers and flutter them. "A twig." And I would understand my place in the vastness of nature.

She would slow down for the big words, stretching them out as if they were elastic. "E . . . co . . . lo . . . gi . . . cal. Pa . . . ra . . . mount." She would draw a finger under them.

I loved the big words and repeated them after her. In no time at all I could recognize them on the page. I began to notice patterns, groups of words that appeared over and over again, curves and straight lines that came together and gave me pictures. I was impatient with phonetics, bored with sounding out letters, but words, glowing above my mother's moving finger, opened up worlds, and my imagination soared, unfettered. I inhaled the grit of busy cities, I had climbed to the tops of snowy mountains, I had crossed the great oceans. I had friends in Europe, Africa, Asia, the Caribbean who kept me company when I was lonely.

My mother indulged me, abandoning sounds for sight. I was just three when I pointed to a sentence in her book, reading it aloud to her. I was three and a half when I read a poem my father had written especially for me. By the time Gardner appeared in my front yard, the morning after that terrible storm had left Lucinda easy prey to his devious offers to help us, there was little I could not read.

When I saw Gardner with his measuring tape measuring the house, I hid my mother's books and my father's poems. Lucinda had dismissed my fears and handed over my mother's money and her jewels to Gardner, but I knew better. My books comforted me when Gardner tramped through my house, changing this, changing that, boarding up the carvings my father had designed for me. They let me dream even in my waking hours.

"Bring me your book," I said to Virginia. "I'll show you how."

She brought her book and I showed her how. Like me, a letter by itself was uninteresting to her, the sound it made on its own meaningless. But she saw pictures when I read to her, and eager for more, she followed my fingers, lapping up sentence after sentence as I read. In two weeks she could read the little book Gardner had given to her.

I believe it was not only the pictures she saw when I read to her that caused her to learn to read so quickly. She was relaxed with me. There was no tension vibrating between us, invisible but ever present to intimidate her. She had nothing to prove with me. She knew no matter what, whether she learned to read or not, I would love her.

Always, I had sworn to her when she said *forever,* and she believed me. I think even if her father had said *always* and *forever,* she would not have been so sure, for she seemed to know, even as a small child, that his love had a price.

As Gardner had threatened, he took me to his garden. He was building a growing house at the edge of the backyard, setting the stage for plans he had already begun to put into effect, converting my house and the land it stood on to his idea of paradise, to his England. The week before, a boatload of glass windowpanes in wood frames had arrived. I thought they were for the house but Gardner ordered the men to stack them in the backyard. They were for his plants, he told me.

"Only primitive man accepts life the way Nature has presented it to him," he said. "The civilized man uses his brain to make his world better."

I was facing the sun and when I squinted my eyes to deflect the glare, my eyebrows converged and he mistook my wrinkled brow for the start of a question.

"I'm talking about brains," he explained. "It takes brains, reason, intelligence, to grow flowers that won't wilt in the sun, plants that will live forever." He pointed his finger to his temple and I understood he meant *his* brains, not any ordinary brains. Not my brains, for example. For in the afternoons, after his midday siesta, he went alone to his garden. To think and experiment, he said to me, making it clear that these were realms quite outside my capabilities.

One morning, many weeks later, as I was carrying a bucket of water to him, which he used to water the tiny shoots that had sprung up from the seeds he had planted in boxes, I noticed he was moving his head slightly from side to side. As I got closer, I realized he was humming. It was not a tune I knew, but it had a lilt to it, a merry rhythm that corresponded with the movement of his head on his neck. I was so shocked to see him in such a pleasant mood that I stood rooted to the ground. The last time I had heard him sing (if chanting can be called singing) was when he pranced like a horse around the fire he had made with the pieces of my mother's bed. He motioned to me to come closer, and, apprehensive, though nothing in his face suggested I had any reason to be fearful, I walked slowly toward him. He patted me on my head when I reached next to him. "You're turning out to be quite a helper, Carlos," he said.

I should have known not to trust him, but I was starved for affection and he was praising me, the first time since he had laid eyes on me. My lips stretched back in a wide smile, my teeth glittered in the sun.

"Yes, quite a helper," he said, and dipped his watering cup into the bucket. "Most suited to this work."

I could have burst into tears at that very moment, but I bit down hard on my lip and my tears retreated. I hated the work he was making me do. I hated fetching things for him, standing by his side waiting for his orders: *Fetch the bag of manure. Fetch the spade. Bring me those seeds.* I hated being his servant, and yet, I must confess, I felt an uncanny sense of pride when I worked next to him.

He had given me a uniform that he had ordered from Trinidad. He wore one, too, his, like mine, khakis—khaki shirt, khaki pants—though

I had shorts and he long pants. "Everyone in his place, everything in its time." (He never passed up a chance to reinforce his lesson about the hierarchical order of the social pyramid.)

The garden he was constructing was a laboratory, he said. He was a scientist, not a common gardener. When he was finished, the world would see flowers that man could only dream of now. Foolishly, I allowed myself to be swept by his fantasy into a fantasy of my own: I imagined that he wanted me to bask in the glow of his glory.

He didn't seem to notice my silence when I did not respond to his twisted praise, or perhaps he assumed my concurrence. "My daughter, for example," he continued happily, "is more suited to work indoors. But you, you will make your money with your brawn, Carlos." He poked his finger into my arm, where the weight of the bucket, heavy with water, had caused my puny muscles to rise. I almost lost my balance.

"Steady, boy. Here. Put the bucket down." He took the bucket from me and placed it on the ground. "Books," he sighed, "books can get you in trouble."

I could only assume that he had excluded himself from the *you* that books could harm, for he was always with his books. Even in the garden, in the afternoons when I was not with him, he had his books, the red leather-bound one always with him.

"Look up. Look up," he said. "There's no shame in making your living with your brawn, boy." He clutched my chin roughly and lifted it up. "Good. That's it." Then he surprised me. "Can't tell you the trouble books brought me," he said. His shoulders sagged.

"Trouble?" I didn't believe him.

He bade me pick up the bucket and follow him, and as he watered the seedlings, he told me his story. He said that while he was preoccupied with his books, learning all he could so that he could be the best doctor he was capable of becoming, his brother was betraying him, ingratiating himself with their parents. He told me nothing about the incident at the hospital that made him a man on the run. He said that somehow his brother got his parents to change their will. "He sucked up to them," he said, "and sucked them dry. When they died, all their money and property were his."

"Why didn't you ask the police to help you?" I asked him.

"My brother bribed the police," he said. "He gave them money to keep them quiet."

"Is that why you came here?" I asked.

His eyes darkened. "Get me the trowel," he barked. "Hurry up. Quick, march."

I ran to the shed, scared that I had made him angry. Lucinda, too, had wanted to know, but she had never dared ask why our isolated island when there was England.

I returned with the trowel. He snatched it from my hand and grunted, "I'll tell you since you want to know." He began digging into the dirt, his back toward me. "I wanted to do my part for the Empire. We have a responsibility, a duty, to take care of our colonies. I wanted to fulfill my obligation. That is it." He straightened up. "Take you." He faced me. "I'll teach you a trade. Book learning, my boy, is not all there is." He tapped the trowel against the side of his pants. "My brother had book learning, but book learning is not what made him rich."

"What made him rich?" I asked quietly.

"Cunning." He turned his attentions abruptly to the tiny shoots that had popped up in some of the boxes. Most of them had wilted, their tops hanging limply over their little stalks. "Too much sun," he grumbled. "When I build the growing house, this won't happen." He put down the trowel and lifted up one of the boxes and had me pick up another. "Can't leave them here. Plants need light, but not this burning sun. Come." I followed him to the shed where my father stored his tools. "That's why I need the growing house. Understand?" He didn't wait for an answer. "The windowpanes. You asked about the windowpanes. They are for the roof of the growing house. To control the temperature."

Something fell on the top of my head, a bird's feather perhaps, for suddenly there was a loud cawing above us and a wide swath of green closed up part of the sky. Green-feathered parrots on their way to the mangrove in Trinidad.

Gardner looked up. "Thank God they don't land here," he said, voicing the opposite of what I was thinking.

I scratched my head on the spot where the feather had grazed it. I must have looked particularly stupid doing that because he laughed. "Not to worry," he said. "I need your brawn, not your brains, Carlos."

I helped him put more boxes of seedlings on the makeshift shelf he had built under the tiny apron of the awning where the roof extended past the wood siding of the shed. When we were finished, he began to hum again, the same merry tune he was humming earlier. He was happy. Something had pleased him. What? In a minute he told me.

"She can read," he said. I was walking behind him. He stopped and turned to face me. He was smiling to himself. "Yesterday," he said, "she read a whole book."

I did not know what to say. I could not say I had taught her, that she had learned to read from me. I did not know what he would do if he found out we had been together.

"I don't mean a baby book," he said.

I wiggled my toes in the dirt under my foot.

"*That*, Carlos," he said, repeating the movement of his finger to his temple, this time probing his skin, "takes intelligence."

I pretended with my silence that I had none of that, but a few days later he would decide that I was not as unintelligent as he had assumed, that perhaps brawn was not all I had.

I had taught Virginia one of my favorite poems. It was not one of my father's poems. It was an Englishman's poem, a poem I called my tiger poem. *Tyger! Tyger! burning bright / In the forests of the night*. When I read it to Virginia she loved it, too, and learned it quickly. I had not thought to tell her that she should not recite it in her father's presence. I assumed that she understood, as I had, that her father was not to know I was teaching her. We had always been careful to hide the books I read to her. So I did not believe she intended to have him hear her. She had gone for a walk with her father and the poem spilled out of her mouth by accident, she said. It was too late, after he had heard her, to take it back.

I remember it was a particularly magical night at the end of the dry season, just before the start of the wet. Four days earlier it had rained, not just at midday, which would not have been unusual, but early in the morning, a soft patter at dawn that rocked me deeper into sleep and earned me ten demerits when Gardner banged on my door. And again in the evening it rained, a sudden outburst as though the floor of the heavens had crashed open, weighted down by the tons of water it had stored for weeks. The vegetation, dry, parched, hungrily soaked up the rainwater. Everywhere green shoots sprouted from dry brown stems, and ropes of vine came alive on the tops of tall spreading trees. So it happened on our island at the beginning of the wet season, this sudden blinding blaze of green, overnight it seemed, exhilarating until weeks later, the rain never ceasing, constant, the green turned into a tangle of impenetrable vines, suffocating big trees, drowning weeds and wild grass in the pools of water that collected between stones and boulders, breeding grounds for mosquitoes. But the rain that had fallen four days ago had not returned. The dry season sun had come out and evaporated the dampness, so there was green without the mud, sun-baked air without a drop of moisture in it, and the path leading down to the bay was dry, passable, though gloriously lined with new bushes.

I would have given anything to walk to the bay that night, to feel the crackle of twigs beneath my feet, to see the green flickering in the moonlight, the stars twinkling above in the indigo sky. But I had to help Ariana in the kitchen. Gardner, his own master, was free to do as he pleased, and it pleased him to take Virginia with him on his walk that night. From the kitchen window where I was gazing longingly at the silvery cobwebs the moon had intertwined across the bushes behind Gardner's garden, I saw them coming toward the backdoor, Gardner's stride long and purposeful, Virginia's short and quick, trying to keep up. Gardner stormed into the house and headed for the kitchen. He pulled me by the scruff of my neck and made me stand before him.

"Who taught it to you?" he hollered.

Virginia, by this time, had caught up with him and began to whimper in the background.

" 'Tyger, tyger, burning bright.' Who taught it to you?" Gardner repeated.

He had to know, not Ariana.

"My mother," I said.

"Your mother?" He brought his face close to mine. "The party girl?"

"She taught it to me." My voice shook.

"Blake? She taught Blake to you? Party girl?"

I could smell his breath. Tobacco and ganja.

"He can read, Father," Virginia was saying to him.

"Read?" The word spluttered from his mouth.

"He knows, Father." Virginia tugged his shirtsleeve. "He knows."

"Knows what?"

I do not think I would have had the courage to have persisted if he had looked at me as sternly as he looked at her, but she was not deterred, my brave Virginia. "Big books, Father," she said.

"Big books?"

"His mother showed him how."

"Showed him?" But he was no longer shouting. I think at that moment he was trying to reconcile his picture of my mother, the whore thrown overboard by sailors, with the other picture his daughter was insisting he see.

"I read my mother's books," I said.

"Your mother's books?"

"He has a lot of books, Father."

"Your mother had books?" He licked his lips and passed his hands through his hair.

I nodded.

He pulled a chair out from under the kitchen table and sat down. "Where? When?"

I stumbled through answers. She bought the books in Trinidad, I said. She read them to me.

How did she know about Blake?

She said she read the books in school.

In school?

Virginia had run to my room and now she was back, waving a book in her hand. Blake's *Songs of Experience*. She gave it to her father. "Ask him to read it, Father."

He shoved the book in my direction. I took it from him.

"Tyger, tyger, burning bright / in the forests of the night . . ." I read.

"He memorized it," he said.

"No, Father."

"Turn the page," he ordered me.

I turned it.

"Here. Read this one here."

I read it: "A little black thing among the snow: / Crying 'weep, weep,' in notes of woe! / 'Where are my father and mother? say?' "

He got up, grabbed my arm, and dragged me to his room. "Here. Here." He picked up a thick book that was lying on his bed and opened it. "Read this page here." I read the passage he pointed out to me, struggling with a word or two, but managing to read it correctly though I did not understand a word I read. It was a passage from Shakespeare, a play that was to become my favorite. When I was done, he sat down on his bed and rubbed his chin repeatedly. A strange smile spread across his face, not a smile really, a grimace, as though something deep inside of him was paining him. "Yes, yes," he said. "Yes, yes." Then not to me, nor to Virginia, nor to Ariana, who was now standing in the doorway wringing her hands, he muttered, the smile lines at the corners of his eyes spreading to his temples, "He can read. The little savage can read."

I became his experiment from that day on. And from that day on I no longer hated him. Before he put me out of his room, he swore he would turn me, little savage that I was, into a human. Nature may have destined that I should make my living with my brawn, but with his help we would confound nature, challenge her, make her bend to his will, not to hers. He would succeed where the alchemist had not. He would turn brass into gold.

Something about England, he said. Something about rats' legs and about a serum to grow human limbs. *No matter. No matter.* He shook his head and his eyes grew misty. He drew me to him. I feared he would kiss me and I stiffened, but he stroked me, caressed my cheek, and made much of me. He would teach me new words, he said, so I would know my own meaning. Yes, yes, that was what he would do.

ELEVEN

BUT I KNEW my own meaning, and the English I spoke conveyed well enough to Lucinda and Ariana all that I meant.

It was true that I did not speak like Gardner. I spoke English with an accent like my father's, with a Trinidadian accent. My mother's English was similar to Gardner's, for though she had been raised by an Algerian nanny, her parents were English, and though she had lived in Algeria, it was in an English enclave there. But my mother loved the music of my father's accent and encouraged me to imitate it. When my father died, it was natural for me to continue to speak the way he did. Then, too, Lucinda was taking care of me and Lucinda was Trinidadian. But I picked up habits from her that Gardner despised. I dropped my *th*s, replacing them with *d*s, and my subjects and verbs rarely agreed.

My vocabulary, no doubt, before Gardner taught me, was inadequate, but my thoughts were clear, rational. I knew who I was; I knew what was mine. I did not forget that the house we lived in and the land it stood on were not Gardner's, that my mother had bequeathed them to me. And when I was old enough to understand my father's poetry, I did not forget the warning so evident to me in his verses: The English had not come to save us; the English had not come to help us.

I was standing next to Gardner when he gave his version of how my house became his to the doctor who had allowed him to stay in his house before he occupied mine. Almost a year had passed and this was the first time the doctor had visited my house. He never came when my father was alive nor in the months before and after my mother's death. Lucinda said he was jealous. Not of our new house. He had his own house in Trinidad. Bigger and better furnished than ours, she said.

"Then jealous of what?" I asked her.

"Of your father," she said.

I thought, perhaps, he was in love with my mother but I could not have been more wrong. He hated my mother, and jealousy was the wrong word to use to describe his feelings for my father. He disliked him; he resented him for living with my mother and hated her for sharing her bed. Later, I understood that it was insecurity, fear, that made him a stranger to my house.

The doctor had attempted to come before. More than once since Gardner had moved in with us I had spied him grunting and puffing up our incline to the house. He was a heavy man, short, his legs two stumps that seemed barely able to carry the burden of his huge stomach. He would pick his way through the rough path, grabbing on to the thin stalks of bushes when he stumbled, and then staggering as he tried to prevent himself from falling when the bushes, too weak to bear his weight, bent almost to the ground. Before he was halfway up the path Gardner would see him and he would send me rushing down, always with the same message: He was not there. He was in Trinidad. Another time, perhaps.

I never thought the doctor much minded when I brought him Gardner's lies, for by the time I would reach him, his face would be so red, his clothes so damp with perspiration, his breathing so shallow that he seemed relieved, not unhappy, to turn back.

That day he managed to reach the edge of my front yard before either Gardner or I had seen him. If Gardner was nervous, worried he could ask questions that would leave a trail to his past in England, he did not show it. He greeted the doctor warmly, though I noted that he was careful to keep him on the porch and not allow him inside.

"Never been here before," the doctor said, lowering his body into the rocking chair, "but I can tell you've improved the place."

"I plan to put down a lawn," Gardner said, gesturing to the yard he had cleared of every single bush and tree.

The doctor fanned himself with his hat. "Just that you know, I didn't approve of what was going on here," he said. "I don't condone that kind of behavior."

His condemnation of my parents pleased Gardner immediately. He sent Ariana to fetch them lemonade but he kept me by his side. "This is their bastard. Carlos."

The doctor did not need to be introduced to me. He had seen me often enough, but he shook my hand. "I don't know why she lowered herself like that," he said.

He didn't seem to care that in my presence he was belittling my mother.

"Oh, she was already lowered," Gardner said, and showing an unusual deference to me (for I was sure he had more to say about my mother), he leaned over to the doctor and whispered something in his ear.

"Ahh," the doctor said, straightening up, "but that black man was also too out of place."

"Yes." Gardner grinned wickedly at me.

They had arrived on common ground though different routes had taken them there. I would hear the doctor's expression *Too out of place* many times on my trips to Trinidad and I would know eventually exactly what he meant. My father was too out of place to cohabit with a white woman. He was too out of place to have a child with her.

The doctor was talking about class, of course, but he was also talking about color. The two were intimately intertwined in the Caribbean, threads of the same cloth. To pull one was to loosen the other, to unravel the fabric completely.

Men and women who insisted on behaving like my father and my mother created confusion for people like the doctor. For the doctor was light-skinned and he counted on the value ascribed to his color to bequeath to his children his place in society.

The European colonists had set the rules. They had discovered that they could use gradations in skin color to replicate a class system that would give them ranking impossible for them to attain in their own countries. Here, they realized, color, not bloodlines, could make one a lord. White skin alone was all the credential they needed for entry to the upper class. The rest followed. Light-skinned natives with straight hair got admitted to the upper middle class; brown-skinned natives with curly hair to the middle class, but black-skinned natives with kinky hair found themselves firmly relegated to the lower class. (Years later I was not surprised to discover that Napoléon reintroduced slavery into the Antilles because he was desperate to quell rumors rampant in the English press claiming that black blood flowed in his veins and Josephine's, gossip based solely on the fact that he was born in Corsica and she in Martinique. Napoleon hoped by his cruelty to prove he had no connection to Africans.)

Gardner had no such problem. He was certain he was white, but he also knew that whatever pretense was made in the colonies, in England, where people were white, his skin color had no value. Yet he believed in the absurd notion of race, the classifications of Homo sapiens based on skin color, hair texture, bone structure. He believed my father's black skin determined his nature, "his race," and so made him a different kind of a man, a subcategory of Homo sapiens. My mother could have been rehabilitated, but there was no hope for my father, confined and defined as he was by nature.

"I could never understand why she would want to change the nature of her own child," he said to the doctor.

The doctor was puzzled. "Nature?" he asked.

"Giving her child African blood," Gardner explained.

The doctor's eyes skated over to mine, I thought in fear that I would say something, strip him naked in front of Gardner, reveal him for who he was: a colored man passing. I could tell that African blood ran in his veins. There was too much olive in his skin, and his cheekbones flared in too familiar a way, in the way I remembered my father's.

"So how did you get the house?" The doctor seemed anxious to redirect Gardner's attention. "His mother was already dead before you came, wasn't she?" Then, as if he were afraid of Gardner's answer, he supplied one of his own. "I suppose you had a previous agreement, yes?"

"Yes, a previous agreement. You could say that. She left the house to Lucinda."

To his credit, the doctor's eyebrows shot up. "To her housekeeper?"

"The boy was too young, you see," Gardner said. "He couldn't take on that responsibility. Sylvia gave the house to Lucinda so Lucinda would take care of the boy. And Lucinda, you see, gave . . . No, not *gave*," he said, correcting himself. "Lucinda *sold* it to me."

"Sold it?"

"She was dying. Cancer. I treated her. She was grateful. The money's Ariana's and the boy's, of course," he said, glancing at me, his eyes hardening, challenging me to contradict him. "I use it to take care of them."

"Ahh," said the doctor.

What had made the doctor say *Ahh* so quickly? Why had it taken Gardner so little to satisfy him? I have pondered these questions many times and each time I arrive at the same conclusion: The thread that connected the doctor to whiteness was too flimsy for him to take the chance of alienating the Englishman. He would confirm that he belonged to Gardner's white race by acting as if he believed that knowledge and truth resided with him, that knowledge, truth, intelligence were intrinsically invested in white skin. Even if he doubted Gardner, he would agree with him. He would say *Ahh*.

As the doctor was about to leave, Gardner said something that shocked me. He said he planned to send me to school. My jaw dropped, my eyes rounded in surprise, but the doctor became animated. I think if he had the slightest doubt of Gardner's honesty, the last traces of his uncertainty evaporated when Gardner declared his intentions for me.

"You hear that?" he gushed, turning to me. "School. The nice doctor plans to send you to school."

Even for Gardner the doctor's enthusiasm was too much. "When he is ready," he said sternly.

The doctor reached into his pants pocket and pulled out his hand-kerchief. "I hope you'll show your gratitude," he said, wiping his mouth and narrowing his eyes at me. "Or else, it's off to the orphanage you go."

My mother had read me stories about the horrors of the orphan-age. I did not want to go to the orphanage.

But Gardner had lied. No money had passed from him to Lucinda. All the money he possessed he had stolen from me, money my mother had given to Lucinda to save for me. I believe that even before the storm brought him to our supposed rescue, his mind was churning out his devilish scheme. For my house was magnificent and the doctor's house, where he first stayed, was old and windswept. There were cracks on the concrete pillars, and tufts of tall wild grass grew in spo-radic bunches across the stone-filled dirt yard.

I do not know when Gardner first thought of making his garden, but if it had occurred to him that it would be here, on our isolated is-land, in the tropics, that he could renew himself, start again, at least through his daughter, he must have found the doctor's stony land discouraging. When he climbed up the hill to my parents' house, he must have been pleased to see my father's fruit trees. Perhaps, though he claimed to despise the fruit trees and had cut them down, it was this fact, the existence of the trees, that had given him hope. The doctor's land was useless but above it he believed he would find fertile soil.

How pleased he must have been to learn that my parents were dead. How lucky he was when that storm almost destroyed our tiny is-land. The gods put a gift in his lap; he used it to trick us.

And hadn't his people done it? Hadn't they left icy winds and chilly rains to come here and everywhere the sun warmed the land? Hadn't they found righteous reasons to justify what they had done?

The first lesson Gardner taught me, when he discovered that I could read and decided he would give me the means to express my own meaning, was about the right of his people, their manifest destiny, to rule the world. He spread a map of the world before me. "Here. Here. There." With the tips of his fingers he jabbed at spots on the map: India, China, Africa, the lands of the Turks and the Arabs, islands and continents spread apart by the great seas and oceans. His people had brought civilization everywhere, he said. "Without us, these places you see would have nothing."

In the years that followed, I learned to wear a mask over my face, an invisible barrier that Gardner could not see. At first, I did not wear this mask to deceive him; I wore it because I wanted to please him. I did not want my face to register my anger when my blood churned from something he said or something he ordered me to do, or to reveal the loathing in my heart when, forgetting his oath, he called me his savage. I wanted to reassure him, I wanted him to feel secure in his presumptions, convinced of his superiority over me and people who looked like me. For he had much to teach me and I was eager to learn. I made a bargain with him in my mind: in exchange for knowledge, I would let him presume. I would let him believe that he understood me better than I understood myself, that he knew my desires before I knew them myself, that he could predict my ambitions, my dreams, the things I would want, the things I would fear, the things I would like or dislike. He could show me who I was and what I was capable of becoming. He could write a book about me and teach me about myself.

He never suspected me. He was too certain of himself, too enamored with the project he had conceived to reinvent me, to care how I felt or if he offended me. I was his chance to redeem himself after his failed experiments in England. He was determined to civilize me, to improve my coarse nature.

The daily schedule he set for me was different now. He wanted me to have time to read the books he assigned me and to be free in the evenings to study with him. I was no longer required to help Ariana in the kitchen or with her housework. I had to wake up earlier, at four in the morning, and go with him to the garden. We returned for breakfast, after which he tutored Virginia in his bedroom for an hour, and then I went back with him to the garden until lunchtime.

But he did not change his habit of napping after lunch, nor of requiring Ariana to spend an hour with him in his bedroom.

When he woke, he returned to the garden. He did not take me with him. I did not know what he did when he went to the garden. I knew he took his gnarled cane with him and his book, the one bound in red leather and embossed with gold letters. Many times, looking up from my books, I saw him dancing around the flower beds, the velvet cloak he had worn that evening when he frightened me flapping in the wind over his back, the cane raised high in one hand, the red leather book in the other.

I never asked him what he did in the garden alone, or why he did not require my help. I was happy to be left with my books, happy to be relieved of the backbreaking work he made me do. For in the garden I was his servant, his slave. He gave orders, I obeyed them even when sweat blinded my eyes, my back ached, my shoulders sagged, and the muscles in my arms and legs tore at the ligaments. I plowed beds for his flowers, planted seedlings, fetched buckets of water, carried bags of manure on my back, nailed, hammered, lifted heavy planks of wood, whatever he demanded. If I was slow, if I didn't fetch and carry fast enough for him, he called me names: tortoise, which irked me but never as much as when he yelled "Slave!" or when, fully aware of the pain he caused me, he screamed out "Hagseed," reminding me, in spite of her books, her education, her British upbringing, what he thought of my mother. It was hard then to keep my tongue in my mouth, yet I did not complain though my blood boiled. I did not complain because while I worked, he talked. He opened up worlds to me. He convinced me that I was with him on the threshold of scientific discoveries that would make it possible to grow sturdier and more beautiful flowers, flowers that could survive a brutal sun or drought that lasted for weeks. "Breeding," he said. "It's all about good breeding. Breeding until you achieve the perfect specimen."

I was not deterred though I had no doubt that he also wanted me to understand that he was breeding me. My seed might have been planted in a hag, but his nurture would make me better than my mother.

He showed me how to create a new flower by grafting the stem of one flower onto the stem of another; how to do the bee's work and spread pollen from one plant onto the stamen of another. But I did not believe that grafting and cross-pollinating were the only magic he used to change the texture of petals on roses, to make bougainvillea bloom in colors that were shocking to me—the polka dots and the stripes especially—or to grow the strange new grass that was springing up in the front yard. I suspected there was more he could tell me. I had my theories but I had never recovered from my initial fear of his book, his cape, and his cane, so I kept my suspicions to myself. I did not pry though I was sure that he did not want me with him when he went to the garden alone because there was power in that cape and in that cane and in the words written down in his red leather-bound book, and he did not want to share that power with me.

He would, he swore, civilize me, but he had set limits, a ceiling beyond which he firmly excluded me. Whatever was written in his red leather-bound book, whatever knowledge it contained that gave him the ability to make flowers and grass bend to his will was knowledge he wanted to keep from me.

And yet he taught me much more than about plants. While I worked, he taught me about astronomy, about the sun and the moon (about which I already knew much), but more than that, about the smaller planets, the ones twinkling in the darkened sky and the ones I could not see. I learned the basics of biology from him and the fundamentals of chemistry. He introduced me to physics and the laws of mathematics. In the evenings, after dinner, and after he had sent Virginia to her bedroom, he spent hours with me playing the music he loved on his gramophone. He conducted when we listened to Mozart or Beethoven or Chopin or Tchaikovsky, and I would lose myself in the sweep and sway of singing instruments, but he wanted me to know their individual sounds. In time he opened up my ears so that I was able to distinguish the cello among the strings, to hear the violin under the viola, to identify the flute and the piccolo among the woodwinds, to pick out French horns from trombones, trombones from tubas, English horns from oboes.

He was especially affected by Beethoven's *Eroica* symphony. Many times I saw a tear roll down his cheek when the needle moved to the adagio, and, it seemed to me, as the somber beat of the funeral march filled the room, that he was in the grip of a memory, mourning the loss of someone he once loved. It did not take long for me to conclude that that someone was his wife, for when we listened to the operas he loved, he would close his eyes and, clutching the ends of his collar, he would pull them tightly together across his neck and sigh. "Only the Italians," he would say, "know the sweet pain of love."

I did not understand a word of the arias he played on his gramophone and yet when a voice swelled to bursting, I was moved, too, as he was, every fiber of my being consumed by feelings I could not explain.

O mio babbino caro.

The music would transform him. The muscles in his face would slacken, and the furrows, seemingly permanent between his eyebrows, would disappear. He was a young man again. I could not find on his face the markings of the bitter despot who was always on a mission to search out disease in every natural thing, or the stern taskmaster who regulated my every day, my every hour.

> *e se l'amassi indarno,*
> *andrei sul Ponte Vecchio,*
> *ma per buttarmi in Arno!*

I would think it was madness that had made me see a devil when he came to my yard after the storm. Madness or a mind not yet healed from my mother's blank eyes, her indifferent dismissal of me, her grief-stricken face before she turned away from me. On those occasions when I witnessed the effect that music had on him, he seemed a gentle man, a kind man, a compassionate man. I could not imagine then such a man capable of the cruelties he was yet to inflict on me.

Sometimes, instead of listening to music, our evenings were spent discussing books he had me read in the afternoons while he was in his garden. He talked endlessly of Shakespeare and Milton, the giants, he said, of all literature written in English, whether American or Canadian. He would quote *Lycidas* to me when he felt the need to explain, when the questions in my eyes pushed him to explain, why he had chosen here, our tiny island, a leper colony, with no running streams, no rivers, to build his botanical laboratory.

Fame is no plant that grows on mortal soil.

He would shake his head and cast his eyes upward, as if to the heavens, when he recited that line. The timbre of his voice would change; it would darken and grow soulful. And hearing him recite Milton, I would forget the man I knew, the man who loved me to flatter him, the man whose ambition, as he reminded me constantly, was to surprise the world with the strange flowers he created. It was not hard then for me to fool myself into thinking of him as he wanted me to think of him: as a spiritual man, a man who did not care for praise, for earthly recognition.

He had me memorize long passages from the works he admired and on our walks at night I repeated them for him, giving him much pleasure, and, I will admit, myself much pleasure and comfort, too. For there were times, especially in my late adolescence, when black clouds pressed upon me and I fell deep into the clutches of an over-whelming grief and longing for parents I had only known briefly. These times came mostly on dark nights when rain thundered inces-santly, drumming a funeral beat on the rooftop. Then I was glad for lines he had had me memorize:

> But when the melancholy fit shall fall
>> Sudden from heaven like a weeping cloud,
>> That fosters the droop-headed flowers all,
>>> And hides the green hill in an April shroud;
>> Then glut thy sorrow on a morning rose,
>>> Or on the rainbow of the salt sand-wave,
>>> Or on the wealth of globéd peonies

I did not know the green hill, a meadow I supposed the poet had in mind. I knew thick forest trees and entangling vines, greens in shapes and shades fanciful and bright, though others so dark, so dense, they could fill me with dread. The rain on my rooftop was not so gentle as an April shower, but it, too, like the poet's rain, set me off to mourn-ing. And though I had no morning roses or globéd peonies, I had the smell of the sea, the salt sand-wave, the rainbow. And I would think of them and find comfort in the poet's verse.

The education I was getting from Gardner was British; it was Euro-pean. But the poems spoke to me and I found myself in them. It bothered me, of course, that Gardner rarely mentioned Africa, that he said not a kind word about the Amerindians who originally populated the islands. On the rare occasions when he did, he made me understand that my history, the history of my island and the islands in the Caribbean, began with him, began with his people. Before the arrival of his people we were nothing—wild, savage creatures who had accomplished nothing, achieved nothing, had made not one iota of contribution to the advancement of human civilization. But I was too eager to learn, too greedy for the knowledge he was giving me to fault him, and for years I forgave him. For years I was grateful.

I look back now and it amazes me that I allowed myself to be so grateful, that I submitted myself to such an exclusively European education, willingly taking the risk of losing faith in my people, respect for the traditions of my forefathers. The year Trinidad gained its independence from England a famous Trinidadian writer living in England published a book about our history. "How can the history of this West Indian futility be written?" he asked, his question resonating with the scorn I had heard in Gardner's voice. "Brutality is not the only difficulty. History is built around achievement and creation; and nothing was created in the West Indies."

TWELVE

I GAVE BACK what I could. I showed Gardner my secret places on the island. I took him over the barbed-wire fence the Americans had built that stretched across the middle of the island from Rust's Bay, near where we lived, around the leprosarium, and down to Perruquier Bay, a mile or so north of the nuns' quarters.

The Americans had come to Trinidad during the war when England was in trouble. Twelve thousand acres they got in exchange for fifty battleships, none new. We were an English colony. There was no need to get our permission. Twelve thousand acres cut across central Trinidad at Waller Field, and along the northwest coast in Chaguaramas, and on the north of Chacachacare, our little island.

We would have been safe from the Germans if it were not for the oil belt sliding under the sea from Venezuela into the south of Trinidad. When their tanks ran dry, German U-boats trolled the Caribbean Sea, searching desperately for fuel.

Naïvely, Trinidad believed it was protected. The Dragon stood guard at the entrance of the Gulf of Paria, and La Remous swirled through her teeth, currents and countercurrents slamming violently into each other, catapulting against the sheer cliffs and tumbling back down like a cataract, the sea turning into a seething pool that rushed with breakneck speed in and out of crevices in the rocks.

Then, one night, under the cover of a starless sky, a German U-boat sneaked into the Port of Spain harbor. Days later, a German officer produced a movie stub from the Globe, a cinema in the heart of the city. He had eaten well, gone to the movies, slept with a woman, he boasted. All done under the eyes of English and American soldiers.

The Americans wasted no time. They laid down mines. La Remous fought back. Cables snapped like dry twigs in her powerful hands. Mines broke free and curled down her whirlpool. Days later, La Remous vomited them in the Atlantic. Some drifted as far as Cuba. Ships and schooners exploded, not all of them the enemy's. One, a wedding party from Grenada, blown to bits, not a single person spared. The Dragon licked its lips and swallowed.

Before the Americans went back home, they swept the ocean. Thirty-five mines had escaped the Dragon. Or so the Americans believed. Not so the nuns, who, though they dreamed of more space for their leprosarium, feared to go beyond the American barrier.

But my father had taken me there. I had ridden on his shoulders when he cut his way through the fence to the road that led to the lighthouse on the highest point, on the north shore of the island. It was from there I first saw La Remous. Years later, whenever I heard her terrifying growl as she swooped through the Dragon's teeth, I would think of the witches' cauldron in *Macbeth*, the sea its lethal brew, bubbling, boiling.

I told Gardner I could take him to the lighthouse. I said that even if some mines had washed up on the beach, it was impossible for any of them to be near the lighthouse, for the lighthouse was on high ground, at the top of the tallest point on the island. He pestered me with questions about land mines, but I reasoned with him that the Americans had no cause to plant land mines. They had their guns trained on the sea; they could shoot the enemy down.

What about the lighthouse? he asked me. I answered that the Dragon took care of the lighthouse. He would see, when he got there, that though at first the land sloped gently downward, after a few yards it fell with a sheer drop into the Dragon's Mouth.

He was satisfied, eager to hear more, pleased when I told him about the barracks the Americans had built. Nine in all, one not far from where we lived, in the bushes, in the back of my house. When I took him there, he ripped off wood, metal, and glass for his greenhouse. A few weeks later, he wanted me to take him to the lighthouse.

The Americans had built a paved road to the lighthouse that began at Perruquier Bay, almost opposite to where we were, behind Rust's Bay. To reach the paved road, we had to pass along a dirt road, in front of the leper colony. Gardner never wanted to be anywhere near the leper colony. He acknowledged that it wasn't as easy, as was rumored, to catch the disease, but he was unwilling to take chances with his life and his daughter's life. He didn't want to bring germs back with him to the house, he said. So we went the way I had gone with my father to the lighthouse, up the hill following the trail that connected the barracks, until near the top we branched off and took the paved road.

It was not an easy climb. It had been years since the Americans had been on the island, and few had used that path since then. It was overgrown with razor grass. Branches of trees, given free rein, dipped down low over us, but in between the canopy of green leaves were splashes of color: bouquets of tiny orange berries; pink, yellow, red, lavender flowers. I spotted a savonnetta tree, stunning with its translucent leaves and purplish flowers. The wood the carpenter had used to carve out birds and flowers in the panels in my house had come from the savonnetta, but I did not tell Gardner that when I pointed out the tree. I did not want him cutting it down for floorboards or using it to make himself a desk or a chair or some other piece of furniture for the house. I warned him, though, about the poisonous manchineel tree. I had seen the berries scattered on the top of the incline ahead of us. They were small, no more than an inch in diameter, greenish-yellow, apple-shaped. *Little green apples.* He must have thought so, too, for when one of them tottered at the edge and began to roll downward, he broke away from me and ran toward it. "Apples." The word fluttered out of his mouth, nostalgia so gripping his heart that he seemed to have forgotten where he was, his war with tropical fruits smothered in that moment. "No! No!" I shouted as he lunged for it. "Stop!" I slapped my hand around his wrist.

I startled him. He jumped back, but he recovered instantaneously. "Don't you ever." He shook his finger at me. "Don't you ever raise your voice at me." His bottom lip was trembling.

Out of perversity, for I was certain he understood that I was trying to warn him about the danger of touching the fruit of the manchineel, or, perhaps, because he saw another occasion to drive home to me that he was the master and I his underling, he stuck out his hand again. I pulled it back.

"No! Don't touch it." I tightened my grasp. "It will make you sick."

Did he thank me?

I told him that even water falling off the leaves of the manchineel would leave blisters on his skin. He took out his handkerchief and wiped his hands, inside and outside, over and over again obsessively. When he was done, he handed the handkerchief to me.

"Tell Ariana to wash it," he said, then changed his mind. "No, tell her to burn it."

Did he thank me? Suppose he had bitten into the berry, suppose it had not only given him blisters but cramps that twisted his stomach into knots. Suppose it had poisoned him fatally.

"Everything on this island is diseased," he said bitterly. He berated himself for his moment of weakness, for allowing nostalgia to betray him.

We saw huge green iguanas on the dirt trail, the spikes on their backs metallic armor. They flicked their long tails and stared at us, the covering over their large protruding eyes opening and shutting like blinkers. I did not think they would move but Gardner stamped his cane into the ground and in an instant they were gone.

Several times we heard swishing sounds in the bushes near us. Something moving under the trees. A snake? The possibility that he might have been poisoned by a manchineel berry had shaken Gardner, but a snake gave him not a moment's trepidation.

We saw the pointed red cap of the lighthouse first, with the weather vane at its peak, a fish made out of black wrought iron, an arrow for its head. Below it, the glass circular enclosure gleamed in the sun behind an iron railing at the edge of a narrow platform. As we got closer, we could see the white tower clearly, thick and solid except for a single opening, a sliver of glass, like an elongated eye, glinting under the platform. The lighthouse keeper was sitting on the green ledge at the base of the lighthouse. As soon as he spied us, he jumped up and came running toward us, his face a ripple of wide grins.

"Don't have many people coming up here." He slapped my back so hard I reached over my shoulders to massage it. "Just me and my partner," he said to Gardner and held out his hand. Gardner shook it but not with the same enthusiasm.

"I so glad to see you. Is only two of us and the sea. It get lonely here."

Gardner wasted no time. "Just the two of you?" He was looking up at the lighthouse, his face twitching with nervous excitement. It occurred to me that had I been able to see him when he first set eyes on my mother's house, I would have witnessed the same twitching, the same nervousness, the same restrained excitement on his face.

"My partner gone to La Tinta."

La Tinta Bay. It was south of where we were, named by the Spanish settlers for its black sand that made the water seem the color of ink. My father used to fish in La Tinta Bay but he had never taken me there.

"And left you all alone?"

"We have to eat," the lighthouse keeper shrugged. "Two weeks we stay here at a time. Somebody have to fish."

"Why not fish here?"

"You ever eat La Tinta fish? Sweetest in the world. And don't talk about crab. They big like lobster at La Tinta." He opened his arms wide.

"Big like that?" I asked, amazed, my arms extended wider than his.

Gardner kicked my foot and looked sternly at me. "How long does he stay there?" he asked.

The lighthouse keeper, momentarily confused, looked from me to Gardner and back again.

"Your partner," Gardner said and drew back his attention. "How long does he stay at La Tinta?"

"Is he you want to see?"

I was looking around me. All the trees my father had planted, all the trees Gardner had cut down, all here: mango trees, breadfruit trees, guava trees, pawpaw trees, lime trees. In a square patch of dirt bordered by planks of wood, not far from the lighthouse, were the brittle stems of dead plants. Tomato or peppers, I thought.

"We does grow our food, too," the lighthouse keeper said, pleased with my interest. "Pigeon peas, tomato, cabbage, things like that. Onliest problem, we have to wait for rain."

Gardner did not have to wait for rain. He stored his rainwater. Created it, my childish mind had once fantasized, awed by all that green in our front yard, even in the dry season.

"When are you expecting him?" Gardner's head was tilted back on his neck, his eyes fixed on the top of the lighthouse.

"My partner?" The lighthouse keeper turned away from me.

"Yes. When?" Gardner was getting impatient.

"Late, late. Sometime he stay at La Tinta whole day. Come back late evening. You know him?"

"No, no," Gardner said quickly. "I came to see the lighthouse. Can you let me in?"

"It never lock. Excepting if both me and my partner gone."

"So you can take me inside?"

"Yes. Come with me rong the corner."

We walked behind him and he led us to the other side of the lighthouse, to a tall, enormous, weather-beaten wood door. Just as he was about to open it, he shook his head sadly. "Not many people does come here," he said. "I tell you it does really get lonely sometimes."

Gardner thought it wise to sympathize. "But you have the sea," he said.

"It pretty now, but don't come back when it storm. Sometimes the lightning here come so fast, the night never have a chance to get dark."

How could I have known that the lighthouse keeper's words were just what Gardner was hoping to hear?

We followed the lighthouse keeper up the narrow black spiral staircase in the middle of the lighthouse tower. At the top were huge round plates of glass that revolved behind a circular glass wall when the light was turned on at night. Along one side of the walls, rising slightly above the floor, was another door, a short, metal one, thick and heavy as the door on a vault, barely wide enough for a man to squeeze through but only if he bent on all fours. When the lighthouse keeper opened it, the wind rushed in, howling and baying.

Gardner was the first to go through the tiny door to the ledge outside. I followed. Over the roar of the wind, I heard him chant: "All this, all this." He was leaning against the railing, the wind whipping his body into a flagpole, his shirt and pants like sails flung stiffly out behind him. Below us was the fourth boca of the Dragon's Mouth, the widest of the four mouths of the Dragon yet no less treacherous. Waves slammed into rocks that rose dark and jagged above the surface waters, pitching white foam high in the air that bounced back down, striking rock and water with ferocious force.

All this, all this.

In the background, the mountains of Venezuela, seemingly within touching distance, and to the north, the Atlantic.

All this, all this.

And it seemed to me that at that moment Gardner believed that the boca, the rocks, the mountains behind them, the ocean, everything, all he could see, belonged to him.

Gardner allowed me to accompany him to the lighthouse one more time. He brought the cane with the prancing centaurs with him and a bag, which he slung over his shoulder. At the paved road he told me to stay behind, but I did not obey him. When I was sure he could not see me, I followed him. Near the lighthouse, I hid behind a tree. I saw him give something to the lighthouse keeper, money perhaps. They laughed and shook hands. Then the lighthouse keeper disappeared into his house. Moments later, he reappeared with a tackle box in his hand and headed in the opposite direction, down the path, not far from where I was hiding. When he turned the bend in the road, I walked around to where the lighthouse faced the sea and crouched in the bushes. I knew what Gardner would do. I had seen the glee on his face when he called into the wind: *All this. All this.* I looked up to the iron railing and waited. I didn't have long to wait. I saw him crawl out of the tiny opening, his cape draped over his shoulders, his book and cane in his hands. I saw him lean forward against the railing. The wind rose under his cape. A wing. A bird. That was what he looked like to me: a giant bird of prey, unnatural in color, unnatural in its singular wing. A red corbeau, one-winged.

Gardner went to the lighthouse alone after that. Each time he returned exhausted, his eyes glassy, his limbs limp, his skin pale. He collapsed into his bed and slept for hours. Whenever a rainstorm threatened, he became agitated. Before the first drop fell, he was off again to the lighthouse, his bag on his back, the cane in his hand. As irrational as it seemed to me then, I found myself thinking that it was he, not nature, who had caused that terrible storm that had brought him to us, he who had engineered it.

But of all my secret places I showed to Gardner, the one he loved me best for was the cove, near Rust's Bay, hidden behind a hill of rocks. I had not discovered it on my own. The horseshoe shoreline of Chacachacare Bay was pocketed with tiny coves and bays. Bushes and trees grew so close to their edges it was not easy to see them. I would never have found this cove if one of the lepers had not taken me there. Like most of the lepers, he distrusted Europeans, though not European women. The French nuns had been kind to them. Most of the doctors, he complained, had prizes on their minds. Even after everyone knew that the sulfuric drugs were working and every day patients in the colony were getting better, there were still doctors who wanted to inject them with oils.

"Treat us like guinea pigs," he said. "They don't care whether we live or die."

He loved my mother. She gave him fish from my father's catch. On the day of her funeral, he presented me with an exquisite flower, an orchid so dazzlingly white I had to shade my eyes. He could show me where the others were, he whispered. The next day he took me to the cove beyond the rocks.

When Gardner told me that his greatest wish was to grow the rarest orchid in the world, I told him I knew where he could find an orchid tree. He laughed at me. "Orchids are flowers," he said, "not trees."

One startlingly clear night, when he was especially pleased with my recitation from one of his favorite books, he agreed to humor me. In the silvery light of the moon, the orchids gleamed like stars on the spreading branches at the top of a tall cedar tree, roots piercing the bark like crab claws, and beneath them, more roots, long, brown, spindly, dangling in the air. Gardner was overjoyed. Epiphytes, he said they were, not parasites. And for the second time since I had known him, he spoke of his brother. He was the parasite, he said, his chest heaving with his agitation. He had wrapped himself around him, he said, like the tendrils of a malignant ivy.

When his breathing slowed again, he put his arm around my shoulders and hugged me. It had taken these orchids years to bloom. Generations. He would make history. He pulled me close to him and he thanked me. He said he loved me, and though, inexplicably, at that very moment the leper's words rang in my ears (guinea pigs, he called the doctors), I said I loved him, too.

Before he eventually decided he could trust me to go alone, Gardner took me with him when he went to Trinidad to shop for food or materials for the house and his garden. I did not think he took me with him because he was afraid to leave me alone in the house with Virginia. That likelihood did not occur to me until years later, when he accused me of attempting to rape her.

At first I thought he wanted me to accompany him because he was afraid of the boca. He had seen La Remous, and though the boatman who brought us to Trinidad always chose his times carefully when there was little chance of La Remous churning the sea to a frenzy, Gardner still gritted his teeth and held on tightly to his seat each time the wash from the third boca flung the boat up with the tremendous waves and slammed it back down on the water. The boatman's insouciance did not help. "Is a little ting!" he would say when he saw Gardner crouched in his seat. If Gardner protested, he would throw back his head and laugh out loud, exposing his chalk-white teeth. "You 'fraid a little ting like that?"

It was not always a little thing. Sometimes the waves were mountainous and the descent so steep and so sudden that I, too, feared for our lives, but these were the times that the boatman became most animated. *"Oui Foute!"* he would shout, stretching his hand over the water and pointing. "See that wave! Wait, wait. Another one! *Oui Foute, Pappy-O!"* There were other times, though, noticing the white ring that formed around Gardner's mouth, that he had the good sense to calm down, but his solicitude seemed to irritate Gardner more than his preening. "Yuh belly go settle down when we reach the shore," he would say to Gardner, offering him a pail and a rag. "If you have to trow up, trow up."

I soon concluded, however, that Gardner took me with him not so much because he was afraid of the boca but because he wanted me to protect him in Trinidad. He told me there were too many darkie beggars there. My job, he seemed to imply, was to keep the darkies away from him. I did not know that he had a more urgent reason for avoiding Trinidad, that he feared discovery.

On one of our trips we ran into the commissioner. The commissioner had heard about the English doctor who was living on Chacachacare and he was anxious to meet him. Would he come to tea next week? he pressed Gardner. Or any time that was convenient for him?

Gardner said yes. He said he would come the next time he returned to Trinidad, but on the boat back home he laughed when he told me he would never accept the commissioner's invitation. He had no time for frivolities, he said.

I was astounded. "You must go," I urged him. "You must. He could help you find your brother. He could track him down and get back your money."

Did I hope that if Gardner recovered his money he would have no need of mine? I am sure that was part of my motivation, why I continued to beg him until he shook me so violently by my shoulders I thought my neck would snap. Never, never, he made me swear. Never say a word to anyone about the story he had told me about his brother.

We saw the commissioner from time to time when we went to Trinidad, but he was never able to persuade Gardner to come to tea at his home or to visit him in his office at the police station. Gardner was always ready with the excuse that he needed to get back early for his precious plants. When the commissioner asked: Isn't it a bit desolate out there, old man? Gardner had a quick response. He was doing important research on tropical flowers, he said. The climate and terrain in Chacachacare were exactly what he needed. He liked the remoteness of the island. He didn't want people poking around and stealing his ideas.

How did you manage to get Sylvia's house? (The commissioner asked this question without malice or accusation.) Gardner's answer was the same as the one he had given to the doctor, and, like the doctor, the commissioner praised me for having the good fortune to be under the protection of an Englishman. I was lucky, he said. The orphanage in Trinidad was not a nice place to be.

One day Gardner surprised me by announcing that the time was right for me to leave the island to go to secondary school in Trinidad. I had never believed his promise to the doctor, but as we were returning on the boat from a shopping trip in Trinidad, he declared suddenly that I needed to go to school to be with other boys. My first instinct when he made this offer was not to trust him. I had grown quite tall for my age and looked like a man. I thought Gardner was beginning to worry that I could get it in my head to call him a liar, claim my mother's inheritance, and throw him out of my house.

He had good reason to think so. Often when we walked down Frederick Street in Trinidad, we saw crowds gathered in Woodford Square. Always there was a man with the wire of a hearing aid dangling from his ear, speaking from a platform under a flamboyant tree. I never could make out the exact words he said—something about black, something about power—but I felt his passion, and when the crowd broke into a roar, I wanted to hear more. Gardner, however, would not let me stay. I found out from the shopkeeper the name of the man who seemed to have a mesmerizing hold on the people there. Eric Williams. *De Doctah*. He had come from America, where he had been teaching at Howard University. He was an Oxford man, the shopkeeper said proudly. Got his doctor title from Oxford.

Gardner told me he did not like this Eric Williams. Stirring up trouble in Trinidad, he said. If the British left, how would the darkies know how to run the government?

If the British left? I was old enough to know that in the past Europeans had made a fortune on our island from cotton and whale oil. That Sir Walter Raleigh's ships would have sunk if the Amerindians had not taken him to La Brea Pitch Lake in Trinidad, where there was more tar than he ever could have imagined, tons more than he needed to caulk his leaking ships. That in the following years the British had worked Africans almost to death on sugarcane and cocoa plantations, and that even as we spoke, British Petroleum, Shell Oil, Esso, and Texaco were drilling oil out of the ground in the south of Trinidad.

If the British left? We would be rich. That was what I thought.

Now he was saying to me that I would love living in Trinidad. "Thank God the British are still there."

"Why would I like it?" I asked him cautiously.

"Why? To be with boys your age," he said.

"I don't need to be with boys my age. They aren't as smart as you," I said.

He grinned. I could tell he was flattered, and I flattered him some more. "Nobody in Trinidad can teach me more than you do," I said.

"But you only have me for company," he protested unconvincingly.

"Nobody knows more than you," I said. I was not lying. I believed there was no one as intelligent or as knowledgeable as he, no one from whom I could learn as much as I was learning from him. But my house was also very much on my mind. Perhaps he was not thinking: *This is it. He'll be gone. This is all I need to do and the house will be all mine.* Yet I was not going to take the chance that that was not his true motive.

"You'll need friends your own age," he said. "The lepers cannot count."

"No, the lepers cannot count," I conceded.

They liked me, but they felt self-conscious with me, more aware of their deformities when they saw me whole, healthy, my arms and legs strong and muscular. Not long after Gardner arrived, they stopped speaking to me altogether. They knew Gardner had only scorn for them. He was always warning me to stay away from them, warning

Ariana not to let Virginia go too far from the house for fear she could get infected. Not wanting to give him reason to lose his trust in me, which every day I could see I was gaining, I never crossed the border that separated our part of the island from the leper colony without his permission. I wondered often, though, how he had been allowed to be a medical doctor, how someone with so little compassion for the sick could have been given this license.

Ariana once told Gardner the story about the priest who used to say Mass in the chapel when the nuns were here. The priest had come into the kitchen just as the cook had turned off the stove and removed the pot that was on it. As he began to give her instructions for a luncheon he was going to have the next day with some visitors from Europe, the priest leaned against the stove and rested his hand on the hot burner. The cook screamed, and the priest looked at her, puzzled. "What? What?" he asked. Then he saw that the skin on his hand had withered and turned bloodred.

For weeks after Ariana told him this story, whenever she brought him his tea, Gardner would place his hand around the boiling hot teapot. "Ouch!" he would say melodramatically. A doctor, but this was the test he used to assure himself that his nerve ends were not damaged, that he had not contracted leprosy.

"Still, there is Ariana," he was now saying to me.

"Ariana is silly," I said.

He laughed, more than my comment warranted, I remember thinking.

"What could I talk about with Ariana?" I said.

"What indeed?" But his face had flushed red.

I took notice that he did not mention his daughter. He did not say, *But there is Virginia. You have her company.* He said he loved me, yet he had never recanted the first lesson he had taken pains to teach me with a bundle of sticks.

I could tell, though, he was pleased with me. Before we stepped off the boat at Chacachacare, he paid me what he must have believed was the highest compliment. I was better than my mother, he said. My mother was a woman, but still she was English. You are brighter and more intelligent, he said.

He never again offered to send me away to school. I had so convinced him that I was grateful to him and he could depend on my loyalty that he let me go alone to Trinidad to shop for him, certain I would return, certain I would bring back his goods and his money. *My goods, my money.* Certain he could trust me to be his servant.

THIRTEEN

*O*N VIRGINIA'S twelfth birthday, Gardner called Ariana into the
dining room and announced that Virginia had learned all that
was necessary for a woman to learn. Anything more would make her
unmarketable. It was Ariana's turn to train her.

I should have suspected that that day would come. Until then, Gardner had given Virginia her schooling in his room. He had not allowed
her to join us in the evenings in the drawing room or to accompany us
on our walks at night. I assumed he thought I was unworthy to spend
such long hours in his daughter's company, but Virginia disagreed. She
repeated what she had told me that first day when I had offered to
teach her to read. "He thinks I am stupid." I stuck to my convictions,
though I also believed that it was not so much that he doubted her intelligence as that he had other plans for her. Still, I was surprised that
he was willing to relinquish some of the control he exercised over her.

Under the pretext that he was protecting her from contracting leprosy, Gardner had confined her world to short distances just beyond
my house. She could not go anywhere close to the area where the
Americans had abandoned their barracks, not even to the barbed-wire

boundary of the leper colony. She could go for walks with Ariana when the sun went down in the late afternoon, but only to the end of the path that led to the pebble-stone beach near the doctor's house. No matter how hot it got, she could go in the water only on Sundays, and then under two conditions: one, that the doctor was on the mainland with his family, and two, that Gardner had the time to accompany her. And since Gardner had made up his mind not to return to Trinidad, she could not leave the island.

Ariana was angry to be given another task. Train her how? she asked Gardner. In the domestic arts, he said. Show her how to cook, how to sew, how to keep a well-ordered house.

He meant to compliment her, but Ariana was not complimented. "What I teach her that for?" she asked sullenly. "When she get married she have servant to cook and clean for her."

I braced myself for Gardner's response, but he spoke to her with infinite patience, as if to a friend with whose opinions he disagreed but nonetheless tolerated. "Teach her so she knows what orders to give her servants," he said.

It struck me later that his tone was not so much one that a friend might use, but rather that of an indulgent husband, for his voice was weighted with much forbearance that sounded to me strangely like the rhythms of courtship. Ariana could have been a wife whose temper tantrums he knew to come and go like a sudden downpour at midday. By evening her mood would change.

"Do it for me, Ariana."

Ariana bunched her lips together and sucked in air through her teeth. *Steups.* A sound of dismissal and utter contempt. It had come to the Caribbean with the Africans. Yet Gardner grinned at her.

When we were alone she complained about her new assignment. "If she slice something and cut her hand with a knife, who you think he blame but me?"

That was when I gave her my name for Gardner. "He thinks he's Prospero," I said.

She liked the sound of the name. She linked it to another word she knew: *prosperous.* "He get prosperous when he fool my mother," she said bitterly.

I never told Ariana where I got my name for Gardner, and the truth was that though the pages were wide open for me to read them, and every day I saw more and more of Prospero in Gardner, I did not believe I was in danger. I did not think he would imprison me or torture me, as Prospero had done to Caliban.

I was not blind to his devious intentions. I saw his ambition clearly. His interest in me, as in his flowers, was scientific. I had piqued his curiosity. But in those days of my delusions, I also allowed myself to hope that somewhere in his heart he believed I could, with his instruction, with his help, become his intellectual equal.

Sometimes when he asked my opinion of books I had read he would listen so closely to what I had to say that it was easy to indulge myself in this fantasy, but there was a price to pay for this indulgence.

"What do you think of Macbeth?" he asked me one evening. "I mean the man, not the play."

Macbeth had killed a king. *I am in blood / Stepp'd in so far that, should I wade no more, / Returning were as tedious as go o'er.* But Gardner liked when I argued the side that was the opposite of an obvious position, and, uncertain of his motive, I pandered to him. "Isn't ambition a good thing?" I asked him.

"A good thing?" We were on the path walking down to the bay. The moon had slipped behind a cloud, and darkness had fallen over us suddenly, like a heavy cloak.

"Without ambition," I said, "where would man be?"

"But to kill a man to fulfill your ambitions?" An oiliness had entered his voice, and I turned to see his face, but under the blackness of the night only the outline was visible.

"Shouldn't there be a limit to ambition?" he asked me.

I answered him with a quote that pleased him. " 'A man's reach should exceed his grasp, / Or what's a heaven for?' "

The cloud slid by and in the moonlight his face glistened. He could not praise me enough. He said I was wiser than my years, more intelligent than many a man he had known. Later that night I returned to the bay. For an hour I swam. It was not enough to wash away my dread, a fear of something worse to come.

It was not fear, however, a premonition of danger, that caused me to give Ariana the name Prospero for Gardner. I was trying to get her on my side. What I really wanted, what Virginia and I really wanted, was more time to be with each other. I told Ariana that she was right to speak to Gardner the way she had. I said I admired her for standing up to him. Prospero, I said, didn't think Virginia needed to learn how to cook and clean, because *they* (and I dropped my bottom lip into a telling sneer) always found people like *us* to do their work for them.

"You could have the whole afternoon to yourself if you left me to look after Virginia when Prospero is in his garden," I said.

I had reason to believe she would find this offer attractive. I had noticed that she seemed listless after her hour, after lunch, with Gardner, that she moved around the kitchen as if heavy weights were strapped to her legs, that she was fretful when Virginia made even the slightest request of her. Usually she would exchange some words with me, mostly to complain about something I had not done well enough to her liking, like not cleaning the garbage pail properly or emptying it when she wanted. Lately, however, she barely spoke to me, grunting only yes or no to my questions.

"You would be able to do what you want," I said, trying to make my case more persuasive.

"Suppose she tell."

"She won't tell. She likes her books. She wants me to teach her."

"Suppose he ask her to show him how she can cook."

"He doesn't want her to cook. He wants her to know *how* to cook. You can tell me what you do and I will write it down for her. Like a cookbook," I said. "She can read it and tell him what he wants to know."

She tossed her thick mane of hair back and forth off her shoulders, considering my proposition.

"We'll be in the drawing room. You can check on us whenever you want," I said.

"He don't want you in the drawing room," she said.

She was right. The year before, Gardner had installed air conditioners in his and Virginia's bedrooms, in the drawing room, and in the dining room. He said Ariana and I did not need air conditioners in our rooms. Like all colored people, we had a natural protection against the heat. Our epidermis was thick, he said. Heat took a long time to pene-trate it. He permitted me to sit in the drawing room with him in the evenings but in the afternoon I had to remain in the blistering heat of the kitchen or in the oven my bedroom became when the sun blazed down on the galvanized roof.

My bedroom would not have been so hot if Gardner had not taken down the Demerara shutters my father had installed over all the bed-room windows. We raised them with sticks anchored on the win-dowsills and they sheltered us from the sun. Gardner claimed they were a perfect nesting place for termites. His tone was unnecessarily gruff, and I suspected that when he took them down he wanted to show me that he was wiser than my father. Many a day I am certain he regretted his false pride, for the sun was so direct at midday that even with air-conditioning his bedroom had to be steaming.

"You could see him coming and warn us," I said to Ariana, deter-mined to answer all her objections. "You'll be free."

"Free?" She looked past me, her eyes glazed.

"Free to do what you want," I said.

"Free," she said it again, dreamily.

And I, not imagining what else she could mean, said, "Free from having to work for Prospero."

Her face brightened, but just as I was about to leave the room, sat-isfied that I had convinced her, she stopped me. "I think she like you," she said.

I turned around. Her slight body seemed to sway under the weight of her hair. I noticed, as if for the first time, how thin she was, how her eyes seemed to consume her face. "You need to eat more," I said.

She did not allow me to distract her. "I sure she like you," she said.

"She wants to know more." I kept my tone flat, devoid of emotion. "She's vexed with her father for saying she doesn't need to know more."

"I don't mean that," she said. "I mean she like, like you. I see how she smile at you. And when she speak to you, her voice go nice, nice, nice."

I brushed her off. "Take those thoughts out of your head," I said.

"You watch out they don't get in *Prospero* head." She pointed her thin finger at me. "You watch out he don't get to thinking she like you and you like her back."

Many times in the long afternoons Virginia and I had together, Ariana drifting in and out of the drawing room like a shadow, those words would return to haunt me: *You watch out he don't get to thinking she like you and you like her back.* But always I managed to shrug them off, convincing myself that Virginia and I were friends, best friends, nothing more. She was too young for us to be anything more. In those afternoons we talked, we listened to music, we dreamed, we read books together, nothing more.

FOURTEEN

"TELL ME HOW we came to be here?" Virginia asked me not long after her father put an end to her education. "Tell me about our history."

Her skin was pale, her hair blond, her eyes blue, but she said *our*. Not *your*. *Our* history, she said.

"My father's people came in chains," I said.

"Chains?" Her eyes widened.

"Before them, before a single African touched these shores, there were Amerindians. Almost every last one of them wiped out by smallpox."

"Infected by something on the island?" she asked.

"Not something. Someone. The Europeans brought disease with them that killed nearly all the Amerindians."

"And your father's people?"

"Brought from Africa, herded on ships like cattle. They were slaves on the plantations."

Her father had told her none of this, and he had discussed none of this with me. All I had were my father's poems. They recounted a merciless sea, a crossing in a ship's coffin, men and women in chains, heads stacked against legs for efficiency. An arrival on a land where European women clutched Bibles and sang holy verses to justify what their men had done.

"When did this happen?"

"Not that long ago," I said.

And did the people in England know what was happening here?

She was reading Jane Austen at that time and had finished both *Sense and Sensibility* and *Pride and Prejudice*. I gave her *Mansfield Park*. Two weeks later, halfway through the novel, she approached me again. Why, she wanted to know, was there "such a dead silence" (she quoted the line from the novel precisely) from everybody who was present when Fanny Price asked Sir Thomas Bertram, who had just returned from Antigua, about the slave trade in the West Indies?

I said they were embarrassed, I said they must have all felt some twinge of conscience, some sense of their hypocrisy, especially Sir Thomas, who had put on such a show about the impropriety of his un-married daughters acting in a play about romantic love with unmar-ried men when he, on the other hand, had committed the worst sin that any human could commit. He had traded human flesh, he had treated his fellow humans as chattel, worse than that, he had done so without pity or remorse, for the sole purpose of extending his prop-erty, adding to his creature comforts, for a household of a wife, two sons, and two daughters that was more than adequate for ten times, no, twenty times, as many. He was a criminal, I said.

She seemed shocked by the strong word I had used. "A criminal?" Her head shot forward.

"Men like him were all criminals," I said. "They committed crimes against humanity." I searched her face for signs that I had offended her. Her father was English, her mother, too, all her grandparents for gen-erations back. "But, of course," I said, "you'd first have to believe that the people they tortured were humans."

If I had shocked her, she recovered quickly. "They *were* humans," she said.

How could I not love her?

I told her that to those people, Africans were less than humans. If they took them away from their homes and families, if they used whips and chains to force them to work, they had done so not to men and women, but to a species they considered less than men and women.

She looked so sad I began to regret that I had told her this. "Not all English people thought so," I said. "Many of them fought to free the slaves."

"But what about people like Sir Thomas Bertram? How could they stand to know that people had to suffer and die for them to live so grand?"

They. She didn't conceive of herself as part of *they.* The very scene in the novel that had arrested me arrested her. She could not read of Fanny Price's query dispassionately. Antigua was in the West Indies and so was Chacachacare. She was not born here, but she had known only here. The landscape, the sun, the sea had shaped her.

I had asked Gardner this question: If a seed came from England but was planted here, would the flower belong here or there? Would the flower be ours or theirs?

He did not hesitate. He pointed to a rose he had bred. It was his labor that had made it so beautiful. It was the sun *here* and the soil *here* he had prepared with a special fertilizer from *here* that had made it so. "Of course, it is my rose," he said. "They couldn't grow a rose like that in England."

I knew what he said was true. And there could not be a girl like her in England.

FIFTEEN

S THE YEARS WENT BY, Gardner became ever more careful about keeping his secrets from me. He did not want me to know the formula for the solution he concocted to clone his orchids and to grow grass that seldom needed watering. I was at his side to help him when he was grafting bougainvillea to sprout petals with polka dots and anthuriums to bloom like calla lilies, but he sent me to the house when he mixed the fertilizer. I brought him berries from Trinidad but he made sure I was never around when he fermented them to make the blue liquid he drank every day.

I was not bothered by these little tricks he apparently believed had fooled me. I was relieved, especially thankful on those predawn mornings when I stumbled groggily to the backyard, fighting sleep, and he sent me away. "Go back to bed," he would snarl. "A brain like yours needs its rest, Carlos."

His insult had no effect on me. Gardening was not what interested me. Literature and music interested me.

I didn't think it crossed his mind that when he was not in the house,

Virginia would welcome my company. For all his sometimes kindly treatment of me—when we listened to music together, when we talked about Shakespeare and Milton—he still thought of me as a sort of special species of Homo sapiens, not quite as human as he. In his version of Darwin, the ugly was always attracted to the beautiful, but never vice versa. And since in his eyes I was ugly and Virginia was beautiful, he believed she would recoil from me. But Virginia did not recoil from me. She liked me. She was polite, perfunctorily pleasant with me in his presence, but in his absence she was my friend.

It was because of her that I showed him my poetry. I had kept it a secret from him, at first doing so out of my longing for some tangible connection to my father, something I could claim was ours, mine and his alone. I wanted to believe my father had passed on his talent to me, given me his gift, and I guarded my poems jealously. One day, pride (I know now it was also love) led me to give Virginia three. They were poems about the beauty of the island, about my dreams of the sea and the land, the sky and the clouds, dreams so intense and real to me that when I woke I longed to sleep so I could dream again. Virginia praised me lavishly. She called me a magician, a juggler with words. Flattered, I forgot my mask and gave the poems to Gardner. "Junk," he said and tore them up.

Later at night I searched for the pieces in the garbage can where he had thrown them. Not a single scrap of paper did I find. Two days later, I came upon the torn edges of one of my poems under a clay pot where he had recently transplanted one of the orchids he had stripped off the tree in the cove.

> woke up this morning,
> had to search for a reason to live,
> look—a bird

I stuffed my poem in my pocket.

I took more risks for Virginia in my desire to see her happy. Because Gardner had declared all tropical fruits diseased, she had never tasted a mango. On a trip to Trinidad, I smuggled one for her in my bag. When

I got off the boat I was careful to hide it under the doctor's house. The next day I retrieved it from behind a concrete pillar. The delight on Virginia's face when her teeth sank into the pulp was more than reward for me. Mango juice spurted out of her mouth and ran down her fingers and wrist to the top of her blouse. She begged me to bring her more.

It was the telltale sign of yellow mango juice on her blouse that betrayed our secret to Ariana. From then on, I had to bring mangoes for Ariana, too, for though she delighted in the name I had given her for Gardner, I could not always be certain of her constancy. There were times, after her hour with Gardner, when a savage anger seemed to burn in her. Instead of moping around listlessly, as she sometimes did when Gardner left for his garden, she would stomp through the house, shouting, "No talking today. Work." She would demand that Virginia follow her into the kitchen and threaten to tell on me if I hesitated to return to my room. These bouts of anger were short-lived, however. In a day or two they passed and Virginia and I were able to resume the pattern of our afternoons, though always we remained uncertain of her moods.

The mangoes did not completely eradicate Ariana's resentment but they did much to compensate for her humiliation when Gardner made her cook and nursemaid to Virginia. On her good days she would concede that it was not Virginia's fault but Prospero's, that "I am she servant." On her bad days she complained about having to look after Virginia "as if she a baby." Then she would turn on me. "And watch you, too." Gardner wanted to be doubly sure of me.

Soon I was bringing back from Trinidad not only mangoes, but oranges and portugals, chennettes and guavas, governor plums and green plums, pomme cythere and pommerac, dongs and tamarind, siki yea figs and bananas. I always hid my bag of treasure under the doctor's house and picked it up the next day when Gardner was in his greenhouse. We took no chances. We buried the skins and seeds in a hole I had dug for that purpose beyond the front yard.

The fruit bought Ariana's silence when Gardner questioned her about Virginia's day, but she let me know that I was indebted to her. "If it ent for me, you'd be in a lot of trouble. He saving her for a white man. You better don't get it in your head to like her."

Foolishly, I still did not think I was in danger of liking Virginia in the way Ariana meant.

Then, one day, shortly before Virginia's fifteenth birthday, everything changed. I should have been forewarned. I had had a sign. But I was not superstitious. Lucinda had told me stories about the soucouyant, the douen, la diablesse, and though I was a child then and readily impressionable, I never believed what she told me. I knew she wanted to scare me, to keep me within her boundaries. I didn't believe there was a soucouyant under the tree outside our yard, an old woman who shed her skin at night and turned into a ball of fire. And Lucinda couldn't make me go to bed when I was not sleepy by frightening me with her tales of la diablesse, a pretty woman with a cloven foot, and douens, spirits of dead children who had not been baptized, all of them waiting in the dark to lure the innocent to their doom. I already knew about fairy tales from my mother, and I no more believed in the stories Lucinda told me than in the ones my mother used to read to me about a giant that lived on the top of a beanstalk or about pigs that talked.

That day I missed the three o'clock boat that was to bring me back to Chacachacare after I finished my errands in Trinidad. Gardner had given me a list for the pharmacist, but when I handed the list to the pharmacist, he gave it back to me. He couldn't help Gardner this time, he said. The drugs Gardner wanted were not the regular kind. No, he said, slapping away the paper I was holding out to him, the drugs on the list were *big-time* drugs, not the kind that a small-fry like him could just mix up in a back room and hand out to anybody. He would need a prescription.

I knew Gardner would be angry if I came back empty-handed, so I reminded him that Gardner was a doctor. If he could prescribe for other people, he could certainly prescribe for himself. The pharmacist mumbled something about dangerous drugs and poison. Afraid he wouldn't change his mind, I made it clear to him that if Gardner did not get what he had sent me for he wouldn't buy from him again. Do you want to risk losing his business? I asked him. It never occurred to me that the deep lines that deepened on his forehead when he took the list back from me were not caused by anxiety, but by fear for my personal safety.

The pharmacist had told me to come back later. It turned out he meant much later than when I arrived, and it was two-thirty before he was ready for me, too late for me to catch the three o'clock boat. At four o'clock I found a boat that was taking passengers to their vacation homes on Monos and Huevos, the tiny islands not far from Chacachacare, but when the passengers discovered I lived on Chacachacare, they spurned me. They did not want me on the boat, they said. Lepers live on Chacachacare. It took the boatman some time to convince them they had no cause for worry. I lived on the other side of the horseshoe, he told them, far from the colony.

Ten minutes out on the sea, the passenger who had most protested my presence, a stout, caramel-colored woman, who, even after the other passengers agreed reluctantly to let me on the boat, still objected, claiming that the boat was too small to hold us all (it was a pirogue), began shouting hysterically and pointing to the sky. Above us, banners of red in undulating waves were cutting across the blueness of the sky. The strange sight of ibis coming home early to the mangrove. A sunset, though the sun was still golden in the sky.

Something had frightened them in Venezuela, the boatman said. They never leave till almost night.

"Is a sign, is a sign," the woman cried. "We going to drown today. I tell the boatman not to take the boy."

Nobody drowned. The boatman docked safely at Monos and Huevos, and brought me afterward to Chacachacare. But when I got there, I had cause to wonder if I had not been given a sign, if the ibis, frightened into returning home early to the mangrove in Trinidad, were not warning indeed of trouble to come.

As soon as I opened the back door, I heard Virginia. She was trying to dislodge something that was clogging her throat. Her head was bent low over the kitchen sink and I could see only shoulders shuddering each time the muscles in her throat constricted. She spun around when I called out to her. Her eyes were red, the skin around her mouth a deep, dark purple, and long trails of spittle dribbled from her mouth. I dropped my bags and rushed to her, but she ran out of the kitchen, and before I could reach her, she locked her bedroom door.

Ariana slunk past me. "Help her," I begged. "Something's happened to her."

"Leave her," she said. Her voice was strangely calm.

"She's sick," I said. I grabbed Ariana's arm.

"Leave her." She disentangled herself from my grasp.

"She was throwing up. I saw her."

"She do like that all the time now," she said.

"Like what?"

"You don't see. I see," she said.

"Is she sick?"

"Ask her."

"Ask her what?"

"You and she talking all the time. Ask her what in her throat."

But Virginia did not answer her door when I knocked, and Gardner asked no questions when Ariana told him that his daughter was not well.

The next morning, by chance, I came upon Virginia in the corridor. I had been working with Gardner in the backyard and he had sent me to the house to fetch him a glass of water. She was standing in front of the mirror. Her mouth was open and she was twisting her head from side to side, peering into the back of her throat. She did not see me, though I was at the end of the corridor, not far from where she was. I came closer to her and called her name. She flinched and closed her mouth.

"I thought you were outside," she said, wiping her lips with the back of her hand. "With my father."

"Are you sick? Is something the matter?"

"No. No," she said. A lock of her hair had fallen across her face. She tucked it behind her ear. Twelve years ago, her hair was blond; now it had turned honey brown. She wore it pushed back from her forehead, in a loose plait down her back, inches above her waist, but a curl or two always managed to slip out.

"Is something wrong with your throat?" I asked her.

"No. I'm fine. I'm okay."

"I heard you," I said.

"A silly infection." She rubbed the side of her neck. "I get it sometimes. My tonsils," she said.

I wanted to believe her because she seemed to want me to believe her. "Put two heaping spoonfuls of salt in warm water and gargle." I gave her Lucinda's remedy.

"Salt?" she repeated the word as if it were all I had said.

"I'll get it for you." I moved toward the kitchen.

"No." She held up her hands. "You have to go back. Father," she warned.

She seemed different. Her skin, normally a golden brown, was dull, lifeless. Her face was pale, the sides of her mouth the color of chalk. She was wearing a flowered print dress, belted at the waist. It did nothing to brighten her complexion.

Gardner had told her that no one was more beautiful than her mother. He had put a photograph of her mother in her room, and when she showed it to me, she asked me, almost in despair, if I thought there was a chance that she would grow to resemble her mother. She had her mother's heart-shaped face, her aquiline nose, her soft chin, even the same crinkles, when she smiled, that formed around her mother's eyes. But what I loved most were her lips, full, wide, generous. They were her mother's lips, though in the photograph those lips were pressed together as if they concealed a secret. I told her I did not think she would grow to look like her mother. I told her she was lovelier than her mother. Now, color drained from her face, she looked exactly like the photograph on her dresser.

"Go," she said again when I had not moved. "He'll be waiting for you."

"Does he know you're sick?"

She reached for the box of salt in the cupboard. "I didn't come out for dinner."

It was a simple statement loaded with a truth I could not ignore. Gardner was told she was sick but he had made no mention of her, not to Ariana when she served his dinner, not to me when he called me later to the drawing room. The record he had ordered had arrived from Trinidad. A Mozart concerto. We listened to it all evening.

"Why didn't you open your door when I knocked?" I asked her.

"He won't like it if you don't go back soon," she said.

"Shall I tell him?"

She turned on the tap and filled a glass with water.

"I'm going to tell him," I said.

She faced me. Gardner had given her earrings. They were an early present for her fifteenth birthday, gold pendants with tiny blue stones at the bottom. They matched her eyes. She was wearing them, but they did not match her eyes now. The stones were clear, blue as a sunlit sea, but her eyes were dark, troubled. A silvered sea on the eve of a storm.

"What?" she said, looking at me directly. "Tell him what? There is nothing to tell."

And for two days there was nothing to tell. If I mentioned her tonsils, she dismissed me with the same impatience, sometimes tinged with anger. She could have had more gagging fits, I would not have known. I never again saw her bent over the kitchen sink or searching the back of her throat in the mirror. When we sat in the drawing room in the afternoon, she wanted me to talk about books or about my last trip to Trinidad. Nothing else. Then, on the third day, while I was telling her about a speech I had heard in Woodford Square, she began twisting her hands nervously on her lap and biting her lower lip.

I thought I had frightened her with my talk about Eric Williams and the independence movement in Trinidad. No, she said. She was glad independence was coming.

Then what? I asked.

"We are going to have visitors. Friends of Mrs. Burton."

I had almost forgotten Mrs. Burton. She had come to the house only twice, and on both occasions I had caught only glimpses of her. She was an Englishwoman Gardner had hired to decorate the house. The year he decided that books would make Virginia unmarketable, he also decided to make the house more suitable. For an Englishwoman, he told me. "Don't forget, Virginia is English."

He sent me with a message to the pharmacist to ask for his recommendation. The pharmacist recommended Mrs. Burton. Mrs. Burton came once to examine the layout of the drawing room and a second time, after Gardner and I had painted the room to her specifications,

and the furniture and other furnishings she suggested had been delivered, she came to hang the drapes and to arrange the furniture. That
second time Gardner was so pleased with the effect she had created in
his drawing room that in a rare gesture of generosity he showed her
his orchids.

Mrs. Burton was the president of the Trinidad chapter of England's
Royal Horticultural Society, and from that day, she began a campaign
to persuade Gardner to allow her to enter his orchids in her annual
flower show. But Gardner never invited her back to the house though
she sent him letters weekly, monthly, and then, sporadically, though
steadily. "She wants to know my secrets," he said. Her letters were a
source of amusement to him.

"Your father laughs at Mrs. Burton," I said to Virginia. "He ridicules
her. He won't have her or her friends in his house."

"He's invited her friends to see the orchids," she said.

"What friends?"

"An American man and his son," she said.

I knew immediately that Ariana was right. "So soon." I mumbled.

Virginia burst into tears.

Sympathy came from the most unexpected quarters. "I sorry for
she," Ariana said as she passed me that evening on her way to Virginia's
bedroom.

It was past midnight when a piercing scream bolted me awake. I
rushed out of my room in time to see Gardner, his open pajama shirt
flapping behind him, running toward Virginia's room. He caught my
eye and signaled me to go back. I heard the door shut and then silence.
For the rest of the night, I could not sleep. At dawn, I crept out of my
room, hoping to speak to Ariana, but she was nowhere to be found. I
looked out of the window and saw Gardner by the flower beds.

"Virginia," he said gruffly as I approached him. "A bad dream."

He didn't wait for me to respond. He gave me instructions to repot
one of the plants and reached for the pot next to the one I was working on. The plant in it, a new flower he was growing, had doubled in
size, overnight it seemed to me. He plunged his hands in the dirt and
pulled it out. "A nightmare," he said, straightening up.

I had been afraid it was her throat. "Is she feeling better?" I asked.

He dusted his hands down the legs of his pants. Cleanliness was next to godliness, he was forever telling me. Now the sides of his pants were smeared with dirt and he did not seem to notice.

"Nerves," he said. He examined his fingernails. They were black, caked thick with dirt. He slipped one nail under another and pushed the dirt away. "Her mother suffered from nerves."

He had told me she had died in childbirth. He had said she was a saint, a piece of virtue.

"Too delicate." He stopped cleaning his fingernails. The muscles around his mouth hardened. He looked away. "Too refined to bear a child."

Refined? My chest tightened.

"She was pure, you understand. Her sensibilities . . ." He raised his hand and circled the air with his open palm struggling to find the precise word. "*Accustomed.* She was not *accustomed,* you see."

Sexual intercourse. I was sure he was referring to sexual intercourse. I averted my eyes, embarrassed for him, embarrassed by the image before my mind's eye: he, sweating, plowing between unwilling thighs, *too delicate* thighs. But I was angry, too, by this reminder of his contempt, the scorn he had for people who looked like me, people who were *accustomed.*

"Virginia suffers from nerves like her." He rolled his shoulders, trying, I thought, to shake himself out of the moroseness that had settled on him, and when he succeeded, he dismissed me abruptly. "Go, get me the bag of fertilizer I mixed yesterday."

When I came back with the bag from the shed where he stored the chemicals and potions he used to make fertilizers for the soil, he was digging out some plants from a row of pots on the shelf. The stiffness that moments ago had narrowed his lips to a thin line was gone. He had a gleam in his eyes. He was practically grinning when he took the bag from me.

He was going to have visitors, he said.

I pretended I did not know.

"Mrs. Burton has referred them to me. They're interested in my orchids. The ones I found in the cove."

I noticed his error, of course. *He* had not found the orchids in the cove. *I* had taken him there. But I had long become inured to errors like this one. At times, as if to test me, he would say *my house, my land.* I swallowed my anger then and I swallowed it now.

"Mrs. Burton says she believes they are the rarest in the world."

I did not respond and he frowned at me, but in the next instant the irritation he seemed to have felt by my silence passed and his eyes shone again. "They are Americans," he said brightly. "The ones who are coming."

I feigned surprise. "Americans?"

"Rich Americans," he said.

He slashed open the bag of fertilizer with his penknife and bade me fetch the spreader he used for scattering the fertilizer on the lawn. When I brought it to him, he winked at me conspiratorially. "Two birds with one stone," he said.

I did not understand him immediately. He came closer to me. "The rich American has a son," he said.

Virginia had told me this already but he made the significance plainer to me. "It's time," he said, "for her to be with her own kind."

I felt it then, the pressure on my heart, the constriction around my throat. *I was not her kind.*

"It's time for her to think of marriage." He slapped me on my back.

He returned to the house, and all the time I worked, spreading the lawn with fertilizer, the lawn that never seemed to need mowing, his words rang in my ears. *It's time for her to be with her own kind. It's time for her to think of marriage.*

A storm raged in me with such fury, it eclipsed tremors already begun deep in my heart. I was not conscious of these tremors. I was not conscious that it was love that was making me so angry. I thought it was this final assault on me, this assault to my humanity: I was not her kind. My kind would always be less than her kind, always be unworthy of her kind.

For the next three days, Gardner kept me busy in the backyard. My afternoons were no longer free. I had to sweep the greenhouse and wash the glass panes above it. I had to repot plants, cut away leaves with the slightest blemish from all the flowers in his garden. I had to clean the gravel around the orchids and clip off the dead tendrils. I had to cut back the bushes that grew over the dirt path that led from the dock to the house. He wanted everything to be perfect when the visitors came, not a blade of grass lower or higher than the other. He wanted his orchids displayed at their best. He wanted to make an impression.

I hardly ever saw Virginia during this time. Whenever I returned to the house, she was already in her room. When she came to the drawing room, Gardner was always there. If by chance I caught her alone in the corridor or outside on the porch, she put her finger on her lips and warned me with her eyes to walk away.

"I feel sorry for she," Ariana said. "Prospero planning a marriage for she."

I took consolation in the nightmare that woke her up screaming.

SIXTEEN

*H*IS NAME was Alfred Haynes. Freddie, Gardner called him, but I renamed him Ferdie in my mind when Gardner's plans were laid bare in front of me. Ferdie for the king's son, trapped with his father on a sea turned treacherous by Prospero's magic, the ship a child's toy in the gargantuan waves, men tossed about like dolls from stem to stern, last prayers flung desperately to heaven until Prospero threw out his seine and pulled them in, fish for his supper, the best saved for his daughter.

I will confess immediately that Alfred was handsome, though when I first saw him, from the kitchen where I was pounding cornmeal for Ariana, he seemed an average man of average height, square-shouldered, not particularly muscular, not at all a god. But I had seen him only from the back that first time; I had not had the advantage of his face.

Gardner had asked me to help Ariana. I had not done kitchen work since he had discovered that I could read. But he wanted everything to be perfect for the Americans so I became busboy, dishwasher, and kitchen helper again. He sent me to Trinidad for special groceries: expensive cuts of beef, bacon, chicken livers, eggs, high-grade butter, cream, almonds, mushrooms. He planned to serve beef Wellington for lunch and began by having Ariana practice making the pâté, which was to be spread over the beef, under a pastry covering. Three times Ariana had to boil the chicken livers, fry the bacon, sauté the onions, and chop the hard-boiled eggs. Each time she chopped the eggs either too coarsely or much too fine, fried the bacon too crisply or not crisply enough, burned the onions, or boiled the livers until they crumbled and fell apart. In the end Gardner had to make the pâté. But when it came to the Wellington itself, Ariana's performance was spectacular.

"Why you ent tell me is beef patty you want me to make?" she asked sullenly when she succeeded on her first try. "My mother teach me that long time."

"Beef Wellington with chicken pâté, not patty! Té, té!" Gardner shouted, spit spraying from his mouth.

When he left the kitchen, Ariana grumbled something about English people always trying to find fancy words for ordinary things. If Gardner had told her in the first place that what he wanted was a big beef patty with chicken livers she would have made that with no trouble at all. It would have taken a little adjusting, that's all.

But the day that Ariana produced a golden-brown beef Wellington, one so perfect that Gardner was rendered speechless, word came from Mrs. Burton that the Americans wanted something local, something Caribbean, something tropical.

If Mrs. Burton had not told him the Americans were rich, I believe Gardner would have scrapped his plans there and then. They were ignoramuses, he said. They lacked sophistication; they lacked class. Haute cuisine was beyond them. But they had money. The allure of all those dollars made his head spin. I would not have been surprised if he hadn't already figured out their worth to the penny and calculated the percentage that would be his daughter's upon her marriage to the son. Factored in, too, the amount he would need to buy amnesia from the people in England waiting for his head.

Ariana, however, was overjoyed. Something local? Gardner had despised her mother's cooking, spoken disparagingly of anything local. Revenge was probably on her mind when, eschewing the simpler meal of rice and peas that Mrs. Burton recommended as quintessentially Caribbean, she chose callaloo, stewed chicken, breadfruit, dasheen, yam, and coo-coo. For days the kitchen was filled with smells I had almost forgotten: sugar burning in oil to brown the chicken for stew, breadfruit steaming in coconut milk, okra boiling in pigtail, dasheen leaves shredded to make callaloo.

But perhaps it was not revenge that allowed Ariana to endure in silence the scratches and scrapes on her knuckles when she grated the hard coconut, or the green stains on her fingers from the dasheen bush, or the hot oil that splattered on her neck. Perhaps it was pride, for pride was what I felt when I was sent back to Trinidad with the new grocery list, pride that made me think more kindly of the Americans. *They wanted something local.* I began to hope that Gardner was wrong. I fantasized that the rich American's son had already chosen his bride in America. I made myself believe that he would not be interested in Virginia. I never allowed myself to consider the possibility that Virginia would be interested in him.

Yet when, eventually, I saw his face and the reflection of his face on Virginia's face, both at the same time, my fear returned more intense than before. I had dismissed him as not a god, too short to be a god, but the awe in Virginia's eyes was unmistakable. This was a god to her, a thing divine, resembling her: skin the color of hers, not mine; hair as blond.

From the disadvantage of the kitchen window, I watched them walk toward the orchid beds. At the white orchids they stopped, the young man and his father huddling close to each other on one side of the bed, Virginia a slight distance away from them. Gardner stood on the other side, his attention, like mine, focused on his daughter. If the son found Virginia beautiful, it was clear to me that for him her beauty was overshadowed by the beauty of the orchid. He spoke to his father, he spoke to Gardner. Only once did he turn to her. But I could tell by the way her head was fixed in his direction that Virginia was enraptured.

The Americans left immediately after lunch. Gardner did not take Virginia with him when he went to the bay to see them off. I suppose, in spite of his plans, he did not want to seem too anxious. I came out of the kitchen and approached Virginia. I did not mince my words. I was so overcome with jealousy that my brain did not allow me to be discreet, to conceal my palpitating heart.

"You looked at him as if he had dropped from heaven," I said. She walked away from me. I followed her. "You were mesmerized." My voice was harsh with resentment. "You couldn't keep your eyes off of him."

She stopped and turned. "Father doesn't want me to talk to you," she said.

If she had spoken to me as harshly as I had to her, I would have despaired. I would not have had the courage to go on. But she did not say those words harshly. She said them softly, gently, her voice full of concern for me. Still, I grabbed her arm roughly. "Are you going to marry him?" I asked.

"Father said . . ." Her lips trembled.

I tightened my hold on her. "Are you?"

She tried to push my hand away.

"Are you?"

"Father said . . ." She struggled again.

I released her, drained, my heart sinking. "What has happened to you? You won't talk to me, you avoid me."

She rubbed the spot where I had held her but she did not walk away. "Father says it's time." Her eyes were moist.

We were in the corridor outside her room. At the far end, near the kitchen, Ariana was looking at us. "I have to go," Virginia said, glancing at Ariana.

"Wait." Ariana had told me she felt sorry for Virginia. I did not think she would make trouble for her.

"He'll be back soon," Virginia said.

"Tonight. Get away tonight," I pleaded with her.

She glanced once again down the corridor. Ariana was still looking at us, but she had made no move to come toward us.

"She won't tell him," I said.

"Father has made up his mind," she said.

"Come with me to the cove," I said.

She did not say yes, she did not say no.

I had promised many times to take her there. She wanted to see the big tree where the orchids used to be, but though Ariana was willing to give us time when Gardner was in his garden, it was time she had calculated, time she supervised. No matter how I had tried to reassure her, she was unwilling, afraid, to take the risk that Gardner would return before she could warn us.

"We could go at night," I said to Virginia.

"In the dark?"

"When he's asleep," I said.

"He sleeps too lightly," she said.

I thought she was remembering the night he heard her scream. "We'll be quiet," I said.

She shook her head. Ariana came closer. "Go," she said to Virginia. "Is the only way."

After dinner, in the kitchen, Ariana told me what she had done. She had put something in Gardner's blue drink, she said. "Nothing make Prospero wake up till morning come."

There was no moon. Once we got past the end of the lawn to the path that led to the sea, the bushes closed in on us and we could barely see. I stretched out my hand to Virginia. She took it, and when her fingers closed over mine, my anger, my jealousy, my fear ebbed away like the tide.

Hand in hand, not speaking, as much because we were afraid to speak, to make the slightest noise (impossible as I knew it would be for Gardner to hear us) as it was because we were suddenly shy, I led her off the path, through a narrow track cluttered with dead branches, stones, and curling vines. The night air was thick with the fragrance of the earth baked in the daylong sun. Dried leaves crumbled beneath our feet and released a vegetable perfume that mixed with the odor of animal droppings, a smell not unpleasant. Organic. Pure. Nature untouched, unchanged by human hands.

Along the way Virginia stumbled, her shoe caught in the tendril of a vine. She reached for me, and when her head brushed my chest, my heart did somersaults. I could hear her breathing, the air coming out of her mouth in spurts. I swallowed hard, trying to loosen the tightness mounting my throat, and placed my arm lightly around her waist to help her climb over the craggy knoll to the cove on the other side.

She saw the orchids immediately. Like stars, she said. And I was grateful that Gardner's fear of the lepers had kept him away. Three trips we had made to the cove and then he got frightened. "The lepers bury their dead here," I had told him, and saved the rest clutching the thick branches at the top of the tree.

We sat on a big stone at the edge of the water. Dark trees hugged the rough-pebbled beach, a sliver only, yet distinct next to the sea black with the night though sparkling here and there where tiny waves broke the surface. Night sounds encircled us: the faint lap, lap of waves stroking the beach, the shudder of leaves in the light breeze, the flutter of feathers, birds stirring in their sleep.

I could tell she was no longer nervous. Even without the moon, I could see that her face had softened.

"Did the Americans like them?" I asked her.

"The Americans?" The surprise in her eyes was genuine, as if she had forgotten.

"The orchids. Did they like them?"

She drew her legs to her chest and hugged her knees. "Yes," she said. Then, looking out to the water, she added dreamily, "Especially the son."

My jealousy returned. "He's handsome," I said. My tone was spiteful.

"As if he came from another world," she said.

I had not expected her to be so blunt. "America," I said, still spiteful. "He came from America."

She wrinkled her brow. "I know from America," she said.

If I had been able to find a way to stop the blood from rushing to my head, I would have been reasonable. I would have been able to assess her words calmly, to have reminded myself that the American was the first young white man she had seen on the island. But I could not stem the flood in my brain any more than I could stop the cold streak snaking down my spine.

"I saw the way you stared at him," I said.

A pink stain rose on her cheeks. She lowered her voice. "Do you think he noticed?"

"Your father noticed," I said.

The stain on her cheeks grew darker. "He's handsome," she murmured.

I wished I could roll back the clock. I wished I could recover the time when all she was to me was a friend, a sort of sister. Then I could have laughed at her, told her he was nothing special. In Trinidad I had seen men handsomer.

"You say that because he is white," I said. I spoke in anger, but it was fear I felt.

She opened her eyes wide and arched her brows. "No. No," she said.

"And I am not white."

"No. I was surprised to see him. That's all," she said.

"You should have more control over your feelings." I spat out the words at her.

"Feelings? But I have no feelings for him." The tips of her fingers grazed my cheek. "Not like the feelings I have for you."

I held her by her wrist and pulled back her hand. "You think of me as a friend," I said.

"My only friend."

"Once you told me you would love me forever."

"And I will," she said. "Forever."

"But you will marry him."

"I will marry you," she said.

I released her hand. I think she was as shocked as I when the words fell back on her ears and the truth penetrated her heart. Her eyes darkened, her lips lost color. I reached for her and kissed her.

Mrs. Burton came for lunch the next day. I was sitting in the place Gardner had assigned me, at a table near the window, where I ate alone. From where I was, it was difficult to hear what Mrs. Burton was saying, but I had my suspicions and I could hardly wait for Ariana, who was serving them, to return to the kitchen.

"She wants Miss Virginia to come to Trinidad," she said. The tray of dirty dishes she was holding seemed to weigh her down. Her legs buckled when she placed it on the counter.

"And what did Miss Virginia say?" I asked her.

"She say nothing. Prospero say she have to go."

Mrs. Burton left around half past two. Gardner went to the dock with her, his arms loaded down with orchid plants. I had guessed his purpose right: He had made a bargain. Orchids in exchange for her promise to orchestrate his daughter's marriage.

I was helping Ariana in the kitchen when Virginia appeared. She had come so quietly I would not have known she was standing by the doorway if Ariana had not nudged me.

"He said I have to leave tomorrow." Her face was wreathed with sorrow. I did not care that Ariana was there. I folded her in my arms and pressed her to my chest.

"He said I must pack tonight."

"For how long?"

"Mrs. Burton is having a party for the Americans. He wants me to go."

"I'll talk to him," I said. I did not know what I meant when I said that. What could I say to him? What could I tell him that would dissuade him from a plan he had fixed for her?

"I'll tell him," I said, my mouth in her hair. "I'll tell him I love you."

She disentangled herself from my arms and pushed her hands with such force against my chest, I had to step back to balance myself. "He will kill you," she said. Her lips were ash white, the blood drained from her face. I pulled her back in my arms. "Don't." Her voice came muffled against my shirt. "Not a word. Not a word to him. Promise me, Carlos."

I glanced over to Ariana. Her hand was clasped over her mouth, and her eyes darted from me to the kitchen door. "I tell you when he coming," she said.

I led Virginia to the drawing room and eased her down on the sofa with me. I had to save her, save myself.

"He has made up his mind," she said. "He will not change it."

"And what about you? What about us?"

"He will not allow it." She held my face between the palms of her hands and drew me to her.

I felt Ariana's hand on my arm. "Let her go," she said. "Come." She beckoned Virginia. "Is time. I help you pack. Is better this way."

Gardner was in a good mood when he returned. He bounded up the front steps, clapping his hands and shouting for Virginia. "Virginia! Good news, Virginia!" Ariana met him in the drawing room. "Have you packed her yet?" he asked her.

"We almost done," she said.

"Then finish, finish. They love her. Do you hear me, Ariana? They love her. Mrs. Burton said the boy is smitten with her."

One day, one visit. It seemed that was all it took. And yet I knew the American hardly looked at her.

He knocked on Virginia's door. "He's smitten. Freddie's smitten." But Virginia did not open her door. He knocked again and when she did not answer, he said in a loud voice to no one in particular, "She's shy. She'll come around." Nothing, it seemed, was going to dampen his spirits. He popped his head in the kitchen and told me to meet him in the greenhouse. "He's in love," he said. He did not wait for my response.

How was I going to tell him I was in love with her? What would he do when I told him? Of all the possibilities before me, the one I never considered was the one Virginia predicted: I did not think he would kill me.

His plans for Virginia were still on his mind when I came to the greenhouse dressed in my khaki gardener's uniform. I had never seen him so excited.

"There's to be a party soon," he said. His eyes were shining and the corners of his mouth twitched in his effort to suppress a smile.

He had changed his clothes. When Mrs. Burton was here, he had worn the same white shirt he had put on for the Americans, which Ariana had bleached in the sun and starched according to his instructions. But now he was in his dusty gardener's khaki pants and rumpled shirt, an old man, a simple gardener, though he thought a scientist in a botanical lab.

"I've given Mrs. Burton money to have a dress made for her," he said. He tightened the knot on his ponytail. "Just a few orchids, that's all it cost me."

I wanted to say that perhaps a dress was worth a few orchids, but not her. I wanted to say that she would be unhappy with this Freddie, this Ferdie. She belonged here, not there, not in America, a place she did not know, with people she did not know.

He sent me to fetch the pots of chaconia. He had pulled up the chaconia bush when he was cutting down the trees in my backyard, but one plant had survived. He would have destroyed it, too, if Lucinda had not given him her name for it. Wild poinsettia, she called it. Its mass of scarlet-red petals blossomed in clusters, mounted at the tips of stems sprouting elegant long, flat, dark green leaves. He would find a way to double the petals, he told her. Now he wanted to triple them. "Getting there, getting there," he said when I brought him the plants. He was pleased with himself. Exhilarated.

I was trying to figure out how to begin, where would be the best way to start.

He clipped off the top of one of the plants and held up the cutting. "This," he said, "is a hybrid of a hybrid. Nothing like it. Nothing like what I am going to make with it."

And suddenly it came to me. Suddenly I knew how I would trap him.

"The flowers get prettier the more you mix them," I said.

He grinned at me. "That's the secret. Mix them, graft them." He reached for another plant, sliced six inches from the top, and took both cuttings to his worktable. I knew the routine. I handed him a lump of moss he had sprayed with his secret solution, a piece of plastic wrapping paper, and twine. He switched the cuttings and attached a clipping from one plant to the other plant, wrapped the moss around it, and secured it with the plastic and twine. "Good," he said, and slapped his hands together. A puff of light dust rose in the air. "Now for the hibiscus." He had tamed the wild hibiscus bush he had found on the island. It was a thick shrub now that lined the back of the green-house and bloomed all year round, but he was still experimenting. "Next year the flowers will be bigger and prettier," he said, when I gave him one of the pots of hibiscus plants he had forced into dwarfs.

"Is it the same with humans?" I asked.

"Humans?" He eyed me suspiciously.

"Can you make them prettier if you graft them?"

I think I was so invisible to him that the thought did not occur to him that I might be speaking of myself, of myself and his daughter. He continued to frown at me for a second more, and then he laughed out loud, a dry, mirthless laugh. "You should have seen the things I did in England," he said. He clipped a flower and shook the yellow pollen on a white piece of paper.

"With humans?"

"Yes, indeed, with humans, my boy." He sounded proud of his achievement. "Would have cured their diseases," he said.

I flattered him. "I know you would have," I said.

"But they were skittish, my boy. Wouldn't let me." He shook the pollen of one plant onto the stamen of the other.

"Could you grow parts?"

I seemed to have startled him with that question. He stopped what he was doing. "Parts?" He fixed his eyes on me.

"A good part to replace a bad part. Like grow a finger if someone had lost a finger," I said.

I did not know how close I had come to his history. "Grow a finger?" He narrowed his eyes at me.

"Or liver. If you could do that, you could cure any disease." It was disease he was fighting when he cut and grafted, when he chopped down the fruit trees my father had planted. "You said that was what you were trying to do in England," I said.

He seemed to have realized that I could not have known more. The tension in his face eased. "Yes, yes," he said. "That was what I was try-ing to do." He bent over the plant and plucked off the dead leaves.

"You could have helped the czar," I said.

"Ah, the Romanovs."

I was closing in on him. I knew I pleased him with my reference to the Romanovs. He liked when I spoke of historical events in Europe. They were tangible evidence, proof of the success of his experiment in civilizing me.

"Alexis," I said, keeping my voice even. "You could have cured him."

"Hemophilia," he said.

"But if they had intermarried . . ." I left the rest of the sentence hanging.

He cut another flower. "You have to be careful," he said, brushing off the pollen. "You have to get it all."

"But if they had intermarried." I forced him back to the place where I wanted him.

He shook his head. "That was not possible, my boy." He picked up the paper with the pollen. "Blue blood, you know, must stay with blue blood."

"But wouldn't the disease have regressed?"

"Yes. That's possible." He emptied the pollen carefully into the centers of the flowers on a row of other plants. "Regressed," he said. "In time, disappeared."

"All diseases, in fact, could be cured that way."

"What way?" He was still concentrating on the flowers.

"By intermarriage."

He straightened up. "Intermarriage?" His eyes were nuggets of steel.

"If an African who carried the sickle cell anemia gene married a European who had the gene for cystic fibrosis, isn't it possible that none of their children would get either disease?"

"Who's been telling you that, my boy?" The paper he was holding fluttered in his hand. Pollen drifted to the ground, gold dust sprinkling the brown earth.

"I read it in your books," I said, not backing down.

He brought his face close to mine. "There can be no improvement of the white race from a marriage with the black race." I smelled his breath. It was sour. Acidic.

"You said I was better than my mother." I reeled him in. All that was left now was to plunge my fingers deep in his gills.

"Your mother was a fool."

"My mother was married to a black man."

"Your mother was a fool for lying down with a black man." The vein in his forehead bulged thick and blue.

"He was my father." I could feel my blood pulsating in my neck. "You live in his house. You live in a black man's house."

He was breathing hard, sucking in air like a donkey. "Liar!"

"*My* house. You stole it from me."

"Liar! Ingrate!" He grabbed me by the collar of my shirt. But I was ready. I reached around my neck and held his wrist. I squeezed it hard until his hand grew limp. He let go and we faced each other, panting.

"I curse the day I lodged you." He bared his teeth, a dog snarling.

"*You,*" I said. I held his eyes. "*You* curse the day, but not Virginia."

It took a second for my words to sink in, so accustomed was he to excluding me, to thinking of me as inferior to him, inferior to Virginia, not quite a man as Englishmen were men, not quite human as Englishmen were human. And then he understood. *But not Virginia.*

"You filthy bastard. You vile savage, you born devil." His eyes were fiery balls blazing beneath his wrinkled forehead. A fine film of dirt had collected on the sweat pearled on his top lip. Spittle dribbled down his chin. "I will kill you. I will kill you if you even try. "

I lashed out: " 'Thou didst prevent me; I had peopled else / This isle with Calibans.' "

Caliban's words. And yet what I meant to say to him was that I loved her. That one day I hoped to marry her, to have children with her. But the world had grown dark when he hurled that string of epithets at me. There was no light for me to see.

He lunged for me. I stepped aside and tripped him. He fell on his knees. I pushed him farther down, face forward in the dirt with my heel.

It was over. We had come to the end.

Why hadn't I left before? Why had I stayed so many years? Why hadn't I fought him for my house and my land? My reasons, when those questions troubled my mind, were always the same. I had no papers, I had no proof. There was no deed. It was my mother's house: That alone was my evidence. As long as the British ruled, an Englishman's lies would trump my truth.

But it was *my* house and *my* land, and I would not leave him here with my house and my land.

Yet gratitude, too, bound me to him. He had taught me more than I would ever have known. He had brought the world to me on Chacachacare.

And there was habit, the sick love that comes from habit. I had lived with him twelve years on this desolate island. How was it possible for me not to have formed an attachment to him, even if merely of the sort one would have for a pet that licked one's hand? I have heard of couples who stay married in spite of the abuse they have inflicted on each other. A woman comes to the police with a broken hand, her face bloodied, her nose smashed, her eyes swollen, and in the end she begs for the release of her batterer. Habit? We are creatures who serve that demon. Change terrifies us. There were times I hated him, but hate is not possible without love. Hate is the ashes, the dying embers of love. Hate is not indifference.

SEVENTEEN

*B*UT HE IMPRISONED ME. I had knocked him down. I could have done it again. I was in the full vigor of my youth. He was thin and sinewy, a middle-aged man dried out by the sun. Yet that was how Inspector Mumsford found me: surrounded by barbed wire, penned up in the backyard, accused of attempting to rape Virginia.

This is what I remember. I remember seeing him on his knees, his face covered with dirt. I remember feeling no emotion for him, neither hate nor love. I was indifferent, my heart a blank slate, all my anger and resentment toward him erased, all the affection that had made it possible for me to endure his insults, his abuse, his casual derision of the fading memories of my mother and father.

I had found myself in his music, in his literature, and thought of his art as my art, belonging also to me, but there was nothing in common between us now. Nothing to stir me to pity when he looked up, hurt and disbelief, not anger, stinging his eyes to water. For he had betrayed art. Art—music and literature (not the artist)—had been my guide to beauty and truth, to what was good, to what was morally reprehensible. He had misused art, subverted it to suit his vanity.

I walked away. I turned my back on him. I did not look back.

Inside the house, I threw myself on my bed. I had done what I had every reason to do, was justified in doing, not just then but years before. The strain left me limp, a rag doll, its innards stuffed with straw. My eyelids dropped heavily over my eyes and a sleep descended on me so thick, so deep, I did not hear him, I did not sense him, not until he plunged a syringe filled with his vile drug deep in my thigh and set my bones on fire.

I bolted upright. Too late. He was standing by my bedside, his lips snatched back high on his gums, his teeth like fangs, gleaming. I strained to reach for him, but a dense fog rolled over me. Through it, the pharmacist's face, wrinkled with worry, shimmered toward me. Paralysis mounted my legs and spread up my entire body, a wave washing inexorably across dry sand. Before darkness engulfed me I achieved a clarity that hubris had denied me. I had bullied the pharmacist. Now with the same poison, Gardner had drugged me.

I was not conscious when Gardner pulled me off the bed and dragged me to the backyard. I did not hear when he pounded nails into the fence he built around me. Only once did my brain break through the fog that enveloped it. He was chanting, words that rose and fell in lugubrious rhythms. They penetrated a place where I had stored a memory: my mother's burning bed; he, a horse prancing, his cape iridescent. I must have said something. What, I do not remember. My lips moved—that I remember—and he plunged the needle in my thigh again.

The sun was blazing down on me when I regained consciousness. He had stripped me to my underpants. Pain seared across every inch of my body as though a million needles had been dug and then twisted viciously into me. Blood had clotted in spots over my naked torso and over my face, my arms, my legs. Where the sores were fresh, the blood oozed, and in its tracks, mosquitoes, glutted, too fat to fly, slipped and staggered like drunks.

The stench of shit burned my lungs. Vomit rose up my throat. I forced it back. I had to wait for him; I had to steel myself.

Then I saw him. He was walking toward me, bouncing a pail of water back and forth in his hand, grinning merrily. My head throbbed, but I knew what I had to do. He had cursed my mother. He had commanded graves to open and wake their sleepers. I knew how to make him afraid of me. *Obeah,* he had sneered when we heard the drums beat in the night from the other side of our bay, where the leper colony began. *Devil worship.* And yet his were the very words that passed through my mind when I chanced to see him in the afternoons walking up and down between the rows of seedlings he had planted in the mounds next to the greenhouse, at the edge of the lawn. *Obeah. Devil worship,* I thought, watching him in his velvet cape shake his cane over the seedlings and mumble words he read from his red leather-bound book.

He was close to the fence now and I summoned up my strength, what little I had remaining. "You will never rest," I said. I spoke slowly and deliberately. "You will never find peace in your life." The words whistled malignantly through my clenched teeth. "You will rot like a leper, you will die in shame, without a cent, without a farthing to your name."

His arm twitched and his hand jerked forward. Water spilled out of the pail and splashed on his leg. I did not stop. "You cursed my mother. I curse you in the name of my mother."

His head had moved downward automatically when the water wet his leg. It had taken no effort on his part, no courage, to look away, but freed from my eyes, he recovered.

He would make me like a honeycomb to bees, he said. The mosquitoes will pinch and sting me until sores and blisters covered every pore of my body. I was a rapist. *A would-be rapist.*

Even in his rage he would remember he was English, his daughter was English. *Would-be,* he remembered to say.

"Your vile race is of such a nature that nurture can never stick." He flung the words out at me.

I let him rant on.

He regretted all he had ever done for me. He was a fool to think he could change me.

But he was afraid of me. His experiment had succeeded beyond his imagining. His real fear, I knew, was that his daughter could choose me.

For two days, until Inspector Mumsford rescued me, I suffered in silence. I knew he wanted me to beg for his mercy, to cry out when the sun baked the sores where the mosquitoes had settled in hordes to bleed me, but I gave him no satisfaction.

"I must eat my dinner." That was all I said, the only consolation he got from me.

Now I sat in the room that the monk had given me. My sores were still raw, my body still racked with pain. How I wished I had said to Gardner what I said to that poor, foolish monk. How I wished I had defied him years ago. How I wished I had let him pick up the poisonous berry from the manchineel tree that day I took him to the lighthouse. I could have split it open, rubbed the juices on his hand. I could have tricked him into biting it.

For the first time in my life I felt free, in control of my thoughts. For the first time I could say without hesitation that I was seeing the world on my terms, not on his terms, not through eyes that had determined that I was inferior, that had marked me, even before I was born, as less than, as incapable of being, the man he thought himself and all white men to be.

That monk was praying for me now. It would be no use. I had stayed in Dr. Gardner's garden too long. I was my own man now.

I undressed. I took off my pants and hung them up. Something dropped out of my pocket. A piece of paper, folded in two. I unfolded it. A letter from Virginia.

My dearest Carlos,

It breaks my heart to think what Father has done to you. He told me he intends to hand you over to the commissioner. He said you tried to rape me while I was sleeping. I told him it's a lie, but he will not listen to me.

What did you say to Father?

Do not lose hope. I will tell the commissioner the truth.
I love you.

Virginia

Dearest Virginia. Before I fell asleep, I had read her last words ten times. *I love you.* In my dreams I breathed them back to her in her ear.

Virginia

EIGHTEEN

SIX YEARS have passed since Father put me on the boat to Trinidad, his head swimming with a fantasy he had concocted, spun out of desperation to cover his tracks, to ease the terror that must surely have hounded him in the minutes before waking when his mind drifted, when his dreams merged with reality before his consciousness could rescue him.

Alfred, he claimed, had fallen in love with me. Alfred wanted to marry me. And I? I had no feelings for Alfred, but my lack of feelings for Alfred did not matter to Father. What mattered to Father were his own feelings, his fear that someone would discover those feelings.

When Carlos returned to the house the day Father bid me to pack my clothes for Trinidad, I knew something terrible had happened. It was not unusual for Father to send Carlos back to the house several times to fetch something for him when they worked together in the garden. But that day Carlos did not go out again. I heard him stomp through the house; I heard him bang his bedroom door shut.

Moments later Father came to my room. He was disheveled. His hair had fallen out of the elastic band that usually held it back. It was dusted with dirt, and tiny pebbles were stuck between the strands. He had a bruise on his forehead. The skin was not broken, but it was red, the edges blue. He was perspiring profusely. Trails of sweat coursed down the sides of his face, pooling on his chin and dripping, drop after drop, onto the collar of his shirt. His pants were torn on one knee, and his shirttails were hanging out of the waistband.

"Father!" I bounded over to him, my hand raised solicitously to his forehead. "What has happened to you?"

He pushed my hand away. "Has Ariana packed your clothes?"

"I'll get the Mercurochrome." I stepped forward in the direction of the door.

"Stay in your room!" The thunder in his voice frightened me. I stopped where I was and remained rooted to the floor. I knew a storm could follow that thunder.

"Where is Ariana?" He did not wait for my answer. "Ariana!" He was at the doorway shouting out her name. "Ariana!" Then he swung back to me. "Be ready to leave early in the morning," he said.

I didn't dare ask where I was going. I was afraid of the rumbling growing darker in the back of his throat. He was happy when he came home after seeing Mrs. Burton off, calling out to me, his voice rising with a gaiety I had not heard in it before, but now his eyes were cold, hard, the folds under them dark blue. Below his cheekbones his flesh drooped into two pendulous sacks at the bottom of his jaw, and the furrows at the sides of his mouth had deepened.

"Ariana!" he called again, but she was already in the room behind him.

"What, Master?" Her voice was silky, seductive. It was the first time I heard her address him in this tone, but she had no secrets from me now.

Father seemed to lose his balance when he spun around to face her. He tottered slightly before finding his footing again. "I did not hear you." None of the roughness he had just used with me remained in his voice.

"You called me?"

I caught Father's eye and for a moment I thought I saw his face crumble with embarrassment, but I could have imagined this, for when he spoke the roughness was there. "She'll eat dinner in her room," he said to Ariana. "Don't let her out of your sight."

What had happened in the garden? Why was Father's forehead bruised, his clothes torn? Why had Carlos banged his bedroom door shut? I was afraid to ask Father these questions, and Ariana had no answers for me.

Hours later we heard Father walking up and down the corridor. After a while his footsteps ceased. When they started again, we heard the swish of the bag, or whatever it was, against the hardwood floor. Father was pulling something behind him, something heavy. He was panting and grunting. When I was sure he was out of the house, I pleaded with Ariana to let me go to Carlos. I had not heard him leave the house and I was worried. Perhaps he is sick, I said to Ariana, smothering the suspicions flickering at the edges of my brain: *Was there a connection between the blue bruise on Father's forehead and the loud bang I heard when Carlos closed his door?* Carlos may need my help, I said to her.

At first she refused to help me, but I continued to beg her and finally she agreed to check on him herself. When she came back, she told me that Carlos was not in his room. "He not sick. Your father take him in the garden," she said.

"Take him?" My nerves were raw.

"Take him. Took him," she said irritably.

But it was not her grammar that I was questioning; it was her choice of verb. Still, I could not imagine what she could have meant by *take*. "Went with him," I said. "You mean Carlos *went* with Father."

"Is that I mean," she said.

"Perhaps the bag Father was dragging had muffled Carlos's footsteps," I said, offering an explanation to calm my nerves.

"Is so," she said. "It make it hard for you to hear him."

Father was standing next to Ariana when she woke me up before dawn. "You have ten minutes," he said.

I swung my legs over the side of the bed. "Where am I going?" I asked him.

"To Mrs. Burton's," he said.

I was not surprised. I was prepared for his answer. "When will I be back?"

"If you're lucky, it won't be soon," he said.

"Can I say good-bye to Carlos?"

"No," he said. He offered me no explanation.

The coldness in his eyes frightened me. "You're sending me away forever?"

"Make a good impression and in two or three years, he'll marry you."

He meant Alfred, but I did not want to make a good impression on Alfred. He was a stranger to me. I did not like him the way Father hoped I would. He startled me when I saw him. He seemed an apparition, a character in a novel that had suddenly come to life. *Darcy.* As handsome as I had imagined Darcy. Even the manner in which he greeted me—politely but not with the enthusiasm Father had prepared me to expect—made me think of Darcy, and I stared at him long after he turned away from me.

Carlos said I looked at him as if he had come from another world. He *had* come from another world—that was how he seemed to me—a world I knew from the books I had read, a make-believe world where seasons changed, where snow fell, where the land froze, where daffodils grew. When I saw Alfred, his skin the color of dough, I knew he had come from that world.

My hair was blond and my eyes were blue but my skin was the color of copper, brown as if that hue were native to me. Alfred must have sensed my difference from him the moment he saw me, standing between the orange and red bougainvillea, in my bright pink sundress, the sun blazing down on me, the sky a brilliant blue above me. Red spots the size of pennies bloomed across his pale cheeks. When he mopped his brow, his handkerchief was soaked. I must have seemed unnatural to him, looking so cool, my skin so dry.

At lunch, he spoke slowly to me as if English were not my language. I did not speak like Father. I did not have his accent. Father spoke like an Englishman; I spoke like Carlos. I loved the way Carlos's words rose and fell in a rhythm that sounded like singing. Father protested at first, reminding me I was English. I had a responsibility to the natives, he said. They should imitate me, not me them. Father gave in eventually, for under his tutelage Carlos's vowels became rounded, his consonants crisp, not flat like Ariana's. So long as I did not speak like Ariana, Father did not correct me.

"Do you always speak so strangely?" Alfred asked me.

"I live here," I said. "This is how we speak."

Father said he was smitten. He said it as if it were in his power to make Alfred fall in love with me.

Several times at lunch Alfred leaned over to me to repeat something he had said, thinking, I suppose, I had not understood him. Father must have been desperate to assume that Alfred was trying to court me.

"Didn't you see how he wanted to get close to you?" Father said, trying to convince me. "He'll do anything to be near you."

But getting near to me was not on Alfred's mind. Orchids were on Alfred's mind. Where had Father found the white ones? Did I know where there were more? When I had no answers to give him, he soon got bored.

Father saw what he wanted to see. "Play your cards right and it'll be easy," he said. "He's got fire i' th' blood."

Fire in the blood. It was Father who had fire in the blood.

When at last Father left the room, I plied Ariana with questions. Had she seen Carlos? Had she talked to him? Where was Carlos?

Carlos in the garden, she said.

Had he said anything to Father? Did Father know about our afternoons together?

She busied herself with closing my suitcase. She did not answer me.

What did Father say to Carlos? My heart beat wildly in my chest. *He had done it. Carlos had told Father he loved me.* What did Father do to Carlos? Yet when I asked this last question, I did not imagine torture. Father was a weak man, but Father was not a cruel man. When I was a child and he lost his temper with me, he always apologized. He hugged and kissed me, though I knew my mistakes had made him angry. If Father found out about my afternoons with Carlos, he would put him out; he would make him leave the house. He would do no more than that, I thought.

Ariana locked the suitcase and came close to me. "Promise me," she said. "Not a word until you get to Trinidad."

I was leaving. I was her only hope. I nodded. I murmured my assent.

"Your father put Carlos in a cage in the garden," she said, "and he fill the cage with manure."

I could not speak. Breath rose from my chest but got trapped in my throat.

"That's not all," she said. "He put a basin full of dirty water at Carlos feet and he bring mosquitoes there. They bite Carlos all over he body. He body have mosquito bite everywhere. It bleeding all over."

She had to clamp her hand over my mouth to stifle the scream that echoed in my head.

"He say Carlos try to rape you. They going to put Carlos in jail. If you want to help him, say nothing to your father." She pushed me down on the bed and straddled my chest. "When you get to Trinidad, you tell the police. You tell them about you. I promise you I tell them everything about me."

I was ready when Father came for me. I had dried my tears. I had managed to stop my heart from galloping. *You tell them about you.* But I didn't know if I had the courage to tell the police about me.

We were close to the dock when Father announced to me that Carlos had confessed.

"Confessed?" I pretended I did not know what he meant.

"You must have seen him looking at you," he said. "Malicious slave!" He spat on the ground.

I drew in my breath. Carlos had shown me his father's poems. Had Father tortured him the way the slave masters in those poems had tortured their slaves?

"And all I have done for him," Father was saying to me. "This is how he repays me."

I was walking beside him. He was holding my bags and I was carrying an orchid in a clay pot, a present for Freddie. Freddie, not Alfred. That was how Father said I should address him. "How would he know you're interested if you insist on Alfred?" he had asked me.

We were close to the dock, only yards away. I kept my eyes straight ahead of me and clutched the clay pot tightly, trying to still my shaking hands.

"You have nothing to say?"

I bit down hard on my bottom lip.

"Ariana said she saw him," he said.

It was a lie.

"She saw him lusting after you," he said.

"No," I said.

"He confessed. He got jealous when Freddie came. Told me he liked you. Said he wanted to rape you."

"He never touched me," I said.

"When you were sleeping," he said.

I could see the boat ahead of us. It was moored to the stone wall. The boatman waved but my hands were trembling so rapidly, I could not lift them.

When you were sleeping. We both knew what happened when I was sleeping.

"The commissioner will know what to do with him," Father said. "If I had not prevented him . . ." He looked up to the sky and drew his hand across his forehead as if overcome with emotion. "If I had not got there in time." He sighed. "God knows what he would have done to you if I had not stopped him."

Lies. Lies. But I sealed my lips shut.

On the boat, I managed to scribble a note to Carlos. I gave it to the boatman. "Put it in Ariana's hands when you get back," I begged him. "Father must not see it."

NINETEEN

ID FATHER really believe his lie? To say he did, I would have to think he had gone mad, and Father had not gone mad. Father was sane, sane enough to figure out a way to save his skin by pointing his finger at Carlos, depositing his sins on Carlos's shoulders and granting himself absolution.

"God knows what he would have done to you," he said to me.

God knew what he, my father, had done to me.

I had warnings, but I say so in retrospect. Guilt blinded me each time a fissure threaded through my brain, cracking open a narrow slit that could have allowed me to see. He was my father. I loved him.

"You are what I live for." He said those words to me hundreds of times. The first time I was a toddler, clinging to his neck and weeping. The book he read to me at night had pictures of children in it. All the children had mothers. I wanted a mother.

He would be my mother and father, he said. "You are what I live for."

So I made myself believe he had not intended to kiss me the way he did on my birthday, that he was caught by surprise, terrified when he glimpsed into that dark pit he had opened up by accident.

We were celebrating. I had turned twelve. He was drunk, giddy with too much wine. "Go on," he said, filling my glass. "A lady should know how to drink wine with dinner."

I did not feel like a lady. I was still a child, but he told me this was the last year I would be a child. Next year I would be a teenager and soon a woman, he said.

To please him I drank the wine, though I did not like the taste. He finished the bottle.

Did I encourage him to embrace me so tightly when he came to my room to say good night? My head felt light, my muscles loose and re-laxed. I opened the door for him, the wine making me feel none of the usual tension that always caused me to brace myself for his nightly lec-tures on what I had failed to learn that day, on what I must be prepared to learn the next. He opened his arms and I glided into them.

Which happened first, I cannot tell. Did I turn my head to the right for his kiss on my cheek while he was turning his? Did we try to correct the mistake both at the same time? In the end, our heads were facing for-ward and the kiss intended for my cheek landed on my mouth. Before I could wriggle free, his tongue, hard, wet, warm, probed my lips apart.

The next day Father made his announcement. He would no longer be my teacher. I had learned all that was necessary for a woman to learn. From then on, I would be apprenticed to Ariana.

Only he and I knew the truth. It was fear that made him relinquish those early-morning hours he spent with me, terrifying me into learn-ing to read and write and do simple arithmetic. I was slow, he said; I was not smart.

Carlos saved me. If not for Carlos, I would have believed what Fa-ther had said about me. I would have continued to think I was stupid. Carlos said I saved him first. Before I arrived, he hated his freckles, he said. They were ugly dots that disfigured his face. He was at war with his body, but when I touched his cheek and smiled at him, he was the victor.

I do not remember touching his cheek, but I remember that day. It was the first time Father had spoken harshly to me. "Never touch *them*," he hissed in my ear. He snapped his hand around my wrist and tugged me so hard, I stumbled. When the door closed behind us, he began hollering at me, words I could not make out except these: "You are white. Do you understand? You are white."

I knew my colors. He had taught them to me. I was pink, but only under my clothes. My face, my arms, my legs, every part of my body that my dress had not covered had turned fiery red on the beach in Trinidad where I had followed Father each morning, waiting for the fishermen to leave, searching afterward for fish they had left behind. Father rubbed ointment on my burning skin and promised the pain would subside. When it did, I was tanned brown.

"I'm not white," I whimpered.

Father clutched my shoulders and shook me. I was better than that boy, he said. Better than Ariana, better than all the people who had given us fish to eat, better than the ones who had put us on the boat to Chacachacare.

"Better? Why better, Father?" Tears streamed down my face.

"Because your skin is white," he said. He let go of my shoulders.

He had shown me white. Snow was white; flour was white. "No, Father," I said. I stretched out my arm. I wanted to prove to him that I had learned my colors. "This is not white."

His eyebrows converged and then slackened. "Next to them," he said. "I mean next to them. Your skin is white next to them."

I did not understand him. "Next to them?"

"Compared to them. Your skin is white compared to their skin."

"And would my skin still be white, Father, if they were not here?"

My question seemed to amuse him. His mouth, rigid when he was speaking to me, relaxed into a smile. "What a clever girl," he said.

Clever girl! I had waited a long time for such praise.

"But you see," he said, "they are colored and you are not colored."

Encouraged, I showed him how much more I knew. "I am colored, too, Father," I said. "I am colored red and pink." I pointed to my tanned legs. "And brown, too."

"Golden brown," he corrected me. "They are colored black."

My black crayon was black. "Carlos is not the color of my crayon," I said.

He was talking about people, not crayons, he said.

"Are colors different for people?"

The rigidity returned to his mouth. He lost patience with me. "You are *better.* You are *superior* to that boy. You are superior to all the colored people here. That is the point. Remember that."

But it was Carlos who had taught me to read, not Father. If Father was so superior, why had he not found a way to teach me to read?

I loved Father but I was afraid of him. Because I loved him, I wanted to please him; I wanted to be smart for him, to know the answers to the questions he asked me, to recite by heart the lessons he taught me. Because I feared him, my nerves became frayed, my brain clogged, and nothing he said penetrated. Words stuck in my throat; they would not come out. When they did, they left my tongue in no order I could recognize.

Carlos put me at ease. With Father, words were lines and loops I grew to despise. I tried to put sound to them so he would not raise his voice at me, so he would not look at me with disgust in his eyes, as if he were ashamed of me, as if he could not understand how a man as brilliant as he could have fathered an idiot like me.

How pleased he was when I read my first little book from cover to cover! But Carlos had made me see the pictures behind the words. He had traced his finger beneath the lines and loops when he read to me, and I saw colors and shapes as clearly as if they were in front of me.

How shocked Father was when I blurted out the poem Carlos had taught me! *Tyger! Tyger! burning bright / In the forests of the night.* I was walking behind Father, spellbound by a moon so bright it looked like the sun.

"Lahjabless walking tonight." Ariana had tried to frighten me.

"Don't pay her any mind," Carlos said. "It's the full moon that makes her talk like that."

And it was the full moon that made me talk like that, that made me sing out the poem Carlos had taught me as I skipped behind my father in the moonlight.

Tyger! Tyger! burning bright
In the forests of the night,
What immortal hand or eye
Could frame thy fearful symmetry?

"*I* not *e*," Father said, not turning his head to look back at me. I had pronounced the final syllable of the last word to rhyme with *tree*. "Symmetri," Father said.

I sang out the poem again, caught in the magic of the dappled light, the treetops covered in lace, like Cinderella's dress. But while I was here, on my beloved island, Father must have been there, in England, a boy reciting the same lines in a forest of maple and oak. My girlish voice must have clashed against the deeper tones of that boy's, for suddenly Father seemed to hear me, to realize it was my voice, not the boy's, that had brushed against his ears. He stopped short and I fell against him.

"Who? What?" His tongue struggled to find the question he wanted.

Too late I realized what I had done. Carlos had warned me: He would teach me but I could not tell Father.

"Who taught it to you?"

Father must have suspected the moment he found the question. He had not read the poem to me. Even if I had opened his books, he knew I did not know enough to read the poem on my own.

"Who?" Disbelief registered on his face, but the possibility was too far-fetched to take hold in his brain. He bounded to the house, anger giving authority to his footsteps.

Carlos said I was brave to defend him. But it was not courage that made me bring Carlos's book to Father. I was proud of Carlos. I wanted to prove to Father that he was wrong. Carlos was smart. He could read. He could read books I could not read. I was not superior to him. The color of my skin did not make me better than him.

When Father declared that my formal education was over, Carlos, pitying me, said he would continue to teach me. He had no inkling of the desperation that had driven Father to his decision. He did not know that Father was afraid to be alone with me.

Not long afterward my body began to change. Startlingly, within just a few weeks after Father turned me over to Ariana, my breasts blossomed into two plump balls that strained against the thin fabric of my blouses. I pulled and tugged at the sides of my chest, trying to adjust my body into dresses that had become too tight for me. Father noticed. Without saying a word to me, he sent Carlos to Trinidad with a note for the shopkeeper to send a bra for me.

"If only your mother were here," Father said when he handed me the package.

I was more embarrassed for him than for myself when I saw what was in it.

"Your mother could have shown you how to wear it," he said, shaking his head and looking so miserable that, thinking to ease his discomfort, I said I would ask Ariana to help me.

"She's a servant," he said gruffly. He felt inept, he felt inadequate, but it was his duty to prepare me to be a lady. "Go." He sat down on my bed. "Put it on. I want to see how it fits."

At the time I did not think this was a pretext so he could remain in the room. I thought he meant what he said sincerely. I went behind the closet door and took off my dress. I put on the bra, and over it, my bathrobe.

"Let's see. Let's see," Father said when I came out from behind the door. "Open your robe. I can't see how it fits if you close your robe." He got up and came toward me. "Come, come. Hurry up."

My body felt hot. My fingers shook when I untied the belt of my robe. Father used to dress me when I was a child but he had long since left me to dress on my own. I felt embarrassed, ashamed, when he eased the robe over my shoulders. But Father appeared oblivious of my body, his attention focused on my bra as if the two cups held nothing beneath them, as if he were unaware that only a mere piece of cotton separated what was visible to his eyes from my new, burgeoning flesh.

"No, the straps are too tight." He stuck his finger between the elastic and my bare skin. My shoulders stung when the elastic snapped back.

"And you fastened it too tightly in the back."

I was standing in front of him, my bathrobe dropped to my waist, my chest bare except for the white bra encasing my breasts.

"Unfasten it. Can't you see your skin popping out below?" The bottoms of my breasts had rolled out beneath the hem of the bra. He flicked his finger across one and then the other. "Turn around. Turn around."

I felt hands on my back. There was a buzzing in my ear. I stopped breathing.

"If only your mother were here . . ." He sighed.

Was I to believe him? And yet he had said nothing nor done anything for me to doubt his innocence. I felt riddled with guilt for my half-formed suspicions. The kiss was an accident; his fingers brushing the bottoms of my breasts nothing more than his awkward attempt to help me. If my mother were here and had done as he had done, would I have harbored dark thoughts?

But in the days and weeks that followed I couldn't avoid noticing that he was looking at me in a way he had never done before. If I chanced to meet his eyes, he turned away or frowned at me. I thought he was displeased with me, disappointed I was not growing up to be a beauty like my mother. At night I used to look longingly at her photograph on my dresser and beg God to make me resemble her. In despair one day I sought comfort from Carlos. You look just like her, he said. Even prettier. I thought my father believed the opposite.

And yet there was something in the way Father looked at me that made me feel not merely inadequate, but ill at ease. It was as if the way my body was developing was a source of embarrassment to him, not merely of disappointment. Frequently when he spoke to me, he would cast his eyes downward to my legs, and a shiver would rush through his body when he turned away.

Soon he began to complain about my clothes. I was still wearing the cotton shifts Ariana made for me on a sewing machine Father had bought her. They were simple dresses with an opening at the top for my head and on either side for my arms. They had no waistline, and the only adjustment Ariana had made to them was to add long darts to make room for my breasts.

Now Father thought there was something else she needed to do.

My bottom jiggled, he said to me one evening after dinner. He had just excused me from the table and I was walking away from him in the direction of the drawing room. I stopped immediately, self-conscious of his eyes on me, and I drew my hands quickly along the sides of my hips as if somehow doing so I could hold my jiggling flesh in place.

"Yes," he said. "We must do something about that."

His remedy was a panty corset. Carlos was sent again with a sealed note to the store in Trinidad, requesting one for me.

"If only your mother was here . . ." Father began with the usual refrain. He loved me, he said. All he did was in care of me, his dear one, his daughter. He had done his best; he had tried to be a good father, a kind and loving father.

How else could I respond but to say I loved him, too, to say he was a kind and loving father?

Ah, he said, he would have done more if he were truly a kind and loving father. He would not have abandoned me.

"Abandoned me?" He had brought me with him from England. He had not abandoned me.

"I should not have left you to figure out by yourself the things a woman must know," he said. He looked directly into my eyes. "You have a jewel."

It was wishful thinking, absurd that I should have allowed myself to believe he was speaking of my mother's diamond engagement ring. He had given it to me years ago, when I was still a child. He had warned me to keep it under lock and key. It was one of a kind, he had said. But so profound was my embarrassment at that moment that I reached for the slimmest straw.

"I still have it, Father," I said. "I have not lost it."

He grimaced. "And you will be worth nothing if you do," he said.

I flinched and he asked: "Do I surprise you? Ah, but you know nothing about the world." He rocked back in his chair. "I can tell you much about the world. The world is evil," he said.

"No one here would steal Mother's ring," I said, still trying to hold on to my childhood.

"Foolish child." His eyes were full of scorn for me.

"But I have it, Father. I can show it to you. I can, Father."

Did I mirror a desire he had managed to suppress? *I can show it to you.* At night, in bed, was this his dream?

He brought his chair to a standstill. "I'm not speaking of your mother's ring." His voice was hoarse. "Your biggest jewel. *That* is what I mean. Your virgin knot." He leaned forward toward me.

Instinctively I drew my legs together and locked them at my knees.

"The jewel in your dower. Your prize," he said.

I prayed the floor would open up and swallow me. I twisted my body in the chair, trying to escape the oily sheen glittering off his eyes.

"You're not like them. *Animals,* that's what they are. They lack self-control. Reason." He drummed his index finger into his forehead. "They give in to every impulse, every desire. Break your virgin knot and you will be just like them. No more than an animal that has no reason, that has no will, that does what it wants to do, when it wants to do it. *We* control our bodies. *We* do not let our bodies control us. *We* control our desires. Our desires do not control us. Do you understand me?"

I clenched my hands hard into each other.

"You will be no different from Ariana if you lose your jewel." The vein in the middle of his forehead was thick and dark. "Guard it or you will have no value."

How could I have guessed then that I would have to guard it from him?

For two days I wore the corset he had given me, and then on the third day a rash broke out across my waist and around the top of my thighs where the elastic, soaked with perspiration, clung to my skin. By the end of the week, a rosary of tiny bumps had spread down my thighs and was working its way toward my knees. He relented finally. I no longer had to wear a corset, but my dresses had to be made in a style that had skirts wide enough to conceal the movement of my bottom and roomy enough for my breasts.

"You're like your mother," he said, rubbing on my thighs and legs a salve he had mixed. "Her skin was sensitive. Your father's skin was tough."

It was possible he was unaware he had said, *your father,* not *my father;* that he had used the past tense, *was,* not *is.* But I needed to be reassured; I needed to be reminded he was my father, my protector. My nerves were strained, my mind in a turmoil with guilt for feelings I could not articulate. What had he done that a parent would not have done? Who else could have prepared me to be a woman? My mother was dead. I should have been grateful he was willing to be both mother and father to me, and yet I was overcome with shame when he spoke to me about these intimate things concerning my body, shame that almost paralyzed me now when he touched my thighs.

"Aren't you my father?" I asked him.

"Your mother was a virtuous woman," he said, "and she told me you were my daughter."

His answer intensified my confusion. I believed that he believed he was my father, but the words he seemed to have chosen deliberately deepened my discomfort, my yet-unarticulated suspicions. He praised my mother, but he also cast a shadow over her.

TWENTY

*B*UT I WAS ALSO HAPPY on Chacachacare. I had Carlos for a companion. From the day he saved the bird Father had almost killed, I felt bound to him by an invisible string Father could not break. In Father's presence we pretended we meant nothing to each other, but we had our secret codes: a wink, a smile, a nod.

Carlos did not eat at the table with Father and me, but from where he was positioned in the kitchen I could see him, and we devised ways of sending signals to each other. When Father bent over his plate, I would look up and wave to Carlos. Sometimes I would accidentally drop my napkin on the floor. From under the table, I would flutter my fingers, reminding Carlos of the time we fed a bird together. I did that twice at dinner one night and Father spoke sharply to me. "I'll have to pin that napkin to your bodice if you can't keep it on your lap," he said. But he must have noticed, too, that from where I sat I could look straight across to Carlos.

I do not think Father allowed himself to imagine that I could have feelings for Carlos, yet something instinctual in him that he could not or would not articulate made him decide that night to block my view.

The next day he moved the table and made me sit with my back to the kitchen. Not long afterward I was a participant in a lecture he staged with a stack of sticks to warn Carlos and Ariana of the consequences of disobeying him. I stiffened against Father when he pulled me close to his chest and pointed out my place on the pyramid he had made with the sticks. My place, he said, was just below his place and above the place where he had put Carlos and Ariana.

"That's why they eat in the kitchen," Father explained to me after he had dismissed Ariana and Carlos.

"But we found them here," I protested.

"Ah," he sighed, "if not for us, where would they be?" He reminded me how much they needed his help. "A tree had crashed into the side of the house, remember? What if I had not moved it? What if I had not fixed the wall? The next storm would have wiped them out. That woman could not take care of them. She was too sick. They would have nothing if I had not helped them."

He claimed Lucinda sold him the house in gratitude for all he did for her. "I let him stay free of charge," he said. "I don't ask him to pay me."

But Carlos insisted the house was his. "It was my mother's," he said to me, "and so it's mine." Yet he never confronted Father, though often I heard Father remind him that he had bought the house from Lucinda, that Carlos was lucky he had permitted him to live with us. What was I to conclude except that Carlos said those things to me because he *wished* the house were his; he *wished* his mother had not let Lucinda have it?

Carlos kept his tongue in his mouth, too, when Father repeated the story he had told us about the fall of Lucifer. I knew Carlos seethed with anger. I saw his face darken, his nostrils flare, but he never challenged Father.

"Why?" I asked Father again when I was much older. "Why do we belong at the top of the pyramid?"

"You do not know who you are," Father said. "Do you think this primitive place was always your home?"

I knew I was born in England. How many times had Father told me that I was an heir to an empire? How many times had he told me about kings and queens and the conquests that vaulted their little island to an empire? But these stories never took root in my imagination. No matter how often he tried to convince me I belonged to the world he described of castles and manor houses, of lords and ladies—*civilized gentry*—to a world of battleships and bombers that had conquered continents, I felt removed from it, distant, a stranger, an alien to the people and places he said were mine.

The winter wonderland he spoke about seemed to me a figment of his imagination, snow and sleet as unreal to me as the turrets and towers he described. The host of golden daffodils, sheep grazing on rolling green meadows, fantasies. But I had seen the ibis return home before twilight; I had seen the sky turn red with their scarlet feathers when they flew past our island from their feeding grounds in Venezuela to roost in the mangrove in Trinidad. I had seen the sky so blue I imagined God. I had seen the sun set it on fire and spread its dying embers in a carnival of colors across the horizon. I had smelled the air after a rainfall, sodden with salt from the sea. I had heard thunder roar when lightning sliced the clouds in two. I had mistaken the songs of birds for the voices of humans singing. This was my world. These were the sounds and sweet smells I knew, I loved.

But this time when he related my history to me again, Father wanted to be specific.

"I was famous in England," he said. "An important man." He waved his hand over his face to brush away my astonishment. "Fame brings envy," he said.

Was he envied? I asked him.

"By everybody," he said. "Especially by my brother."

The story he told me was different from the one he told Carlos, though calculated also to gain my gratitude. My father wanted people to be beholden to him. He thrived on their gratitude. He did not give me the lie about doing his bit for the Empire. He wanted me to know he had sacrificed his life for me.

"I was a better doctor than my brother," he said. "He was jealous of me, of the praise I got constantly. When your mother died, he figured out a way to hurt me. He was married and had no children. He took me to court on a trumped-up story that I was too busy and had no time to raise you. You were a baby, just three. He said you needed a mother, and his wife would be the perfect mother for you. I had enemies. I knew there was a chance he could win the case, so I ran. Nobody would look for me in a leper colony."

I did not dare ask: What caused your brother to think you had no time for me, Father? Why did you have enemies?

"You are a third of my life," he said. "That for which I live. You preserved me."

I clung to his flamboyant declaration of paternal love, hoping to chase away the dark shadows drifting between us. Would a father who so loved his daughter, who lived for her, given up friends, comfort, England, all for her, do anything to harm her?

"I am fair to Carlos," he said. "I treat him better than befits his station. His mother was a party girl, his father a black nobody. You come from better stock." My station, his station, Father said, was higher than Carlos's station.

We were on an isolated island. A cell, Father sometimes called it. Across from us, a leper colony, hidden only by the bend in the horseshoe darkened by low hills dense with trees. On an island like ours, what did station matter?

"Ah," Father said. "Everything."

Everything was the natural order of the universe.

I heard Ariana use Father's very words to the fisherman who brought our fish on Mondays. I used to go with her in late afternoon to meet him at the edge of the bay. He was infatuated with her but she would have nothing to do with him. He smelled of fish guts, she said, and his clothes were filthy.

I thought he was handsome. His pants were torn, his sleeveless vest, once white, was stained with dried blood. Fish scales glinted across his bare arms, some tangled in his matted hair, but his face glowed with a sheen that made me think of a newly minted penny: clean, washed, unused, bronzed. When he spoke, it was easy to ignore his smell and his tattered clothes, to be drawn to him by his wide smile and bright, twinkling eyes.

"Ah always save the best fish for you," he said, winking at Ariana.

She took the fish from him without a word. "He too boldface," she told me later. "He forget his place."

Did Ariana learn about place from my father, or did the concept of her place and the fisherman's place in relation to her place come naturally to her? Did she think she had a right to a better place on the social ladder because she wore clean clothes and smelled of soap?

Carlos would quote Milton to me: *Better to reign in Hell than serve in Heaven.* Yet he never contested Father's perverted notions about the natural order of the universe that placed him below Father and me. There were days I waited anxiously for him to return from his errands for Father in Trinidad, all the time thinking that this would be the day, this would be the day he would not come back. But he never stayed. He always came back.

Father said he could go to school in Trinidad. Why didn't he go?

"I would never learn as much as I am learning from him," he said. "Your father gives me his books. I listen to his music."

Was he really so grateful to Father? I heard the bitterness in his voice, I saw his jaw clench and his eyes turn cold in my father's presence, but I pretended it was my imagination that made me hear and see such things, an illusion created out of my anxiety. I was selfish. I did not want to be left alone with Father on the island.

I could have had another friend. There was a girl who had tried to befriend me. I was with Ariana when I first saw her. Ariana was quarreling with the fisherman about the size of the fish he had brought for her. My father wanted baked stuffed fish for supper and had given her his orders.

"I tell you it have to be this long," Ariana was saying to the fisherman. She stretched out her left arm and with her right hand measured its length, from her elbow to the tips of her fingers. The fisherman, giddy with his attraction for her, reached out to touch her.

"Ah," he cooed, "yuh arm sweeter than sugar."

Ariana pounced on him. He was too fast, she said, an expression alluding not to his physical dexterity but to the speed with which he had assumed familiarity with her. He had forgotten his place. He had crossed the line. "Monkey should know which tree to climb," she said. She steupsed and flounced her body away from him.

Embarrassed for the fisherman, I looked in the other direction, away from the sea, toward the trees that grew up the incline on the right side of the doctor's house, opposite to the path that led to our house. Something caught my eye, a branch swaying back and forth though there was no breeze. I squinted in the fiery light of the descending sun and peered into the distance. I saw arms first, then legs. That was all I saw before Ariana grabbed my hand and pulled me away.

I did not tell Ariana or Carlos what I had seen. I was sure the arms and legs belonged to a girl, and if I was right, she had broken the rules. She had gone beyond the boundary of the leper colony. If she was caught, she would be punished.

For two weeks, I searched for the girl among the trees, but there was no sign of her, not the slightest movement in the branches to give me hope. Then one day I looked down instead of up, and there I saw, propped against one of the tree trunks, a tiny bouquet of pink and yellow wildflowers tied with brown string. While Ariana bargained with the fisherman, I edged toward the trees and picked it up.

The next Monday, in the very same place, there was a single red hibiscus, tied once again with brown string. This time I saw her. She was crouched in a cup of the tree, her bare feet, bony like a bird's, curled over the edge of a branch. She could have been my age but she was much thinner. The pink cotton petticoat she was wearing hung over her shoulders, a dress on a clothes hanger, the space seemingly empty beneath it except for knees, legs, and feet, spindly twigs, protruding. Her hair was cut short, just to her ears. It was thick and curly, the curls denser and tighter than Ariana's. Her nose was small but her eyes were big, saucer-shaped. What I noticed most of all was her skin, and I let out my breath, relieved. It was flawless, a silky flow of brown chocolate, nothing to mar it, no telltale signs of the dreaded disease.

When our eyes met, she put her finger to her lips and pointed in Ariana's direction. I picked up the hibiscus and stuffed it in my pocket.

The following Monday, while Ariana was distracted, I put my best yellow ribbon under the tree. The girl returned it to me the next Monday tied around five yellow buttercup flowers. I left her a pink ribbon the next time and she gave it back to me wrapped around a pink ixora. I left her a white one next, and I got it back with a bow on a white seashell. And so we did this exchange once a week, Ariana never finding out until, suddenly, the girl disappeared. Weeks went by and one by one the ribbons I left for her lost color, bleached by the blazing sun. Rain fell and the ribbons sank in the mud. In a month they were unrecognizable, tattered and torn.

Six months passed, and I had almost despaired of seeing the girl again, when one late afternoon something blue fluttered out in the breeze from behind the shadows of a pillar beneath the doctor's house. The skirt of a dress! My heart pumping fast in my chest, I hurried toward the pillar. Ariana was too absorbed admonishing the fisherman about something to take notice of me. I was just a short distance away from the pillar when my friend came out of the shadows. I gasped, shocked when I saw her. Afraid Ariana had heard me, I turned around quickly, but the sound I had made as air rushed down my throat, almost choking me, had filtered through the fisherman's teasing laughter and was lost in the soft lapping of the tiny waves upon the stony beach. In that split second when I turned back again, my friend was gone. She had evaporated into the air like the wet slick of rain on concrete when the sun came out. But her image remained, branded on my brain. Across her forehead and below her cheekbones I had seen blisters clustered together like tiny cherries, dark, firm, her flesh beginning to rot on a face alive, animated with excitement to see me until it met its reflection in the mirror of my eyes.

Never before had I been so close to someone with Hansen's disease. I had had glimpses of some patients from the colony, but they were dark silhouettes against the afternoon sun, crammed next to each other in an open pirogue behind the government boat that towed them across the bay to Trinidad to visit relatives, their children, perhaps, who had been taken from them. These were the cured ones but the ones still treated as pariah, made to sit on benches in a rudderless boat. I should have felt pity for them, but the fear my father had instilled in me was too strong to leave room for compassion. I shut my eyes and wished them away. Now, seeing my friend's face, her flesh rotting, I shuddered with revulsion.

For nights I could not sleep, terrified that I could contract her disease. I had worn the ribbons she had returned; I had breathed in the scent of the flowers she had touched. Unable to put my fears out of my mind, I told Carlos what I had done.

"You can't get leprosy by touching someone's clothing," he assured me. "Don't worry about the ribbons."

But I felt guilty. And I missed her. Only my deepening friendship with Carlos eased my longing to see her again. Now I lived for those hours when Father went to his garden and I had Carlos to myself. Ariana alone spoiled my happiness then, though I did my best to ignore her. I could not help but hear the sighs that came, sometimes in rolling waves, from the kitchen where she sat. But Ariana had always seemed morose to me. I used to think it was because her mother was dead, but my mother was also dead. Ariana was more fortunate than I. I would have preferred to have known my mother even if for a short time. That would have been better than not to have known her at all. I said so to Ariana and she replied that at least my mother had not abandoned me. "Your mother did not *want* to die," I said to her. "She did not *want* to leave you." And she answered, "She should have find some place to leave me then. Not here on this godforsaken island."

I thought she was happy living in the house with us. I thought she liked Father. I thought she wanted to please him. "The food the way you like it, sir?" she would ask him as she cleared the table. The slightest praise from Father seemed to brighten her eyes.

I used to think Father made her feel important when he called her to his room after lunch. She would announce what we would eat the next day as if the decision were hers, and she would make poor Carlos wash the dishes for her and mop the floor. I thought she liked me, too. When I was a child she seemed happy to play games with me when Father went in the garden and left her to entertain me.

I thought the reason she began to resent me was that I had told Father that Carlos could read. It was my fault, she seemed to believe, that Father no longer required Carlos to help her in the kitchen. I became a burden to her after that. She began to see herself as Father had defined her: my servant, my nanny at my beck and call, his eyes when he could not be with me. So I convinced myself that I was doing her a favor, giving her long hours to do whatever she wanted while I sat in the drawing room with Carlos.

Yet it became more and more difficult for me to turn a blind eye to the gloom that seemed to have settled over her. Permanently, it appeared to me. She would sit in the same spot in the kitchen while Carlos and I talked and laughed in the drawing room. From time to time, she would sigh or glance up at us with a vacant expression in her eyes. On our afternoon walks now, she barely said a word to me. Even with the fisherman, she was strangely subdued. No more did she complain about the fish he brought her. When he teased her, she looked away from him, her eyes drifting aimlessly across the bay. Nothing he could say—about her hair, her eyes, her arms—could nudge her into her usual response. It was as if he had become a stranger to her. She paid for the fish and let his teasing wash over her.

Worried, the fisherman asked her if she was not well. "Mind your own business," she said. There was no snap of anger in her tone, only a deadening dismissal of his concern for her.

"The Tobago love is over," Carlos said.

Tobago love. Tobago, on the northwestern coast of Trinidad, was the most populated of the islands annexed to it, the butt of jokes about its smallness and the supposedly futile ambition of its people to imitate the sophistication of Trinidadians. Ariana liked the attention the fisherman was giving her, Carlos explained. She just didn't know how to accept his compliments.

Perhaps Carlos was right, but I thought there had to be a bigger reason for the change in Ariana. There were times I came upon her sitting in the kitchen, her eyes downcast, twirling a strand of her thick, black hair absentmindedly around her fingers. She seemed to be in another world, a world miles away from where we were. And yet I never inquired. I never asked her if there was something I could do to help her.

I preserved him, Father said. I was soon to discover that Ariana preserved me from him.

TWENTY-ONE

*T*HE FIRST TIME Father came to my room, I had just turned fifteen. I was sleeping. I thought I was dreaming. Something was stuck in my throat and I could not get it out. But I was not dreaming. Something *was* stuck in my throat. I gagged and it sank in deeper. I gagged again and tried to get up, but a great weight pressed down on me and I could not budge. I flailed my arms. It held me down.

I saw skin.

I saw hair.

Then it was over.

Father was sitting at the side of my bed, his head buried in his hands. "I'm sorry. I'm sorry." He said the words again and again. Tears were in his eyes.

"Humankind," says T. S. Eliot, "cannot bear very much reality." I am human; I, too, cannot bear very much reality. I need my dreams, my illusions, my fantasies. I lose part of myself when I glimpse back to that first time when Father violated me, the self I need to believe is lovable, is good, is pure. The self I need to believe was not soiled, was not defiled. The self I fantasize had a girlhood like the girlhood of those innocent girls, those pretty women, in the stories I read. This fantasy keeps me steady; it holds me back from tumbling down the tunnel of despair from which I fear I may never return.

I loved my father. Even now I want to love my father. Isn't that the wish of every daughter? Who wants to know, who wants to believe, that the flesh and blood that gave life to her flesh and blood would wish to ruin her?

I know with my reason that Father crossed a line no loving father would cross. I know with my heart that Father loved me. These two truths exist side by side, one unbearable, the other making it possible for me to hope, to believe I can be loved.

My reason urges me to expose him, to reveal to the last detail all he had done to me. He with his books and his learning; he with his pale skin, his books, and his learning, presuming himself superior to Carlos.

He can read. The little savage can read. I had heard him clearly that day I proved to him that Carlos could read. I had not forgotten.

Who was the savage now? Who, in spite of his learning, had transgressed that universal taboo embedded in the souls of all of us who call ourselves human?

I am afraid to recall the sounds, the grunts Father made that stopped up my ears. I am afraid to recall the smells, the musky odor of sweat and semen. I am afraid to recall the touch, a father's body on his daughter's. I tell what I can tell, what I can bear to tell.

Father made me a promise. "It won't happen again," he said.

Five times. That is the number, the numeral for the actual times that it happened again. One million, eight hundred, fourteen thousand, four hundred. That is the number, the true times it happened to me again. For there was not a second in those three weeks before Father wrote to Mrs. Burton, afraid of what more he might do, that I could build a dam strong enough against the raging force of memories, insistent that I feel all over again his hardened flesh in my mouth, his fingers in my hair, leeches drawing blood.

The next time he bruised my lips. I twisted my head to the right; I twisted it to the left. He twisted it back again, fingers in my hair.

When he was finished, he pleaded for my pity. "Look at what I have become," he said. "My child, my own child."

My child. My own child.

The third time, he wanted my compassion. "I have no friends, no family, no one who looks like me. Only you. I get so lonely."

The fourth time, long after he was gone, a bone, the ghost of a bone, lingered in my throat. Ariana caught me looking for it. "Here." She handed me a jar of honey. Shame, like molten tar, coursed through my body, burning me up.

"It make you feel better," she said. "I know he do it to you, too."

I could barely speak. "Too?" I asked her.

"What you think he do with me when he call me in he room after lunch?" she said.

"Since when?"

"Since I was nine," she said.

Bile stung my throat and I coughed to push it down.

She handed me a towel. "I want to throw up, too," she said. I pressed the towel against my lips. I swallowed hard.

"Since you turn woman, he do it to me worse because is you he want, not me."

Did he put it in your mouth?

I must have asked the question for I heard her say, "Not only there. It don't matter to him I not a virgin. I black. He say you still a virgin."

My jewel was in my dower; my virgin knot was unbroken. That was what mattered to Father.

Did Father fear that he would cease to exist, that he would no longer be who he deceived himself to be if Ariana was not who he defined her to be? Was it so essential to this deception that I, his English rose, remain untouched, her jewel safe in her dower? Was Father's construction of his worth so dependent on his construction of the lack of worth of people whose skin color was darker than his?

Father said Ariana and her kind were primitive. He meant no malice, he told me. And I used to think *primitive* was a kinder word than *savage*. Primitive people, Father said, were like children. They gave no thought to the consequences of their actions. They did what they wanted to do because it pleased them to do it when they did it. But we were civilized. *We* white people, *we* English people, used reason to control our desires. If this was true, Father had become too civilized, his desires so controlled, so repressed, that like a boil rounded and glistening with pus, his desires had grown ripe. Freed from the eyes that could have restrained him in England, Father lanced his boil and it spewed out the years of obscenities he had hoarded, defiling Ariana, defiling me.

The morning of the fifth and last time Father came to my room, he left lesions in my mouth. This time he placed the blame on me. He could not help himself, he said. I reminded him of my mother. "Such beautiful hair, such beautiful eyes." He stroked my neck. I tore away his hand.

It didn't take much to convince Carlos that all I suffered from was a sore throat. But Father knew better. Terrified that the fifth time might not be the last time, he reached out for salvation to Mrs. Burton.

TWENTY-TWO

I BARELY NOTICED the crossing by sea. Yet there had been days, standing at the edge of the bay, I could not move though Ariana stamped her feet and shouted my name threatening to leave me, so entranced was I by the tiny ripples across the silken water, the shimmering reflection of greens and browns from trees overshadowing the bay. Now on the boat on my way to Mrs. Burton's I was blind to all that beauty. Now questions consumed me: What would the police do to Carlos? What could I say to save him?

"Tell them about you," Ariana urged me. Did I dare, though Father had abused me?

I had liked Carlos from the first day I saw him. Loved him before he knew. Twelve years, not five or six, *twelve* years we had lived together on this isolated island, our only neighbors, the lepers, bound together by their infirmities and keeping their distance from us and we from them. What boy or girl would not have clung to each other?

My childish self had said the words when Carlos saved a dying bird for me, but now the words had meaning: I loved him. All those afternoons sitting next to him in the drawing room. All those afternoons listening to his stories, pretending to pay attention to the lessons he wanted to teach me, and most of the time watching the slope of his chin, tracing the lines of his lips, his broad brow, his wide chin, finding the reflection of my eyes in his. How could he think I would consider marrying Alfred?

It was Father, not I, who believed that the color of Alfred's skin would make Alfred more attractive to me. A child does not think less of another child because the color of that child's skin is different from hers. Adults are the ones who plant the disease; adults are the ones who nurture it.

Malicious slave. I burned with anger when Father spat out those words as I walked next to him on the way to the boat that was waiting for me. Carlos had made me understand that slavery was a crime against humanity. Did Father believe that Carlos was less than human; that Alfred, but not Carlos, was human?

Guilt-thickened tongues, stopped-up vocal cords when Fanny Price asked Sir Bertram about the slave trade. I had read feverishly to the end of *Mansfield Park,* hoping to find evidence of their remorse. But though Sir Bertram was ready to admit his mistakes in raising his daughters, not a word of repentance crossed his lips. And yet he had made his fortune trading human flesh. And yet he had purchased and furnished Mansfield Park with money steeped in human blood. Was his conscience not stirred because he believed the Africans he enslaved were less than human? Was Father's conscience not stirred because he believed Carlos was less than human?

Mrs. Burton had arranged for a car to meet me at the Yacht Club. When the driver opened the back door, I slid inside, barely managing to thank him. My fears for Carlos still hounded me, questions bombarding me that I had no answers for. I clutched the clay pot with the orchid for Mrs. Burton close to my chest and lowered my head. I must have been a pitiful sight, for the driver turned to me and said, "Not to worry, miss. I get you there in an hour." He had misread my silence, but it was then, when I raised my head to answer him, that I saw the world Carlos had described to me.

The sun had risen only a sliver above the horizon when we left Chacachacare, and in the dim light, the trees and the sea seemed covered by a veil, gray though translucent. Now, an hour later, the forested hills on the left side of the road were flecked with gold, and on the right, where the land dropped sharply, the sea was dazzling. Half-naked fishermen, their brown torsos glistening in the sunlight, their legs spread wide apart, balanced themselves on the bows of colorful pirogues and threw huge nets overboard that sent long sprays of water in the air that sparkled like diamonds.

I had imagined all this. I had reconstructed this world, made paintings in my mind with the words Carlos had given me, but what I saw before me was a thousand times better. I sat up in the car, breathless now with anticipation. I knew what was to come, and yet when we reached it, the surprise was fresh. The bauxite factory: intricate nests of pink bridges and funnels, pink towers rising above them, and below, pipes pouring rivers of pink dust into ships, larger than houses, anchored in the harbor below. Guiana, its coastline choked with mud from the delta of the Orinoco River, had sent its bauxite on flatbed boats here to be exported from the deep waters in Trinidad. Even the trees were covered with pink dust—lethal for the people, I know now—but the factory seemed a giant dollhouse to me then, and everything around it a pink wonderland.

We drove past the fishing village of Cocorite, where policemen on horseback had rounded up the first waves of people sick with leprosy and shipped them to our island. There was a story about a group of Indians who had managed to escape. A boatload of them drowned on their way back to India. I, too, would have been on that boat. I, too, would have preferred to take my chances than to be pried from my family, huddled and roped like cattle to the market. Now I saw Indians, Africans, douglas—people mixed with Indian and African blood—standing in front of wooden shacks that tumbled upon each other on the land side of the narrow, winding road, opposite the sea. Not so many would have survived had the sick ones not been sent to Chacachacare.

We passed another village. Under the rusty awnings of broken-down shops, men in sleeveless vests sat around weather-beaten tables drinking rum. On the seaside, more men, but these pulled in seines from the sea while women, holding empty basins, waited for them under sea-almond trees.

For fish. It was here I had come that first time. I remembered the fishermen who had followed me. Under my chest, tiny muscles fluttered like the beating of butterfly wings. A distant memory. A photograph. I hardly had time to savor it before we left the village behind and before us loomed a grand cream-colored manor house as if lifted out of a Victorian novel.

"The Poor House," the driver said, and deflated my hopes. "You wouldn't want to go there, miss. It smells."

I craned my neck backward and peered through the rear window. A scattering of people in ragged clothes, some so thin they looked like crooked sticks, were huddled at the black, imposing iron gates.

"They waiting for they breakfast," the driver said. "We in St. James now."

When I faced forward the scene had changed. People everywhere: Chinese, Indians, Africans. Europeans who looked like me. They were laughing, shouting, hands gesticulating in the air. The car slowed down with the traffic, and I breathed in the sweet perfume of overripe fruit and the pungent odor of fried fish and curry that came from open stalls in front of shops and stores that lined the street. I saw a church and then a temple.

"The temple for the Hindus," the driver said when I asked.

The road widened into a circle. On the right was a cinema, a huge white building with columns and balconies, Roxy spelled out in bright red letters. We rounded the circle and veered off to a road on the left of a small, triangular savannah. On the opposite side, running parallel to the savannah, was another road, and along it a stretch of houses followed by a long, high wall. "The back of the Oval," the driver said. "Is there the West Indian team give the English a licking. Teach them a lesson."

I had listened to that cricket match on the radio with Father and Carlos. When England lost, Father snapped off the dial.

I could not see enough, I could not hear enough. But my excitement was not to last.

"Did you notice when we pass the police barracks?" the driver asked.

My anxiety returned. *The police. Did he know about Carlos?* I had seen the sign; I had not missed the palm trees, the bottoms of their trunks stained with whitewash, three feet high. Like sentinels, they lined sides of a great lawn, guarding the path that led to a long green-and-white building sprawled out in the background. My eyes had seen this, but my brain refused to process what it knew, preferring instead the marquee at the Roxy.

"My brother train there in the barracks," the driver said.

That was all he wanted me to know, but my mood had shifted as we turned into another street and I was thinking of Carlos again, fearing for his safety.

"We nearing Mrs. Burton's house," the driver said. "Ellerslie Park. Is where your people live."

He meant white people. Even before I saw the grand houses with the manicured lawns and the flowers blooming in the well-tended beds, I knew we had arrived where the rich people lived. The quiet here was a sharp contrast to the bustle of St. James, the only sounds the rustle of leaves on the trees and the occasional whistle of a bird; the only people, two black women dressed in blue uniforms and a black man on a bicycle. They looked straight ahead. They did not turn when we passed them by.

There were no "No Trespassing" signs but the walls and gates sent the message strongly enough: *Here, the vulgarity of the road stops. Here, you enter a different land.* Houses were set far back behind wide lawns; tall iron gates were shut tightly at the entrances of driveways.

Anticipating my arrival, Mrs. Burton had left her gate unlocked. The driver opened it and drove up the circular driveway. In front of us, rooms fanned out on both sides of a covered entranceway supported by white Grecian columns. The house itself was also white, but not as bright. It was built close to the ground, and though pocked with several windows, it seemed oppressive to me, a thick concrete structure, unsuited for a hot, tropical climate. The spreading green lawn gave some relief to this impression, but, like the other houses, it, too, was bounded by an iron gate.

The driver opened the car door for me, took out my bags, and deposited them on the front steps. Then he returned and stood next to the car door.

I rang the doorbell. The curtains were drawn and I could not see inside but I could hear Mrs. Burton calling, "Coming, coming."

Father said that years ago she had arrived from England with her husband, who had some important position in the colonial government. After her husband died, she decided to stay. When I told Carlos that she must have stayed because she loved the island, he curled his lip. All English widows decide to stay, he said. Where else would their skin color have such value? Mrs. Burton, he said, could make a living in Trinidad as an interior decorator though she had no training. Being English was the only credential she needed.

I hadn't waited long before Mrs. Burton opened the door. She was a slim woman with enormous breasts that sagged sadly to just above the waist of the blue cotton dress she was wearing. She had lived in the tropics for more than thirty years, but her skin was the color of parchment, and blue veins were visible across her cheeks and hands. She had red hair, obviously dyed, and she wore it in a short bob with bangs over her forehead that nevertheless did not hide the bald spots, close to the front of her head, where her hair had thinned. The red hair against her pale skin gave her an air of being foreign, a distinction she seemed to have nurtured, for her accent was very British.

It was my accent she commented on first after I greeted her. "Wherever did you learn to speak like that?" She made tut-tutting sounds with her tongue. "Living with servants! I told your father. It won't do for you to keep living with servants." She dismissed the driver, and, putting her arm around my shoulder, guided me inside. "Leave your bags here," she said, and took the clay pot with the orchid from my hands. "Jane will get them. Jane! Jane!" she hollered.

A woman came toward us from the back. She was dressed in a uniform similar to the one I had seen worn by the two women we had passed on the street. Mrs. Burton introduced me. "Miss Virginia. She is English."

Instinctively I shot back, "But I grew up on Chacachacare."

"Yes, miss," the uniformed woman said and took my bags. When she was gone, Mrs. Burton admonished me. "That was unnecessary," she said. "Servants don't have to know the details. You're English and that is that. It does not matter where you grew up. Chacachacare, for God's sake! Don't go around announcing that to everyone. Chacachacare!"

Fearing I had made her angry, I tried to distract her. I asked her if she liked the orchid Father had sent her. She twirled the pot in her hands and examined it. I could see she was pleased. "Your father has a real talent with them," she said. A weak smile began on the corners of her lips. "Come, I'll show you mine."

I followed her through a corridor leading to the backyard. On the way, I glimpsed the drawing room. It had not taken much imagination for her to replicate her decor for my father. Her drawing room was exactly like Father's: damask curtains, polished wood floors, Persian rug, floral love seats. Father's England.

In the backyard, she spread out her arms lovingly toward her garden. "These, my dear, are my children. Mr. Burton and I, you see, were not blessed with babies."

Ten orchids in clay pots hung on pipes that ran across tall metal posts. I could identify some by name: the striped and spotted white-and-pink phalaenopsis; the yellow venosa; the greenish yellow dendrobium with its vivid pink center. I bent over the pale violet phalaenopsis violacea and inhaled. Mrs. Burton was delighted. "Not many people know it has a fragrance."

"Father grows them," I said, straightening up.

"Yes, he has the best garden in the West Indies." She hung the orchid I had given her on the tubing and stepped back to admire it some more. "For the life of me, though," she said, "I can't understand why he has not named this one after him. I would have. The Mrs. Burton, I would have called it."

"Father prefers the Latin names," I said.

"Your father is too modest."

But fear of discovery, not modesty, was Father's motive. Yet, even then, I did not know the whole truth: He was not in hiding to protect me. I was a third of his life, he claimed, but it was the other two thirds he wanted to save.

"Of course I have more orchids than you see here," Mrs. Burton was saying. "I've sent them off to Chelsea. Last year . . ." She paused, pushed away her bangs, and threw her head back. "Last year, my anthuriums came in second. Come, I'll show them to you." She led me to a canopy of vines where dozens of anthuriums bloomed in clumps on beds of coconut husks, their colors ranging from cotton white to a deep purplish red. My father had anthuriums like these, prettier than these, but I told her I had seen none better.

She cupped her hand under my chin and gently raised my head. "But you," she said, "must be the loveliest flower in your father's garden. Surely your father must have told you so."

Father would have been afraid. Father kept his secret locked up tight in the daylight. In the daylight he could pretend he was my father, but he took no risks. He was careful not to let his eyes linger, to stray to places on my body where he could be betrayed. One look, one wrong glance in the daylight could unsettle him, loosen the tight hold he kept on his incestuous longings.

"Wanting in refinement, but lovely." She fingered the collar of my dress. "Not much time to have a dress made for you," she sighed.

It was my best dress. It was pink. Pink looked good on me, Carlos said.

"I can wear this dress," I said.

She continued to inspect me, her eyes traveling up and down my body, from my head to my toes. "Perhaps something in blue to match your pretty eyes. Mr. Haynes and his son will be here for supper tomorrow. You must look your best."

"I like this dress," I said.

She patted my cheeks. "No need to be ashamed, my dear. I can't expect you to find a seamstress among the lepers."

I made a feeble attempt to protest, but she grasped my hand firmly. "Come. Enough of this chatter. You must be exhausted. Jane! Jane!" She called out to Jane again and turned back to me. "Rest. I know you must have had to wake up early." When Jane reappeared, she instructed her to take me to my room. "I'll come for you at lunchtime," she said.

By lunchtime, she was even more solicitous. By lunchtime, Inspector Mumsford had telephoned.

She entered my room without knocking. I was lying on my back on the bed, staring at the ceiling, trying to fight off the intense feeling of powerlessness that was closing in on me. In my letter to Carlos I had urged him not to lose hope, but what did I have to offer him? Tomorrow, and Father would have his way. Perhaps a rare orchid would not be temptation enough for Alfred and his father, but Father's plan to dispose of me was already in motion. He had put me in good hands, Mrs. Burton said. Her hands. And if not Alfred, I knew there would be another.

I sat up the moment I heard the doorknob turn. She came toward me in fast little steps, her hand clasped to her mouth. "You poor girl. You poor, poor girl." Her cheeks quivered. "Did he hurt you? Did that savage hurt you?"

I knew right away that Father had contacted the police. "No. No." I locked my legs together and smoothed the folds of my skirt over my knees, determined to hide my fear from her.

"You can tell me. I understand these things. I'm a woman." She stood over me, her face grief-stricken.

"He did not hurt me," I said.

"You poor girl," she said again.

The fluttering began again in my chest and rose to my neck. "What did Father tell the police?" I asked her.

"Inspector Mumsford is investigating."

"He didn't do anything," I said.

"Your father wants us to keep this quiet. You're lucky. Inspector Mumsford is an Englishman."

I shifted my legs over the edge of the bed. "Carlos did nothing to me," I said.

"He's a savage," she said.

"He's my friend," I said.

"Friend?" she snorted. "A servant."

"He was always kind to me."

"They get ideas when you are kind to them. They take advantage."

"He did not hurt me." But she was not listening to me.

"Your father said he caught him in time. He said he prevented him . . ." She sat down on the chair next to the bed and put her fist in her mouth. "You don't know what this can do to your reputation." She stifled a cry. "This is a small place. People gossip. You give them a little and they make hay with it."

"What is Inspector Mumsford going to do to Carlos?" I asked, the fluttering in my neck and chest galloping now.

"It's your reputation I'm thinking of, not this Carlos. We have to be discreet. I'll say you are sick. I'll tell Mr. Haynes you're sick. I'll say you caught a cold coming over on the boat. I'll postpone the party."

"What did the inspector say?" I needed to know. I wanted to be prepared.

"What he didn't say, but what I am going to say to you, is that you must not, *must not*." She wagged her finger in my face. "You must not repeat to anyone that that boy, that servant, was your friend. People will read something into that. You must not give them anything."

"He's innocent."

She stood up and her sad breasts swished from side to side above her waistline. "You were on that island too long, little miss," she said.

"You don't understand."

"It is you and your father who don't understand. Well, your father understands now."

"Carlos didn't do anything," I said.

"I told him he was wrong to let that monster live in your house. But he insisted he was a good boy, a fast learner. He was not like ordinary boys. He was intelligent. But he was a *colored* boy. I reminded your father of that fact."

"Nothing happened," I said.

"Your father did his best, but a girl needs to be brought up by a woman, a woman who can teach her the ways of the world. You'll be ruined if any of this gets out. Just the suggestion that he could have, that he might have, is enough to damage your reputation."

I tried to defend Carlos again but she stopped me. "You think you know these people, but you're wrong." She sank back into the chair and her body folded like an accordion, her neck into her collarbone, her breasts grazing the top of her belly. "Your father was too good to that boy, too generous. These people are never grateful. They are the most ungrateful creatures."

"Carlos is not like that," I said.

Color came into her pale face. "You don't know what he's like. You don't know anything about them. Do you know what is going on here? Independence, that's what. They want independence. After we've done so much for them."

Done so much for them? I could hear Carlos striking back: "You got rich from our sweat. We planted sugarcane and cocoa for you. Now you're taking our oil."

"The ingratitude! They want to be free from us. Bush! That's what this place was like. A jungle! We made it what it is, and now it's decent, now a decent person can live here, they want us to give it to them. Yes, Virginia." She held up her hands to stop me again. "I can tell you about these people. They want to destroy us. If we let a thing like this leak out, they will destroy you. I'll say you're sick. We'll put off Alfred's visit until Inspector Mumsford has this under control."

For the rest of the day and the next day, and the day after that until late in the afternoon, when Inspector Mumsford finally arrived, Mrs. Burton lectured me on the ingratitude of the natives and on the burdens resting on the shoulders of English people in the colonies. "We Englishwomen bear a particular responsibility," she told me. "They look up to us. We have to set an example. We are their guides as to what is proper and what is not. We can't fraternize with them. Look where fraternizing has got you."

It did not matter how many times I said to her that Carlos had done nothing wrong. She brushed me away. She said I did not know *them* as she knew *them*. I had been fooled. They are cunning. Sly, she said. Malicious. I had allowed Carlos to trick me into becoming too friendly with him. "If you had not fraternized with him, he wouldn't have dared. You can't fraternize with these people. It goes to their heads. And now they want independence."

Her lectures to me switched back and forth from her disapproval of the Independence Movement that Carlos had praised so much to me to her disapproval of my behavior toward Carlos and then to her fear of my ruin. "Thank God," she said, "your father stopped him in time. Coming into your room when you were sleeping!"

In my room when I was sleeping! How clever Father had been.

"Whether a woman is ruined by force, or whether she gives herself freely to be ruined, or whether, like in your case," she lowered her voice, "there is a suggestion that she could have been ruined, her life is over. No man of any distinction would marry her."

I wanted to tell her that my knot was unbroken, my jewel was still in my dower. Father had used Ariana to protect my jewel, and Ariana had saved me from Father.

We were having tea when Inspector Mumsford rang the doorbell. At four o'clock, Mrs. Burton insisted I put on a proper dress and sit with her in the drawing room while Jane served us scones and jam, and poured tea from a china pot through a tiny silver strainer.

Mrs. Burton had not lost the English habit of tea in the afternoons. "One must not yield to the bush," she said to me.

My father had lost the habit of tea in the afternoons, but he had not yielded to the bush. The bush had yielded to my father.

The proper dress Mrs. Burton wanted me to wear was the white blouse and navy skirt that Father had made me pack. He had thrown out the bright prints and florals I had put in my suitcase. I needed to wear something more understated in Trinidad, he said. Something *English*. "I've left you to yourself too long," he told me, not a trace of irony darkening his voice.

Jane answered the doorbell and came back with the news that Inspector Mumsford was here to see Miss Virginia. Mrs. Burton motioned to me to stay where I was, and, sending Jane back to the kitchen, she went to the door alone. I strained my ears to hear what she and the inspector were saying, but I could make out very little. I heard Inspector Mumsford mention Carlos's name, and then *investigation,* and soon afterward Mrs. Burton clapped her hands and Jane came running toward her.

"We are not to be disturbed. Do you understand, Jane?" She was approaching the drawing room and I could hear her clearly now. "We'll be in here. Keep the door closed. Bring some tea and scones for the inspector and then remain in the kitchen, out of the way."

Inspector Mumsford said something to Mrs. Burton and her voice rose to a petulant wail. "And why not, Inspector?" There were murmurings from the inspector and then Mrs. Burton said loudly and irritably, "Bring a fresh pot of tea for the inspector, Jane. A cup and saucer and a clean plate. And clear my dishes. Hurry up!"

When she was gone, the inspector clicked his heels at the doorway of the drawing room and introduced himself. "Inspector Mumsford," he said. "Here on an investigation."

I was surprised he was so young. I expected him to be my father's age, someone who had spent years in the English colonies, a man with formed opinions about "natives," not likely to be sympathetic, but his face was smooth and pink, the hair thick on his head and on his mustache. I felt hopeful. Perhaps he would understand. Perhaps he would believe me. I invited him into the room and pointed to a chair, but he remained standing. "After you, miss," he said.

He waited until I sat down, and then, flipping up the back panel of his belted khaki jacket, he took the chair next to me. Carefully he pinched the creases in his pants and then as carefully, with his hands resting lightly on his thighs, crossed one leg over the other at his knees. Some of my hope drained away as I watched him sit with so much ceremony. Young, but an English officer, I thought.

While Jane moved about the room, he made light conversation with me about the weather: how little rain we had been having this year; how it seemed hotter than last year; how, in spite of it all, Mrs. Burton managed to keep her drawing room cool.

"She draws the blinds at midday," I said, trying hard to match his tone though my heart was sinking.

"Your father's house is cooler, of course," he said.

"Yes. We have air-conditioning."

All the time we spoke, he was following Jane's movements while she removed Mrs. Burton's cup and saucer from the cocktail table between us to the tea trolley in the back of the room.

"I can pour your tea for you, sir." Jane paused before him. "Do you want milk and sugar, sir?"

The inspector turned to me. "What about you, miss?"

I said I had had my tea. "Then just tea for me. Milk, no sugar."

"A scone, sir?"

"No scone."

When she left the room and he seemed sure she was out of earshot, he put down the cup of tea she had given him, and informed me, his tone officious now, that he had been to Chacachacare and had brought Carlos back with him to Trinidad.

My lips felt dry and I moistened them with my tongue. Was he in jail? I asked. Oh, no, he said. He had taken him to the monks at Mount St. Benedict until the inquiry. The monks have a boarding school for boys there, he said.

"A reformatory?"

"Oh, nothing of the kind, miss. A school, not a reformatory. Carlos, I mean Mr. Codrington, will be well taken care of."

"Is he still in pain?"

He seemed surprised by my question. "You saw him, Miss Gardner?"

"No, not myself," I said. "Ariana told me."

"They are only mosquito bites," he said, not unkindly. His eyes softened, but I could have imagined this; I wanted so much to trust him. "They will heal."

They will heal, but he had suffered. Father had made him suffer.

He fished into his jacket pocket and pulled out a small notebook and pen. "I have to take a statement from you. Then we'll decide what to do with him."

I took a deep breath. "Father made it all up," I said. Slowly I let the air out of my lungs. He was on the point of opening his notebook when I said this.

"Made it up?" He seemed uncertain whether he had heard me correctly.

"What he told you about Carlos. He made it up."

"Why would he do a thing like that, Miss Gardner?" He looked at me directly.

"Carlos is my friend," I said, not backing down.

"Your father said he tried to be more than your friend."

"He would never hurt me," I said.

"Your father said he wanted to."

"He didn't," I said.

He placed the notebook on the table and picked up his cup. Holding the saucer in one hand and the cup in the other, he eyed me above the steam rising from the tea. "It is my understanding, Miss Gardner," he said, "that Mr. Codrington expressed a desire to hurt you." He spoke slowly and I had the distinct impression he was choosing each word carefully. The effort stiffened his lips, and his mustache cast a dark shadow over his mouth.

"It's not true," I said. I had made a mistake. I had placed my hopes in him too quickly.

"Your father told me he prevented him just in time," he said.

"My father did not tell you the truth," I said.

"You mean he lied?"

"Carlos loves me," I said.

"So your father's servant claimed," he said drily.

"Ariana?"

"She sent a letter. She wrote that Mr. Codrington is in love with you."

I dug my right hand into the palm of my left hand and pressed my fingernails deep into my skin to stop both my hands from shaking.

He placed the cup gingerly on the saucer and, bending over to put them both on the cocktail table, he asked quietly, "You're engaged, are you not, Miss Gardner?"

I was taken aback by the question for I had readied myself for Ariana's accusations, her condemnation of my father. "Engaged?" I asked, relieved.

"Your father said to a Mr. Haynes," he said, straightening up.

"I'm not engaged," I said, loosening my hands. My right palm was streaked with the pink prints of my fingernails.

"An American, I believe he is."

"I saw Mr. Haynes once," I said.

"Once?"

"Father was trying to arrange for me to marry him."

"Arrange? Surely, miss . . ."

"Mr. Haynes was not interested in me, Inspector Mumsford."

"That was not what your father said." His fingers circled the rim of the saucer on the table.

"Father says what he wants to believe. He and Mrs. Burton wanted Alfred to be interested in me."

"A pretty English girl?" His hazel eyes glistened.

"Alfred came with his father to see Father's orchids. That was his only reason for coming."

"And where's Mr. Haynes now?" he asked. "Can you tell me, miss?"

"I don't know. I haven't seen him since I've arrived. Mrs. Burton says it would be best to wait until this is over."

He brushed his mustache back and forth and studied me. "Yes," he said finally. "Yes, I would say that would be best." He reached again for his notebook. "Do you think, Miss Gardner . . ." He tapped the notebook against his chin. "Do you suppose that Mr. Codrington presumed to speak that way to your father because he knew of your father's plans for you and Mr. Haynes?"

"What way? Speak what way?" My hands felt suddenly cold and clammy.

"With such insolence," he said.

He was an Englishman. A generation ago a black man would have been killed on the spot if he had so much as raised his eyes to an Englishman's daughter.

"Carlos is never insolent," I said.

"He told your father he wanted to have children with you," he said.

"He loves me, Inspector. I told you that."

"Begging your pardon, miss. The suggestion was sexual."

"Did Father say so?"

"It was unbecoming of a gentleman, miss."

I felt emboldened by Carlos's courage. He had done as he had said. He had spoken to Father. "Enough for Father to do what he did to him?" I asked.

"No, miss," he said. "No. That was not right, miss."

We were both silent. I could feel him searching for some justification, something that would help him understand why my father had been so cruel. "Is it possible, miss," he asked at last, "that Mr. Codrington was jealous of Mr. Haynes?"

"He had no reason to be," I said quietly.

At first he looked puzzled and then my meaning sunk in. "Surely," he said, "you don't want me to understand . . . Surely, miss, you could not have any interest in Mr. Codrington?"

"I like him a thousand times better than Mr. Haynes," I said, making the effort to keep my voice calm.

He reddened. "Surely . . . " he stuttered.

"Even more," I said.

"He is a colored man, Miss Gardner." His face was scarlet.

"That does not matter to me," I said.

"Does not matter? You're English, miss."

"I don't remember England," I said. "I was a little girl when I left England."

"But you are white, miss."

"Carlos and I love each other," I said.

He stood up. "This is bad. Very bad." He shook his head.

"It's not a crime for Carlos to love me," I said. He shot an angry glance at me. "Or for me to love him," I added.

He turned away and walked the length of the room. Had I said too much? Had I made more trouble for Carlos? But Carlos was not on the inspector's mind when he walked back and stopped abruptly in front of me. Ariana was on his mind.

"How well do you know Ariana?" he asked.

"Ariana?" My heart flip-flopped in my chest.

"How long have you known her?"

"Since I came to Chacachacare. She was living in the house when Father and I arrived."

"And do you think she tells the truth?"

I did not know which truth he meant. I avoided the one I feared. "What she wrote about Carlos is true," I said. "And I love him, too."

A spasm of pain crossed his face. "She came to see me," he said.

"See you?"

"Yesterday. In my office."

What had she told him? I shifted uncomfortably in my chair.

"She claims she was more than a servant to your father," he said.

I felt as though he were towering over me, but he was not towering over me. He was standing several feet away from me, gripping the back of his chair.

"Did you know that?" He paused, waiting for my answer.

"Did she talk about me?" I asked him.

"Talk about you? Oh no, miss. She did not come to see me to talk about you. She came to talk about your father. Do you know why?"

I pressed my hands on my lap and looked steadily down at them. *Tell the police about you, she said. I'll tell them about me.* "Whatever she told you about my father is true," I said.

"I felt so," he said. "I felt so."

The sadness in his voice made me look up. His fingers were curled tightly around the top of the chair, his shoulders slumped.

Did I understand what he meant when he said Ariana was more than a servant to my father? he asked me. Yes, I said. I understood him completely.

"And did she tell you all he did to her?" he asked me.

I nodded without a word.

He spared me the details, though in truth I thought he was sparing himself, that he could not bear to hear himself recite the horrors Ariana most likely had told him.

"He was blackmailing her." His voice was infinitely heavy. "Did you know that, miss?"

I said I did not know that. How could Father blackmail her? What could Father have that she could want, that would put her in his power in that way?

She loved jewelry, he said.

I told him that the only jewelry I saw her wear were earrings.

Did I know they were diamonds? he asked.

I laughed. She loved shiny things, I said. They were probably shiny stones, but not diamonds. She had no money for diamonds. Then he told me the story Ariana had told him and I remembered how she loved to gaze at fireflies.

My father had betrayed all England, he said. All decent Englishmen. How could he have taken advantage of a child?

How could he have taken advantage of me?

What would the inspector think if I told him that betraying decent Englishmen was the least of what my father had done? What would he think if I told him my father had betrayed his daughter, my father had stolen his daughter's youth?

But the inspector thought decent Englishmen in English colonies did not sexually molest young native girls. He thought English fathers protected English daughters. He thought English fathers did not sneak into the bedrooms of English daughters while they were sleeping.

What would he say if he knew I woke up more mornings than I wanted to remember, the back of my throat aching from my father's probing? What would he do if I told him my father's real reason for arranging a marriage for me?

Mrs. Burton had warned me that I would be ruined if people found out, if the slightest suggestion reached their ears that Carlos had attempted, as she put it, to compromise my virginity. If I told the inspector the whole truth about my father, would he think I had been compromised, that I was ruined? Would he feel disgust for my father but still feel scorn for me?

The inspector thought pretty English girls should marry pretty Englishmen. He thought native men in English colonies could not fall in love with English girls and English girls with them. He thought English girls raised in English colonies remained English girls, and the people, the land, the sea, and the sun had no effect on them.

"What is going to happen to Carlos?" I asked him.

"I have your word, and I had Ariana's," he said. "I will have to speak to your father, of course. Mr. Codrington will have to come with me and face your father to tell his side of the story, but I expect in the end he will be free to do as he wants, though I would think he would want to leave the island."

"He was born in Chacachacare," I said. "He will not want to leave."

"I don't think your father will let him stay in the house," he said.

"We found him in the house when we came," I said.

"Yes," he said flatly. "He told me it was his mother's house."

Out of guilt I defended my father, for I, too, had known that the house first belonged to Carlos's mother. "His mother left it to her housekeeper," I said. "Father bought it from her."

The inspector arched his eyebrows. "He paid for it?"

"Father said so."

He did not respond.

"The housekeeper was dying," I said. "Father took care of her."

Whether I convinced him or not, I could not tell. His face betrayed no emotion. He put his notebook and pen in his pocket. "I better get going, miss. It's getting late."

"And Father? What will happen to Father?" I asked him.

"I expect when I confront him with your statement, he will withdraw the allegation," he said.

"But what about what he did to Ariana?"

"It's unfortunate. A dastardly thing for him to do. She'll stay here. The matron at the station will find a place for her in Trinidad."

"And Father will be free?"

"So long as he stays on the island, we won't interfere."

"And me? Where will I go?"

"Your father must determine that," he said.

I did not think for a moment he thought I could be in danger. Ariana was in danger. My father had taken advantage of her, but he could not allow himself to think that my father would take advantage of me. Not an English father. But I was in danger and I could not be left alone with my father. I had to see Carlos. I had to make certain that Carlos would stay with me on Chacachacare.

"I want to go with you when you take Carlos back," I said.

"What about your visitors? The Americans? Mr. Haynes?"

"They will not miss me."

"And Mrs. Burton?"

"I will speak to her," I said.

He adjusted the belt on his waist. "Are you sure that is what you want to do?"

"Yes," I said.

"I don't think it's a good idea, miss."

"I *must* go," I said. I could tell he was ready to object again, so I added quickly, "Father would want me to come."

He considered my answer and seemed to decide it was reasonable. "Then nine o'clock. On the dot. I will send a car for you. "

Before he left, he told Mrs. Burton that the matter with Carlos was settled. He was taking him back tomorrow to make his statement in the presence of my father. He didn't expect my father to press charges.

That would be best, Mrs. Burton said. There was nothing to be gained from a scandal. Virginia was not harmed, thank God.

"What will you do with him when he comes back?" she asked. "We can't have him running loose here."

"We can't lock him up without charges," the inspector said. "In any case, I believe he may want to stay."

"Want to stay?" Mrs. Burton snorted when we were alone and the rumble of the inspector's car had long faded. "What does it matter what *he* wants? He cannot be permitted to stay. Not with you on the island. Your father was lax, lax to have a colored boy living in your house. I'll speak to him. You must remain here with me, my dear. You can't return with that boy on the loose."

I told her I was going back the next day with the inspector to Chacachacare.

She lost her temper. An ungrateful wretch, she called me.

TWENTY-THREE

HE INSPECTOR was true to his word. At nine o'clock the car arrived to take me to the boat to Chacachacare. The inspector did not come out of the car. He sent his driver to fetch me.

I had seen Mrs. Burton earlier that morning in the dining room. Jane had rung the bell at seven for breakfast. The night before, her pride stung when I opposed her, Mrs. Burton informed me, with all the scorn she could muster in her voice, that in the civilized world—and I don't mean here, she said, or in your backwoods on that leper colony where no one knows manners—we don't shout and yell. So tomorrow, at seven, and I don't mean one minute to seven, but seven exactly—for time means nothing to these people here; you say seven and they come at eight—Jane will ring the bell. I expect you to be dressed and at the table for breakfast.

My father did not need to use a bell. He told us when we would eat and Ariana obeyed and served us on time.

At breakfast Mrs. Burton was tight-lipped. When Jane put the platter of scrambled eggs and ham on the table in front of her, she pushed it away. "Too hard," she said. "Haven't I told you often enough not to let the eggs get hard? Take it away. We'll just have the ham."

I knew she was taking out her anger with me on Jane, and I met Jane's eyes and tried to convey my sympathy.

"Be quick!" Mrs. Burton tapped Jane on her arm as she placed a slice of ham on her plate and another on mine. She seemed hardly able to wait for Jane to leave the room. No sooner had the door closed than she began to harangue me.

"You're making a serious mistake," she said. She reached over for the butter plate and cut down hard into the solid square of butter. "The inspector can deal with the situation quite well without you. You don't know what you're doing to your reputation to go on the boat with that boy. People will see you. They will talk."

"I will be with the inspector," I said defensively.

She swiped the butter across her toast and did not answer me.

I tried again to reason with her. "The inspector is taking Carlos back home. If Carlos had done anything wrong, the inspector wouldn't be taking him back to Chacachacare."

She stopped buttering her toast and pointed her knife at me. "*I* know where the inspector brought the boy. If I know, don't you think other people know? The people here gossip. One servant tells your business to another servant and before you know it, everybody knows. Jane told me the boy was at Mount St. Benedict. Yes, don't look surprised. She knew even before you knew. If you aren't here when I have my party for Mr. Haynes and his son—and I am going to have the party whether you are here or not—I can't vouch for what people will say about you. I can't keep making excuses for you. People will put two and two together. Jane has already put two and two together, what with the inspector here yesterday. And if you leave with him this morning, she'll be sure to figure it out. You can't go. I just *won't* let you go. What will your father say?"

In the end I thought it was her promise to my father that worried her more than the loss of my reputation. It had taken her a long time to persuade my father to give her one of his orchids. She had come in second at the Chelsea Flower Show the year before. She wanted to come in first.

In the car the inspector told me that Carlos would meet us at the dock at the Yacht Club. I was excited to see Carlos again, but I was nervous, too. Doubts that had not been there before crowded my mind. Suppose Carlos changed his mind. Could he still love me after what my father had done to him? Would he despise me? I looked out of the window, barely seeing the town and villages we passed, their newness overshadowed by my worries and fears.

The inspector patted my hand, trying to comfort me. "Everything will be all right, miss," he said. "Your father will see reason. He won't press charges."

He had come dressed in full uniform: belted khaki jacket, khaki shorts stopped at the knees, tasseled high brown socks, polished shoes, baton, and pith helmet. Her Majesty's representative. An Englishman. He could not conceive that I could love Carlos and Carlos could love me. He could not contain in his brain that my fears were not only for Carlos's safety, but also for my happiness. I was my father's daughter. What that irrefutable truth would cost me weakened my knees and sent my heart racing.

Carlos was waiting for us on the pier. I broke away from the inspector and ran to him. At first all I saw was his familiar shape, his broad shoulders, his slim hips, his long legs. Only when I got close did I see the sores. I flung my arms around his neck horrified by the red blotches that had spread across his handsome face. He tightened his hold on me and I buried my head in his shoulder, my tears soaking his shirt.

"It's okay, Virginia," he whispered. "It's okay. I'm well. I'm fine." But when I raised my head and saw the red, raw bumps around his ears, his nose, climbing up his neck and in between the brown freckles that I loved, my tears fell again.

"Shhh." He brought my head to his chest and held me still. "Shhh."

"Must be getting on, miss." The inspector had reached us. He stood next to me, his legs apart, planted firmly on the ground, striking his baton on his open palm. "No time for lollygagging."

The childish word he used, his subdued tone, betrayed his embarrassment, his discomfort at witnessing our intimacy, our open display of affection, but he seemed moved, too, his heart softened. "One more minute then," he said. "That is all I can give you." He walked away and left us alone.

Carlos disentangled my arms from around his neck and took my hand. The long pants he was wearing covered his legs, but his arms were almost bare under his short-sleeved shirt. There were mosquito bites on almost every inch of his skin, most of them concentrated at his elbows. How many mosquitoes at one time had sunk their probes into his flesh? Ariana had seen him when he was bloody. What would I have done if I had seen blood oozing from his sores?

Tenderly, not wanting to cause him more pain than he had already suffered, I brought one arm and then his other arm to my lips and kissed them in turn, lingering on the spots where the mosquitoes had clustered. "Father will pay for this," I said. Yet at that moment, I did not know how.

Carlos pulled his arms gently away from my mouth. "The inspector came to see me last night," he said. "I know what you told him."

"I will say it again in front of Father," I said.

He looked away from me.

"I *will*," I said.

Why should he have believed me? I had not defended him when Father tried to teach me I was superior to him, that the color of my skin made me better than him. I was a child then when Father first gave me that lesson, and perhaps I could be forgiven, but I was no longer a child when Carlos told me the house was his, that Father had stolen it from him.

"My mother loved this house," he had said. "Every room my father built, he had built to please her." He reminded me of the carvings at the top of each of the wood partitions that had separated the rooms. "My father had those carvings made for me. Why would my mother not want me to have the house my father had spent so many days and nights building for us? Your father is a liar. My mother would never have given the house to Lucinda. She left it for me."

Father said Carlos's mother was a party girl. She was careless. Party girls did careless, irresponsible things. Things like leaving their houses to servants.

When I said to the inspector that Carlos's mother had left the house to Lucinda, I knew I was trying to hold on to the last shred of hope that the father I loved as a little girl had not always lied to me.

Shame, and feelings more paralyzing than shame, had stopped me from exposing Father to the inspector. I owed my life to Father. I would not have survived without him. He loved me. He loved me so much that he gave up his life in England for me. All he did, he said, he did for me. And yet Father had betrayed me. And yet he had abused me.

I put my hand on Carlos's chin and forced him to face me. This time would not be like other times. This time I would not keep silent. "Father will hear the truth from my lips," I said. "The inspector will be my witness."

"And afterward?" he asked me.

But it was I who wanted to know what would happen afterward. I needed to be sure. "Will you go back to Trinidad afterward?" I asked him.

He shook his head. "We belong in Chacachacare."

We. I knew he had not ceased to love me. "Don't leave me alone with Father," I said.

The inspector had restricted us to a minute, but we had taken more than a minute. When I looked back, he was standing on the dock, tapping his baton against his leg, peering steadfastly into the water.

The boat waiting for us was not a government launch. It was an ordinary pirogue, unpainted and covered over in the center with a piece of dark green tarpaulin held up by four bamboo poles. The boatman appeared to be one of the local fishermen. He was barefooted, and wore a rumpled yellow T-shirt and brown cotton shorts. The inspector explained later that he hadn't taken the launch because he did not want to attract the attention of the locals. The commissioner had cautioned him to be inconspicuous, but, of course, in the full regalia of a police inspector, the inspector was anything but inconspicuous.

The boatman had already untied the rope that was attached to a metal ring at the edge of the pier and was holding it tight, trying to keep the boat from rocking. From time to time he looked up expectantly at the inspector, but in spite of his urgent glances, the inspector did not move. I thought the inspector was losing his patience waiting for us and I said to Carlos that we needed to hurry. It was Carlos who figured out that the inspector was afraid, not impatient. He let go of my hand, and, without saying a word, though by then I noticed that the color was drained from the inspector's face, he walked over to the inspector and took his elbow. Clinging to Carlos's shoulder, the inspector tentatively lifted his leg over the rim of the boat and let Carlos guide him inside.

Carlos took the backseat in front of the boatman and put me to sit next to the inspector. I could tell from the brief smile that broke on the inspector's lips that he was pleased with this arrangement, pleased, too, that Carlos had been discreet, that he had placed his hand under his arm with such little ceremony that it appeared as if he were extending a courtesy to a government official, not rescuing him from his dread of slipping into the water.

The tarpaulin over the boat was not wide enough to spare the inspector's right arm and leg from burning under the fiery sun. The inspector did not complain, but I felt sorry for him and moved closer to the edge of the boat to give him more space. He was grateful and he thanked me, and slid to the middle of the seat. Squashed somewhat, I leaned over the boat and let my hand trail in the water. When I looked down I saw tiny fish—blue, purple with blue; red, yellow with red; green, orange with green, all the dazzling colors of the rainbow—darting through the emerald-green reeds of sea plants shimmering above the speckled white sand. I did not know what the inspector and Carlos were thinking at that moment. Perhaps they were thinking of their impending confrontation with my father, but I was not thinking of my father when I saw those fish, when I saw those green reeds, when my eyes traveled farther across the silken blue water. I was thinking: *This is my sea, my place in the world. This is where I belong.*

As if on cue, a school of dolphins arced in unison in front of us. Eight in all, their silver-gray bodies glistening and then disappearing under the sea.

The inspector perked up. "I didn't think they came so close," he said excitedly.

"Dey like people," the boatman said. "Watch, dey go come up again and follow we."

The dolphins reappeared on the side of the boat, leaping into the air, nodding their heads back and forth at us, their eyes shining in their expressive faces.

"Dey showing off. Dey like you," the boatman said.

Even the inspector laughed.

I belonged here, in this place. A feeling of pride surged through me like an electric current.

The dolphins left us when we reached the outskirts of the boca between Monos and Chacachacare. The currents there, spilling out of the Dragon's Mouth, pitched the boat up and down, and I gripped my seat to steady myself.

"Lucky you come today," the boatman said, his white teeth gleaming behind his lips spread apart. "Tomorrow the sea here go be rough, rough." He pointed to the north where in the far distance gray clouds had gathered at the edge of the blue sky.

"Are you certain we'll be back before it rains?" the inspector asked nervously.

"We come back long time before dat, sir. From the looks of those clouds so far away, it don't storm till way after midnight."

And indeed directly above us the clouds were bright white. Soon we were on calm waters again, approaching my island. In front of us a nest of trees rose up the incline above the narrow shore. We rounded the bend and the doctor's house came into sight with its rusty red galvanized roof and A-frame second story. The salt in the sea air, the wind, and the sun had wreaked havoc on it, but it signaled home to me, home, where I wanted to be.

For the first time I noticed how gracefully the cement steps curved upward to the pillared veranda. For the first time I noticed that the peak of the A-frame resembled the spire of a church. *Holy ground. Home.* To the right of the stone wall that protected the house from the sea, I could make out the gray rocks I had climbed with Carlos when he took me to the cove on the other side.

I could not leave here. I could not return to the busyness of Trinidad, to the stuffiness of Mrs. Burton's way of life. And yet with Father on the island, how could I stay?

"The house is farther back behind the trees," Carlos said to the inspector.

He didn't have to remind him, the inspector replied. But Carlos had guessed, as I had, that the inspector was uneasy.

"I'll walk in front of you and clear the way," Carlos said.

"What about snakes?" the inspector asked. "The last boatman who took me here said there were snakes."

Carlos grinned. "He was trying to frighten you. I've seen a snake here only once and it was a thin, green one we call the horsewhip snake. It's harmless."

The inspector mumbled something about lizards, and Carlos put him at ease again. "They scatter when they hear us," he said. Then, just as we got close to the house, something—I thought it was a giant iguana—scampered through the bushes and the inspector jumped in horror to the middle of the path.

"It's gone," Carlos said, calming him down.

The inspector turned to me, his lips ashen. "How do you manage it, Miss Gardner?"

I gave him the only answer that was true for me. "I live here, Inspector. This is home for me."

Before he knocked on the front door of the house, the inspector warned Carlos to hold his tongue. "Leave the talking to me, Codrington," he said. "I'll deal with Dr. Gardner." His words were harsher than his tone and I thought he spoke more out of concern for Carlos than to make the point that he was in charge.

But Father was not there. The inspector knocked on the door a couple more times and then tried the knob. It gave in easily.

"He must have known we were coming to have left the door unlocked," the inspector said.

"If he knew we were coming, he would want to be here," Carlos said.

The inspector frowned.

"He'd want to tell us his lies," Carlos said.

The inspector glared at him. "No point adding fuel to the fire, Codrington," he said.

I, too, was surprised by Carlos's tone, that he would speak in this manner about my father to an English inspector. But something was different about Carlos. The times I caught a glimpse of him in the boat,

it seemed to me that there was a hardness in his eyes I had not seen before. I had attributed the stiffness around his jaw to his determination
to confront my father, to force him to acknowledge his innocence, but
now I was beginning to wonder if he had not come for more than that,
if he did not have another purpose for being here with the inspector.

We searched the entire house. We looked in every room, in the garden, and in the greenhouse but Father was nowhere to be found.

"I'll wait here for him in the drawing room," the inspector said.
"The air-conditioning is on. He wouldn't have left it on if he hadn't intended to return soon. We'll hear what he has to say when he comes."

Carlos was behind him. "Perhaps he won't be back before night-
fall," he said.

The inspector swiveled around. "You say that as though you know
where he is, Codrington," he said gruffly.

"I do, Inspector," Carlos said.

"And where is that? I am not going to the leper colony, if that is
where you mean."

I could tell that the inspector was irritated and I rushed quickly to
intervene. I did not want the inspector angry with Carlos. I wanted
him on our side when we faced Father. "Would you like something to
drink, Inspector?" I asked him.

He fanned himself with his pith helmet. It was cool in the drawing
room, but the red blotches on his cheeks had not subsided, and there
was a string of tiny bumps on the back of his neck.

"Water, if you don't mind."

"I can get you something stronger," I said.

"Oh no, miss. Not on duty, miss. But perhaps Mr. Codrington?"

"I never touch alcohol," Carlos said.

The inspector seemed surprised. "Never touch it?"

"Never," Carlos said.

"Would you like some water, too?" I asked Carlos.

"Thanks. I'm thirsty."

"But Dr. Gardner told me . . ." The inspector was not done.

"I served him. I bought the berries for him," Carlos said, "but he
fermented them himself in secret. He hid his drink from me."

"Never?" the inspector asked again.

"I never tasted it. I never wanted it," Carlos said.

"Then why did he tell me . . . ?"

"That I drink? To make you think the worst of me," Carlos said.

The inspector sat down and stroked his mustache. I left the room to get the water and when I returned, he was saying softly to Carlos, "We'll see about that when he comes, Codrington. We'll see if he doesn't make *me* think the worst of *him*."

Weeks later, the inspector confessed to me that my father himself had planted doubts in his mind. I listened in shame as he told me that the very first day he met him, my father raised his suspicions with his indecent talk about virgin knots, spoilt meat, fire i' th' blood. Not suspicions of his abuse of me, to be sure. Suspicions of a sick mind that had transferred to Carlos his lascivious longings for a woman.

I took courage now from the sympathy he extended to Carlos, his seeming willingness to consider his side of the tale my father had poured in his ears. I felt that if I said more, if my father caused me to say more, to accuse him of more than the lies he invented about Carlos, the inspector would defend me, he would support me.

"You don't have to keep standing, Codrington." The inspector took the glass I offered him. "There's a comfortable armchair over there. Sit."

But Carlos was not ready, as I was, to trust the inspector, and he remained standing. "When we were in his bedroom," he said, "I noticed that Dr. Gardner's cloak and cane were missing. I didn't see his book on his desk."

"I suppose he took his cloak and cane with him wherever he went," the inspector said drily.

I handed Carlos the other glass I had brought. "Virginia knows about his cane and his cloak," Carlos said. He twirled the glass around in his hand. "She's seen him with his book."

Sometimes when Father worked in his garden, he wore his velvet cloak with stars on it. He took his cane, too, the one with the metal top engraved with men with human torsos and hips and legs of a horse. I had seen him reading from his red leather-bound book. I asked him about the cloak, the cane, and the book. He said they came from England. They were his father's. He told me not to touch them.

"They belonged to my grandfather," I said to the inspector. "Father's father."

"Dr. Gardner makes magic with them," Carlos said.

"Poppycock!" The inspector drained his glass and put it down on the side table next to him.

"He takes them with him when he goes to the lighthouse," Carlos said.

"Nonsense!" the inspector said.

"I've gone with him. I've seen him." Carlos bent his glass to his lips and swallowed.

The inspector faced me. "Do you know anything about this, Miss Gardner?"

"She never went," Carlos said. "She's never seen him at the lighthouse."

"Humph!" the inspector sneered dismissively.

"It's going to storm tonight," Carlos said. "You heard what the boatman said. Dr. Gardner likes to go to the lighthouse when it's about to storm."

I knew that was true. Father often went to the lighthouse before a storm.

"I'm certain that's where he is," Carlos said.

"Certain?" The inspector raised his eyebrows.

"I can take you there." Carlos drank the rest of his water and handed me the empty glass. "That is, if you want to find him," he said.

"Of course I want to find him," the inspector said stiffly.

"You'll need to change your clothes," Carlos said. "You can't go like that. With shorts."

"I'll go as I am," the inspector said.

"You'll need to cover your legs and your arms." Carlos ran his eyes over the inspector's uniform. "They could get scratched. You have to go through the bush to get to the lighthouse."

The inspector flicked away an invisible speck on his collar, and Carlos, thinking perhaps as I did that he was attempting to camouflage his nervousness, said, not unkindly, "It won't be too bad. Dr. Gardner has probably already cleared the way."

"It's not a matter of the way being cleared, Codrington. He may not be there."

But Carlos was not about to let him off so lightly. "He's there," he said. "If you go, you can see him do his magic."

"Magic!" the inspector snorted.

"Don't be afraid. He won't do anything to you, I'm sure," Carlos said.

"I'm not afraid," the inspector shot back. "I'll go, if you're so certain."

"I'm certain," Carlos said.

"But I won't have another word about magic," the inspector said.

"You don't believe me?"

"Dr. Gardner said you were intelligent. I'm surprised you'd say such nonsense. I suppose the next thing you'd want to tell me is that he uses black magic. What is it you call it? Obeah? Yes, obeah."

"I didn't say obeah."

"He's an Englishman, for God's sake."

"I said magic. Did you see his orchids? His bougainvillea? Have you ever seen such colors?"

"Dr. Gardner is a scientist. He does not need magic."

"Nobody else has grass like his. He hardly ever waters it."

"Scientists are making discoveries every day," the inspector said. But he did not look as confident as his words implied. He ran his finger around the collar of his jacket and asked me for more water.

I was about to leave the room to get it for him when Carlos stopped me. "Wait," he said. He turned back to the inspector. "Ask Virginia."

"Ask her what?"

Carlos was looking steadily at me. "You remember, don't you, Virginia? You remember when he burned my mother's bed?"

"I don't understand. What's this about your mother's bed?" the inspector said.

"Tell him, Virginia," Carlos said.

I was a child. I did not see. Father made Ariana keep me inside.

"You remember how it smelled, don't you, Virginia?"

For weeks after Father had cleared the spot, months after it was covered again with grass, the pungent odor of burning wood lingered in the house. Father said he was burning old furniture. We were getting something better, he said. I wanted to believe him. And years later we did get something better: couches, chairs, tables, and other pieces of the furniture Mrs. Burton ordered for us.

"You heard him chanting." Carlos came closer to me.

My head spun. I clamped my hand over my forehead and breathed in deeply.

Carlos brought his mouth to my ear and began to chant softly. Not words I could recognize. They were not English words he chanted. Made-up words, unintelligible words, and yet oddly familiar words. They coursed through the twists and bends in the canal of my ear, poking at the rock I had laid over a memory.

"Don't you remember?"

I was afraid, but not of Carlos. I was afraid of the memory that was leaking through the crevices in the rock, surfacing.

"What is it you are doing, Codrington?" the inspector barked.

Carlos's breath was warm and moist on my skin. He was chanting again, in a whisper now, his voice soft, gentle in my ear. "Try, Virginia."

The inspector got up. "What's that noise you are making, Codrington?" He fluttered his baton in Carlos's direction. "Move away from her. At once, Codrington!"

"Try to remember, Virginia," Carlos whispered again.

And then the rock became dislodged, and riding on the smoke that had slipped through my bedroom shutters, I heard my father's voice: an eerie, frightening chant that curled around the edges of my room and settled in the corners.

I had hidden under the bed; I had covered my ears.

I must have covered my ears when I remembered, for Carlos's hands were on my arms and he was lowering them to my sides. "Tell the inspector, Virginia."

It was true: the chanting, the magic, the fire.

"Tell him, Virginia."

I was in the grip of a whirlwind of emotions. "He's told you the truth," I heard myself say.

"What? What truth?" The inspector was near me.

"Father burned the bed."

"What bed?"

"His mother's bed."

The inspector reached for my hand. "Come, Miss Gardner. Sit down."

I stepped away from him.

"Please sit, miss," the inspector said again. "We'll wait here for your father."

"No." I wanted to see Father. I wanted to look in his eyes. I wanted to ask him about the fire. About that night. About his lies.

"He won't be back tonight," Carlos said to the inspector. "If you want to speak to him today, you have to go to the lighthouse."

The inspector raised his hands over his face and drew them slowly downward over his eyes and nose. He looked tired. Ready to surrender.

"I want to go with you," I said.

"I can't let you do that, miss," the inspector said.

"If we are going, we must leave now," Carlos said.

"She'll have to stay here," the inspector said.

"No," I said. "I must go. I need to go." Father would admit what he had done to me.

"She'll be safe," Carlos said. "I won't let anything happen to her."

The inspector pressed his fingers into his chin and closed his eyes.

"I'll get you a pair of my pants," Carlos said. "And an old shirt. You can wear them over your uniform."

The inspector shook his head. "I won't need your clothes," he said.

"They'll protect you from the razor grass," Carlos said.

The inspector opened his eyes. "Stop." He held up his hand. "No more. We'll drive."

"Drive? Drive in what?"

"We'll take the lighthouse jeep."

It turned out that the maritime division of the Ministry of Works and Transportation kept a jeep on the island. I had never seen it and if Father had, he had never mentioned it.

"They hide it in the bushes," the inspector said. "So the lepers can't take it."

I would have laughed out loud if there were space in my heart for levity. Why would the lepers take the jeep? Where would they go? They couldn't cross the sea in a jeep! But the memory Carlos had awakened consumed me, and I could not force my lips to stretch into a smile. *Had I so totally forgotten that day Father burned the bed?*

Loving Father required forgetting. It required erasing from my consciousness all the things that had caused icicles to enclose my heart: the acrid smell of smoke, the ugly crackle of the bed frame burning; Father dancing around the flower beds with his cloak and cane and book; Father shouting orders to Ariana; Father making Carlos work under the burning sun and denying him a place at our table; Father insisting that I was superior to Ariana and Carlos. Carlos saying to me, but to me alone, that the house was his. I had erased all these, for I could not love my father otherwise. I could not face these truths and have the father I wanted. *Needed*.

"Oh, the lepers wouldn't be able to get off the island," the inspector was saying, "but they could go to the lighthouse. The lighthouse keepers wouldn't want that, of course. The disease, you know. They wouldn't want to catch it."

Two lighthouse keepers stayed on the island in one shift, the inspector explained, and were rotated every fortnight. They left the jeep near the bay for their replacements but they rigged it so that only a key like the one he had in his pocket could start the engine.

If we had forced him into acquiescing to our demands that I go with him to the lighthouse, the inspector seemed determined now to show us that he had not lost the English stiff upper lip. On the way to the bay, he trudged stoically forward, his shoulders erect, not giving the slightest indication of concern though at least twice I heard the scuttle of animal feet through the trees, and he could not have missed the huge iguana that peered at us from the side of the path.

The boatman was waiting for us. The inspector waved him away when he stretched out his hand to help him climb into the pirogue. "Do you know how to drive a jeep?" he asked him.

Not only a jeep, the boatman boasted, but a vehicle bigger than a jeep. A big truck. A big lorry. A bus. Anything with wheels . . .

"Can you take us to Dingsee Bay?" the inspector rudely interrupted and wiped away the grin plastered on the boatman's face. But the boatman had his revenge.

"Dinghy Bay, you mean?" he asked. "I surprise you English people know that name. Ordinarily," he said, speaking now directly to Carlos and me, "when the tide low, the only ways to get there is by dinghy. But the tide high now. We could pull up next to the jetty."

"Dingsee or Dinghy," the inspector said. "Can you take us there?" The jeep, he said, was hidden between the trees and tall bushes, not far from the shore.

"I take you there before you could say Jack Robinson," the boatman said.

To get to Dinghy Bay, we had to cross Chacachacare Bay, in front of Sanders Bay and Coco Bay, the main settlements of the leper colony. I was glad the boatman avoided the coastline. We never came close enough for me to see the buildings distinctly. From the distance, out in the bay, they seemed unreal, drawings for a fictitious story: the weatherbeaten leprosarium with its peaked roof, and behind it, lodged in a thicket of trees, wooden shacks climbing unsteadily up an incline, oddities on a desolate island.

I could have seen all this and felt nothing were it not for the group of sticklike figures standing close to the water, their arms thrust upward, waving.

"Not too many still here," the boatman said, pointing to them.

Could she be one of them, my wordless friend whom I had spurned?

"Most of them cured and gone back to Trinidad," the boatman said.

What had I been afraid of?

Father said: "Get too close and you get the disease. Do you want your face to rot like theirs?"

I looked away, guilt choking me.

"Wave back," the boatman said. "They like that. Wave!"

Carlos stood up and waved, but I was frozen in my seat.

Soon they were behind us and the boatman was pointing to an-other spot. "Up yonder. That's where the nuns and them use to live. Their chapel not too far."

A cluster of cream-colored two-storied concrete buildings rose up the hill. Over the drone of the engine, the boatman shouted, "Those nuns was saints. Ten of them buried in the cemetery there. Dey was French, you know. Not English."

"If you keep on talking, we'll miss the bay," the inspector shouted back. I could tell he was angry. He must have known, as I did, that the boatman meant to imply that the French had done more for the sick on the island than had the English.

But the boatman was already steering the boat toward the tiny jetty, its sides buttressed with huge black rubber tires. On the shore, a group of large black vultures, the pink flesh on their long necks crimped like a turkey's gullet, stared us down. Corbeaux. When the boat docked, they scattered. Some flew up into the trees; the rest settled stubbornly back down on the ground just a few feet away from us.

"They don't 'fraid us," the boatman said. "They hoping we leave them dead fish."

Around us, stuck on the rough edges of stones on the pebbled beach, were the remains of fish, their dried guts splayed out in macabre shades of red and blue. A shudder snaked up my spine. Death everywhere: among the lepers, in the nuns' cemetery. Vultures biding their time.

The inspector gave the boatman directions to the whereabouts of the jeep. He handed him the key and the boatman disappeared. Alone, the three of us, I felt as if we had been left stranded on the nar-row shore, no way for us to get back. Across from us, a short distance through the trees, La Tinta Bay, and facing it, the fourth boca, Boca Grande. On the other side, Venezuela and the vast South American continent. The boatman could keep on walking; he could take the jeep; he could warn Father. There would be no one to help us. I fought off this feeling of dread, reminding myself that the boatman did not know Father. Why should he want to protect him? Why should he warn him? And if the boatman did not come back, we could leave when we wanted; we were not stranded. Carlos, I reasoned, could start the boat engine. But panic seized me. What if the boatman had locked the engine? Then I heard the sound of the jeep accelerating, and my heart slowed down.

When the boatman pulled up, the inspector hopped in front, in the covered closed cab of the jeep. "You two can sit in the back," he said.

Perhaps he simply wanted to please me, perhaps he was moved by the affection he had witnessed between Carlos and me on the dock in Trinidad. Whatever his motive, I was glad he left me alone with Carlos.

There was no covering over the back of the jeep, and the wind whipped my hair and plastered it to my face. Carlos pushed it back and drew me to him. I snuggled against his chest and tried not to think of what lay ahead. *What would I say to Father when I saw him?*

The boatman shifted gears, and the engine strained to climb the steep hill. Carlos tightened his arm around my shoulder. "Do you see?" He cradled my chin and turned my head to the right, where the land plunged to the sea. Below us, waves crashed against black rocks, and in the distance, the sea, a sheet of blue-green organza, shimmered.

"Look." Carlos moved my head to the other side. Green upon green, every shade from light to dark, and mounting on tall trees, the tendrils of vines twisting and curling around branches. In between, sparks of color: orange berries, delicate lilac clusters, flowers in tints of yellow, pink, and red.

Antiseptic was the adjective I silently kept to myself for the flowers in my father's garden that grew out of pots and on weeded beds, their colors so unnatural to me, so artificial. But nothing here was antiseptic, nothing here artificial.

"Smell," Carlos said.

I breathed in the sweet perfume of flowers and new greenery, the metallic odor of clean earth, the salt scent of the sea. Thoughts of Father began to slip away.

"Hear that. Listen. *Cha-ca-cha-ca-Ree.*" Carlos's voice rose softly, carried on the rush of a single breath. "*Cha-ca-cha-ca-Ree.* Listen."

A bird whistling.

"They say the Amerindians named the island for the cotton they used to grow here. I like the other story better, the one about the Indians naming the island after a bird."

Cha-ca-cha-ca-Ree. I heard it now everywhere, and in between the greenery I saw the flash of yellow feathers, then blue, then red.

We wound around sharp bends in the road. More precipices, more flashes of blue sea, black rocks, white froth curling on the edges of glistening waves. More thick greenery. Color. Flowers, birds. Carlos next to me.

I could pretend we were alone, I could make believe no one was with us, no police inspector in the seat in front, next to a driver, taking us up a road leading to my father. No purpose for my being here except for Carlos. No reason to prove the innocence of the man I loved.

The boatman shifted gears again. We slowed down; the engine coughed. The boatman looked back at us through the open rear window of the cab. "Last lap," he said. "Not to worry. We go make it." And then, there, looming in front of us, was the lighthouse.

It was smaller than I had imagined, or it would not have seemed so small if not for the sea behind it. I saw the white tower—the black railing on top, the glass enclosure, the red cone above it, the weather vane—but all this was dwarfed by a wide slate of blue-green glass, the sea glinting, bright and mysterious. Boca Grande. Beneath its surface, La Remous simmered, and beyond, the Atlantic, the ocean I had crossed with Father.

My throat constricted with the intensity of the feeling that rushed over me: Three years old. I was begging Father to stop the ship from rolling.

Through a dark haze, I could hear the inspector asking: "The drive too much for you, too?"

I was bent over, gagging, my stomach heaving.

"All those twists and turns in the road," the inspector was saying.

I had wrapped my arms around Father's neck. With one hand, he was clutching me to his chest, with the other he was holding the table steady. Wave after gigantic wave pitched the ship up and down. The table broke free from Father's grip and slid across the room. Cups, saucers, the pot of tea, the plate of biscuits, everything crashed to the floor. "Careful," Father said. I was on his lap, my feet dangling inches above the shards.

I pressed my hand against my mouth and swallowed. Nothing

there, none of the liquid that had stung my throat when I vomited, tea
and biscuits trailing down the leg of Father's pants.

"Luckily, I didn't have much of a breakfast." The inspector's voice
again.

*Father cleaned me up and I curled into his arms. I felt safe, protected. I was
with my father.*

"Is there something I can do to help?" the inspector asked.

I peeled my eyes away from the Atlantic and forced myself to
speak. My dizziness had passed, I said. I blamed my nausea on the
winding road.

"Well, if you feel okay . . ."

My mouth was dry. I moistened my lips with my tongue. "It's
over," I said.

"Okay, but stay in the jeep."

"I want to go with you," I said.

"No, miss," he said.

"Please," I begged him.

He shook his head.

"Please," I pleaded with him again.

He drew his hand through his hair. "It's not wise, miss."

"She's reached this far," Carlos reasoned with him.

The inspector glanced sharply at him, but he did not contradict
him.

"I want to go," I said.

"It's against my better judgment," the inspector said, but I could
tell he was weakening.

"I need to go," I said.

"Then if you must," he said. "But you have to hide in the bushes. I
don't want your father to see you until I've spoken to him."

Across the blue sky, a big black bird, a vulture, a corbeau. It
swooped down low and landed, its long, ringed legs trembling as it anchored itself on the branch of a thick-trunked tree. Around it, more
corbeaux, cemetery gargoyles guarding the dead.

The inspector looked up.

"Plenty corbeaux here, too," the boatman said.

"I wouldn't have thought they'd come this high," the inspector said.

"They come wherever they think they can find the dead," the boat-man said.

I wanted to be brave, but the corbeaux staring down on us chilled my heart. I clasped my hand to my mouth.

"Don't be frightened, miss," the boatman said. "I don't mean dead people. I mean dead fish. Guts and fish head and things like that. Crab claws. Whatever the lighthouse keeper does throw away."

"Come," the inspector beckoned me. "We have no time to waste."

The boatman stepped forward.

"Not you," the inspector said and sent him back. "Wait for us in the jeep. I'll call you if I need you."

"Hide there," he told me, pointing to a place where the bushes had grown thick. "If your father is here, I will get him. Don't move until I call you."

I crouched down low behind the bushes. I was here to save Carlos, to make Father admit Carlos's innocence. But the birds had stopped whistling, the leaves on the trees had stopped rustling. I had imagined this, of course, this strange quiet that descended around me, for the sound I was listening for was the sound of my father's voice. But I did not hear my father's voice; I did not see him. What I heard was the voice of the inspector complaining. He could hardly breathe in the sti-fling heat, he was saying. And the fishy smell drifting onshore from the ocean was making him nauseous. "I don't see Dr. Gardner. Fine wild-goose chase you've taken me on, Codrington."

"He's inside the lighthouse," I heard Carlos say.

"Then we'll speak to the lighthouse keeper," the inspector said.

"He bribed him," Carlos said.

"How do you know that, Codrington?"

"When he comes here, he pays the lighthouse keeper to stay away."

"Did you see him do that, Codrington?"

A wind blew inland from across the boca. It was a warm wind but the bushes in front of me shivered. Their leaves, thick, dense, clustered on thin stems, swayed back and forth, brushing against each other. *Swish, swish.* The sounds they made muffled Carlos's answer.

"Well, you can't be certain," the inspector said.

"I'm certain you won't find the lighthouse keeper here," Carlos said.

I parted the bushes just wide enough to see in front of me, leaving as little open space as possible so as still to conceal me. Carlos was walking behind the inspector. They were looking upward, to the top of the lighthouse, to the platform with the black railing, below the glass enclosure. The sun was in my eyes. I squinted when I looked up, too. Nothing. No movement. Under the platform was an opening cut out of the lighthouse wall, a slit like a giant vertical eye. Behind it, darkness, an oily black thickness glinting against the whiteness of the tower.

Then, suddenly, something fluttered out from the opening under the platform. A piece of cloth. Red.

"He's there! He's there!" Carlos shouted.

The corbeaux perched on the tree flapped their wings and craned their necks. The loose skin under their helmeted heads trembled.

"It's his cloak."

My heart was a drum thumping in my chest. More red. It slid through the slit on the wall.

Red: my father's cloak. Red: the fire outside my bedroom window. My father chanting. A glimpse of him before Ariana pulls me away. There are silver stars on his red cloak. They flicker in the sparks breaking loose from the fire. His hair rises. Red, too, like the fire. I scramble under the bed.

I crouched down lower now in my hiding place, terrified, blinded by the tumble of images crashing down on me. "Carlos!" I called out to him. I could hear him running toward me.

"Stop!" The inspector's voice was commanding. "Halt!"

Carlos's footsteps ended.

"Stay!"

I peeked out from the bushes. Carlos had turned toward the inspector.

"Leave her. Let her be, Codrington."

But Carlos turned around again.

"I am an officer of the law, Codrington. Do not give me a reason to arrest you."

I would have cried out to Carlos to come no farther, but he, too, heard the determination in the inspector's voice. There was no doubt he would do as he had threatened. He would arrest him.

"She's safe, Codrington," the inspector was saying now. I saw him place his hand on Carlos's arm. It was the gesture that a friend would make. "It's better this way. Better that he doesn't see her right away." His tone was soothing, and once again I felt that though the inspector was a pompous man, he was a decent man, and in the end he would not abandon us.

When they were a few feet away from the base of the lighthouse, the inspector cupped his hands around his mouth, cocked his head upward, and called out to Father. "I know you are there, Dr. Gardner!"

More red fluttered from the slit in the lighthouse wall, then vanished.

"Come down, Dr. Gardner!" the inspector called again.

The door to the lighthouse was on the other side of the tower, facing the sea. Close to it, in viewing distance of the door, was a large tree laden with green fruit. A mango tree. I recognized the fruit. When I saw Carlos leading the inspector around the tower, I moved from the bushes and hid behind the tree trunk.

"Come down now, Dr. Gardner!" the inspector shouted. "I say, *now!*"

The door cracked open. A flash of red, and then my father appeared. I barely recognized him. His red velvet cape with the silver stars flowed over his shoulders and draped down the length of his back. It was tied around his neck with a gold ribbon. *A magician's cloak.* In one hand he held the cane with the silver top, and in the other, his red book. His hair was clumped in thin locks that fell down the sides of his face like wet straw. "Filthy slave!" he yelled. I could hear him distinctly. "Ungrateful whelp! Send him away. Lock him up!"

He was standing too far away for me to see his face clearly, but I could imagine his crinkled brow, clogged with dirt from the long walk over the hills above our bay; I could imagine the rivers of black sweat coursing down his reddened face. I could imagine his eyes, a wild boar's eyes before the kill, hardened, pitiless.

"Bloody devil! Bastard! Lascivious slave! You think you fooled me? You think I didn't know who you were? Filth! Pervert!" He stepped closer to Carlos.

The inspector pushed him back.

"Pervert!" he spat out again.

I cringed. The inspector must have cringed, too. Ariana had told him what Father had done to her. But he did not know about me, what Father had done to me. He did not know how well my father knew which one of them was the pervert.

"No need for nasty words, Dr. Gardner," the inspector said. "We can settle this business now and we'll be gone."

"Settle?"

"We have a report from someone that says Mr. Codrington is innocent."

"*Mister* Codrington? *Mister?* Do you see it's a black man in front of you, Inspector?"

"Someone reported . . . " the inspector began again.

"Lies!" My father cut him off. "I told you, Inspector, what this beast was plotting to do to my virgin daughter."

Carlos stepped toward him. The inspector raised his hand and signaled to him to stay back. "Remain where you are, Codrington," he cautioned him.

"Let him come. Let him come and I will beat him to a pulp." My father shook his cane at Carlos.

"Give me that." The inspector held out his hand for my father's cane. "Hand it over, Dr. Gardner."

My father tightened his grip on the cane.

"I'll have to file charges against you, Dr. Gardner, if you don't give me that cane."

"File charges? File charges against an Englishman? Do you see this beast here, Mumsford? Tie up the beast, Mumsford."

"Hand me the cane or I'll have to take it from you, Dr. Gardner."

"Bastard!" My father shook his cane again at Carlos.

"Hand it to me!"

"You forget yourself, Mumsford," my father said.

"You forget yourself, sir," the inspector said and grabbed the cane.

Stunned that the inspector had sided with a brown man against him, my father released his hold on the cane like a man in a trance.

"There, there, Dr. Gardner. That wasn't so hard, was it?" the inspector crooned.

My father found his voice and glared at him. "You do not know what you are doing, Mumsford," he hissed.

"Pardon me, sir," the inspector said, "but I do know, sir."

"Filth!" My father lashed out again at Carlos.

Satisfied that he had disarmed my father, the inspector tried once again to get him to admit to Carlos's innocence. "Someone has reported that Codrington never harmed your daughter, sir."

My father was still holding on to his red book, clutching it to his chest in the bend of his arm. "I prevented him," he said. "The bastard. He thought I would let him ruin my daughter."

"Someone said he never would have harmed your daughter, sir."

"Someone? Someone? Who did the lying beast get to help him tell his lies?"

"Ariana, sir. She said Codrington would never hurt your daughter, sir. She said he was good to your daughter, sir."

"She is one of his kind. They lie. Lying is in their nature."

"She said you did things to her, sir," the inspector said.

I thought my father would back down. I thought guilt would silence him, but he threw back his head and laughed. "Things to her? The slut! Things to her?"

"She said you did these things to her when she was only a child," the inspector said. It must have taken all the effort of his training for him to say those words to my father without emotion, but then he was a policeman on duty, conducting an investigation. And my father was an Englishman. For the Englishman's sake, somewhere in his head, he must have still held on to a sliver of doubt.

"Liar! Slut! The both of them, lying slaves," my father screamed.

Carlos had his back to me, but I could see his fists opening and closing at his sides.

"*He* did things to her." My father pointed his finger at Carlos.

The fists Carlos made with his hands were tighter. I knew it would not be long before he would lose his patience, before he would explode and knock my father down.

"*He* screwed her!"

It was the last straw. If he had not told such a bald-faced lie, if he had not made such a malicious accusation, Carlos might have been able to stand there a little longer, bottling his rage, squeezing it tight in his clenched fists.

Carlos lunged forward and grabbed his hand, twisting it with such force that my father lost his grip on his red book and it fell with a dull thud to the ground.

For a second both men stopped, paralyzed by the sight of my father's precious book, his sacred book, sprawled in the dirt. Carlos recovered first. He stuck out his foot and aimed at the book. The kick he gave it sent it tumbling over clumps of broken bits of coral and rock. When it settled, it lay on its back, its spine broken, its pages fanning in the breeze that had risen from the sea.

My father's eyes welled with tears, but they were not tears of sorrow. They were tears of indignation, tears of frustration. Tears of humiliation. He wanted revenge now, and he cried out to the inspector to use his baton to strike down Carlos. "Stripes will move him not kindness. The cat-o'-nine-tails is what he needs. Beat him!"

Carlos was still holding on to my father's hand, his fingers wrapped around his wrist. "You stole my house," he shouted. "Did you think I would forget you stole my house?"

Now I knew. Now I understood the stiff jaw, the hardness in his eyes on the boat that brought us here. I could no longer deceive myself: I had accepted my father's lies to staunch my own needs, to hold back the dam that would have split open, tears running down my cheeks forever if I had confronted the truth.

In my heart of hearts I must have always known, always believed what Carlos had said to me: The house was his. But I could not choose. I needed them both, Carlos and Father. I was afraid Carlos would put us out if I agreed that the house was his. And I could not be left alone with Father.

"It was my mother's house!" The words roared out of Carlos's mouth.

My father swung at him with his other hand. "Stop the brute, the devil, the beast!" he yelled out to the inspector. The inspector jumped between them, wielding his baton.

To this day I do not believe the inspector intended to hit Carlos. I believe he intended to use his baton as a shield to pry Carlos away from my father. From what I could see, the baton would have struck my father's head had he not ducked. It came down instead on Carlos's shoulder. When I saw Carlos double over, I knew the pain that ripped through his body would make him lose all sense of caution, all fear that he was in the presence of two Englishmen, one, though he appeared to be defending him, an officer of the law, an English inspector. Carlos had withstood my father's insults; he had suffered torture at his hands. I knew his rage would blind him.

He grasped my father's neck and I bounded out of my hiding place. I had to save him. I had to prevent him from strangling my father. He would go to jail if he harmed my father. "Stop! Stop!" I shouted.

My father saw me before either the inspector or Carlos heard me. "Virginia!" My name warbled through the strained strings of his vocal cords. "Virginia!" His jaw fell open; his eyes shot out of their sockets.

Carlos dropped his hands from around my father's neck and backed away.

"Virginia!"

The inspector clutched my father's arm and tried to steady him.

No one but my father and I knew what thoughts were going through our minds. No one but my father and I knew his perverted secret.

I came closer to him and looked directly into his eyes. "Tell the inspector that Carlos is innocent," I said.

"You," he breathed.

"Tell him."

"Forgive me," he said.

"Tell him."

He reached for my hand. I flinched and pulled my hand away. "Say you lied."

"I'm sorry. I'm sorry," he groaned.

I gritted my teeth. "Say you lied."

"Forgive me." He dropped to his knees.

"No," I said.

He looked over to the inspector, his eyes pleading with him. Not understanding, the inspector reached into his pocket and pulled out a folded sheet of paper. "Here," he said. "You just have to sign this paper, Dr. Gardner, and I'll leave you with your daughter."

But my father was not listening to him. He was repeating "Forgive me, forgive me," on his knees still before me.

Clearly disturbed by my father's odd behavior, the inspector begged him to stand. "You'll scrape your knees. Up, Dr. Gardner."

My father placed his opened palm on the ground, and the inspector, thinking he was trying to brace himself up, bent down to help him. "That's it," he cooed. "Up, Dr. Gardner. You just have to sign the paper."

My father knocked the paper out of the inspector's hand. Dirt rising with the wind rolled toward it. Before the inspector could retrieve the paper, it fluttered away, carried on the tiny puffs of dirt swelling beneath it.

Again my father asked for my forgiveness. Again I told him he had to confess. Tears in his eyes, he stumbled to his feet, his hands outstretched, a mendicant, a common street beggar.

"No!" I could not bear his touch, his fingers on my skin.

He stumbled back.

The inspector tried again to calm him. "We'll go back to the house," he said. "We'll talk there."

A terrible light flashed across my father's eyes, the sun striking the blue, the cold steel edge of a sword, malevolent. He grabbed the hem of his cloak and twisted it around his body. A mummy. The ribbon at his neck cut deep into the creases in his skin.

Afraid of the light in my father's eyes, the desperation he must have seen there, the inspector hollered, "Wait!" But my father had already spun around and was running through the bramble in front of the lighthouse, heading for the edge of the precipice.

Before he curled himself into a ball, my father looked back. Did he hope I would stop him? Did he hope I would forgive him?

By the time we reached him, he was already rolling downward. A ledge midway down the slope broke his fall. He stood up, looked back at me again, and then, extending his arms, he threw himself forward down the steep drop to the sea. Above him his cape fluttered like wings in the wind. The corbeaux screeched and swooped down from their perch on the thick-trunked tree, his ceremonial guards lined up behind him.

"He looked like a crucifix," the inspector said. "His body falling down like that."

"A corbeau," Carlos said.

"A bird," the inspector conceded. Later he told me he believed that at that moment my father had gone mad; he had lost his senses. He thought he could fly.

Magic. This time it failed him. His cape, buoyed by the warm air, ballooned behind him, but in seconds gravity pulled him downward. His body struck the sharp edges of the rocks and broke into pieces. A wave gathered force, swelled high, and pushed toward the shore. It reached his body, pulled, sucked, and dragged him—head, torso, arms, and legs, his magical cape around him—deep into the Dragon's Mouth.

My father's contrition was hollow. He had no remorse for what he had done to Carlos or what he had done to Ariana. He believed that my life, the life of a person born of English parents—a white person—was worth more than Carlos's life, the life of a black man, the life of a man in whose veins ran the blood of Africans. My life, the life of a white girl, was worth more that the life of a brown-skinned girl. In his perverse way he protected my virginity, but the virginity of a brown-skinned girl had no value for him. He would penetrate Ariana, but he would leave me intact. My father did not deserve my forgiveness.

"Why did he ask *you?*" Carlos asked me. "Why ask for *your* forgiveness?"

I was not ready to give him the answer.

As the boatman had predicted, it stormed the night my father flew over the cliff, below the lighthouse. In the eerie light from the lighthouse tower that arced across the dark waters, his body must have glinted, the phosphorous remains of a carcass caught in the narrow crevice of a rock. To La Remous he must have seemed already a ghost, the shadow of the dead that was not her business. But nothing would have distracted La Remous that night when lightning bolts sliced the black sky and thunder roared. She was riding the swollen waves in the driving rain, swirling the waters into her ferocious currents. She had no time for my father. He was debris on the rocks, and she was busy making a whirlpool in the center of the Boca. Four days later the Dragon spied my father in the crevice where he had spat him out. He lifted him up and pitched his mangled body on the craggy shore. Corbeaux circled above him.

We buried my father in the nuns' cemetery, behind the old convent, near Marine Bay. The inspector had feared a scandal. He did not want my father's body brought to Trinidad. The nuns pitied me: *Poor orphaned child. No mother, no father. No family anywhere in Trinidad.* No one told them my father's death was a suicide. An accident, the inspector said.

I cannot say I rejoiced when my father killed himself. I felt that an injustice had been righted. My father had paid the price for the harm he had done to Carlos, the harm he had done to me, the harm he had done to Ariana. But at his funeral I found myself a child again, trailing behind my father on the beach at Cocorite. The wall I had built around my heart cracked, split open, and my tears flowed when the memories rushed through. The neck of my dress was soaked, plastered to my skin, when they lowered his body.

In the convent school in Port of Spain where the nuns arranged to send me, I learned the truth. I learned that my father was not thinking of me when he ran out of England, a man pursued. He was thinking of himself, desperate to save his skin. Afterward, after I learned this, nothing was left in my heart for my father, neither pity nor sorrow nor anger.

I spent one year in the convent school. Carlos remained on Chacachacare. The house was his again, the money my father stashed away from the sale of his mother's jewelry his, too.

The inspector did not contest his claim. Independence was on the horizon, politics in the favor of people born here. Englishmen were returning home. By the following year they would lose another colony.

Carlos and I made a pact before I left for Trinidad. In one year I would come back. In one year we would marry.

In that one year I learned of my father's history. The nuns, trying to find family for me, tracked down a man who said he had helped my father. He was a friend of a friend of my father's brother. He was the one who had put my father and me on the boat to Chacachacare.

Had my father been so heartless? Had he really given a woman a drug he had not tested?

My father had changed his name and yet still he feared discovery. Poor deluded Mrs. Burton. It was fear, not modesty, that had prevented my father from attaching his name to the white orchid. All that hypocritical talk about *Lycidas* he had poured into Carlos's ears! My father was ambitious, greedy for praise and recognition. It was fame he was striving for in England.

Peter and Paul Bidwedder. One was as bad as the other.

TWENTY-FOUR

*M*Y FATHER IS DEAD six years now. Four years ago, Carlos and I got married and I returned with him to Chacachacare. I had heard from Alfred. He wanted to apologize for leading me on. He said that at the time he came to my house, he already had a girlfriend. If he had not had a girlfriend, he would have been happy to date me. He swore he never would have taken advantage of my innocence. Father, it seems, had sent two letters by the boatman: one to the commissioner and the other to Alfred full of threats and warnings, cautioning him to be careful with my virtue, my purity. "You are lucky to have a father who protects you," Alfred wrote. If only Alfred knew!

Inspector Mumsford came to see me during my year at the convent school in Trinidad. He was leaving for England and wanted to say good-bye. He asked about Carlos. I told him of our plans to marry. He was not happy for me. He said he had hoped I would return to England. Not that Carlos did not seem a good man, but we were different. "Them," he said, throwing open his left hand. "Us," he said, throwing open his right hand. "Kind should stay with kind."

"Carlos is my kind," I said.

He narrowed his eyes at me.

"Carlos is human and I am human," I said.

Othello and Desdemona. Was Shakespeare thinking of the prejudice of his day when he wrote their tragic story? It was no coincidence, Carlos said to me, that not long after Queen Elizabeth I issued a Royal Proclamation ordering the arrest and expulsion of "Negroes and blackmores," Shakespeare told his story about a white woman in love with a Moor. It was fear that drove the queen to this extreme: too many English men and women marrying Africans. But love had its way. By the end of the eighteenth century there were half a million black people living in England.

I had not missed the shy smile that crossed Carlos's face when he told me this. Nor did I forget that more than once he had commented that my mother's sealed lips, in the photograph on my bureau, seemed to conceal a secret. Was that secret the lips themselves, full lips I had inherited, which, when they parted, made fishermen forget they wanted to burn candles?

The inspector scratched his head, perplexed. "It's a new world," he said. "I do not understand it."

"A brave new world," I countered.

In six months, Carlos and I will have our first child. It's in a brave new world we hope to raise him, a world courageous enough to face the truth: We love with the heart for what is within, not outside, of us. Not for our superficial trappings. This truth had eluded the inspector and Father. Yet I do not know why Father had to be so cruel. Why did he have to torture Carlos?

"Why was Iago so evil?" Carlos responds when I struggle to puzzle out Father's motive. "Racism needs no more incentive than the difference in the color of our skins."

He had given Father the Miranda test, Carlos says, and Father had failed it. He believed no degree of education, no accumulation of knowledge, though surpassing his or that of any of his countrymen, would make a black man equal to an Englishman, would make him worthy of his daughter.

"What set him off?" I ask Carlos.

"One word," he replies. *"People."*

But it was Father who was obsessed with my future progeny. Fear had brought him to a crisis. Fear had made him try to sell me to a stranger. Fear that if he could not find a way to stop himself, to put a barrier between his lascivious desires and me, it would be he who would be the father of my progeny.

There are nights I cannot sleep, worrying that a day could come when Carlos would shift my father's sins from my father to me. "I am his daughter," I remind Carlos.

He answers that he does not share my father's twisted logic; he does not believe that my father's blood, the color of my father's skin, makes me who I am.

"But we owe you. Father owed you," I say.

"I have what he stole from me. That is all I want," he says. "I have my house."

Would he have married me if he had not got back his house? Would he have wanted me to be the mother of his children if Father still occupied his house?

"I cannot change the fact that he was my father, but I am not English," I say, needing reassurance.

And he responds: "Your skin is English."

I do not pretend. I know my white skin gives me privileges. Doors would open for me if we lived in Trinidad. For my sake, the commissioner had promised to find Carlos a job, but we stay here on Chacachacare. Carlos is a poet. Like his father, the sea, the sun, the sky, the birds, all flora and fauna on the island are his inspiration. I do not want him to leave.

On our wedding day, the nuns presented us with the old boat they had used when they lived on the island. Carlos has repaired it. He has built a cabin in the middle of the boat with seats we can convert to a bed. Around the back and front of the cabin he has added benches. He has painted the boat yellow and white and named it after me. *The Vir-*

ginia, he calls it. Almost every day he ferries people back and forth from the mainland to their vacation homes on the other small islands. No one has built a vacation home on our island. They fear the lepers, the living ones and the dead.

I, too, am afraid of the lepers though I know that there is a cure and that the disease is not contagious. I was in Trinidad when the lepers helped Carlos rebuild the boat and dismantle many of the changes my father had made to the house and yard. One of the patients, a carpenter—an artist, Carlos says he is—restored the carvings of birds and flowers on the tops of the interior walls that my father had destroyed. When the sun shines through our house, it casts shadows of birds, hibiscus, roses, and lilies across our polished floors.

We have no need of the air conditioner. Carlos has installed fans with long wood blades on the ceilings, and when we turn them on, air flows from one room to the other through the spaces in the carvings in the walls.

We have kept many of Father's flowers. Bougainvillea still blaze across the pillars on our front porch, orchids still climb the gray stumps of coconut tree trunks dug into graveled beds in our backyard. Under the shade of the greenhouse, we still grow anthuriums. But Carlos has restored the white orchids to the tree in the cove, where they belong.

We have fruit trees—mango, plum, grapefruit, orange, sapodilla, pomme cythere, chennettes. The chennette tree was the first Carlos planted, the first of the fruit trees my father had cut down. Every foot it grows, Carlos says, diminishes the memory of his pain.

Our lawn is different, too. It is not as green as my father's grass, nor as sturdy. In the dry season it burns and turns a deep brown, but when it rains, it is green again.

Carlos earns a good income from overseas tourists who hire him to take them to the bigger islands: Tobago, Grenada, Barbados, some as far away as Antigua. I always go with him. I feel closer to Carlos on our boat, especially at night when the tourists are ashore. I lie with my head on his lap, the sea endless before us, the land behind us shadowed except for the flickering lights, and Carlos reads his poems to me. He says we remind him of his parents. Our love, he predicts, will be just as enduring.

I think I am the most fortunate woman in the world. I think our child will be the most fortunate child in the world.

Today, in the late afternoon, we sit on the porch watching the sun fan a fire across the horizon. Carlos has returned from the market in Trinidad. He has brought me mangoes. Julie, my favorite. He has planted three Julie mango trees in our yard. None so far has borne fruit. I believe him when he says they are awaiting our child. A present from nature, he tells me.

My fingers are yellowed with mango pulp; the skin around my mouth is wet and sticky. Mango peel falls to a basin at my feet. I reach for another. I tear away the skin with the edges of my teeth. I do not use a knife. Carlos laughs. "Like a true Trini," he says to me.

A true Trini. I laugh with him. Trinis—Trinidadians. That is what we call ourselves, though we also say we are Chacachacarians.

"Guess who I saw this morning near the market?" Carlos puts down the mango he is eating.

I guess right away. "Ariana," I say.

"She's a cadet in the police force," he tells me.

I am pleased the matron has taken such good care of her. "She's so brave," I say. "If it wasn't for her letter to the commissioner . . ."

Carlos takes my hand.

"She told him I love you," I say.

He squeezes my hand. "And I love you more," he says. We laugh. We have played this game before. He says he loves me and I answer, "I love you more." He lets go of my hand and I ask, not suspecting that my question would lead me to tell him what I have been so afraid to reveal: "How does Ariana look?"

"Fat," he says.

"Fat?"

"Well, not fat really. But you know how she used to be all skin and bones. Now she has some flesh on her."

Skin and bones. We avoid each other's eyes when he says this. We both know why she was skin and bones. We had witnessed her withdrawal into herself, but I know better than Carlos why in the last year even eating seemed a chore for her.

I should tell him now, I say to myself. I am going to have his child.

There should be no secrets between us. I have tried before. How many times have I wanted to give him the true answer to the question he had asked me when my father despaired, lost hope of being pardoned?

Why did he ask *you* to forgive him? Carlos had asked me. Why *you*?

Each time I begin to tell him the truth, each time the words bubble up to my lips, I swallow them. Mrs. Burton's warning rings in my ears. *No man of distinction.* Would Carlos be like most men of distinction? I had heard the girls in my school whispering. After hours, when the maternity clinics are closed to the public, mothers bring their daughters. But nobody talks. Nobody exposes the fathers.

Shame keeps them silent, as my shame kept me silent, shame that should have been my father's shame, but was not. Was not, except for those false seconds when he warbled his pathetic contrition under the cover of darkness, the truth inescapable before him. He would deny it in the light of day, demanding with a look, *never a word,* that I wipe my memory clean.

How easy it was for him to walk away, to forget or pretend to forget. To deposit his burden on me. But I lived in the body he had violated, the body he had plundered. I could not escape.

Carlos believes he has part of the answer to his question to me. He says my father did not ask for his forgiveness because my father did not believe he had done him any wrong. He says that my father expected his gratitude. He had fed him; he had educated him. "For his so-called kindness to me, he thought I should adore him, bow down to him. But it was *my* house. He met me here." He quotes a line from *Hamlet,* Claudius's desperate plea: " 'May one be pardoned and retain th' offense?' If he'd lived, he would have kept my house and my mother's jewels."

But *Why you?* continues to puzzle him. Why had my father asked for *my* forgiveness? Now I try to find a way to tell him.

"Ariana was unhappy here," I say, thinking to start with Ariana. Thinking this route would lead me to myself.

"Yes." He does not say more, but he has turned away from me, and I know if I could see his eyes and the curl I am certain his lips have formed, his face would reveal the disgust he feels.

She was only a child! I have heard him repeat these words, sitting on the porch in the rocking chair, staring blankly into the night.

"And yet my father was so concerned about my virginity." I move dangerously close to the heart of what I need to say.

He bends down and picks up a mango from the bunch he has laid on the floor. Slowly, shining its skin on the leg of his pants, a gesture that prepares me for words I am afraid I will hear (for he does not eat the mango skin; no one does), he says, "It's the ones who preach the most about such things who are often the most guilty."

A memory floods my being, Father answering me enigmatically: *She said you were my daughter.*

Carlos continues to polish the mango. "Such men are always on the lookout for the slightest breach of modesty in their wives. Yet they want them to be whores in bed."

My heart beats rapidly in my chest. "My father said my mother was the most virtuous woman he knew," I say.

"He was probably the one who named you."

Now, I think. *Now.*

"Do you think Ariana will marry?" I ask.

He puts down the mango. He is looking at me. "Why do you ask?"

I begin. "Because Father . . ." My voice falters. "Because Father . . ."

He stands up. His eyes have darkened and he presses his lips tightly together. I think he knows what I am about to say. I feel his love enfolding me, spreading roots beneath me, anchoring me. *He will hold me up. I will not fall.*

"Ariana was not the only one," I murmur.

He comes over to where I am sitting. He gathers me in his arms. He understands. He knows. He takes me to his chair and puts me on his lap. I lean my head against his chest. I feel his breath moving in and out. I feel safe, I feel secure.

"Father made sure I did not lose my virginity," I say. "But he took everything else."

The baby kicks in my womb and turns. I move my hand instinctively to the place where my belly rolls: a gentle, undulating wave.

Carlos covers my hand with his.

MORE ACKNOWLEDGMENTS

Sister Marie Thérèse Rétout, O.P. spent a morning with me at my parents' home in Trinidad, sharing her handwritten notes about the experiences of the Dominican nuns in Chacachacare. Her book *Called to Serve: A History of the Dominican Sisters in Trinidad and Tobago* (Trinidad: Paria Publishing Company, 1998) was indispensable for many of the details about Chacachacare in this novel, and so, too, the book *Western Isles of Trinidad* (Trinidad: Litho Press, 2000) written by Father Anthony de Verteuil, C.S. Sp. I am also indebted to David Tindall, who gave me my first guided tour of Chacachacare, and to Raymond Habib, who took me on his magnificent launch, along with his beautiful daughter Natalie and handsome young son Matthew, to see the lighthouse on Chacachacare. My thanks to Superintendent Mark Fisher for permitting navigational officers Otis Tippin and Christopher George to open the lighthouse for me. I am grateful for the invaluable information they gave me. Thanks, too, to Rawle Birmingham, who drove us up that winding road to the lighthouse.

Kevin Browne, one of my past students at Medgar Evers College, is the true author of the two poems in the novel. I owe the spelling of folklore characters and the fruits, flora, and fauna of Trinidad to John Mendes's remarkable compilation in *Cote ci Cote la* (Trinidad: Mendes, 1986). I am grateful for the support and leadership of Edison O. Jackson, the president of my college, Medgar Evers College, who generously gave me invaluable time to write. My gratitude in particular to my friends Pat Ramdeen-Anderson and Anne-Marie Stewart for their critical eye; to Elisabeth Dyssegaard, my first editor, who asked the right questions; to Melody Guy, who guided me to the final draft; to my sister Mary Nunez for her loyalty and friendship; and to my agent, Ivy Fischer Stone of the Fifi Oscard Agency, for her continued support. This acknowledgment comes late, but I am forever grateful to the master poet Walter James Miller, who was my first mentor.

As always, my life would be bleak without my son, Jason Harrell.

AUTHOR'S NOTE

I had finished this novel when I finally read Stephen Greenblatt's absorbing book *Will in the World* (Norton, 2004), which links Shakespeare's life to his work. Naturally, I was anxious to read his comments about *The Tempest*. As other critics have done, Greenblatt sees Prospero as a stand-in for the playwright. Thus, confounded by Prospero's appeal for forgiveness (to Greenblatt, Prospero's "guilt does not make entire sense"), Greenblatt asks, "Why, if he [Shakespeare] is implicated in the figure of his magician hero, might he feel compelled to plead for indulgence, as if he were asking to be pardoned for a crime he had committed? The whiff of criminality is just a fantasy, of course, but is a peculiar fantasy, of a piece with the hint of necromancy" (376–377). At the end of the book, Greenblatt makes the alarming observation: "The woman who most intensely appealed to Shakespeare in his life was twenty years younger than he: his daughter Susanna. It cannot be an accident that three of his last plays—*Pericles, The Winter's Tale,* and *The Tempest*—are centered on the father-daughter relationship and are so deeply anxious about incestuous desires" (389–390).

What difference it would have made had I read Greenblatt's book while I was writing this novel, I cannot tell.

ELIZABETH NUNEZ is the author of *Grace, Discretion* (short-listed for the 2003 Hurston Wright Legacy Award for Fiction), *Beyond the Limbo Silence, Bruised Hibiscus* (winner of an American Book Award), and *When Rocks Dance*. She was born in Trinidad and immigrated to the United States after secondary school. Nunez is a CUNY Distinguished Professor of English at Medgar Evers College. She cofounded the National Black Writers Conference, is executive producer of the acclaimed television series *Black Writers in America* (nominated for a 2004 New York Emmy), and now chairs the PEN American Center Open Book committee. Named Author of the Year by the Go On Girl! Book Club for 2002, Nunez is the recipient of numerous awards and honors, including fellowships at the Yaddo and MacDowell colonies and the Paden Institute, the YWCA Woman of Distinction Award, and the Sojourner Truth Award from the National Association of Black Business. She lives in Amityville, New York. Visit the author's website at www.elizabethnunez.com.

whispering his name, the name of his father also, she breathed her last breath?

I believe that Gardner spoke of my mother in this disparaging way to ease whatever shred of conscience he had left that pricked his soul in the night. Perhaps I give him more credit than is warranted. Perhaps he had no soul, or if he had, it was so tattered and torn with sin as to have barely existed at all. But it is also possible that in his diseased mind he had convinced himself that my mother had polluted the house and, therefore, had not deserved it.

My father thought my mother bewitching; Gardner called her a witch.

I grasp at straws no doubt, but there are days I seem to need to find some logic, *something,* that would help me make sense of Gardner's unrelenting arrogance, his overweening hubris. He had come to us homeless, an unwanted lodger in the old doctor's home, and yet he believed that we should be indebted to him and not the other way around. His bold-faced presumptions still astound me to silence, that he should act as if he thought he had discovered us, as if before his arrival we had not existed at all!

EIGHT

$\mathcal{B}$UT I LIKED his daughter right from the start, and not only because her eyes were the color of mine and reminded me of my mother's. That first day, while Dr. Gardner was trying to persuade Lucinda that we needed his help, I caught her looking at me. When my eyes met hers, she ducked behind her father's back, but later that day, when Gardner returned with all his belongings, which were few—two duffel bags and a satchel strapped to his back, which led me foolishly to hope that his stay with us would not be long—she looked up at me again and this time she smiled. Her two front teeth were missing, and the pink gap on her gums was wide. I would have kept my lips closed if my front teeth were missing, but she spread hers apart and waved at me. At the top of the front steps, she stretched her hand toward me. I bent down and she touched my face.

"Freckles," she said.

She was walking behind her father. He spun around and pulled her hand away. "Freckled," he murmured gruffly. His eyes were stern, threatening.

That was how Virginia and I began—with a bond struck instantly between us by the similarity of the color of our eyes, and a kindness she extended to me that I greedily accepted.

For I *was* self-conscious of the tiny brown dots that covered most of my body, though less so on my face. Only a few months earlier Ariana had convinced me that they were hideous. I had been accustomed at the time to bathing outdoors, from the standpipe at the back of the house. I would strip off my clothes regardless of who was there to see me: Ariana or Lucinda or anyone else. I thought no more of the appendage hanging between my legs than of a convenience necessary when my bladder needed emptying, and my freckles, no different from my blue eyes, odd, because I had seen them on no one else, but familiar because they were mine. One day, probably because she was tired of the attention Lucinda was paying to me (my father had just been killed and my mother had died soon after), Ariana pointed to my sex and jeered: "Look at that teeny, weeny little thing you have."

"So what?" I said. My penis had shriveled under the cold water and was a knob lying limp next to my scrotum.

"So what, you stupid boy? Girls not going to like you, that's what."

"I don't care if girls don't like me," I struck back.

"You wait and see. When you get big, you going to want them to like you, and they not going to like you because your thing too small."

Instinctively, I cupped my hand over my penis.

"And, mostly," she added, taking pleasure in my discomfort, "girls not going to like you because you polka dot."

I looked down at my body, my thin arms and legs, the stump between my upper thighs, the brown spots that marred my skin, and for the first time I felt ugly, for the first time I knew shame. I became conscious of a self apart from the self of the carefree boy I was, a boy who spent his days and nights with no awareness of his physical self except when the need required it, except when the urges of his bodily functions demanded it, a boy who reveled in the delights of the world around him: white clouds drifting with the wind across a sun-filled blue sky; the bay still, silent, and glittering before the coming of a rainstorm; birds whose whistles he was learning to imitate by heart; trees he climbed without fear; cicadas whose crying in the night brought him comfort when grief over the death of his parents seemed unbearable. The thousand twangling instruments he heard in the whisper of a breeze, in the rustle of leaves in the bushes.

I was too young, of course, when Ariana made me ashamed of my freckles to have arrived at the conclusion that shocked that monk at Mount St. Benedict, but it was likely that the seeds of the war I would wage with the story in Genesis were planted then. I date the awakening of my conscious self to that singular event at the standpipe. There were penalties: the loss of innocence, the loss of bliss—the same penalties doled out to Adam when he was expelled from the garden and felt ashamed of his nakedness. But by the time I was seventeen, the age I was when Gardner imprisoned me, I had come to believe that the advantages far outweighed the penalties, and Adam became my hero. The exchange he made for Eden seemed to me better than the alternative: happiness with no cognizance of bad and ugly, and therefore no consciousness of good and beauty. For how to know good except by knowledge of what is bad, of what it is not? How to know beauty except by knowledge of what is ugly, of what it is not?

Sometimes, baffled by Gardner's outrageous arrogance, his cool assumption of superiority over me, I would try to make sense of his behavior in the light of this logic. Perhaps Gardner thought this way, too. Perhaps he said to himself: *I am unfreckled and pale, and Carlos is what I am not, and therefore he is ugly. I am good, and Carlos is not what I am, and therefore he is bad. I speak with an English accent, and Carlos does not, and therefore he gabbles like a thing most brutish; therefore he does not know his own meaning.*

But shame was all I felt that day at the standpipe, and I began to see my freckles as a sort of disfigurement (Ariana, when her mother could not hear her, would keep reminding me that they were). The next time I bathed at the standpipe, I put on my underpants.

Virginia's smile and touch restored in me the possibility of ease with my body, for when her hand caressed my face, brushing it with her sunshine, I was no longer that ugly boy Ariana said I was. "Freckles," Virginia said, and smiled at me. Gardner countered, *Freckled,* but he was already too late.

I was not the only one, however, who profited from Virginia's generous smile. The boatman who brought Virginia and her father to our